THE PROSPEROUS THIEF

Andrea Goldsmith is the author of four previous novels: *Gracious Living* (1989), *Modern Interiors* (1991), *Facing the Music* (1994) and *Under the Knife* (1998). She lives in Melbourne. Andrea Goldsmith's website is at *http://purl.nla.gov.au/net/award/andrea-goldsmith*

THE PROSPEROUS THIEF

Andrea Goldsmith

ALLEN&UNWIN

This edition published in 2004
First published in 2002

This project has been assisted by the Commonwealth
Government through the Australia Council, its arts
funding and advisory body.

Allen & Unwin
83 Alexander Street
Crows Nest NSW 2065
Australia
Phone: (61 2) 8425 0100
Fax: (61 2) 9906 2218
Email: info@allenandunwin.com
Web: www.allenandunwin.com

National Library of Australia
Cataloguing-in-Publication entry:

Goldsmith, Andrea, 1950– .
The prosperous thief.

ISBN 1 74114 469 8.

1. Jews – Australia – Fiction. 2. Holocaust, Jewish (1939–1945) –
Fiction. 3. Jews – Fiction. 4. Australia – Fiction. I. Title.

A823.3

Printed in Australia by McPherson's Printing Group

10 9 8 7 6 5 4 3 2

for Dot

Virtue and crime weigh the same
I've seen it:
in a man who was both
criminal and virtuous.

—Tadeusz Rózewicz

We all live in a phantom dwelling.

—Basho

Part I

THE PAST

A Thief with Aspirations

On a balmy night in the summer of 1910, not far from the gutter in Berlin's Scheunenviertel, Heinrik Heck was born. Twenty-four hours later his mother was back at the bar downing her beers and buttoning Heini to a nipple whenever he threatened to bawl. His father, typical of the wanderer-fathers in the Scheunenviertel, had moved on months before the birth. He had promised Heini's mother he'd be back, but was either dead or in gaol or had chanced on some good luck he wasn't about to share with a woman who meant only shackles and misfortune. Greta didn't care, she'd moved on too. First there had been Johannes, followed by a messy month with Johannes and Bulle, and finally, not long before the birth, sentimental Heinrik, who was honoured, he said, to offer his name to the child. Seven weeks later and the sentiment had soured; soon Heinrik, too, was gone, leaving behind nothing but his name.

Heini was weaned from breast to beer in the three or four bars of his mother's preference. Berlin's white beer was a favourite along with a nice piece of sausage, although Heini learned early not to be choosy. When there was nothing better to eat he would climb on a chair and from there to the table, dip his fist into the mustard pot and lick.

While not an ideal diet, it seemed to do the trick, for Heini grew into a smart little boy blessed with a cunning more valuable than gold in this district, and certainly longer lasting. He knew how to scrounge for food and could always find a safe place to sleep. And even before he could walk he could gauge the mood of his mother and the other drinkers in the bar. On good days he was bar mascot with ample attention and plenty of food, but when moods turned sour, all he was good for was slapping and kicking and knew to keep his distance.

The Hecks and people like them filled in the cracks in the underworld. Pickpockets, thieves, prostitutes, pimps, bludgers, fighters, gamblers. And drunks, always drunks. They hung out in gloomy bars and bedded down in grimy rooms, several crammed in together and no one as brave as the rats or as well fed. Heini, his stomach hurtling in its emptiness, would see the rats gnawing the doorframes and know he'd have to turn himself into a stranger to have a life as good as them.

'They don't come much lower than us,' his mother once said. 'But someone's got to hold up all the rest.'

Down in the Scheunenviertel it was the quick or the dead and Heini fortunately was a fast learner. By the age of five he had acquired the basic skills for survival in this district. He knew to trust no one but himself, he knew when to take advantage, and he was learning the hard way how to deal with fear. Younger than most of the boys who prowled the streets, he nonetheless possessed fingers fine-tuned for gain. One day when the baker's back was turned, he grabbed a loaf and made off with it. He slipped into the first alley, then into another, and from there through a dank portal across a courtyard to an alcove on the far side. He squatted down among the weeds and, with his back pressed against a scrap of wall, he sank his teeth into the still-warm bread. His stomach clutched with delight. He took two more bites, then knowing to prolong the pleasure, changed to a neat nibbling round the edges. Such an expert with a loaf, he could make it last till midday.

The sun was shining but not too strong, the wind was a cool shuffling on his face, and the loaf as good as any he had tasted. He squirmed against the bricks until he found a smooth patch, was nibbling the loaf and squinting into the light and thinking as far as days went this was one of the best, when he saw them, two of the toughest, on the other side of the courtyard. Quickly he shrinks into the weeds and wraps himself up like a snail. He's sure they haven't seen him. And neither can he see them, although he senses them drawing near. His ears strain to hear, but apart from cursing, the boys' words blur in the breathy air. Tighter, he tells himself, curl up tighter. But fear fills his stomach and then it's rising and with it the bread, and if the boys haven't noticed him already they will now, although these toughs could see a cringing kid at a hundred metres in poor light, so he probably never stood a chance. And here they come, loping across the ragged ground, closer and closer and laughing as they grab him.

They're as big as grown-ups, they taunt with insults, they throttle with fists, they toss him around like a ball. Heini can't stop his grizzling, he's all pain and snivelling fear. These boys will flay the life out of him, then they'll throw him in a hole where no one will find him, and he'll lie there sore and starving and too weak to move. He may even die.

He may even die.

And suddenly his fear loosens and his blubbering stops — no point to nothing if he's about to die. And now he's kicking the boys and swinging his fists, and spitting from his bloodied mouth. He's not fool enough to think he can hurt them, but neither will he go down without a fight. And almost immediately their blows slacken, their taunts lose enthusiasm, and in another minute they've had enough. But they'll be back, they say, as they turn to leave, and they'll finish the job next time. Heini hears their laughter as they make their way across the courtyard. And though he's sore and bleeding and his loaf is ground into the dirt, he vows there won't be a next time.

It is less than a month later when next he sees them. He is coming down the stairs of his building carrying a bucket full of slops. His head is down, his mind on the job, and under his breath he's cursing his mother who's too drunk at the end of the day to walk, and too desperate to get to the bar in the morning to bother with the buckets, when a flicker at the edge of his vision makes him look up. And there they are, the two brutes waiting for him at the bottom of the stairs. Their fists are raised all ready to punch, their faces are mean with smiling. Heini is all fear and floundering, nowhere to run and certainly not with his hands full of filth. He's the loser this time and all out of luck, when suddenly he realises his advantage. He's standing on the stairs high above them, and in his hands a weapon far more powerful than their big beefy fists. He raises the bucket slowly, so slowly, raises it while keeping his gaze pressed hard to them. For a moment they waver, surely this kid wouldn't dare? They even move forward, then decide not to take the chance.

Heini acquired a reputation in the streets as a kid not to be messed with. Not that he had abolished fear, he needed a certain amount to keep him alert, but after the business with the toughs it was so well disguised no one would recognise it, much less turn it to their advantage. And along with the reputation, he developed a practical wisdom. Whether dealing with danger, or the basics of eating and hygiene, even the more complex business of making a living, Heini had a nose for the necessities. Not all children had the knack; his sister who was a bit younger and his brother who was a bit older certainly didn't. They relied on him and he did his best to look after them.

Once when his brother complained about one of the drinkers in the bar and bared his backside to show the marks, Heini explained that sometimes you learn more than you bargained for.

'Although it'll toughen you up,' he said, inspecting the damage. 'This,' he said, pointing to the broken skin, 'this isn't unbearable, it's just bad. And there's plenty of bad in this life, so best you get used to it.' He paused before adding, 'And you stink.' He put an arm around his brother who was trying not to cry and suggested they go for a swim together. 'I stink even worse than you.'

When everyone smells there's no point to washing, but Heini knew when the worst smell is your own, when you reek like your guts are spilling through your skin, it's time to act. With so many horses in the streets there were plenty of troughs – often a safer bet than the pond in the park. Not that anything had ever happened to him, but he'd heard about other children who had been hounded by a monster-man down there, or so went the story. Summer was best. Summer meant swimming, and how he loved moving through the cool, cool water, the ease and stretch of his body, or just floating on his back beneath the sun, his eyes shut and not a care in the world. A person could do a lot worse than be a fish, he had often thought.

Heini was the dependable member of the family, and better him than Walter who was a bit simple, or his mother who was becoming more and more useless. Heini took his responsibilities very seriously, and by the age of eight he had become a truly gifted thief, much better than any of the other boys he knew. Affe Werner, who had been a thief longer than living memory, would gaze on Heini with pride. 'That boy,' he would say, 'has been touched by God.'

Heini felt it himself. He was a natural. How else to explain the ease with which he would nip through an opening, sniff out the money and valuables, have them safe in his pouch plus a little something for himself, and be back in the street before Werner had finished his cigarette. He was adept at purses too, and worked Alexanderplatz and the Friedrichstrasse theatres with the stealth of an old pro. He wasn't bad at begging either, although it seemed such a waste of his gifts and besides it spoiled his pride. Although what he had squeezed out of smart ladies in their furs was no one's business.

'Quite a boy you have,' people would say to Greta, who may or may not respond depending on the time of day.

It was a life and Heini wasn't about to complain. The worst was his teeth, but fortunately they were falling out and stronger ones growing in their place. He always had somewhere to sleep, although never flash and often changing because his mother would drink the rent or one of her men would disappear with the purse. But still a place, either at the very bottom of the building or the very top, just the one room for five people, Heini, his sister and brother in one bed, and Greta with her latest in the other. And in between, the stove and the table and the stinking lamp and a string for the clothes and a bucket for the water and another for the slops. And bloating the air the familiar stench of fuel mixed with piss and foul breath and mould.

Heini far preferred the attics to the cellars. It was not just the filth from the street which oozed endlessly into the basements, nor the thick, prison-like bars that smothered the basement windows; he liked the way the windows bulged beneath the sloping roof of the garrets, and beyond the glass, the queer comfort of the endless sky. It was a bit like swimming, he would think, as he lay on the bed gazing out. He was fascinated by the clouds, how some stretched like smoke through the blue, and others were feathery like birds' wings, and others were puffed up and fat enough to carry a boy – although goodness knows where he'd go if ever he had the chance.

As lives went, Heini could pinpoint a lot worse. He knew of kids who spent their days coughing up their lungs, and others with umpteen brothers and sisters to squeeze into a life the same size as his own, and the dumb girl with the small head who dribbled and laughed and would be dead if she didn't have a mother to look after her. And while the current room might be smaller or colder or more lice-infested than others, Heini knew what was possible for people like him and what he needed to do each day to exploit the meagre possibilities. Even the places he robbed, with heaters that worked and two, sometimes three rooms for just one family, didn't rankle. They were robbing material pure and simple, and not for living in by the likes of him.

It is possible his mother may have once shared his views, but by 1918 nothing much mattered to her except the next drink. Greta and her mates had hardly budged when the machine guns first sounded, and most were still in their places when the war was over. But opportunities were not thick on the ground in the post-war period, and Heini, with a sister and brother to support, found himself stretched to the limit.

One morning while placating his aching teeth with the tip of his finger he noticed a group of children heading off to school. He followed at a distance, saw them enter through a gate and disappear into the building beyond. He had never thought of going to school before. But why not? There was money to be made in reading and writing, particularly down in the Scheunenviertel where plenty of people couldn't even sign their name. And if he was as smart as people said, he should manage book-learning as well as anyone. He looked more closely at the children, they were just like him, same rags, same ill-fitting shoes, same dirt on their faces. If it was all right for them, why not for him?

It took a month to organise. He chose a school near the market in order to be in close proximity to the shoppers, a little more evening work around the theatres, and most of the house-stealing he'd leave to his brother. The way he'd worked it out, he said to his mother, they shouldn't be any worse off. She thought it a god-awful idea. Everyone she knew had managed perfectly well without going to school. But Heini knew her friends, and if ever there was a reason for school it was them.

Although he nearly changed his mind on the first day. Everyone knew what to do and where to go and he didn't. He had always managed by being a step ahead of the rest and was jittery with all the strangeness. He decided to give it a month.

Well before the trial period was up, Heini had learned the ropes. He had learned the pecking order too. To be popular with the kids you had to be a leader in the playground without being a bully, and to win over the teacher you had to be clever. In fact, the teacher made his preference for the smart kids so obvious Heini wondered why the dumb ones bothered to turn up. Years of managing the family finances put him near the top of the class in arithmetic, and once he learned his letters there was no stopping him with reading and writing. The writing surprised the teacher, so neat and well shaped despite his large hand, and while Heini could easily have demonstrated where the credit lay with the teacher's wallet more often than not poking out of his pocket, he never did.

Heini settled into the new routine quickly. His mother hardly mentioned his going to school; in fact, he'd find himself wondering if she even remembered, and then she'd burst out with a snide remark about children who were too big for their boots and rising above themselves. Heini didn't care. He loved school and was determined to make the most of it. Within two years, and still only ten years of age, he was earning regular money reading and writing for those in the neighbourhood who couldn't. He passed on his learning to his brother and sister. Walter couldn't get the hang of it and as soon as he acquired the basics begged to be let off. But Hilde was just like him and took to the lessons like a drunk to drink.

Six years later when he left school, Heini judged it as time well spent; there were, after all, other ways of stealing than bag-snatching and housebreaking. But tough times meant his plans fell in a heap along with those of most other Germans. The war might have ended in 1918, but losing it went on for much longer. There were strikes and starvation, and what few pockets were full were hidden behind fortresses. And while Heini knew most people were suffering, when you're already on the bottom, the crush is that much worse. Day after day, month after month, year after year the same dismal story: not enough food, not enough money, and no prospects. Each day, he would go to the market with Walter; but even for expert scavengers, when the food is in short supply and the scavengers are not, you're lucky to come away with anything much at all.

With a month's rent owing and the landlord bellowing, the Hecks were forced to move again. If it hadn't been winter, Heini would have chosen the park rather than their new home. It was a corner of a basement, no window, and the worst room by far in a long sequence of bad rooms. The bricks were mouldy and damp, the stove gobbled coal and swallowed heat, the air wasn't fit for breathing; even the rats, Heini noticed, stayed away. And if the room was not bad enough, Walter's lungs were playing up, the drink was turning Greta's feet numb, and his sister, after falling prey to one of Greta's boyfriends, was not good for anything. They had always managed before, but now it was difficult to see anyone who was worse off.

With thieving proving unprofitable and his years of school not yielding the cash Heini had hoped, his life was an unremitting burden. For the first time ever he was desperate to escape. He had heard there was work to be found on farms, so he decided to try the countryside – although having never before ventured more than a couple of kilometres from Alexanderplatz, he could not have described a farm, much less the type of work he expected to find. But life was so miserable he simply didn't care.

He planned to slip out early one Friday before anyone was awake, but the morning was clogged with problems. There was his brother's cough to attend to, and his mother's feet were so bad she needed help to the bar. So instead of being out on the open road, he was lugging her down the street, her numb feet buckling beneath her, a barrel-shaped woman above her spindly legs, and no lightweight that's for sure. At last he gets her settled and returns home for his pack and there's his sister swearing she's seen the man who hurt her. She's clinging to him and crying and Heini knows if anyone can hold him here it's Hilde. Yet he has a premonition that if he doesn't leave now he'll never get away. Though his stomach churns for her, he tenses against the turmoil and calms her down, and as her grip loosens, he moves to leave. Immediately her body is pinning him back, and again he feeds her soothing words. But this time when her hold begins to weaken he makes sure he is prepared. He promises her a special treat.

He knows his sister, she's young and easily tempted. What treat? she asks. He tells her it's a surprise, that if she lets him go she'll soon find out. A minute later he is alone in the street and if he has any sense he'll make a run for it. But it's his sister and he has made a promise. It takes him almost an hour but eventually he tracks down a large, fragrant orange and returns to the room. Hilde is delighted. He sits on the bed with her and Walter and removes the peel slowly and delicately so as not to pierce the transparent skin, all the while telling about lands where oranges are so plentiful people can pick them from trees whenever the fancy takes them. With the peeling finished, he separates the segments. One for you, he says, handing a piece to his sister, one for you, he says to his brother, and one for me, and soon everyone is sucking a segment of orange. Then the process is repeated, and after that one more time.

'What happens if there are the wrong number of pieces?' Hilde asks.

'But that's the magic of oranges,' says Heini. 'There's always exactly the right number.'

With the orange finished and his sister calm and happy, Heini finally leaves. There are no goodbyes, he doesn't want to make it harder for himself, instead he trains his thoughts to the future. He'll find work and make enough money to send for Hilde and Walter, and the three of them will live together in a nice room in the country with a stove which works and sufficient food never to be hungry. The thoughts give him courage as he travels westwards, moving quickly through the familiar streets and into the broad strip of Unter den Linden. He crosses over Friedrichstrasse, he's practically running he's moving so fast, but any slower and he might change his mind. His pace slackens only after he passes through the Brandenburg Gate and, for the first time in his life, he enters the Tiergarten.

It's another world in here. The air is as fresh as rainwater and the light looks like it has been washed in gold. Even the sound is different, with muffled rustlings of birds and trees and the burr of distant traffic. The clunk and grate of his boots is thunderous, and he tries to tread more lightly. He's surprised at so many smart people with nothing better to do on a Friday afternoon than stroll beneath the trees and talk. He feels the scratch of their gaze and a prickling of heat down his back. He smoothes his hair and settles his jacket, but still they stare at him. A minute or two later he can't bear it any longer and takes the next path out of the park to the road.

It is late morning and not knowing how far he has to travel he sets himself a pace. With winter just around the corner the day is surprisingly warm. He stops at a fountain to drink, then he is off again and striding it out. In these bustling streets no one takes any notice of him and Heini far prefers it that way. He keeps his gaze to the ground, skirts the lumps and pits in the pavement, the garbage too, and expert scavenger that he is, easily sees the tiny coin even though it's coated with grime. It is not German money and useless to anyone with an empty stomach. He wipes it on his sleeve and studies the engraving. It's English, he thinks, and judging by the size not worth much, but still he folds it in a shred of paper and puts it in his pocket. It's an omen, he decides, to bring him luck in his new life.

He walks onwards until he reaches the district of Charlotten-burg. It is such a short way from home but it might be another country; it makes him think he wouldn't feel right in heaven if there turned out to be such a place. He stops in a quiet clean street lined with pale, palatial buildings. His boots are gross on grass that looks like it has just been to the barbers, and through the silence he hears a frantic panting – his own, he suddenly realises. He feels the danger creep down his spine; it's like being caught with your hand in a lady's purse. He raises his head, and his nostrils flare to the possibility of another life, but if there is a scent he fails to pick it up.

He has been away from home for just over an hour, yet knows this is not for him. He longs for the safety of noise and jostling crowds, he longs for the familiar smell of his own life. He recalls all he has heard of the country, the broad open fields and tranquil lakes and how you can walk for a whole day and not see a single person, and he imagines himself alone in the middle of a vast empty silent landscape buffeted by the same terror filling him now. But still he does not move. It is not until he sees a *Kinderfraülein* with two young children in her care that he turns back – not out of love for his family, in his short life love has never been sufficient reason to do anything, but someone has to look after them.

• • •

When Greta's next boyfriend arrived, a box of possessions in one hand, a flagon in the other and the usual empty pockets, Heini took a stand: he paid for the room, so he should decide who could stay. He made it clear that while his mother was welcome, her boyfriend was not. Greta packed her things and left, but returned within the week. With the arrival of the next man she left again, for a month this time. With the third man, when she had not come home after five weeks, Heini set out to find her.

Greta was neither happy nor unhappy to see him. She asked after Walter and Hilde, and before returning to her drink and her loser, muttered that Heini knew where she was should he need anything. The following week Heini found a better room. He pulled his mother out of the bar, sobered her up and dragged her off to the landlord because no one would rent a room to a fifteen year old with two children to support. It was one of the few services she had ever done for him, and, as it turned out, the last.

It was easier with only three: Heini, Hilde and Walter, attached to one another like fingers to a hand. Heini knew he would die for his sister or brother – no boast this, just never put to the test. Hilde's fears kept her indoors. It was not the one man who hurt her that filled her with terror, it was all men. She stayed home while the boys went in search of a living. Walter made a poor house thief, and was not much better as a bag snatcher; but as the twenties progressed and more goods and produce became available, he proved a champ at shopping. The things he paid for and the things he didn't meant they scraped by. Heini took whatever reading and writing jobs came his way, but with more children going to school he knew there was little future in it. As for thieving, if he had a cart he might have tried the large houses near the Tiergarten, he may even have ventured as far as those places he'd seen in Charlottenburg, but he had no cart, not even the possibility of one. As for bicycles, he'd never had any luck with them: as quickly as he stole one so it would be stolen from him. And with the roads such a mess and many of the streetcar tracks running on planks because of the new underground construction, even streetcars were no longer fast or reliable. That left only his feet.

The old rooming houses, like those the Hecks had always lived in, had never been worth a thief's attention, so Heini concentrated, as he had always done, on those buildings in neighbouring districts where access was easy, locks were limp, and valuables, if not thick on the ground, sufficient to make the risk worthwhile. In short, he robbed the flats of the nearly poor. He robbed the coalman and the clerk, he robbed the streetcar driver and the leather dyer. He robbed people who could not afford to lose a pfennig. But what choice did he have? He might prefer to rob the rich of their wallets and handbags, but in the long aftermath of the Treaty of Versailles, the rich were in short supply and pickpockets as numerous as flies.

Month by month the pickings were ever more slender. As a last resort Heini decided to try the huge new apartment blocks which were springing up in the district. These buildings, erected for people much like himself, were just a fancier type of slum and he had previously avoided them. He had watched when the bulldozers moved in, watched as they destroyed everything – shops, stalls, corners for talking, benches for loitering, eaves for smoking under, watched as a good chunk of daily life disappeared. These buildings held few attractions for the thief but now it seemed he had little choice.

One morning while he was enjoying a quiet smoke just a couple of streets from one of the new apartment blocks and thinking that as soon as he was finished he would wander over and try his luck, a huge explosion occurred, rocketing smoke and debris high into the sky. And following the first explosion, smaller aftershocks. There was a long pause between the roar of the explosions and people rushing into the streets, a quiet, queer moment like the world had just stopped and was not yet ready to begin again. When the shouting began, Heini joined the throng running towards the new building. It was all smoke and ruin when they arrived. A huge gas explosion had ripped the guts out of the place, ripped the guts out of the inhabitants too. Heini had been a cigarette away from death, and as he walked away he wondered how much luck he had left.

Prospects

Since his earliest years, Heini had known that the essence of satisfaction was living the right-sized life. And while it didn't take much nous to realise that where poverty reigns, the right-sized life is very small indeed, you have to make a go of it. He knew this all the way down to his fingertips, but for reasons he couldn't explain, the knowledge started to slip. He became aware of a growing unease, a bit like two rusty cogs grinding inside him. It was on the day he first met the Jewish pastry-cook he realised that what he was feeling was none other than wanting more – more than was possible.

It was a bleak, dirty day, and he was tired and hungry. Hilde hadn't left the room all week and Walter was coughing and spluttering and too sick to work. There was little food around and the small change in his pocket so small it wouldn't yield half a cabbage. Three mouths to feed and neither food nor money, and he was tired of it all. He was sixteen years old, the sort of lad who in different circumstances might have made a mother proud, strong and solid with a crop of blond wavy hair, rather like a lion in appearance, so he had been told. Sixteen years old, yet all out of energy. He couldn't have said exactly what he needed, but it wasn't this filth, this gutter, this room, this hunger, this cough. And it wasn't the winter cold, the howling pipes, the savage itch of his skin, and his bloody teeth which wouldn't fall out, just clung to their boiling abscesses until he begged the barber to pull. He would see people sashaying through the streets or riding in cabs, their stomachs full, their teeth good, he would watch these people and be prepared to make any bargain to be them – not forever, just while he regained his energy and found the money for some decent teeth.

He was wandering the streets chewing on his dissatisfaction, no longer wondering how best to manage for Hilde and Walter, no longer planning where the next meal was coming from, just writhing around in the rottenness of his life. It was only when he entered Münzstrasse and the black-coated Jews with their straggly beards flapped across his vision that he became aware of where he was. He looked around at the decaying buildings and poked his head into dingy courtyards: these Jews with their tatty clothes and bent bodies were nearly as poor as he, yet seemed not to have it so hard. And suddenly he felt the unfairness of it all: his poor was the worst poor of all. Even Jews had jobs and families, even Jews had teeth. And so lost himself in wanting or else would not have attacked the pastry-cook, not in this area with the pastry-cook a shout away from friends. Not anywhere for that matter, Heini was a thief not a brute.

The Jew wasn't hurt, nor did he seem particularly scared. He steadied Heini with a clean hand on his sleeve and calming words. And Heini would never understand how it happened, but there he was minutes later walking down the street with an old Jew he'd just attacked, and he's talking like a burst drain with no hint of running dry, talking when he should have been out of there.

Heini had never been one for conversation. He was partial to a smoke and the occasional chat, but mostly was happy with his own company. As for complaining about his measly life, it would only make him look weak, and besides, no one would be interested. But the old Jew not only listened he actually encouraged, asking question after question in an odd clotted speech that sounded like he'd swallowed German and brought it up thicker. And whether it was the novelty of it all or Heini was simply at the end of his tether, the words gushed out of him like they'd been lying in wait for just the right moment. By the time they stopped outside a pastry shop, Heini felt as if he'd spilled his whole life.

'This is my place,' the old man said, indicating the shop. 'If you want, you can come in.'

Heini wasn't thinking straight. He'd attacked a Jew, he'd talked more in the past few minutes than he had in the past few months, and now without a moment's hesitation he was entering a Jewish shop. The smell of baking knuckled into his nostrils and shot straight to his glands. The old man offered a dish of small pastries each shaped like a crescent moon. Heini took one if only to stop his talking, then another and another; they melted in his salivary mouth. Such special food made him feel important, much the same, he suspected, as owning a shirt collar or a second pair of shoes. And in that moment he knew that if ever the day came when he ate pastry regularly, he would have left the Scheunenviertel far behind.

'Choose,' the old man said, waving an arm at his cakes. 'Anything you like for your brother and sister. Choose.'

Heini was used to taking what was available and never anything left over; surrounded by such plenty he was at a loss. The old Jew saw his trouble, and after a moment he selected a tart large enough for ten brothers and sisters and put it in a box.

'This,' he said pointing to the tart, 'is the best in Berlin. A perfect *Pflaumenküchen*.' He uttered the word as if he were tasting it. 'I know because I have tested. Some make the pastry too thick, or the plums they slice too thin, or they make mean with the fruit. But this,' and he was triumphant, 'this is the real *Pflaumenküchen*.' He closed the box and pushed it towards Heini.

In his whole life Heini had never tasted a plum much less a cake full of them. And probably wouldn't now, for surely the man would want something in return. With a glance at the box, he said nothing, just turned to leave. But the old man persevered.

'Take it,' he said.

Heini felt himself hesitate. 'You sure you don't want any money? You don't want anything at all?'

'No, no. I give it to you. I can tell, you're not a bad boy.'

And Heini wanted to say, and you're not a bad Jew either – but was unpractised with compliments.

The cake was delicious. And even though he, Hilde and Walter ate a piece whenever they pleased, it lasted a full two days.

'I bet if you went back to that Jew's shop, he'd give you another,' Walter said.

And probably he would, but Heini had to decide first whether the old man with his talking was good for him. It was like that initial time at school when he didn't know the routines: he was attracted but also unnerved by the strangeness. In the end he returned – for the conversation more than the food, and returned many times after that, pausing a moment at the threshold of the shop to step out of the stab and grind of his usual life into his very own make-believe.

The old Jew always seemed pleased to see him. He liked people, he said, and he liked to talk.

'I know plenty of people you wouldn't like,' Heini said one day. 'Rough people, bad people.'

'Bad? Good? Only God judges.'

God certainly wasn't working overtime, Heini thought, and must have allowed the thought to rise to his face.

'You have to forgive, Heini,' the old Jew said.

He liked it best when the old man told him stories from his own life. Compared with Heini's family who had always lived within a shout of Alexanderplatz, the Jew's life could fill an adventure book. His ancestors had come from a town called Gollancz near the border of Poland and Russia – he showed Heini the exact spot on his very own map. A long time before the Jew was born, his family had left Gollancz and slowly moved west-wards. They would stop in a town for a few years until the local people started attacking Jews, and then they would move on to another town until the attacks started there too. It was in one of these towns that the old Jew had been born. Step by step, attack by attack, they had moved westwards. Finally, when the man was about the same age as Heini, his family had arrived in Berlin.

The Jew leaned back against the cooling racks, a fine shower of flour dusting his cap and settling on his shoulders. 'And here I've stayed. A pastry-cook like my father. A fine wife, no sons but four daughters, all good girls with good husbands, a grandfather of ten.' He shrugged, not so much with his shoulders, Heini noticed, but more with his arms and hands. 'I'm not complaining.'

The old Jew told about his cousin who had gathered his family and taken them across the world to Australia. 'There,' he said, indicating a pink mass on the map about as far from Germany as you could go. 'My cousin, he writes me letters. He likes to tell me how well he's doing. In *schmutters* he is.'

Heini didn't understand.

'Clothes, he makes clothes – and these Australians, they must want to buy. Last I heard he was driving around in his own motor car.'

Heini wondered why the pastry-cook didn't go to Australia.

'Too old,' he said, stroking his ragged beard. 'But you're not.'

Heini laughed. Germany didn't think he was worth much, otherwise he'd have a better life. So why on earth would Australia want him?

'I'm telling you,' the old man said, 'if they take my cousin, they'll take anyone. The country, it's too big,' and again the odd shrugging with the hands, 'they have to fill it somehow.'

Over the next several months, until just after he turned seventeen, Heini visited the old Jew. Except for Hilde and Walter, he told no one, for while there didn't seem much reason to hate Jews more than you'd hate anyone else, nearly everyone did. In fact, if Jew hatred were a business, Heini found himself thinking, a man could make a fortune.

For the first few visits Heini wasn't allowed to touch anything. His was a kosher shop, the old man explained, Jewish food for Jewish customers. But later he gave Heini a space of his own well away from the other workbenches, with his own bowl and implements. He would make him scrub his hands until they looked like someone else's then show him how to beat a mixture or roll out pastry.

'Perhaps one day you'll be a pastry-cook like me,' the old man said.

More likely just an older thief, Heini thought, but nonetheless enjoyed the work, how you start with a little bit of this and a little bit of that and in the end you have a whole cake or tart. And the talk, he enjoyed the talk. The old man was a gift. In his words, in his kindness, in the cakes he gave to Heini to take home, he was a gift. And in return? Heini did not know and neither could he ask.

He returned to the shop again and again. He found himself wanting to be with the old man more than he wanted to do any-thing else. The old man was pleasure for pleasure's sake, something

Heini had never before experienced, something he knew that in his sort of life couldn't possibly last. And there was a grating against his heart. Heini wasn't accustomed to kindness and the old man's kindness was making him soft. The Jew was just like his cakes, a luxury Heini couldn't afford, so he tried to visit less often. But he couldn't stick to his plan, and in the end – it was hard, so hard – he forced himself to stay away altogether.

The twenties had been so bad for the inhabitants of the Scheunen-viertel it was hard to imagine it could get any worse. But when the Depression hit, bad took on a whole new definition. The Scheunenviertel swelled with newcomers. Heini saw men in good coats with nothing but their hands in their pockets, men who were strangers to being poor and very bad at it. And children with hunger clinging to their bones crowding the streets and courtyards. Heini stopped thinking about the old Jew, he stopped thinking about a better life; just surviving each day took all his energy.

By 1934 when things began to improve, Heini had done two short stints in prison for stealing from the wrong pockets – although hard to know what pockets would have been right when practically all were empty. Walter had fared much better. He had joined Hitler's Stormtroopers and was rising through the ranks. Hilde was still Hilde, under Heini's wing and still afraid. As for work, Heini might have joined the SA himself but they were not his type of men. He'd seen them in action all his life, first with his mother then with Hilde and now with anyone who stood in their way.

The long years of the Depression had been bad for thieving, and at a time when it should have been easier, with so many people in uniform, Heini still was out of luck. No matter how much he planned, there was always someone on the lookout, someone paid to keep the law. With obstacles looming at every turn, Heini no longer had the heart for thieving, so again he decided to try the countryside. He felt more prepared this time, older, wiser, and his stints in prison had taught him how to survive away from the noise and bustle of Berlin. He found a motherly type to keep an eye on Hilde, gathered his belongings and followed the path of the river out of the city. As soon as he was beyond the city limits, he took off his clothes and washed away the crawling grime from his body, then lay his clothes and himself on the ground in a small clearing to dry.

It was quiet, only the sound of birds and the intermittent chug and shout from the river. He lay on his back, shading his eyes from the sun and feeling cool droplets of water snaking over his scalp; they tickled in a pleasant sort of way. With the city now behind him, he decided to put a wall between his old life and the new. A fresh start, he told himself, and no turning back.

But the countryside was not kind to him. Heini didn't know the life nor did he know how to work for a boss. He was hired to cut grass, and so he did until he was tired, and then he rested. But sitting was permitted only after all the cutting was finished. He would cut much better after he regained his breath, he said, and soon found himself out of work. In his next job he was dismissed for felling too many trees. He was just providing the firewood he had been asked for, he said, and was told he had cut trees enough for the whole village.

At his next position he hoed a vegetable garden and planted the seeds in rows exactly as directed by Frau S, a fat, shrill woman with a pretty daughter.

'In rows,' she shouted periodically from her kitchen just to make sure.

And in rows they went, just like he was told. And such delight when the sprouting began, like the thrill when the old Jew's pastries puffed up in the oven. As Heini watched the seedlings grow, he was thinking he might become a farmer. The farm was large enough for more than one family, and daughters who would not see twenty again needed a husband. He was dreaming of staying forever, learning to ride a horse, learning to plough a field, sending for Walter and Hilde and marrying the pretty daughter, when he was grabbed by the mother and dragged to the vegetable garden.

What had he done? The rows were perfect, all the vegetables sprouting. What had he done?

She was yelling at him and calling him stupid. Corn, she jabbed at one plant, beans, she jabbed at the next, potatoes at the next.

'It's a salad of a row,' she screamed at him, and told him to get out before she set the dogs onto him.

The best two months of his life and he was booted out with

even less than when he arrived, although fortunately not the daughter's virtue. Two more jobs in the country and he tossed it in and returned to Berlin. He may have lost the heart for stealing but at least he knew what the job required. And Hilde was so happy to have him home, and there was more money about and better food. Even Walter marching in his black boots was happy. Everyone seemed happier.

And perhaps that was the problem, things became too easy and Heini stopped looking over his shoulder. When he was arrested in the spring of 1936 just before the Berlin Olympics and put away, not for a few months but for two years, Heini knew he'd run out of luck. And when they sent him not to the old prison but the new camp at Orianienberg-Sachsenhausen, he knew he was done for. And when two years later he was released, and Hilde had disappeared along with life as he had known it, he thought his luck was still running backwards. But only briefly. With a past so tarnished you couldn't even give it away, he decided it was no great loss. Not even Hilde. He searched for a few weeks and then he gave up. He'd provided what protection he could, now she had to manage without him.

Only two years, but so much had changed. Everywhere were men in uniform, boys too, poor people like him making a go of it. Life was better, much better under Hitler, and only a Jew would dispute it. Without any difficulty Heini found himself a proper job in a munitions factory building gun carriages for the thousand-year Reich. It was a far cry from the pastry-cook of his old dreams, but he liked the work and for the first time in his life he felt he was doing something worthwhile. And his country seemed to value him, that was a first too. Heini would look around and feel a sense of belonging – not that he made friends, it had never been his way, but he felt part of a big important movement. Life was good, life was very good.

Occasionally he thought of the old Jew, the only person ever to think he might amount to something, and one day, dressed in his first ever new coat with a nice lambswool collar, he made his way into the Jewish streets. Heini hardly recognised the area. The shops were daubed with slogans, the Jewish star in careless paint was slapped on walls and windows, the streets were largely deserted, shutters were drawn, shops were boarded up; the air was stilted and eerily hushed. He felt the furtive glances of Jews behind their windows: they did not want him here, although would want a German in uniform even less. He pushed on regardless until he reached the pastry-cook's shop. The shutters were drawn, the dust on the slats lay thick and hard. No one had been here for a long time. Heini peered through a gap in the shutters; there was nothing but blackness within.

Suddenly he was aware of what he was doing, a German in a new coat peering like a thief into the darkness of an old Jew's shop, and turned sharply away – from the old Jew, from these streets, from the past. He should have had more sense: with a life such as his, sentimentality was not a terrain he had explored or was ever likely to. And yet as he hurried away he was aware of his disappointment. He had wanted to show the Jew he had made something of his life.

With a clogging in his throat, Heini pushed himself fast from the old familiar streets, past Museumsinsel and into Unter den Linden. He walked briskly up the broad avenue, crossed over Friedrichstrasse and Wilhelmstrasse, pushed himself away from his old life, past the swirl of rich foreigners at the Adlon Hotel, right up to the Brandenburg Gate. There he stopped and looked back.

The thoroughfare stretching before him was bursting with activity. The new linden trees, planted when the underground construction was completed, were now nearly as high as the banners. Heini breathed deeply and the pain in his throat eased. The old Jew, together with Hilde and Walter, the only people ever to have cared about him, were his past, but this – the grand buildings, the smart people, the green lindens, the bright red and black banners – this was his future. Little remained of his old life, and soon it would be just a scuffling at the back of his mind. There was still the problem of his teeth, but he had a job, and a room shared with just one other fellow, and with so many opportunities for people like him, it was anyone's guess what the future had in store. Heini looked down the broad avenue. Mingled with the fancy tourists were men in uniform going about their business, men who looked no different from himself. Men who had turned to the new Germany and seen it had a place for them.

He stood in the crowd, absently rubbing his sore gums. At twenty-eight years of age he was no angel, but neither was he useless. He'd been to school, he had a proper job, he made honest money. There was opportunity in the air, he could smell it. He might find a wife, settle down, he might even join the army. And suddenly he realised that he, Heinrik Heck, could do anything. His country wanted him and in return it would look after him and, with a stab of pain deep into his jaw, his rotting teeth too.

Out of a Job in the
New Germany

About a kilometre from Heinrik Heck and the hubbub of Unter den Linden, a well-dressed couple enter Tiergartenstrasse from the southern edge of the park. Across the road at number seventeen is the British Passport Control Office. Martin Lewin points it out to his wife who scarcely glances at the building. And when he urges her forward, she holds her ground, so he loops his arm through hers and leads. As they step onto the road the wind swipes her scarf; straining against her neck, the ribbon of underwater blues streaks back towards the park. With the intransigence of her gait, the granite set of her face, her husband pulling one way, the scarf streaming the other, Renate Lewin looks to be in flight against herself. But still Martin leads, a small man, shorter than his wife, but determined. When they reach the other side of the road, Renate refuses to go any further. Martin pauses a moment before taking her hand and removing her glove, ever so slowly. He presses his mouth to her palm, then turns the hand and glides his lips across the bony stretch of her fingers. Suddenly she smiles, an attractive woman in a modern, stylised way, and he smiles back.

With his features now animated, Martin Lewin appears younger than at first sight. Indeed, he would be much the same age as Heinrik Heck, although there any likeness would end. Where Heini is large and blond, Martin is compact and dark. And there is a roughness about Heini that not even a new coat with a fine lambswool collar can disguise. Martin Lewin, in contrast, is all neatness and formality, from his clipped brown beard and dark-rimmed spectacles to the overcoat which drapes his small frame without a wrinkle. He bears a resemblance to the famous Dr Freud, younger of course, but with the same serious mien and tidy composure.

Martin Lewin is a businessman, or used to be back in the days when Jews were still allowed to work, a bookish silk merchant from Krefeld via Düsseldorf who still carries himself with the customary ease of more prosperous days. But times have changed. While Heinrik Heck from the Berlin gutter is facing the future with eager optimism, Martin Lewin knows there is no place for him and his family in the new Germany.

He raises an anxious face towards the British Passport Control Office. Here he hopes to find a new home for his family somewhere in the vast British Commonwealth. Perhaps England, or Scotland or Wales, even India or Australia. It doesn't really matter, Martin has decided the Lewins will go anywhere.

His wife, however, has very different ideas. Renate Lewin does not want to be here at the British Passport Control Office; in fact, she does not want to be in Berlin at all, dashing from embassy to legation to specialist foreign office in search of visas. She wants to be home in Krefeld safe behind closed doors, with her husband, her daughter, her mother, and her silk-designing materials. But Martin has insisted: for their lives, he keeps saying, for their lives they have to leave Germany. Renate disagrees as she has for a number of years now, but even if he were right, she does not see why they have to emigrate so far. She might adjust to Paris or Amsterdam, but India and Australia simply do not figure on her map of the world. She has said as much to Martin, but he is among those who believe Hitler will not stop at Austria and the Sudetenland. Not only should Jews leave Germany, he is convinced they should move as far from Europe as possible.

'I don't want to live in England,' she now says, pulling on her glove. 'I don't want to live anywhere in the British Commonwealth.' She launches each word with a tug on the soft kidskin.

'And I don't want to live in Brazil or the United States either,' a reference to the other visa applications Martin has lodged recently. 'Please, Martin, reconsider.'

He shakes his head sadly. This is a man who loves his wife with a deep and passionate love, a man who is distressed by seeing her unhappy, a man who hates being the cause of her misery. But he has no choice. Renate refuses to see that Jews have no place in Hitler's Germany; she says the Germans will come to their senses. But what senses are these, Martin wonders, given the Germans are happier and more productive than at any time since the war?

And besides, they have their daughter to consider. Only six years old but deprived of a normal childhood, Alice Lewin can't go to school, she can't even go outside to play with any guarantee of safety.

'We have no choice,' Martin says to his wife. 'It's not just a matter of our preferences. It's Alice we need to think about.'

The mention of their daughter softens Renate as Martin knew it would. And while he is not fool enough to confuse a temporary lull in their differences with long-term compliance, at least Renate now enters the building without further argument.

Once inside they give their names and are directed to a waiting area. The room is crowded with men and women, young and old, and a number of children too. Renate and Martin are shocked to see children here. Alice is safe at home in Krefeld with her grandmother, protected as much as possible in these dark days from a country and people who wish her harm. But other parents are clearly less vigilant. There's a baby cradled in its mother's arms, a toddler holding tightly to a doll, and four other children, all much the same age as Alice, sitting silent and solemn next to their parents.

'Perhaps there's no one to look after them at home,' Martin whispers to Renate.

But Renate will have none of it. 'There's no excuse for exposing children to this.' She scans the array of people, all of them white-faced and watchful. 'If parents won't protect their children, who will?'

The woman with the baby is sobbing quietly, and now the baby starts to grizzle – not a normal baby's complaint, more a quiet keening, a sound that might belong to any of the people gathered in this room.

The Lewins find two vacant seats against the far wall and there they sit waiting their turn. Fear, hope, desperation, all are running savage here, and a starched white tension, tight and still. Movements are smothered, the papers grasped in so many hands are checked and checked again, always surreptitiously. No one disturbs and yet everyone is disturbed. No one forgets for a moment that one family's luck will be another family's loss. People steal glances at the competition as if it could be determined by manner and appearance whose application will be successful. There is a background murmur of well-modulated German, and an occasional English phrase, but not a word of Yiddish. These Jews are quite a different type from those Eastern European Jews of Heini Heck's experience. In fact, there is unlikely to be a pastry-cook anywhere in this room. Here are gathered secular Jews from Germany's middle-class: doctors, lawyers, academics, business people, all of them indistinguishable from other Germans.

Martin takes them in. 'They're just like us,' he whispers to Renate.

And just like Martin and Renate, they would have lived a comfortable German existence before the rise of Hitler. They would have eaten at restaurants and patronised the theatre and the opera, they would have enjoyed lives which Heini Heck could only dream about. These are well-educated people, discreetly Jewish and proudly German, yet in a few short years they have been reduced to circumstances worse than anything Heini has ever experienced. Heini has known hunger and violence, he has known neglect and poverty, but he has always known there was a place for him in Germany, no matter how menial. But not so today's Jews, not so Martin and Renate Lewin: their very lives are being squeezed. Deprivation, humiliation, threats, violence, and what was distressing but tolerable even as recently as last year is now an ever-present and life-threatening danger. Martin sees his own fear and desperation reflected in the faces and demeanour of the other Jews in this room. It's like being on the deck of a sinking ship with not enough lifeboats to go around.

Suddenly there is a shattering of the brittle air. A woman on the other side of the room is on her feet and waving her arms. 'We were here before you,' she shouts. 'We were here before you.' And turning to the elderly couple next to her, 'You saw us, I know you saw us arrive before them,' and points with her fist in the direction of two girls, neither of them more than sixteen, making their way to one of the desks at the top of the room. The woman follows them, 'They're pushing in,' she shouts, as she pushes past chairs, crushing toes and scraping shins. The toddler's doll falls to the floor, the woman scuttles it yet presses on. Her husband lunges, but she's too quick. He lunges again and this time he manages to grab her jacket, and with apologetic glances to the rest of the room drags her back to her seat. The woman's voice is quieter now but still audible. 'It's not fair,' she says over and over. 'It's not fair.'

And neither it is. Not this place, these queues, this Germany, this *Führer*. And not the laws against Jews, nor those countries that guard their visas like gold. Nothing is fair any more. And when one Jew makes a fuss twenty Jews suffer. Martin wonders if this woman has spoiled their chances. He looks around the room trying to read the faces. But whether spy or Jew is watching, it is impossible to judge.

Over the next two hours there are other outbursts, people for whom the fear or anger or confusion or the sheer unfairness of it all can no longer be contained. Martin and Renate sit locked inside themselves, both knowing it is safer this way. When at last their name is called, Martin approaches the desk alone. He has told Renate he will impress better with his English if he does not have to translate for her, but in truth he is afraid her antagonism to any place that is not Germany will spoil their chances. Yesterday with the Americans and the day before with the Brazilians she made no attempt to hide her lack of interest in their countries, nor her intention to return to Germany as soon as circumstances improved. Not wanting to jeopardise their chances with the whole of the British Commonwealth, Martin uses his unstable English as an excuse to talk with the official alone. Although it is difficult, in this the most crucial move of their lives, to be acting without her.

He has been told that a knowledge of English will help their chances, but as he talks with the officer, he learns their prospects are not good no matter how proficient his English. It was much the same story with the Americans yesterday. So many other German Jews are ahead of them in the emigration queues, people with skills and qualifications much more in demand than those of a silk merchant and his silk-designer wife. Their case seems so hopeless, and their lack of money makes it even worse. And such committed Germans are he and Renate that they have no contacts in Britain, no contacts anywhere in the world, no one to sponsor them or provide guarantees.

The interview is brief and dismal. The Lewin application is placed with others in a tray and Martin walks back to his seat. Everyone watches, everyone is trying to read the result in his face. One man actually speaks: 'The English,' he says in English, 'it helps?' Martin shrugs, who knows what helps? And takes Renate by the arm and together they leave the building.

Back in the fresh air, he feels as if a thresher has plunged through him; all wilt and dust, he's never felt so useless nor so weak. And when a couple walk past on their way into the building, the man familiar from the press and obviously someone of distinction, Martin feels a further slackening: with people like that applying for Britain, what chance do they have?

'We'll be all right,' Renate says.

If only it were true, Martin is thinking. If only merely wishing for something could make it happen, there would be no Hitler, no Nazis, and German Jews would not find themselves outlawed in their own country. It would be so much easier if he could talk with his wife, properly talk about the current situation. But she refuses, and sometimes quite violently; in fact, if it were any less important, Martin would have given up trying a long time ago.

He glances across at her, she is looking more relaxed than she has since their arrival in Berlin, and he decides to let things settle for the moment. He steadies himself with a few deep breaths, he doesn't feel strong but will pretend and, linking his arm through hers, steps into the street. He knows they should contact Erich, Renate's brother, but with no good news to report there seems so little point. Besides, they discussed all the options last night with him and his wife Dora, and again over breakfast this morning, and for now Martin wants no more talking. He feels such futility as if he and all the Jews in Germany are trapped in a maze to which there is neither entry nor exit, all of them in a haphazard scampering while Nazis take potshots at them from strategically placed watchtowers.

With a couple of hours to spare before their train to Düsseldorf leaves, they decide to spend it in the Tiergarten. After three days in Berlin clogged with official buildings and official people, with every waking moment dogged by the struggles of staying in Germany and their struggles to leave, and spiking it all the unaccustomed strain between them, there is every reason to revisit a place that has in the past provided them with so much pleasure.

They cross the road and enter the park. It is a mild day with autumn in full splendour. The sun is shining and the air is crisp and golden. The paths are full of promenading people chattering and laughing as if the world has not changed. And brilliantly coloured leaves lifting in the gentle breeze and fluttering through the air like exotic butterflies. Martin plucks one from Renate's hair and slips it into his pocket.

The park provides a buffer between them and the world outside; Martin feels himself loosen and Renate too. They walk the paths in a slow sauntering beneath branches deeply black against a pale mauve sky. And carpeting the lawns, leaves so richly red that if you were not there to see, if you could not bend down and place them so bright against the white of your skin, you would not believe such colour possible. Martin finds himself wondering where they might be next autumn, and immediately a single, urgent plea: not here, anywhere, but not here.

They remain in the southern section of the park, brushing easily against each other as they walk, an arresting couple with her grace and height and his perfect neatness. They wander past lakes and the river and numerous mounds of dirt made by burrowing beasts, and once even the pale flash of a rabbit. And at last, in this russet and gold place they feel themselves ease back together again. They continue deeper into the park. No traffic penetrates here, just the rustling of leaves, the scrape of their shoes on the gravel, the occasional shout from distant children.

'It's not so different from our first visit,' Renate says, recalling their honeymoon of ten years ago. She leans in closer, touching her face to his neck.

A little further on, in a sheltered area by one of the smaller paths, they notice a man asleep on a bench. He's ragged and filthy and even at a distance they can smell him.

'So Hitler hasn't put everyone back to work,' Renate says looking at the man.

'Jews and derelicts, who would have thought we'd have so much in common?'

It's a poor joke and the spell is immediately broken. Martin's face is grim as he checks his watch, and though they have plenty of time, they make their way back across the park and directly on to Zoo Station. With their pleasures so few and fragile these days, Martin should have thought before he spoke – though Renate appears undisturbed, her brow is clear and her hand on his arm is relaxed. She seems to see what he sees but somehow manages to dispatch the fear more easily. He looks around at the crowds and traffic and so many Nazis, far more than in Düsseldorf or their own town of Krefeld, and feels so exposed.

'We'll be fine,' Renate says again, squeezing his arm. 'Just as long as we stay in Krefeld and keep a low profile, we'll make it through this period.'

She sounds so sure and so like her old self, but she's wrong, he knows she's wrong. Renate has always been the more practical of the two of them, the more realistic too, and the more decisive. It was she who decided when it was time to have a child, she who guided him through the first hollow months when his business was taken. It was she who, after her father died earlier in the year, arranged for her mother to leave Düsseldorf and come to live with them in Krefeld. In fact, all the major decisions of their married life, with the single exception of where they would live – Krefeld, where Martin's business was, and not Düsseldorf where Renate grew up – have been made by her. And Martin has been happy for this to be so. For not only is Renate practical and efficient, she is usually right. But not in this matter of emigration, and the reversal of roles is not comfortable for either of them. Several months ago, despite her opposition, he lodged their papers with the Palestine Office, and in the past couple of days, added America, Britain and Brazil. But still she refuses to face the reality of being Jewish in today's Germany, refuses to see that Hitler is having a dream run. The entire country is now behind him, even here in Berlin where not so long ago the people regarded him as something of a joke. And much of the rest of the world is behind him too. Just a few months ago Hitler marched into Austria and no one stopped him. And a couple of weeks ago he announced the Sudetenland would become part of Greater Germany and still no one stopped him. The British leader Chamberlain comes and goes and as long as Hitler is happy, he is happy too. Everyone seems to love Hitler, everyone except the Jews.

Fake Coffee and
False Promises

Several weeks later, four hundred kilometres west of Berlin in the provincial town of Krefeld, Martin Lewin lay beside his sleeping wife lulled by the familiar sounds of a new day. There was the clatter of horse hooves, the clang of milk cans, the coalman's curses and the grocer grunting as he struggled to raise the iron grille of his shop. A bus wheezed to a stop, a car strained in the frosty morning, and then, as the other sounds fell silent, Martin heard the flap and whip of the swastika banners in the early morning breeze. Suddenly he was alert, the sounds of the new day drowned out by noise from the new Germany.

There had been no word on their visas, and with every day bringing new restrictions and deprivations it felt as if life were going backwards. At the same time, Germans kitted out with new hopes, new opportunities and new uniforms were living better than ever before. Even Heini Heck was prospering under the new regime. Having learned that a spell in prison was no bar to the army, he had dropped in at a recruitment office to investigate his options. When asked what he could do, he said he could cook. And why not? he thought, when there was opportunity for all Germans smart enough to take advantage. His days were now passed on the army parade grounds learning to be a soldier and in the army kitchens learning how to cook.

While Heini's life was hurtling down paths unimaginable before Hitler came to power, in the Lewin household life was reduced to subsistence level. As Martin lay in bed this November morning, he was already totting up the most pressing of his problems while trying to ignore the scrape of anxiety in his stomach. He wished he could pull the quilt over his head like he used to as a child, knowing that when he again emerged the problems would have dispersed. Instead he turned towards Renate and buried his face in the curve of her neck. Gently, so as not to wake her, he ran his hand over her shoulder, down the quiet ripple of her ribs, across the rise of her hip and the familiar swell of her thigh. Not everything had changed, he reminded himself. He might be without work and freedom of movement and his life might be reduced to bare bones, but no one, not even Hitler, could silence his heart.

He pressed in closer and must have dozed, for when next he opened his eyes it was dawn and the sky a wintry pale. Renate was still fast asleep, rare in these jittery days, and Martin not about to wake her. He slid to the edge of the bed, pushed his feet into yesterday's cold shoes, pulled on his old, wilted dressing gown, and with a last glance at his sleeping wife left the room.

He stopped outside his daughter's bedroom. All quiet within, but Alice, who had never needed much sleep, more than likely awake. Such a solemn child she was, with far too many burdens for a six year old and far too little childhood to temper them. He pressed his ear to her door, still no sound, just the sharp and all-too-familiar pang of having failed his child. He hesitated a moment longer before continuing down the dim hallway to his mother-in-law's room. Here there was a filament of light beneath the door; Amalie Friedman was awake but Martin knew she would not want to be disturbed. He moved to the edge of the runner where the carpet was less worn and headed towards the kitchen.

He turned on the light then thought better of it, he could make his coffee just as well in the gloom, and the heater wasn't even a consideration despite the steely air. He should have worn his coat over his pyjamas, instead was left to pull the flimsy gown tighter and worry as he did most of the time these days how best to eke out their meagre funds with no job, hefty expenses and silence on their visas.

Martin Lewin had always been a man of order and what he was wanting now was a plan to follow. He wanted to know they could spend X Reichsmark this week, and Y Reichsmark the following week, and in the third week they would sell the rest of the silver cutlery, and in the fourth week … and so on until, say, week eight when they would hand over the last of their money for visas and bribes and board the boat for America or Britain or, if there were no other choice, Palestine or Brazil. He was wanting a sure-fire strategy for survival at a time when uncertainty was the only reliable player.

He had sought help from foreign silk buyers and sent letters to foreign embassies. He had asked favours from more fortunate friends as they were leaving the country and had maintained regular contact with the various German-Jewish organisations. His days were choked with efforts to leave Germany and for his pains there had not been a flicker of hope. He knew there would be more violence, he knew there would be more restrictions, but the nature of the violence and the extent of the restrictions made a mockery of his tidy mind. He used to believe that people, good people, had a limited tolerance for behaving badly – How to live with oneself? How to justify one's brutality? What to say to one's children? – but today's good Germans were showing a remarkable tolerance and breath-taking stamina. Such strength they displayed and how it crushed.

He sat at the table in the kitchen, his chin cupped in his hands, staring at an old oil stain in the wood. His life was unrecognisable from a few years ago. Nothing had remained untouched, not even here in the flat where he had lived most of his life. And it would only become worse. Winter had begun early this year and how they would manage Martin simply did not know. As a boy he had loved this season: the slingshots made from acorns, the skating rink opening, the first snow, and no matter how cold the weather, it would always be warm at home with stoked boilers and hot drinks and wet clothes dried without a fuss and dry ones always available.

How different it was for his daughter. Today's acorns were German acorns and best left where they lay, the skating rink was banned to Jews, and snow meant never being warm and dry. And summer promised no better. As a child Martin had passed the long hot days down at the river with a mob of boys and girls, Germans and Jews all together and no one bothered by it. But now even the water had been Aryanised and another slice of childhood denied his daughter.

He pulled himself from his seat and busied himself with the coffee, or rather the stuff that passed for coffee these days, put the pot on the stove and cupped his hands around the bowl for warmth. As he stood there he tried to recall the taste of real coffee, to summon it up by association: the grinding of the coffee beans, sitting with Renate at the table while the coffee brewed, the rich aroma filling the kitchen. And for his pains a spurting of sour saliva and the disappointing smell of – what was it? Chicory? He thought that was it, although Renate insisted it was roasted sawdust.

He could recall so much about the old days, but not the sensations, not the actual smells or tastes. And it was no consolation to know he would recognise the old pleasures should they ever return because he needed them now. And immediately chided himself. His daughter had never tasted real coffee, cake was a rarity for her, and chocolate had gone the way of all luxuries. She had never been to a puppet theatre, nor to the swimming baths; in fact, she had hardly ever played with other children. There was so much his daughter had been deprived of, and little for her to recognise if life should ever return to normal.

She had been born in March 1932, a year before Hitler became chancellor but with the National Socialists already on the rise. With each passing year their lives had been whittled away, first the luxuries then the necessities, until there was little left to lose. Even those life rhythms Martin had always presumed as natural had been ambushed so that nothing seemed natural any more, neither birth nor death, nor growing old with the woman he loved – and certainly not childhood.

He and Renate had wanted so much for their daughter, their first child, and the first grandchild as well. As for politics, they simply did not figure back when Renate became pregnant. But even if the pregnancy had occurred later, they still would have gone ahead with much the same joy. For despite the restrictions, or perhaps because of them, back in those days he and Renate, like most of their Jewish friends, thought things couldn't possibly become worse. Back in those days they all wore blinkers.

Martin sighed, hindsight's wisdom has such a ruthless genius for accusation. While the country changed he kept fooling himself it wasn't changing so very much. Yet it was perfectly clear almost from the time Hitler took power that he was to be Germany's salvation. He put Germans back to work, he built German confidence and re-instated German pride, he took the pathetic remnants of Germany after Versailles and modernised and industrialised. He showed the world that Germany was once more to be treated with respect. And if he didn't like Jews, neither did a good many Germans, and even among those who did, most were quite prepared for Jews to be a casualty in an otherwise excellent programme of national recon-struction. It was perfectly clear back then if only Martin had wanted to see.

Yet to be fair to himself, what was happening defied logic. He would look at the anti-Semitic cartoons and read the anti-Semitic propaganda and have to remind himself that this vile material was about him, that suddenly and through no fault of his own he had become a person to be despised. It was as if without warning or explanation the sky turned green, or the grass purple, and you wouldn't believe your eyes and neither could Martin believe his. Children deprived of a childhood; doctors, lawyers, professors and businessmen now portrayed as vermin; veterans from the last war treated like criminals. These things simply made no sense.

He carried his coffee into the living room, wrapped himself in an old cashmere rug – crimson and black, the Nazi colours, he suddenly realised, and quickly banished the thought – settled into its faint luxury and sipped slowly, drawing as much warmth and solace from the stale steaming drink as memory and imagination would allow.

In another life he would have been at the factory by now, not sitting in his nightclothes drinking ersatz coffee. He had worked since the age of fifteen and hated being without a job, hated not being able to provide for his family, hated not having an identifiable place in the world. Although it had been far worse when his business was first taken. Whole days would pass when he couldn't even bring himself to dress, there seemed no reason, and besides, he could entertain Alice just as well in his nightclothes. But gradually he picked himself up, or rather Renate did, as his private loss became overshadowed by the larger and more threatening changes which marked Hitler's Germany.

He could easily identify all the changes, but oddly, the most pervasive and the most merciless tended to be those which had infiltrated here, into home and family. Once a haven, his private world was now permanently infused with anxiety and tension and a pain deep in his belly that he knew to be a rehearsal of future losses. And there had been changes in himself too, which had left him sharply depleted. He had always been a sociable person, a people person, but his renowned amiability was now not simply irrelevant but downright dangerous. It was increasingly difficult to know who he was, much less which of his old qualities would help in these impossible times.

Back in the old days his life had been full of people. Rich people, poor people, artists, tradesmen, Germans and Jews. Outside of family and work, he liked nothing better than chatting with friends or acquaintances over coffee and cake. There was something in his manner, not unrelated he had often thought to his small stature and nondescript looks, which made him comfortable to be with in a way more handsome men were not. And he found people interesting, so he would invite confidences when most other people simply couldn't be bothered. That he neither expected nor sought the same in return merely added to his attractions.

'You're like a priest in the confessional, the way you listen to people,' Renate once had said. And then she'd laughed. 'A Jewish priest.'

He had not set out to be Everyman, a sort of friendly neutral. Rather, growing up the elder brother of a musical genius meant he'd had to learn to endear himself to people in ways different from his brother. Fritz had been compared with the young Mozart even before he could walk, and while he had been pompous in short trousers and insufferable in long, Martin saw that everyone was prepared to forgive because of the music. And Martin, too, forgave, but his task did not end there, for he knew that unless he wanted to end up as page-turner to his famous younger brother, he would have to carve out a niche for himself. One of his school teachers had once described him as possessing a talent for friendship, his very own talent just like Fritz. So Martin chose what his brother lacked, he chose to be liked and, given its rewards, was well satisfied. But there were costs too. He was not much more than twenty when he realised that being so attuned to the needs of others meant relegating any urgings of his own to the background. He had become so efficient at gratifying other people's passions his own had withered on the vine.

This explained, he now realised, why as a Jew in Germany he had done so well. Germans welcomed him to their circles because his Jewishness was not obvious – as one German friend once said: 'You're more like us' – and Jews liked him because he was less self-concerned than they were. He became as much a genius at friendship as was Fritz at the piano. But as the days and years passed, he knew something was awry; his life was out of kilter, he felt numb with all his niceness, he needed someone to quicken the heart.

He had met his future wife ten years ago at a recital given by his brother. Renate's family was well known in the arts. Her father was one of Germany's foremost art dealers and the most highly regarded in Westphalia. A patron of the avant-garde, he was one of the reasons why Düsseldorf had maintained its reputation as a centre for the arts while other cities had lagged behind. Renate's mother, Amalie Friedman, was a well-known pianist and an associate of Fritz's. At the conclusion of the concert, Martin had watched Renate being scooped up and presented to his brother, watched this shimmering young woman dressed in an oyster-shell pink gown made from the highest quality silk – Martin was a silk merchant even while falling in love – and was reminded of the women in Modigliani's late work: the slick crop of black hair, the pointed face, the long, full-hipped body, the casual sensuality of the whole, and his heart beat hideously with wanting.

Suddenly he was fed up with being nice. He would far prefer to be like his brother, an object of admiration for beautiful women despite being bereft of every positive quality other than a genius for music. But Fritz was Fritz and Martin was Martin and with no chance of a miracle, Martin decided to preserve his self-respect and grind away at his envy and desire alone. He collected his coat and hat and was about to leave the hall when Renate turned away from the brilliant brother and walked out of the crowd towards him.

And so began a life unlike anything he had ever known. Suddenly he found himself in a perpetual fireworks storm, his life of order shattered in cascades of colour and heat. He neither wanted nor needed sleep, all he wanted was Renate. And she to his utter astonishment wanted him. His friends laughed at him: he was in love, they said, but would settle. And they were right, but only to a point. From the time of meeting Renate, the bland likeable Martin moved to one side to make space for a new Martin, Renate's Martin. It was as if he had become two people: the pleasant singalong tune to the world, and the full orchestra at home.

The dual Martins continued for many years, but a singalong tune was easily drowned out in today's blaring propaganda, and with the tensions at home the full orchestra had somehow lost its beat. When life was good Martin hardly gave it a second thought, but now it had soured, the loss was as intrusive as chronic pain. If only he could silence memory, he was thinking, but how to fuel his hopes and manage the bad times if he did? And to compound all the losses were the ever-present assaults: the violence, the abuse, the shafts of hatred slamming into him no matter what he did or where he went or how insignificant he tried to make himself. And it was hatred of *him*, he who had never before known hatred. Better he had been more like his brother, Martin found himself thinking for the first time in years, although not even Fritz, with a network of protectors in the music world, had been spared the violence of these times. A couple of weeks earlier he had telephoned from Berlin asking if he could visit for a few days. He gave no further information, so when he disembarked from the train it was a shock to see his fine, even features pummelled almost out of recognition. 'SA,' was all he said and, despite Martin's urging, refused to elaborate. This was the first time his brother had ever needed him, so Martin stifled his curiosity and did not press. Besides, the warming of their relations had been timely: with no one in the world clamouring for Jews, unless like Fritz they were exceptional, Martin hoped that once his brother was settled in America, he would help Martin and his family emigrate. With persecution of Jews ever more violent and their own prospects for emigration day by day more dismal, Fritz was their best hope.

Although something had to be done now, Martin said to himself, he couldn't just sit here waiting for the next horror to strike. He pulled up the collar of his dressing gown against the chill, pushed the coffee aside and reached for his ledger – still in its green leather folder, and still the gold fountain pen, all these possessions from lost times, like the flat itself so solid and established, so German if the truth be known – studied the figures and made some more. He used to think life could be lived like a balance sheet, credits on one side, debits on the other, and as long as he was in credit there was no cause for complaint. He used to think a lot of things he now knew to be wrong. But unfortunately, knowing his mistakes did not rectify them, particularly when circumstances had put most of his resources well out of reach.

The anxieties were relentless, although sometimes he would experience a small pocket of relief as he listened to his mother-in-law playing the piano. The music seemed to insert itself at exactly the right level, somewhere beneath the grid of rationality yet close to the soft flesh of his hopeful soul. And he still turned to his books, but was all too often left wanting when it came to sense and coherence. With rational thought an anachronism in the fervour of Nuremberg, he wondered whether even he, a Jew, had been infected. Renate disagreed, suggesting instead he was creating his own defeat. 'You're going to the best Germans to make sense of the worst,' she said, pointing to his books of German poetry and philosophy. 'The devils define the gods, but rarely the other way round.' So he broadened his reading, but was forced to accept that the problem lay with the circumstances themselves. There was no sense, no rational, civilised sense to be made of a nation gone mad, a people gone mad, men, women and children gone mad.

Martin stood up and went to the window. It was light outside now, and through the glass he could see the banners lining the street, the same banners which lined every street heralding certainty for Germans and the opposite for Jews. Times had changed and Martin had to change too. It was not enough to love his wife and daughter with all his heart, it was not enough to want their happiness, and it was certainly not enough to wait for better times. But while he struggled in the absence of money and connections to secure their visas, he had to determine a way of living now, in the present, a better way than the fear-riddled existence of recent months. Of course the times were unpredictable, the violence, the restrictions, the visas themselves, but surely the next few hours, the next day would bring no surprises. Not even Hitler was that organised.

Martin smiled, not for a moment was he fooling himself. He, Renate, Alice and Amalie had planned an outing to Düsseldorf today. It was the annual Munich Putsch holiday, and with all good Germans occupied with the celebrations, it had seemed as safe a day as any to venture out. But when news came in early yesterday about the shooting of an official in the German Embassy in Paris by a Jewish youth, Martin had immediately cancelled. There would be repercussions, there always were; in fact, Jews suffered when there was no reason at all. Now he wondered if he had acted too hastily. They hadn't been out as a family for weeks, all of them were desperate for some respite. What could possibly happen to them? And in these unpredictable times, would it make any difference if they stayed home or went out?

A Genius for Reprisal

It was the ninth of November and the anniversary of the Munich Putsch, an ill-conceived and clumsy mistake if ever there was one, which in a mere fifteen years had metamorphosed into a glorious act of martyrdom and one of Nazism's most formative moments. Martin put such revisionism down to the Nazi talent for a shrewd type of lying, one that reeked of sincerity and the public good. Renate, however, subscribed to a more fundamental view.

'Laundry,' she said. 'Our leaders are meticulous launderers of the public memory.'

On this particular ninth of November the Lewins had planned to take the train into Düsseldorf. Defy the odds, they had decided, don the blinkers and experience life as it used to be. But that was before young Grynszpan, a Jew as obscure as his name, had gunned down the German official in Paris. Over breakfast they had listened to the latest news on the wireless and discussed the possible repercussions, and Martin now believed they should go ahead as planned. Renate was not so sure. They knew nothing of this Grynszpan, she said, except he was a Jew who had shot a German, and events of the past few years showed it required a lot less for Nazis to turn on Jews.

She had left the dining table and was now standing by the window. In the street below, people in groups, including many in uniform, were making their way to the local Putsch celebrations. There was no sign the Grynszpan incident had diluted the party mood, indeed nothing Renate could see to indicate there would be trouble. And a few hours in Düsseldorf strolling in the gardens and looking at the shops was exactly what she needed. But while Krefeld looked peaceful enough, the situation in Düsseldorf could be very different. It had been reported on the wireless that the wounded embassy worker, vom Rath, came from Düsseldorf. Not a good day for Jews to be on the streets, and particularly not in the injured man's home town.

Martin, still seated at the table, was watching her. He could see she was struggling; in fact, ever since their return from Berlin there had been a change in her. She now seemed so much less certain about their current situation and much more aware of the dangers. Yet knowing her as he did, he was sure she would not let this incident in Paris keep them at home. Renate had always been the more courageous of the two of them; in fact, he had no doubt that the bare-fisted menace which defined Germany in these days was bearable primarily because of her. His Modigliani woman with her lavish hips smooth like the belly of a cello, her narrow shoulders and sleek neck, and despite the dangling decision, just seeing her across the room made his nerves mollify. That's what she did for him, had always done for him, and why he was so reluctant to acknowledge that if not for her they might have left Germany long ago.

His Renate. Lively, warm, artistic, a woman who would enter each day like an explorer on virgin territory. She would gaze at the familiar landmarks of their life in Krefeld and see them as a marvellous and changing exhibition. For her, the routines of life were forever new. This was a woman who would step into each day expecting to be surprised and invariably was.

'So shouldn't we stay home? Won't we be courting trouble?'

He started with the sound of her voice, and in the moment he needed to collect himself took stock of how things had changed, the quality of life in Germany, the quality of *their* life, and most particularly his lush-with-life wife, that she should opt for the safe decision. She sounded so uncertain, miserable too, and the flat felt so crowded with all of them treading on each other's moods, oddly hostile too.

'We'll be fine,' Martin said, surprising himself. 'They promised bigger and better celebrations this year. There'll be so much excitement no one will notice us. Besides,' he said, looking at their daughter white-faced and silent on the couch, 'Alice desperately needs a change.'

Amalie Friedman decided to stay home. She was too old and too German – properly German, she added – to tolerate what was happening out there. And despite pleadings from Alice that her Oma change her mind, would not be persuaded. Amalie had seen quite enough of what her compatriots had become. 'I don't know these people,' she said. 'And I don't know my country.'

She withdrew to her room and a short time later the sombre beauty of the second movement of the *Pathétique* emerged, softly, ever so softly so the music wouldn't escape the flat, because Beethoven had been taken from the Jews too.

Not long afterwards, Martin, Renate and Alice slipped quietly from the building. They had learned that the less one's gentile neighbours knew the better. Hitler, an inspired innovator in so many respects, was a genius at wielding the threat of reprisal. It took a courageous German these days to defend a Jew, and best not to test it.

It was quieter now in the streets and the Lewins assumed everyone was either at the local Putsch celebrations or in their homes listening to the broadcast from Munich. But as they approached the station they saw the Putsch had been poached by the vom Rath attack. 'JEWISH MURDER ATTEMPT IN PARIS – MEMBER OF THE GERMAN EMBASSY CRITICALLY WOUNDED BY SHOTS – THE MURDERING KNAVE, A 17-YEAR-OLD JEW' read yesterday's headline in the *Völkischer Beobachter*. And today beefed up to: 'THE SHOTS IN PARIS WILL NOT GO UNPUNISHED'. A glance at the text showed that all German Jewry was being blamed and not just a seventeen-year-old boy. The newspaper demanded immediate action against the Jews, calling on all good Germans to respond according to their conscience to this savage assault not simply on a loyal servant of the Fatherland but on the Fatherland itself.

Renate read the headlines over and over. A call to violence if ever there was one and they probably should return home. Yet here they were at the station about to embark on a much-needed holiday and what was wise and sensible no longer seemed to have much muscle. Nothing did. Besides, they could pass. Their colouring – neither blond and blue-eyed, nor dark and Semitic – was unremarkable, and as assimilated Jews, their clothes were indistinguishable from those of other middle-class Germans. To go or return home? Renate forced herself to read the whole article properly. Ernest vom Rath, fortunately injured not dead, an unknown German functionary at the Paris Embassy; how much unrest could result? She looked at the other families gathered at the station, the Lewins were interchangeable with any of them, and she looked at Alice, a live spark hopping about on the pavement.

'All right,' she said. 'We'll go.'

Once they were on the train, she felt much better. Not simply relief at being out of the flat, but the familiarity of this journey, connecting as it did the two places which had formed the backbone of her life. Ever since her marriage and the move to Krefeld she had made a weekly visit to Düsseldorf. Every Thursday she would see her parents, would browse the familiar shops, perhaps meet a friend for coffee or take lunch in the *Alstadt*. The weekly trip helped her adjust to the move – not that she wasn't aware of the advantages almost from the beginning. There was the proximity of Düsseldorf, but as well she had the excitement of a new life in Krefeld: Martin, marriage, new people, and work – this last the most surprising of all. For with marriage to Martin, Renate had discovered silk.

Renate had always wanted to be a painter and from her earliest years had seemed to possess the talent. As a toddler she had produced paintings of such astonishing form and maturity her father used to joke that in addition to the usual limbs and blood and bodily organs, she had arrived in the world complete with an innate understanding of western art. She painted her way through childhood and became one of the first women to enter the Düsseldorf School of Painting. But there the dream had started to fade, or perhaps had faded earlier though no one noticed because of the long afterglow of the extraordinary work of the child.

She had been a prodigy at four and a genius at ten. At fourteen she was extraordinary and at sixteen when she entered the School of Painting, her work was described as brilliant, although no one talked about genius any more. Her technique could not be faulted, but her work lacked animus and the angels never panted at her door. It was not that her paintings were stillborn, they were simply limp on the canvas, and perhaps had always been, but one looks for different qualities in the work of a seven year old than a seventeen year old. Renate knew something was missing. She would study her mother at the piano, would sift through the sounds and isolate an out-of-this-world exhilaration which passed from Amalie through the music. Renate loved to paint, but the passion she detected in her mother's music was of a different order. She returned with new hopes to her work, but the painting would not yield. In the end she gave it up, not being the type to dabble in something she revered.

Then soon after marrying Martin she discovered silk. Silk fired her imagination in a way canvas had not; it was as if colour itself had suddenly spilled its mysteries. As the months and years passed, it became very obvious that Renate had finally found her passion.

Krefeld, like Lyon in France and Como in Italy, had long been a centre for woven silk. For several generations the Lewins had been counted among the most prominent of the silk families, so when Renate married Martin she found herself at the heart of the Krefeld community. Just a few years ago it would have been unthinkable that a Lewin could ever be an outsider in Krefeld, but now, not only were they barred from the silk business, they were routinely shunned by people who had once been friends. Experience, history, none of it matters when the whole cultural and moral landscape of your country has changed.

Everyone in the Krefeld community had always known the Lewins were Jewish, but it was a background issue and rarely acknowledged. Renate and Martin attended synagogue in Düsseldorf for the high holidays and for the occasional wedding or barmitzvah, and that was about the extent of it. Before Hitler came to power, neither would have hesitated in putting their Germanness ahead of their Jewishness. Now as they travelled the familiar journey into Düsseldorf, keeping themselves separate but not too separate from the Germans in the compartment and trying to render invisible a Jewishness they had never strongly felt, Renate had a sense, experienced often these days, of an identity ripped out of her and shoved through a grinder. She was raised to be German, had been taught to be proud of being German, and suddenly not only was she no longer German, the whole definition of what it meant to be German had changed. She did not like what she saw of her neighbours and neither did they like what they saw of her.

She and Martin would often discuss, as if speech could render it sensible, their disbelief when people they had known for years, people with whom they had worked and socialised, revealed themselves as cold, insensitive, even brutal strangers. Had they always harboured these tendencies? And if so, what blind spot common to her and Martin and so many other Jews had caused them to miss the signs. How could they have not known? It was like discovering you've spent years living adjacent to a toxic chemical plant when you always thought it manufactured perfume.

Renate gazes through the window at the passing countryside. A much-needed holiday and already her thoughts driving it into the ground. But it's not easy to forget what you once were, what in your heart you still believe yourself to be. If people could moult like animals, shed part of themselves, would she shed her Germanness or her Jewishness? And even now, after all that has happened, she is torn between desire: German, and reality: Jew. As for her daughter, today's Germans leave a stain on her. She sees Alice trying to equate them with the Germans of her storybooks and family lore. Tell me about the Kaiser, Alice will say to her grandmother, tell me how he gave a medal to Opa. She watches her daughter struggling to understand how it was possible for the Kaiser, the highest German in the land, to honour her grandfather, a Jew, when Jews are now the lowest of the low. The other day Alice asked Renate whether they were bad Jews – Renate and Martin, Oma, even Alice herself, unlike her grandfather who was a good enough Jew to receive the Kaiser's medal. Her daughter struggles, but how can you explain to a child she is what everyone hates?

She glances at Alice kneeling on the seat, looking out at the passing scenery, her little girl so happy to be out and about, and makes a pledge to turn her back on all grim thoughts for today. She scoops her daughter onto her lap, slides up close to the window, and together they identify the familiar landmarks. And Renate talks as if things are as they once were, activating a type of selective vision which sees the trees and not the banners in the branches, the houses and not the swastikas in the windows, the people in ordinary clothes and not those in uniform.

Once in Düsseldorf they take a tram to the Königsallee, not for the shops, the usual reason for promenading along the Kö, but for Alice to see the four-sided clocktower which they must circle slowly to make absolutely sure the time is the same on all four sides, and then to stand at a very particular spot near the moat which runs down the centre of the Kö so Alice can make a wish over the sea god Triton spraying water into the stream.

'What will you wish?' Martin asks, knowing even as he speaks that his daughter, a powerful believer in the secrecy of wishes, won't reveal. Although a few days after her last birthday, long enough, she believed, for her wish to be safe, she confessed she always made the same wish: that everyone and everything would be as it used to be, including her grandfather alive again, Martin at his business, and she allowed to go to school. Now as she tries to change the world, her eyes closed and lips silently moving, Martin feels the tears bulge and a choking in his throat. It would make a fine and moving scene in a film, if only it were not his daughter.

It is a perfect day of bright sun and soft breeze, more like late September than early November. They head off towards the *Aldstadt*, not to take coffee because most of the cafés display signs warning off Jews, but to buy an ice for Alice from a more lack-adaisical or less nationalistic street vendor. Alice walks between her parents and every now and then they swing her high in the air. One, two, three and over the crack. One, two, three and over the gutter. Such a lovely day and so pleased they have come, and no one is taking any notice of them and Martin finds himself thinking that perhaps things are not so bad, perhaps Renate is right and the worst is already in the past. He feels lighter, freer, as if he'd been in pain for months and only now as it eases can he appreciate how very wearying it has been.

They reach Heinrich-Heine-Allee and are about to cross when their attention is caught by a flurry of activity on the opposite corner. The Breidenbacher Hof is dripping with swastikas; there's a swirl of high-ranking SS at the entrance and a crowd milling on the footpath. This is the hotel where Hitler stays when he visits Düsseldorf, and for a brief terrifying moment Martin thinks that Hitler is here. In Düsseldorf. Today. A brief moment before reason prevails: Hitler, of course, would be in Munich for the Putsch anniversary, and the officers gathered outside the Breidenbacher Hof would be meeting for the local celebrations.

Martin takes in the mix of uniforms, all so sharp and ordered and portraying an air of authority not possible with normal clothes. There's brown SA and black SS and a sprinkling of grey-garbed army men, and a huge contingent of fresh-faced and eager Hitler Youth in brown and League of German girls in blue. Such a collection of good Germans a mere twenty metres across the road, so many smiling youths and smiling officers together with their proud wives and adoring mothers. So many people united by a cause.

And suddenly the terror returns. Martin pulls in the air but it won't come. His guts want to spill to the pavement, he's faint but must conceal it. Must appear normal. Hundreds of Nazis across the road, and his wife and daughter to protect. Who does he think he's fooling with his 'we look no different from other Germans'? Superficially there might be nothing to distinguish them, but these days even a child can sniff out a Jew. And as if his thoughts were blazoned on the sky, suddenly everyone on the opposite corner seems to be looking their way. Martin feels no less conspicuous than if he were wearing the black hat and shaggy beard of an orthodox Jew.

He grabs Renate with one hand and Alice with the other and turns them in the opposite direction, not running but striding away from the Germans in uniforms. With Alice struggling to keep pace, he swings her into his arms. Through the streets they go, away from the gathering of happy Nazis, as fast as they dare without drawing attention, until they reach the entrance to the Hofgarten. They do not pause until they are well inside the park, and at last they stop, out of breath and tight with fear. Alice, too, is white and stiff, but asks no questions.

It is blessedly quiet in the park, just strolling couples and family groups enjoying the unseasonable sun, and slowly they unwind, slowly they catch their breath. The trees are practically bare of leaves, but there are thick clumps of bushes lining the paths, and holly trees too, glossy green and loaded with berries. As they walk down the main path they feel less exposed; it is as if the park wraps them in a green protective armour. And there are no Germans in uniforms here.

'Probably all flexing their muscles around the Breidenbacher Hof,' Renate says to Martin. 'Just waiting to scare a few Jews.'

Martin smiles, but only weakly.

Tiny bushy-tailed squirrels scamper across the paths, others nuzzle in the lush quilting of fallen leaves. Alice now asks whether she might go and play. Renate lets go of her hand and gives her a small parcel of bread. The child squats at the side of the path and immediately three squirrels appear. They crouch a couple of metres from her, waiting.

'Clever little creatures,' Renate whispers to Martin. 'Close enough for food but far enough to run should they need to.'

'Jews should be so smart,' Martin says.

Renate shakes her head. Enough, she is thinking, enough. Can't you let it go for an hour? And Martin, no less keen than she for some respite, determines to keep such observations to himself. They stand close together while Alice feeds the squirrels, and then the three of them continue through the park, Renate and Martin strolling arm in arm, while Alice gambols across the grass, kicking up the leaves into what she calls snow-leaf storms. Each of them in their own way is making the most of an experience which may not happen again for quite some time, although the possibility of never walking here again would not occur to them.

On the other side of the park Alice dashes ahead to the kiosk. She missed out on her ice before, perhaps now she can have one. But she sees the sign, 'Jews undesired', before her parents have caught up with her, and knows there'll be nothing for her here.

'It doesn't matter,' Martin says, guiding her away from the kiosk. 'We'll be at Katz's soon for lunch.'

As they exit the park they see their tram and make a run for it. They are out of breath and laughing as they trundle down the broad Kaiserstrasse and then into Nordstrasse and the area where Renate grew up. She knows all the shops and houses here, all the landmarks. Martin glances at her, she looks just like her old self.

There are more uniforms about when they leave the tram at Goebenstrasse. Martin, now determined that this should be as normal an outing as possible, guides them to the end of the short street so Alice can identify the building where Oma and Opa used to live – 'And where I grew up,' adds Renate – the second and third floors now hung with banners, and the sound of a wireless where once had been Amalie Friedman's music. The wireless is playing military music, German military music with a strong seductive melody, impossible to resist, and so majestic that to sing along is to swell the heart. Martin has heard German music these past few years that could mobilise the hordes no less effectively than the Pied Piper of Hamelin. Even now, standing in the street below the Friedmans' old flat, he can hear the thud thud thud of boots behind the heavy beat of the orchestra. It's annihilating and unstoppable and he doesn't want to hear any more. He gathers his wife and daughter and hurries them back to the main thoroughfare.

They set off in the direction of Katz's restaurant, but Alice, already very hungry, says her legs don't want to move any more. So with half a kilometre to go, Martin swings her onto his shoulders. They continue on their way, Renate and Martin with arms linked and Alice surveying the world from on high, so she sees the Jews first. Martin feels a flinching of her body and in the next moment, in a space ringed by onlookers, he sees them too: two observant Jews and not a common sight in Düsseldorf, bearded men with long black coats and hats, not Homburgs like Alice's grandfather used to wear, but − she's so taut and still − to her eyes probably much the same. Two observant Jews similar in age to her grandfather, here in an area which Alice associated with him, being cornered by four Brownshirts. Martin doesn't want to see what is happening, he doesn't want to get involved. He just wants to protect his wife and daughter from the situation up ahead and deflect any danger that might spill onto them.

There is only one way clear, and that's back the way they have come. In front are onlookers and buildings and the two Jews with the four thugs taunting them in snarls from the gutter. They tug at the men's beards, pull on their curled forelocks, knock their hats and skullcaps into the filthy gutters. Four young thugs and two wizened old Jews.

'Bloody Jew scum,' they jeer. 'That's what you get for attacking a German.' And start to throw punches, deliberately missing the old men's faces by millimetres.

It won't stop there, Martin knows it won't stop there. He should help them, they're old, they're defenceless, they could have the life beaten out of them, they're scholars not fighters, Martin should go to their aid. And in the next moment: why should he? If these Jews didn't look so obvious no one would be threatening them now. These sorts of Jew with their ancient clothes and ancient customs make it worse for all Jews.

One of the stormtroopers, he doesn't look more than seventeen or eighteen, lands a punch on the bare head of the shortest Jew. The man staggers but doesn't fall. Another swipe and he is on his knees. Filth from the gutter spatters his spectacles.

'Your hats, you Jew bastards, on your heads.'

They reach out, they replace their hats, mud dribbles down their old faces and snares in their beards. Again their hats are knocked off and trodden in the slushy gutters. And then the flash of a knife. Renate seizes Alice and pulls her off Martin's shoulders, shoves her face into her skirts. Alice starts to wriggle, she twists around, she wants to see. Renate and Martin hold her with a grip so tight it must hurt. Now Alice is pulling – it's not like her – she's pulling in the direction of the old Jews. She has no idea of the danger. Martin hauls her onto his hip better to stop her from running off. Her curls slap his face as he swings her up. There's a stillness in the onlookers as the blade of the knife catches the light and slices into the curls of one of the old men.

'Cut mine,' Alice cries out, tugging at her ringlets. 'Cut mine instead.'

Martin slaps his hand across her mouth. Was he quick enough? Did they hear? Did anyone hear? And hisses in her ear she has to be quiet. Alice must catch his terror, because when he loosens his hand from her mouth she no longer struggles, just watches the thugs with the old Jews. The man with the knife finishes the job and is about to start on the other Jew when a clock tolls. He stops and checks his watch. Turns away from the Jew to face – surely not them? Surely the thug is not looking their way, surely he's not going to single out a child for a silly mindless comment. Quick quick. He's coming their way. Excuses. Her grandfather. Yes, her grandfather, a decorated soldier, just died. She's a little girl. She doesn't know some old men are good and others aren't. And she doesn't understand about the Jews.

The thug draws closer, Martin knows he will say anything to save his child. He holds her hard to his hip. The thug has stopped in front of them and Martin tells himself to smile, smile into the face of danger. Renate is stiff, if only she did not look so terrified, and Alice, well Alice is just watching. And now the thug is smiling, not at Martin but at Alice, and in that moment Martin realises he didn't hear her call out. His daughter is safe.

'How old are you?' the man asks. And Alice, revealing an understanding of the situation that many adults don't have, smiles back and tells him she is six. It's the same age as his daughter, he says with a pat to her head. 'And she has lovely long curls just like you.' Another pat to her hair and he turns away, beckons to his mates and moves off.

The old Jews are sprawled across the gutter, one is bleeding from his mouth. Two women, plain-dressed like Quakers, leave the crowd and attend to the men. The rest of the people disperse. Martin can't think of the old men, only his daughter and how close she came to the knife. He and Renate put Alice between them, holding onto her tightly. As they head down the road towards Katz's, he feels the knife ripping into his child, ripping into them too. They have to get out of Germany as soon as possible. Anywhere. Any way. Now. Before harm comes to them, his daughter most of all.

They hurry down the main thoroughfare and turn into the smaller street where Katz lives. There they stop and both Martin and Renate kneel down to Alice's height. They explain the dangers to her as they have so many times before, explain what brutes these Nazis are. They tell her she must never shout out like that again, she must never under any circumstances invite attention from Nazis. And it is not that Alice doesn't understand – she does, all too well – rather she knows the men wouldn't hurt her.

'What? At six, you have intuition?' Renate says.

'What's intuition?' her daughter asks. And then a moment later: 'They would have looked silly cutting a little girl's hair in the middle of the street.' And that is her final word on the subject.

With Katz's building now in sight she runs ahead of them. Martin and Renate pick up their nerves and follow more slowly.

'She has to learn to be more careful,' Renate says.

And while Martin agrees, he doesn't want her to be so careful that like her father she can't breathe without fear.

How best to protect his daughter from the SA and the SS? he finds himself thinking. Indeed, how to protect her from the entire military might of Germany? It is an utterly ludicrous situation. His daughter is only six years old. He looks at her running ahead, tiny in her neat navy blue coat, her legs thinner than his wrist, her feet much smaller than his hands. She's just a child, he keeps saying to himself, knowing that many Germans see just a Jew.

She has stopped in the doorway of Katz's and is waiting for them to catch up. As they approach, her face opens into a smile, and Martin shoves his anxiety aside. The three of them enter the building together.

This is not Katz's restaurant as in the old days, not the huge timbered space filled with tables and noise and separated from the street by a wall of steamy windows, but Katz's apartment building. When the restaurant was forced to close earlier in the year, Katz moved the business into his own home. It was fortunate for him that most of the other residents were Jewish and long-time patrons of his restaurant, for while some Jewish doctors have transferred their practices to their homes without complaint from gentile neighbours, a restaurant is quite a different matter.

They walk up stairs worn concave from more than a century of feet. As they climb, Alice runs her hand over the delicate chill of the wrought-iron rose pattern, looking as always for the unicorn in the middle of every third panel. With each unicorn she makes a silent wish. On her very first visit here she missed a unicorn and a week later her grandfather was dead. Now her attention does not wander even for a second.

Two floors up and they reach Katz's apartment. The former dining and lounge rooms, both with high ceilings, huge chandeliers, heavy-framed paintings and an intricate frieze forming a band around the rooms, are crammed with tables. When his customers first came here, they took in the surroundings and accused Katz of overcharging them at the restaurant. Such grandeur, they said, such riches. And where, they would ask, are our chandeliers? Where our priceless paintings? And Katz as genial as ever would soothe them with sweet words and a sweeter muscat and soon they were settled to food and conversation with the same gusto as of old.

There are few seats left by the time the Lewins arrive, yet the atmosphere is oddly subdued. Jews fill every available space with as many words as possible: as the old saying goes, two Jews, three arguments. But not today. There are newspapers spread on the tables and Herschel Grynszpan's attempt on vom Rath's life is the main topic. As they wait for seats, Martin and Renate listen to the conversations around them. Of major concern is the manner in which the attempted assassination has been reported and the consequent repercussions on Germany's Jews. Of major interest is the identity of this Grynszpan and why he chose a nobody like vom Rath.

'Of course it might have been a simple act of desperation,' a woman seated nearby says. 'Look at his name. The reports say he was born in Germany, but the name's Polish. I suspect all his family have been banished to that place just over the border – can't remember what it's called except it's Polish and unpronounceable. A town where the Nazis have been transporting Poles who've been living in Germany.'

'Zbaszyn,' her companion says. 'It's called Zbaszyn and I hear it's dreadful. Shocking overcrowding, and an epidemic of suicides.'

'Exactly,' the woman continues. 'Imagine how you'd feel if you just heard your family had been dumped in some godforsaken foreign hole. And for many of them it would be foreign. Some of these Poles have been here for generations. They're as German as we are.'

'I doubt that,' the man says.

The woman shakes her head. 'Forget your prejudices, Karl, just for a moment forget them and imagine how you'd feel if the children and I were imprisoned in some backwater, where if disease doesn't finish us, despair will.'

The Lewins listen and imagine and are grateful that between them there is not a single drop of Polish blood.

'But a hundred per cent Jew,' Renate says. 'So how lucky is that?'

Martin is saved a response with the arrival of Katz. Hermann Katz is a short, rotund man with a glossy hairless head. Among Jews he is known as the funny man of Düsseldorf – although today, with his drooping features and solemn greeting, it is hard to believe and, under the circumstances, greatly regretted. For Jews need their comedians. Perhaps in biblical times when, apart from a strict and irritable Yahweh, the going was pretty good for Jews, they might have had little need for humour – certainly the Old Testament is not known for its laughs. But as soon as persecution began in earnest, with life swinging between despair and impending death, Jews seized on humour as a useful ploy for living with perpetual disaster. So it happens that in any Jewish community from Düsseldorf to Dresden there are jokes, and at any one time the latest joke. 'Have you heard the one about – ?' someone will ask, and whether you have or not you'll listen, because with each retelling there are embellishments and improvisations which make the original joke funnier. God resides in the details as any Jew knows, so a joke that takes a minute on Monday will have inflated to five by Friday. By Sunday, listeners might think they're listening to a novel, and a few days later the new joke will have sunk into the general swirl and another emerged as the latest.

Katz was a legendary joke-teller, and as a very funny man many jokes actually originated with him. Hermann Katz was the reason why the Lewins chose to eat here today: with an appeal both to adults and children he was always good for a laugh. But there are no laughs today, not as he guides them across the room, nor when he seats them at a table. No jolly Herr Katz today, just the information with a mournful shake of his shiny head that he'll be closing early.

'This vom Rath business,' he says, with a hand to his pate and polishing, 'it's not good for Jews.'

'Surely it can't get any worse?' Renate says.

Katz shrugs, nothing is for certain but he's heard rumours. 'Go home when you leave here,' he says. 'Go straight home.'

Kristallnacht

Over in Paris, Ernst vom Rath died that afternoon. Not that the authorities would have been surprised, as one of the bullets had ripped clean through his spleen, pancreas and stomach. A mere forty-eight hours separating wounding and death, but for an efficient people like the Germans who had already recorded the habits and whereabouts of every Jew in Germany and Austria, it was time enough to ensure a neat spontaneous outbreak of violence. *Kristallnacht*, such a pretty word: Crystalnight. Not Firenight. Not Deathnight. Not Truthnight. But Crystalnight. Death and destruction dressed up for the ball.

When vom Rath's death became public, the Lewins were travelling back to Krefeld, and by the time they arrived home, Amalie Friedman was full of the news. There had been sporadic violence against Jews since Grynszpan's attack on Monday but now there was talk of serious and widespread reprisals. The reports on the wireless howled with shock and righteous anger; if this vom Rath had been Hitler himself it would be hard to imagine greater outrage. The Lewins began their cold supper with the wireless bleating in the background. But soon Renate was on her feet – such threats couldn't possibly be good for the digestion, she said – and turned the machine off with force enough to dislodge the knob.

They finished their meal in silence, and afterwards engaged in a flurry of activity as if that might ward off danger. But Martin's reading, Alice's puzzle, Amalie's crocheting and Renate's sketching neither filled time nor dampened their fears. As the night deepened, there was a tautness in the air and a rustling behind doors. It was felt in Düsseldorf as a background distraction, but in Krefeld it was an eerie threat, like living in the shadow of a smoking volcano.

Most Jews in this region of Germany chose to live in the large, established communities of Düsseldorf, Cologne and Bonn, so there were only a few Jewish families in Krefeld, none of whom lived close to the Lewins. Two families, rebounding on rumours, had packed their bags and bolted west. They had business connections in Arnhem, and while they knew it would be risky at the border, hoped their Dutch colleagues would vouch for them. Martin thought it doubtful anyone would protect a handful of German-Jewish business acquaintances who were no longer in business, but kept his thoughts to himself. After all, when comparing the unknown risks of staying with the equally unknown risks of leaving, logic was no more reliable than hope and provided a good deal less comfort. Two families decided on flight and a reliance on strangers, while the remaining Krefeld Jews shut themselves in their homes with their wirelesses and telephones and waited.

'How much revenge does this vom Rath warrant?' Martin said. 'How many Jews can possibly be punished?'

He had left the table and was pacing the lounge from window to table and back again. He surged through the room, his overcoat flapping, his pipe jammed in the corner of his mouth. Back and forth he went, his tread heavy on the floor, and only when his coat clipped Renate's easel, almost toppling it, did he realise the danger. The dull regular pounding of his shoes and the Fischers downstairs, and so little required these days to awaken the suspicions of good Germans. He stopped and dangled in the middle of the room, at a loss to know what to do.

'Ring Erich,' Renate said. 'He'll have the latest news.'

Erich Friedman, Renate's brother in Berlin, had an ear so attuned to current affairs that he had once been depicted in a cartoon in the Jewish press as a human strain of telephone exchange. Over the past few years he had managed more than most Jews to maintain friends in high German places, good contacts with good information. Although not yielding much tonight as Martin discovered when he was finally connected. Yes, Erich had heard there would be violence, but more than that he could not say. Though it didn't take a genius or a Jew to guess Hitler would use the vom Rath death as yet another springboard to put the Jews in their place.

'You should rethink your visa applications,' Erich said to Martin. 'Your preference might be for America or England, but you may find that Argentina or Shanghai prefer you.' And just before hanging up. 'Stay at home tonight. Make yourselves invisible.'

How useless and defenceless one feels when waiting for certain but unspecified disaster. The criminal condemned to die knows what to expect and knowing can make certain choices: to go quietly or not; to conceal his emotions or not; to hang himself beforehand or not. But waiting for an unknown disaster is to be tortured by an imagination attuned to the worst. The best one can do in such a situation is toy with possibilities. So if the apartment were stormed Martin would deal with the intruders while Renate, Alice and Amalie would flee. And should there be fire, they would escape via the bedroom window, not because the fire-escape was close by but because the courtyard was poorly illuminated. And if Martin were summoned –

'A dog receives better!'

Renate rose so suddenly her chair fell to the floor. She'd had enough. She hated what was happening and she hated the Germans. But most of all she hated being Jewish: it had never done anything for her and now she was being persecuted for it. She grabbed their knapsacks from the sideboard, hurled them to the table and started to fill them. It was incomprehensible what was happening. Threat after threat, and incumbent on her, on Martin, on all the other Jews to shuffle the various dangers in order to determine what posed the greatest threat at any particular time. Would it be the Nazis at the door? Would it be the neighbours downstairs? Would it be the thugs in the street? What would be the major threat in the next five minutes? What in an hour's time? So much threat, and all directed at them, at Jews, a people for whom violence extended no further than tossing a few words around.

She yanked the straps of each of the knapsacks and carried them into the kitchen. Nazis on a rampage would rip into sideboards and credenzas, display cabinets and dressing-tables, they'd rip into upholstery and bedding, they'd rip into you, but the party fed them well so Jewish food held no interest. She tossed the bags in the bottom of the pantry, shoved them right to the back behind her largest jars of pickles, and slammed the door. The sound sheered through the still, grey room, and Renate, like Martin a while earlier, suddenly recalled the Fischers downstairs. She stood motionless in the kitchen, wrapped in the noise of her own bitter breathing. Anger, loss, betrayal, even fear, all were indulgences to be rationed in these contemptuous times; she felt bleak, chilled and empty: the emergency bags were packed and there was nothing left to do.

And finally she acknowledged things would not improve, not today, nor tomorrow, nor in the foreseeable future. Oddly, this knowledge so assiduously avoided afforded her some relief, for when you accepted the worst, anything less meant not only were you ahead but you knew you would cope.

Besides, there were others to consider. Her poor mother would sit for hours rigid in her corsets, her tightly waved hair framing a face set in stone. If you were to detonate that face, what an eruption of grief and disbelief would spill. Amalie Friedman, always so proud of being German, had a whole history to lose – had lost most of it already. Then there was Alice, her only child, whose past was thinner than a fingernail and whose future was day by day more fragile.

Renate collected herself and returned to the living room. She sat in one armchair and Martin in another, both of them to wait out the long night. Amalie withdrew to her piano and brief improvisations in memory and hope before going to bed, while Alice slept fitfully on the couch. As the hours passed, Renate waited with Martin in a far from comfortable silence, for it was largely her fault they found themselves in this situation. Not that Martin would ever blame her, but the facts were clear. As early as 1935, before he had been forced to give up the business, Martin had wanted to emigrate. But Renate truly believed there was time enough for such radical decisions, and a year later, with the brief spring surrounding the Berlin Olympics, she comforted herself on a decision well delayed.

The remission was cruelly brief. The Olympic flame was hardly extinguished, and the voices of foreigners still fresh in memory, when the persecution returned more punishing than ever; the violence and humiliation too. But despite the increasing dangers, she still did not want to leave. Even when she saw how sublimely sensitive were the Germans when it came to humiliating Jews, how great their talent for Jewish vulnerability, she believed they could remain in Krefeld and still be safe.

'We're German,' Renate would say. 'What is there for a German in Palestine or America or God forbid Australia? If we were to settle in those places, settle properly and forever, we'd have to stop being German.'

'But we can't be German here,' Martin would say. And more quietly, 'Who would want to?'

Now as she sits waiting for disaster during the long night of the ninth of November, Renate sees the future with bruising clarity and knows she would go anywhere.

'Even Shanghai? Even China?' asks Martin, naming the only place in the world without a Jewish quota.

And Renate recalls the joke, worn thin after its marathon through German-Jewish circles, about Oskar Landau in China on Rosh Hashanah and wanting to attend synagogue. All around are temples and shrines and Chinese people going about their business. Finally Oskar stops a man dressed in traditional silk jacket and cane hat, a plait trailing down his back, and asks if there is a synagogue anywhere in the city. To his surprise he learns there is. 'But what do *you* want with a synagogue?' the Chinese man asks. Oskar explains he is Jewish, that today is the Jewish new year. 'Of course, of course. What Jew doesn't know it is Rosh Hashanah,' the Chinese man says. 'It's just you don't look Jewish.'

And of course, of course, Renate says to Martin, if Shanghai is their best option – their only option, Martin now says – then they'll go to Shanghai. So they sit in the shade of night, wrapped in overcoats and regret, Martin planning the various steps to take them from Krefeld in Germany to Shanghai in China, Renate trying to determine if it is possible when all hope is gone to exist under the raised fist of persecution. Alice sleeps on a couch nearby, her whole life in front of her should she ever have the chance, and in her bedroom, Amalie Friedman, elegant even in nightclothes, is lying in bed waiting for the pain in her chest to subside so she can slip into dreams of the past.

When the fires begin late on the night of the ninth of November, the clouds over the Jewish districts of Germany and Austria are sheathed in reds and pinks. The next day, dawn comes late to Jews. The sun is a perfect burnished disc in an evenly charred sky and a smell of burning gorges on the ruins. No secret network is required to spread the news, no clandestine telephone calls nor underground telegraph, for German radio and newspapers are proud to report the spontaneous uprisings across Germany and Austria as good Germans vent their anger over vom Rath's death. Synagogues, schools, community centres, Jewish hospitals, kindergartens, all of them described as sites of anti-German ferment, have been plundered and torched. The few Jewish shops and businesses to have survived the onslaughts of recent years are now destroyed. Jewish homes are stormed and wrecked, and Jews themselves have been beaten, tortured and dragged off to concentration camps.

Around dawn on Thursday morning, Martin, Renate and Alice Lewin are gathered at their dining table. Alice has finished breakfast, the others could not eat. They sit in silence while the wireless intones triumph after German triumph and they hear loss after loss. City by city, town by town, a litany of destruction. And such delight taken in burning the Jewish books of prayer and learning. The way the paper burns, differently according to the German press than Christian scriptures, and the Hebrew script described as if the letters themselves harbour sinister intent. Five thousand years of learning is now nothing more than a Jewish plot to take over Germany. The people of the book are going up in smoke and the most civilised people in the world are fanning the flames.

The beating of boots on a wooden stair is terrifying when you know they're coming for you. Slowly, firmly, closer, louder, a relentless beat in perfect unison, at least two men, possibly more, closer, louder, and coming for you. Through the street door, up the first stairs, their tight-throated voices barking and laughing; no need for silence, no need for surprise when there's no escape and everyone realises it. Then a splinter of silence that digs deep in your body, and you try to breathe but the air has gone, and the pounding in your gut is tearing you open, a moment of silence but it feels like forever. A fist to the door on the flat below, a fist thudding hard till the door is opened. And you breathe again, they're not here for you. But of course for you, who else would they want? Herr Fischer receives a blast from Bavaria: it's Lewin they want, which flat is Lewin's? Asks not for the answer, they know where Lewin is, but as a warning to anyone who might help a Jew.

Upstairs Martin and Renate stand close and frozen. They've planned numerous escape routes, but when the boots are on the stairs, all plans are useless. Alice is alert and watching, they reach her together, but with one of them needing to confront the thugs, it is Renate who lifts the child and holds her tight.

The boots start again. They're on the stairs. They're on the landing. They're outside the door. Three crisp knocks. Martin slips the bolt. The door whips open. Three men burst in. Martin is hurled to the floor. They lift him up, they slam him to the table. Crash goes his head against the mahogany. Crash go their fists into his sweet earnest face.

'What do you want?' Renate is shouting. 'We'll give you what you want.'

They laugh at her, they'll take what they want. They've been working for hours, they know exactly what they want. Alice is softly crying. Renate covers the child's eyes while cupboards are emptied, crockery is hurled against walls, jewellery pocketed, books torn apart, chairs thrown through windows, quilts and pillows slit open. And now the men turn, they turn on Renate, they advance towards her with their filthy taunts. She shoves her daughter behind the sofa, shouts at her to stay still. The men approach, they're peeling off their gloves, such white hands, such slender fingers, reaching towards Renate, about to grab.

And suddenly through the storm of feathers is the stony presence of Amalie Friedman. She's strong this Jew and as German as their mothers, she glides into the room glacial and ghostly. She stands and stares, the thugs stop and watch. No one is moving, no one is speaking. She mounts a chair then steps on the table. She looms over them, large and marmoreal. Quilt feathers puff in piles about her bare feet. The men stare up at her, her face is blue, she raises her arms, she holds the world, she's huge, she clasps her chest, she's falling, slowly falling, a shadowy spectre in her white robe. She strikes the table, the noise is explosive, the table cracks, a little moan, a little splutter, and then an unearthly silence.

One man is on his knees, he doesn't understand what is happening. His leader pulls him to his feet.

'We'll leave these ones,' he says to his men. And to Martin he adds, 'For now.'

Martin can be repaired. A doctor attends him, not their usual Dr Rosenbaum, the Nazis took him away, but the Fischers' doctor – called by them and paid by them too. He works silently, washing, stitching and dressing the wounds, and when he leaves he tells them he'll not be back, nor can they, he nods in the direction of the Fischer flat, do anything more for you.

Amalie Friedman is dead, one of the hundreds of *Kristallnacht* casualties. She cannot be buried until late the following day as there is no one available to perform the ceremony, and when finally the burial does occur, it is in a small wooded area outside Krefeld and not in the plot next to her husband in Düsseldorf cemetery as Amalie always intended. The service, attended by Renate and Martin and two strangers to dig the grave, is conducted by a cantor not a rabbi, who worries he won't make it back to Düsseldorf before sunset and the start of the sabbath. Martin can hardly walk, but insists on being with Renate. She is distraught. Her adored mother is dead, her mother who thrived on love and generosity and music, killed by brutes who wouldn't know goodness if they were choking on it.

Martin tries to reassure her it is better, safer, to bury Amalie here in this secluded wood. Cemeteries were a favourite target on *Kristallnacht*, headstones reduced to rubble, fragments of Hebrew littering the ground, as if desecration of the dead, of the past, of memory, strikes a firmer blow at the souls of the living. And who knows what has happened to Jewish graves in Düsseldorf? Who knows whether Renate's father's grave still exists?

'It's no way to farewell your mother,' says Renate as they stand by the fresh mound of dirt.

It is worse when they are back at the flat, the wreckage such raw testimony to the violence of Amalie's death. Martin starts to sort through the ruins, but Renate sees no point. She clears the debris off an armchair, lays a small cloth over the torn cushion and sits herself down. There's a raw pain where her mother used to be, a gouged-out emptiness and no one can fill it. It would help if her brother were here, but Erich doesn't even know his mother is dead. Erich is imprisoned in the Buchenwald camp. They came for him at three o'clock the same morning his mother died. They would have taken his son Willi too, but their instructions were clear: only males over sixteen to be arrested. 'Another month,' they said, having read Willi's papers, 'and we'll come back for your birthday.'

Renate can be repaired, but not yet. For the moment she doesn't want to think, doesn't want to feel. She wants to crouch in a shadowy crevice of her own making, a precarious sanctuary separating the past when her mother was still alive from a future which appears hopeless. She wants to pull down the shutters on thought; she wants to black out the blistering image of Amalie rising above a bunch of thugs in a last heroic act to save her family. She wants to forget until time has given her strength to remember.

As for Alice, she's only six years old, but after what she has seen, even if she were sixty she would be forever changed. Can a child watch her father being bashed to a bloody husk and not be affected? Can she see her grandmother rise like a phoenix and crash to her death, or witness her mother so immured in grief she is no longer in the world? Can a child see all this and not bear scars? Can she domesticate such horrors and continue with life? Or does she try to snuff out memory and decide that whatever she saw simply did not happen? It's hard to know with Alice, but if she does remember, she wears her horrors chastely.

It helps she is a practical child who has already learned that if she's labouring for others she can't be gnawing at herself. She assists her father with his wounds and her mother with hers. She insists on being the one to go out for food and other essentials – not that there is any alternative in the days following *Kristallnacht* with her father hardly able to walk and her mother closed to the world. Alice stuffs her terror behind usefulness and tries to convince herself she'll be safe. She knows she is pretty in a German sort of way, and she's making a point of shopping in neighbourhoods where her family is not known. And although she's always been scared of the dark, she is prepared to brave the strange streets late in the day, because no German child of her age would be shopping during school hours. There's danger everywhere, and as she makes her way home through the dark streets, she fills her head with stories in order to thwart the terrors.

And there's the trick. In order to do the shopping, to walk the dark streets, to help her mother and her father, to forget her Oma falling down dead, there are some things she cannot allow herself to think – not for a moment, not even for a blink of an eyelid – for, if she did, she too might collapse.

But it is not easy, neither in the streets nor at home. There is a smell to despair and it is distressingly human. It is acid and mould and a smoky sweat, and no matter how much she washes or dabs herself with her mother's cologne, Alice cannot escape it. She is doing her best not to think about that horrible morning, but her mother's despair clings to them all.

At night Alice lies in her bed wondering what her family has done so offensive to God that he has made them Jews. If she knew, she would make amends and all of them would be saved and go to America. Being born a Jew is worse than anything Alice can imagine. And it's never been any different. By the time she was old enough to talk, Hitler was running the country. Hitler, the all-seeing, all-hearing monster you could complain about only at home, and then only in whispers. Hitler who hates Jews so much he won't let Jewish children attend school or Jewish grown-ups go to work, who wants Jews out of Germany never mind how long they've lived here. Alice has never known anything different. So when her father says with each new repressive law, 'It's not good for the Jews', and repeats the same old refrain with the huge new concentration camps, 'It's not good for the Jews', and now, with vom Rath's death and still he's saying, 'It's not good for the Jews', Alice wants to know when has it ever been good for the Jews?

The flat seems to be shrinking. Renate's despair occupies a lot of space. Not wanting the burden of that dreadful grief, Alice gives her mother a wide berth. She wants to open the windows and let out the smell, but Mutti is always cold and Vati says they mustn't draw attention to themselves. He says they must be quiet as mice and act as if invisible. He says that if the SS come again, he wants the Fischers to say the Lewins have gone. The wireless, pitched at a murmur, is never turned off. They eat their cold food, they drink their ersatz coffee, they read, they whisper and her father tries to pull strings down the telephone. But no one in Berlin is listening, much less in Palestine or America, Britain or Brazil.

When she is older Alice will say her childhood ended on *Kristallnacht*, but at the time, while she looks after her parents and negotiates the hostile streets and endears herself to hostile people, she is convinced things will soon return to normal. But even when Martin is feeling better he still does not go out. It is not simply the mess of wounds and bandages, the people are enraged. Vom Rath has achieved a status in death inconceivable when he was alive. And while the transformation of this ordinary functionary into hero and martyred son has occurred across Germany, his home town of Düsseldorf just twenty-five kilometres away has embraced the task with particular fervour. It would be a foolhardy Jew who took to the streets for anything other than essential business.

Martin has tried to contact his brother, but he has disappeared. It seems inconceivable that Fritz with all his connections would have been arrested, and equally inconceivable he would have left for America without telling them. Fritz's disappearance, Martin's own injuries, Renate almost comatose, no contacts, poor prospects for visas, no money, and any day now no place to live. In the right hands it would make a good Jewish joke, but as the stuff of your life, it feels like hell.

Some hours speed by, others bog down in futility. As the days pass, Martin's wounds settle into tolerable aches, the bruising stretches into a palette of murky yellows, greens and browns. Occasionally emotions flicker and spark, but mostly they are leaden on the heart. Life does not exactly go on nor does it peter out, rather it hangs like one of those painted backdrops at the theatre, noticed at first glance, but soon subsumed by the drama being played out in the footlights.

Early the following Wednesday, vom Rath's body is brought by train to Düsseldorf. It is a dank, foggy day, and as the train passes through the towns from Aachen on the Dutch border to Düsseldorf where the body is to lie in state, the flags are limp at half-mast and the people lining the railway tracks bedraggled in their clothes. Just the right weather for a funeral, Alice decides as she sits on the couch turning the pages of her legends from Greece and Rome, not reading, just looking at the coloured plates. Martin is perched by the wireless, while Renate dull and dazed is in her usual place by the window. Alice glances at both of them before returning to her book, turning the pages ever so slowly until she comes to a picture of the River Lethe flowing through a grey-green light, with the boatman rowing the souls of the dead. The mood of the picture exactly matches the mood outside, and in both the dead are travelling to a final resting place. Although, unlike the poor souls in the picture, vom Rath is going nowhere near Hades. His path goes straight to heaven, with a brief stopover at the *Rheinlandhalle* where Hitler himself will pay his respects.

Alice suddenly closes her book. A movement by the window. Her mother has roused herself, is shuffling towards the wireless. She's thin and crumpled but at least she's moving. And now propped on the arm of a chair, her bony whiteness bent to the machine. The body of vom Rath has arrived in Düsseldorf and is already in place with people filing past. The announcer describes the scene as solemn, proudly German, and explosive.

While her parents clasp each other and listen to the wireless, Alice goes to her room and, without really understanding why, pulls out her jack-in-the-box. With the word 'explosive' hard in her head she opens the lid and the figure bursts out. She pushes it down, closes the lid, and another explosion when she releases it again. Over and over, close then open, until the report on the wireless is finished. Then one last time she opens the lid, this time to give the jack-in-the-box his freedom. Out he pops and there he will remain nodding and smiling on her bedside table, long after she and her family have left Krefeld.

While vom Rath lies in state in the *Rheinlandhalle*, the violence and arrests continue as they have since *Kristallnacht*, with the exception of the previous Sunday which Hitler decreed a day of rest. Throughout the day of vom Rath's homecoming, Renate remains bent to the wireless, refusing food and ignoring conversation. At around six o'clock the telephone rings; it is Dora, Erich's wife in Berlin, and suddenly Renate is back in command. She takes the handpiece from Martin and speaks to her sister-in-law.

There's no news of Erich, but word is out that the incarcerations are only for a limited time. It appears that the terror of *Kristallnacht* is far more concerned with filling the Nazi coffers and persuading Jews to emigrate than the slaying of Ernst vom Rath. In fact, Dora knows of two men who have already been released.

'They both had valid visas and convinced the authorities they'd leave Germany immediately,' she says. 'They've already gone.'

'And the conditions at the camps? What have you heard?"

Renate wouldn't want to know, Dora says, but Erich is strong and in good health and should manage better than most. Although this is not the reason for her call. She wants, indeed is insisting the Lewins join her and Willi in Berlin. It will be a tight squeeze in their flat, but the Lewins in Krefeld are far too close to the current ferment.

'And besides,' she says, 'with all the foreign embassies in Berlin, you'll find the visa situation just that much less frustrating.' There is a short pause, and then with undisguised urgency: 'Catch the early train from Düsseldorf. Just get out of there before Hitler arrives for vom Rath's funeral.'

The flat is unliveable, the landlord is demanding recompense for damage, otherwise he'll evict them. It's like living on a bomb site with bombs still to be detonated, but nonetheless Renate and Martin decide it is far too risky to leave prior to Hitler's arrival. Already, with twenty-four hours until the funeral, there has been an influx of dignitaries from all over the country. The station at Düsseldorf will be overrun with Gestapo, SS, SA. They decide it is best to leave their journey until vom Rath is buried and off the front pages. They telephone Dora in Berlin and tell her to expect them the following Monday.

At seven o'clock the next morning the SS come again for Martin. There is no dying grandmother to distract them this time, and no beatings. Martin takes a hasty leave of Alice and Renate. 'I'll be back,' he says. 'Don't worry.' And to Renate: she must do whatever is required to secure visas, 'To anywhere,' he says, then a final kiss before being hustled through the debris of the living room and frogmarched out the door. Within twenty-four hours Martin is in Sachsenhausen concentration camp, while twenty-five kilometres further south in Berlin, Renate and Alice have moved in with Dora Friedman and her son Willi.

On the very same day Renate and Alice were travelling east to join Dora and her son in Berlin, Private Heinrik Heck was travelling in the other direction to Hamburg, together with several other new recruits. His past had taught him the importance of the present moment, but nothing could have prepared him for the excitement he was now feeling. Such prospects he had. For the second time in his life he was leaving Berlin, but so different were the circumstances he might as well be another person. He was well clothed and well fed, and not only did he have money in his pocket, he was being paid to sit on this train, being paid as he smoked his cigarette, being paid to look out the window at the passing scenery. And most exciting of all, he was being paid to cook.

He had always been a quick learner. From early boyhood when he was the best young thief around, during all those years of looking after his sister and brother, and of course his time at school, he had learned faster than anyone. And now, after only a couple of weeks in an army kitchen, he'd picked up enough knowledge to be sent to Hamburg as a cook. After a lifetime of keeping a watchful eye on the present, a glance at his future revealed plenty of possibilities.

And he'd met a woman, Agathe, a good sort who really seemed taken with him. She said she liked a man who was going places, and she could see he was. What a laugh: Heini Heck, late of the Scheunenviertel, suddenly a man with prospects. Agathe worked in a factory, but her main interest was as a leader in the BDM, the girls' section of the Hitler Youth. She was going places too. Heini had known plenty of women in his time, but Agathe was one out of the bag. And she liked him, she liked him very much. She would slip him into her room and there she would love him like he was the last man on earth.

As the train chugged along, Heini was thinking that when he was settled he would send for her, he might even marry her – now that would be a turn-up for the books. But then everything was different when you've got prospects, he decided. And he lit another cigarette, inhaled deeply and settled back to enjoy the journey.

Preposterous Migrations

The Friedmans lived on Bamberger Strasse, a short twenty minute walk from the clang and bustle of the Kurfürstendamm cafés and shops. It was a typical residential street of the area, quiet, tree-lined and crammed with sturdy blocks of flats four and five storeys high, many with a weary, big-city, middle-class shabbiness of a kind not seen in Krefeld or Düsseldorf. Renate had always enjoyed Berlin with its energetic crush of people, its marvellous shops and inexhaustible entertainment. But it was different this time. What had formerly been inviting now felt strange and hostile, and the once-vibrant crowds seemed cold and aggressive. As for the cafés and theatres, most were now forbidden to Jews. Even if she could ignore Martin's absence and forget for a moment the danger he was in, Renate needed only to step into the street to be reminded this was no holiday visit.

Erich and Dora's flat was located in a mushroom-pink block of five storeys, a distinctive building owing to the unusual scalloped facings of the garret windows – as if the windows were wearing bonnets, Alice had once said. All the flats had floor to ceiling windows providing a view to the street, and attached to the better flats were heavy balconies decorated with plaster moldings and flower boxes. On the ground floor was a delicatessen-cum-hardware shop – cheese and sausage for supper plus some solder to fix the leaking heater.

Erich and Dora Friedman and their son Willi lived two floors up from the street in one of the more modest flats. Their immediate neighbours were the Müller family: husband, wife, sullen son and a lumpy daughter. Years before, Willi Friedman had made the mistake of talking to the daughter as they climbed the stairs together. This had resulted in an angry visit from Herr Müller and a threat of trouble should Willi ever approach their daughter again. The Müllers had adhered to a policy of non-engagement with the Friedmans long before Hitler came to power, and had always made it clear they would be far happier sharing a wall and staircase with anyone other than a family of Jews.

The Friedman flat had seen better days but not for a while, or so it seemed to Renate who was accustomed to a home spacious enough and comfortable enough to accommodate a diverse family and social life. It was a two-bedroom flat, but as Willi's bedroom was no more than a cubicle off the kitchen, it was really a one-bedroom flat with pretensions. The one bedroom had also served as a study for Dora as she continued to work on her biography of Heine, even though both she and Heine had long been banished from German universities. The living room was only marginally bigger than the bedroom. At one end was an armchair and couch, both with weary upholstery and flabby cushions, and at the other, a small dining table scored with ink and burns and irregular patches of mustardy shine where the original varnish still remained. All but one wall of the room was covered with books, both Erich's medical and scientific books plus a substantial library of German language literature belonging to Dora, with gaps where the Jewish authors had been removed and hidden.

'A lot of gaps,' Dora said about both her own library and German literature generally. 'And only a matter of time before the whole structure of German culture collapses.'

A tiny place, even more so given the Friedmans were large people, but of little concern before Hitler and his restrictions. In the old days, Erich, a doctor with the public health service, would return from the hospital and Dora from the university and together they would spend their leisure time in the neighbourhood. Even when Willi was a baby they would take their meals at a local restaurant, practise their politics on the promenades, and go hiking – their term – in the Tiergarten. So although they could have moved to a larger place while Erich and Dora were still in work, the flat and its location suited them.

The Friedmans were no more religious than the Lewins but a good deal more Jewish. Both Dora and Erich were active in political and cultural groups associated with the Jewish community, and Willi was prominent in the Zionist youth movement. Now nearly sixteen, Willi had never felt much allegiance to Germany and, while he differed in this respect from his parents, all three were convinced their future lay with Palestine and had been working strenuously towards that end.

If the Friedman flat had been small for three people who spent most of their time away from home, it was a pigeonhole for four people who went out only when necessary. There were the extra possessions to accommodate too, not that Renate had packed much in the panic of leaving Krefeld, nor, for that matter, wisely. In the weeks and months to come she would long for a particular skirt or a pair of walking shoes while looking with dismay at the box of drawing materials she had neither heart nor time to touch. Then there was the anxiety, bulky and ever present, and sometimes so raw that if you were to scrape against it the fear would spurt out in a rush.

Their situation was not particularly unusual. After *Kristallnacht* many Jews were evicted from their homes or the damage was too great for them to return, so it was common for two or three families to squeeze into a flat meant only for one. And while everyone seemed to cope, some did extremely poorly. Fortunately Dora, Willi, Renate and Alice were not among them.

Privacy as they had known it was no longer possible, but rather than turn themselves into entirely different people, they were quick to develop some creative alternatives. They would turn the armchair to the wall when there was a problem to solve or a worry to scratch; or slot themselves behind the couch with a book or dreams. Use of the desk was strictly scheduled so no one need miss out, as was the bathroom – more for thought than for bathing. Each would find a space a little larger than their own body and make of it a place of solitude.

Renate's most strenuous worries occurred at night, not simply because privacy was assured then, but she couldn't sleep. As soon as she shut her eyes her head was rushed by terrifying thoughts of all the possible dangers confronting Martin. Such awful thoughts slamming into her night after night. And she would struggle to push them away, each danger worse than the last, and the worst possible danger enough to bleed her of all reason and hope. For how would they manage without him? A woman and a child, no money, no country, it was too dreadful even for glancing at. And she would try to drown the horrors in a flood of words spoken to her husband to stiffen his stamina. She would tell him, beg him, her open-hearted husband, to put himself first. 'Think of us,' she would say. 'Think of us, Martin. Alice and me. And come home safe.' Hour after hour, night after night, she would talk to him, as if she really believed her thoughts could reach him. For he had to be safe, he had to come home, and the three of them would leave Germany and make a life somewhere else.

Her nights were riddled with fear, but the days spent hustling for visas were even worse. Such a desperate business it was. Day after day spent in a frantic rushing, no money to waste on buses and streetcars, just perpetually aching legs, and shoes more suited to the sedentary life of an artist than the harried existence of the newly despised. Renate would dash from this embassy to that foreign office, and when she stopped, rather than the relief she craved, was further beleaguered by the interminable waiting. She joked that if she were to be given ten marks for every hour she had spent in the queue at the American Consulate she would have money enough to pay the family's way out of Germany several times over. She joked because it was important to appear strong, but in truth she felt like a living, breathing target, out in the open because her family's life depended on it, yet always having to conceal her fear. The dashing across Berlin disguised as a leisurely saunter, the studied nonchalance whenever she passed a German in uniform, the once-normal business of walking down a street now as fraught as crossing a battlefield; each day, each hour demanded of her a first-rate performance.

And it was no better closer to home. The district around the Friedman flat had long possessed an easy, assimilated Jewish presence, yet Renate felt conspicuous as a Jew in a way she never had in Krefeld or Düsseldorf. There were several Jewish families within close proximity, one family actually lived in the same building. A couple of kilometres away was the Jewish community centre where Dora would go several times a week for the latest news, and there was the large synagogue on Fasanenstrasse. Renate felt the Jewishness of the area in a way a Berliner did not. Where she came from, Jewishness was miniscule and politely hidden. As the days passed, she found herself wondering whether she had done the right thing, by her daughter most of all, moving from the anonymity of Krefeld to Germany's most Jewish city.

Dora harboured no such doubts. 'You're ignoring the facts, Renate. The SS found Martin in Krefeld just as easily as they did Erich here in Berlin.' She paused a moment to allow the point to sink in. 'The days of the assimilated Jew are finished. A Jew, no matter how you look, no matter how you live, is a Jew. Even a tiny bit of Jew is a Jew.'

'Shows how powerful Hitler thinks we are,' said Willi with a laugh. 'Even a fraction is to be feared.'

Dora flashed a smile at her son before continuing. She had seen how things were with Renate. She, too, had her dark days and knew how important it was to climb out of the trough before sinking too deep.

'If you feel conspicuous here, imagine how you'd feel –' and she waved in a vague easterly direction, 'over there where there are streets full of Jews, not our sort of Jew, but Polish and Russian Jews. Long black coats, ridiculous hats, their appalling Yiddish, a makeshift synagogue set up every few houses, food you wouldn't want to touch. You want conspicuous, Renate? Take a ride to Rosenthaler Platz, or walk down Grosse Hamburger Strasse past Willi's school, and you'll see Jews who are Jewish from the tops of their heads down to the soles of their shoes.'

Willi offered to act as guide. Since being forced to leave his state school two years earlier, he had attended a Jewish boys' school in the east of the city. 'I've become quite familiar with the area,' he said.

'Not too familiar I hope.' All smiles were now gone and there was a warning in his mother's voice.

'You sound just like a German.'

'Not at all, I'm just not the sort of Jew who lives over there.' And again the vague wave of Dora's hand.

And so the old argument threatened, with the son sounding quite different from the parent, an argument easily stumbled upon in so many German-Jewish homes.

'We're all Jews together, no matter what our origins,' Willi now said. 'You made much the same point a moment ago: even a bit of a Jew is a Jew.' He spoke slowly and deliberately with more than a drop of adolescent venom. Then he turned to Renate. 'I'd be happy to show you around the Jewish district,' he said. And with a stubborn glance at his mother, 'I like it over there. It's like entering a different world, and such a strong world too. Not even Hitler can make them change their ways.'

Renate had never visited the area and, given her self-consciousness among the most secular of Jews, had no desire to. There were Jews and Jews, and while Hitler might not differentiate, Jews themselves did. Renate had seen a few of these *Ostjuden* in the various foreign office waiting rooms in which she now passed her days. They stood out like beggars at a banquet, and not just their appearance, although that was bad enough, their German was a mangled mess to cultured ears, as if it had been subjected to a firing squad. Most of them seemed to be manual workers – tailors, leather workers, dyers and the like, with even less chance of obtaining visas than the Lewins. And poor too, far too poor to pay their way anywhere but back east to the countries of their forebears. Secretly Renate was glad, less competition at the foreign offices meant improved chances for the Lewins, but she would have been gladder still and more at ease if these *Ostjuden* stayed away completely.

Although money was a problem for her too. Within a few of days of arriving in Berlin, hard decisions had to be made. Her small stash of cash was needed for visas and bribes and exit penalties. The only items of value Renate possessed were her mother's jewels. She was merely delaying the inevitable and she knew it. A week after arriving in Berlin, Amalie Friedman's watch, her rings and brooches, and the pearls which were so much a part of her that Renate used to joke her mother wasn't dressed until she had put them on, were given away for a song and a sausage.

Along with her mother's jewellery went so much that had comprised their life in Germany. Change after change and every one requiring just a little more effort. And such a sense of futility as Renate pushed and pushed like Sisyphus with his rock, but in her case the mountain itself kept shifting. Waiting at the foreign offices and embassies day in and day out, she would look at the other women, some so shrivelled and fading, others with the strength and determination of a general, and wonder how it was that people coped so differently. She would see the same women over and over, would see that a week, even a couple of days could make a person weaker or stronger or more desperate, sometimes violently so.

Alice squashed into the flat along with Willi and the adults, and while nearly everything was different from life in Krefeld, she learned to grasp on to those few aspects which had not changed. She had her legends book and her Käthe Kruse doll. And each morning Mutti still brushed her long curls, so different from the short bobs of other girls, and the stroking felt so good and not just on her head but down her back as well. And on Saturday her hair was washed as usual, and even though the water heater was a monster that fizzed and sparked and threatened to blow so that even Mutti wasn't allowed to light it, the Saturday routine and the clean hair to twirl in bed made her feel safer.

Most days she stayed at the flat while her mother and Aunt Dora scoured Berlin for visas. She preferred it this way. She couldn't keep pace with her mother's dashing, and she hated seeing her and all the other mothers so worried. And during the hours of waiting in the foreign offices she didn't want to make new friends, not here in Berlin. Secretly she wanted to be home in Krefeld, and during the long days alone it was easier to pretend she was.

Renate was relieved, not only was it safer for Alice to stay at the flat, there were times when her own nerves were so barbed and her frustration so bullish that if Alice were a witness, it would only distress. As the days ground on, Renate felt as if she were working against a highly integrated machine forever trying to find a way of breaking into the cycle. If she had more money it would be easier to obtain visas and exit papers; if she had the visas it would be easier to secure Martin's release.

As for visa approvals, people were leaving all the time. Some people left with nothing more than a suitcase of clothes from Jewish welfare, having cashed in everything to pay the huge amounts required to leave the country. Others were more fortunate. Renate and Dora had seen the entire contents of a flat being loaded onto a cart or lorry, once even a huge shipping container. Everything from sofas to saucepans, beds to washing blue, even nonperishable food was packed, not simply because good German food would not be available in America or Argentina or Australia, but being unable to take money out of Germany, any cash left over after taxes and permits was converted to material goods.

'There'll be small communities of German Jews all over the world,' Dora said one day, having just farewelled some old friends. 'I can see them now nestling among the kangaroos in Australia, raccoons and red Indians in America and God knows what in Argentina.'

Dora joked, but with silence on their own visas she was worried. Her sister, Hannah, was married to an Oxford don. Dora knew she would sponsor the family, but she and Erich and most adamantly Willi had believed their future lay with Palestine. They had also thought, perhaps naïvely, their chances for Palestine would be strong. So they hadn't sought Hannah's help. But now Dora was wondering whether she should.

'All this German red tape,' Renate said one evening. 'Why are they making it so difficult? It's clear Germany doesn't want us.'

'And neither it seems does the rest of the world,' said Willi, his face pressed into a wry smile.

For all her efforts Renate had little reason to hope. Yet day after day she persisted, channelling her energies into an exile which continued to terrify her. And through it all she tried to be a step ahead of the dangers that pockmarked her days. One afternoon when walking home from the Palestine Office with Dora, she saw approaching on the same side of the road three SS men just like those who came the morning her mother died. Closer they came, young men with the same blond features and the same clenched-fist demeanour as those responsible for her mother's death. And closer still, and it was the same three, she was sure of it, the very ones who killed her mother, just twenty metres away, now fifteen metres, now ten. The rest of the world fell away. Renate saw only the killers. She'd fight them, she'd fight with her bare fists, all rage and muscle she'd kick the life out of them, her mother's killers now nine metres away, now eight, now seven. She stopped in their path, Dora was pulling at her, Dora didn't realise who these men were. Renate shook her off. Five metres, four metres, and she's ready, oh yes she's ready. Come on, killers, come on. Two metres, one metre and now passing. And they're not the ones. They're someone else's brutes not hers.

Dora was frantic. 'What are you doing?' she said. 'What on earth are you thinking of?'

Renate couldn't speak. Only later when they were safe at home and preparing the supper did she tell Dora about the three SS men who were not the ones who killed her mother.

Hunted and hunting all at the same time, concocting a set of convincing lies for this official, a slightly different set for another, and hoping she was on the right track but never quite sure. And although Dora's involvement with the Jewish community meant she was among the first to know where next to direct their efforts when the last avenue had fizzled out, three weeks after Renate's arrival in Berlin, the two women acknowledged they were no closer to obtaining their husbands' release or of leaving Germany.

It was late in the evening of another long day, and all too easy in the dark and cold to succumb to a longing for times past.

'I'd love a glass of muscat,' Renate said. 'And a foot bath.'

'How about a cup of hot water and a cushion instead?'

Renate smiled as Dora pulled out one of the couch cushions and propped it under her feet, then headed for the kitchen.

While Dora was busy with the kettle, Renate settled back into the armchair and closed her eyes. It had been a hellish day. She must have walked close on ten kilometres, much of it through sleet and bitter wind. She had been home for more than an hour but still she was cold and all of her hurting, legs, back, arms, head, even her jaw, and not a scrap of energy remaining even if her life depended on it. Although of course that wasn't true, not with Martin still incarcerated. Her kind, amenable husband and not of a nature to rise to the extreme challenges of these times, how she feared for him. And now the familiar fist at her throat, and tears riding on the fear, and just as quickly she squeezed the tears dry and swallowed hard. Terror, desperation, anguish like you were being disembowelled, and you have to keep it down, keep it quiet. Can't afford to feel a little because the little inflates and soon it swamps and you can't look after your daughter, you can't look after yourself, can't remain strong enough to engineer your family to safety. And it is up to you, up to all the wives and mothers to deal with the officials, handing out bribes like cakes at a party. Up to you to obtain the visas that will save your husband and your family.

Up to you, she now told herself, and by the time Dora returned with two cups of steaming water, was composed again. The urge to survive is bottomless, she was thinking, and despite how bad you feel, there's always a grain of energy left to excavate. She sat with Dora sipping her water while they planned their schedules for the next day. More letters to write, more phone calls to make, more embassies to visit, more functionaries to plead with, more Germans to fear.

It was Willi who first learned of the *Kindertransport* scheme. Apparently British Jews were providing the necessary finance to transport German and Austrian children at risk to safety in England. And Willi was at risk. His father was political and so was he, and soon his age would put him beyond the scheme and directly in the sights of Germans wanting to do their best for the Reich.

But Willi didn't want to go to England, not under any circumstances. 'It's clear what the English think of us,' he said, slamming his fists against the table. 'If not for the English we'd be in Palestine now.'

Dora had just that morning been to the Palestine Office on Meineckestrasse, her fifth futile visit in the past two weeks. She was quiet but firm. 'There's no time left for waiting.'

Willi was now on his feet, a stringy youth all jitters in the cramped flat. As he spoke the sun caught the pale fuzz on his face. 'The visas will come through any day now, I know they will.'

His mother was brusque. 'You know nothing of the sort. None of us do.'

Palestine, Willi kept saying, they'd worked so hard for Palestine, it was the only place for Jews. But Dora had already made up her mind. She put through a long-distance call to her sister and brother-in-law in Oxford, while Willi kept repeating that he wouldn't go and no one could make him. Dora put an arm around her son's shoulders.

'England now,' she said quietly, 'doesn't mean England forever. And given Palestine is British territory, you might well find England provides a quicker route than does Germany.'

Willi was still arguing when the call to England came through.

He stood stiff and glaring while his mother explained the situation to her sister. It was no longer a matter of taking the whole family, she said, rather there was a scheme to get children out, children who would need to be sponsored and provided with a home once they arrived in Britain. Hannah relayed the information to her husband, and in less than a minute Hannah and Jonathon Moser of Oxford, England, had agreed to sponsor Willi and take him into their home for as long as required.

'And Alice too?' Dora said.

Renate was immediately out of her chair and protesting, but Dora, already engaged in a robust accounting of Alice's qualities, ignored her. Such a mature child, she was saying to Hannah, and no trouble at all. Wise beyond her years, quiet, academically inclined, blessed with the Friedman flare for art, and would slip into Oxford life as if she had been born to it. Besides, she had nowhere else to go and no future if she stayed.

'We simply can't predict what will happen here,' Dora said to her sister. 'But Hitler is adamant his Germany will have no Jews.'

A little more persuasion and she must have convinced, for suddenly she was detailing the *Kindertransport* sponsorship procedure: who the Mosers would need to contact at the London end, the documentation required, the importance of speed given the worsening situation in Germany. She wound up the phone call in a profusion of gratitude, replaced the receiver on the hook and turned to face the music.

'How could you?' Renate was holding tight to Alice. 'She's my daughter. You had no right.'

And Willi: 'How could you? It's my life.'

Dora rehearsed the impossible answers before speaking. She started with her son. 'Unless you leave Germany you'll have no life. It's as simple as that. Of course you want Palestine, but Palestine is taking fewer and fewer of us. And while you're waiting, you could well find yourself in Buchenwald like your father.' She put her arm around him but he shrugged her off. 'You're going, Willi, and the sooner you accept it the better.'

Then she turned to Renate. She was brief. When you hear a wavering on the end of the phone, when you know that if given time your sister may decide a six year old is too much for two fifty year olds who know nothing about children, and your English brother-in-law may conclude he's already encumbered with quite enough of things German, you press on, desperate not to lose the opportunity.

'Alice has no future here,' Dora continued. 'No Jew does. Even if Hitler and his National Socialists were defeated tomorrow, too much damage has already been done. It'll be years, if ever, before Germans will feel comfortable around us.'

This same thought had occurred to Renate but she had quickly brushed it aside: too terrible to think that once having left Germany she might never return. Now she forced herself to consider that bizarre phenomenon whereby a perpetrator of wrongdoing through some extraordinary twist of logic comes to resent and eventually blame the victim. She had seen it in certain bad marriages when the philandering husband turns his resentment on his patient and forgiving wife, blaming her for his reprehensible behaviour. And in commerce too, when gains were made dishonestly and the person who benefits resents the one who was cheated.

People don't like to be reminded of their wrongdoings, it introduces conflict into a character otherwise at ease with itself. Renate knew Dora was right, that when all this was over, Germans would want to forget their foray into barbarism, or at least convert it into something justifiable. They would not appreciate the presence of Jews to remind them of the truth.

So it happened that by the close of day, both Willi and Alice were registered for the *Kindertransport*. Willi's chances of being accepted were, they believed, good given his age, his own political activism and his father in Buchenwald. Alice was less of a certainty despite Martin's incarceration; however, Renate and Dora believed her chances would be increased if she were partnered with Willi.

'It won't be for long,' Renate said to Alice. 'And soon we'll all be together, you, me and your father, probably in England –' she and Dora had checked their applications at the British Passport Control Office last thing that afternoon, 'but if not England, somewhere safe.'

Thus she reassured her young daughter, herself too, all the while wishing Martin were here to share the decision and take some of the pain.

They then settled down to wait. The first *Kindertransport* left Berlin early in December with most of the two hundred children being boys of Willi's age and circumstances. So, too, for subsequent transports. Renate despaired Alice would ever be chosen and at the same time despaired she would. It was a terrible cruelty to send your child away, to plan for it and work hard that it may happen, knowing you'll miss her like your soul has been wrenched out of you. Each time a list was posted, Renate would search for her daughter's name, sickened by the same distressing brew of hope and loss. And when her name was not on the list, an even worse brew of joy that Alice was not leaving and terror of what might happen if she remained. She would see the relief on the other mothers' faces and think: Why not my daughter? What must I do to save my daughter? And soaking through her a sense of foreboding, a sense that the worst was still to come, a sense that the last *Kindertransport* to depart really was the last.

Several times Dora rang her sister in Oxford. Was she sure she had done everything required of British sponsors? Would she contact Bloomsbury House just to make sure all the papers were in order? Yes, contact them again, for until the travel permits arrived from England there was little chance of Willi or Alice being included on a *Kindertransport* list. And there were daily visits to the headquarters in Berlin to gather with the same panic-stricken parents waiting to ask the same questions of the same community workers who said they were doing all they could. Every day the same distressed parents, some quietly nursing their fears, others loudly accusing the workers of favouritism, everyone acting as if their children were more important than all the others. Selflessness, Dora and Renate soon learned, was counter-productive in a time of crisis. It was a harsh but simple fact that when survival was threatened there was a hierarchy, and those you loved were on top. Within a week, Renate and Dora were as pushy as the other parents. But without travel permits it was useless.

In January, within two days of each other, Martin was released from Sachsenhausen and Erich from Buchenwald. In a mere eight weeks, Erich, long known as Papa Bear to his family – Dora was Mama Bear – had shrunk to a fraction of his normal size and had aged ten years. His face was a mess of sharp, grime-filled wrinkles separated by patches of tight, grey skin. He and Martin compared notes on food, shelter and treatment by the guards. Sachsenhausen won hands down.

'I'll book in there next time,' said Erich.

Erich had suffered diarrhoea for the entire eight weeks, and would never, he said, rid himself of the stench of his own excreta. In the camp he was forced to rise hours before dawn, drag his rancid body out to the mustering ground to line up with the other prisoners on the freezing asphalt. Aching, starved and silent he would stand while roll call was conducted with bullying slowness, all the while cursing his loose bowels. Should anyone want to go to the latrines – although never want, always need – he was more likely to be punished for asking, rather than given leave to go. The clock above the watchtower totted up his pain, fifteen minutes, forty-five minutes, one hundred and twenty minutes, slow-motion time yet the only movement in the grim morning. And through-out the long bleak days of chill and dust quarrying stones for Hitler's new Germany, the same punch punch punch of pain.

Some of the *Kristallnacht* Jews at Buchenwald had been put to work in the latrines. At first Erich had counted himself fortunate to have been spared what was indisputably the worst of the camp labour, but as his bowels rebelled he was no longer so sure. Soiled all the time and with precious little water, if he had the choice of water to clean himself or relieve his thirst, he would drink and hope he stank no worse than anyone else. Although the guards, all of them such experts in humiliation, were quick to remind that every last one of them was shit.

'Belongs in an abattoir,' a young guard had said about Erich. 'Not that his carcass is fit for eating.'

Physically Martin had fared better than his brother-in-law, but in other respects his suffering had been worse. Every facet of human functioning had taken a beating in the camp. Kindness, respect, selflessness, caring for others, all those qualities necessary when strangers were thrown together, were soon under threat.

Most of the men at Sachsenhausen had been incarcerated since *Kristallnacht*, and by the time Martin arrived many were sick and weak. In his barracks there was one man whose wounds had become septic. Martin tended the wounds using his own allocation of water and bandages made from his own underclothes. The man needed more food than the usual prisoner rations in order to regain his strength, so Martin gave him some of his food, and initially he managed to persuade a few of the other men to part with a little of theirs. But soon he was caring for the man alone. And when the man eventually died, no one thanked him; even the man himself had blamed Martin for prolonging his agony.

Weakness was dangerous in the camp, and too often kindness was seen as weakness. Of course men would look after family members, and friends would look after friends, but when you're starving and cold, when your life trembles on a tightrope, only a fool is a good Samaritan, or so one of the other prisoners said of Martin. Gradually it dawned on him that goodness in the camp was a bit like a tub of water in the middle of the desert, and he too began to dry up.

The cold bored into him, his stomach shrieked for food, kindness was washed away along with the diarrhoea. And through it all, the incessant cruelty of the guards, most of them members of the Death's Head Squad of the SS. They were the basest of beings, true barbarians, as far as Martin was concerned. And so young, many of them not much older than Willi, and chilling to see boys, their values not yet fully formed, behaving with such savagery. Martin would watch them puff themselves up and stride around like young sadistic gods, so proud in their uniforms, the ghastly human skull on their collars.

'You'd never dare look them in the eye,' Martin said one evening soon after he was released. 'So the skull, I always imagined it was my skull, always seemed to be staring at me.'

'They've thought of everything,' Erich said. 'Train men in the art of brutality while they're still young and receptive, and in time there'll be an entire population willing to torture and kill on command.'

The same thought had occurred to Martin while still in the camp, but he had kept it to himself. These were Germans after all, his countrymen. Could he, Martin Lewin, be capable of the same violence if exposed to similar training? The question plagued him as he saw how brutality flared randomly like sparks from a fire. It was as though the German reverence for order was being deliberately sidelined to allow the guards to express whatever primitive violence lurked within. Let off the leash, away from their families and without any civilising restraints, these young fellows were running wild. Martin would see them look around to make sure they had an audience before they laid into some poor fellow. He would watch a group work together, each taking turns to thrash an inmate until they'd thrashed the life out of him. It was a lesson in pack mentality, each man gunning his performance to greater extremes. Sachsenhausen taught him there were no certainties about human behaviour, and no limits to human brutality.

Martin and Erich spoke little about their experiences, they wanted to protect their families and they wanted to forget. Although it was easy to surmise from the almost indecent alteration in their appearance and behaviour. Erich spent hours every day on the toilet. He could be heard groaning behind the closed door and sometimes the voiceless gasping of a grown man crying. And sniffing, always sniffing at himself. It was different for Martin. Winter dug its heels in earlier than usual, according to Martin, and saved its worse for Sachsenhausen. He hovered around the stove and Erich around the toilet, and now and then they would talk in whispers to each other as they regained their health.

Dwelling on hardship is the prerogative of either the malingerer or the one whose suffering is past. Within twenty-four hours of arriving home, Erich returned to his political work and Martin joined Renate in the struggle for visas. It helped blot out the camps, but more to the point, there was the present to attend to and a future to fix.

Fritz, the Lewins' best hope, had disappeared. Martin approached people in the music world, but if anyone had any information they had decided not to reveal it; in fact, very few people were willing to speak to him at all. Then one evening he received a phone call from a man describing himself as a friend of Fritz's, not a musician but a friend – this said with emphasis. He talked low and quickly and Martin had to strain to hear. It emerged that Fritz, Martin's distant abrasive brother, had led a secret life. Prior to *Kristallnacht*, he had been arrested for perversion at a haunt where men went for sex with other men. He had not been seen since.

His brother, his own flesh and blood. Martin could hardly take it in. And yet there was no time to dwell, no time to make sense of the revelations – how to make sense of such revelations? – and certainly no time to mourn, not with so many other losses threatening, not with his wife and daughter to protect. He would deal with it afterwards, he told himself – always assuming there would be an afterwards.

When the next *Kindertransport* list was posted both Willi and Alice were included. Then such a rush, photographs to be taken, medical examinations to be performed, and Alice with a cold and Renate and Martin terrified she would be rejected, entry certificates into Britain, identification numbers assigned. And there they are at Anhalter train station in the middle of a January night, along with several other parents and a couple of hundred children, most aged between ten and sixteen but also a few younger ones like Alice. Many are already alone, having arrived at this point from other destinations in Germany. Police order the children onto the platform while the parents are forced to remain behind the barriers – there'll be no emotional scenes on this German station, although who would be observing at two o'clock in the morning is anyone's guess. Willi and Alice each have a knapsack, a small suitcase and a woollen blanket, each grip the other by the hand.

'Stay together,' the parents say to the children. 'And remember, we'll be seeing you soon.'

There are more hugs, Renate straightens the identification card around her daughter's neck, Willi tells his parents yet again that as soon as he arrives in England he'll contact the Palestine people. Then he and Alice pass through the gate onto the platform and into an eerie silence.

Of all the extreme circumstances on that extreme night, including sending a six-year-old girl to a foreign country to live with people she doesn't know, most bizarre of all is a couple of hundred children, many of whom have never before been separated from their parents, making no noise. And in that solemn silence, a fear and tragic awareness that the worst one can imagine may in fact eventuate.

There are police and guards and *Kindertransport* escorts directing the children: the miserable ones who know the truth of this journey, and the smiling ones who have been told they are going on holiday. As Renate watches her small daughter she wonders what makes one parent lie and another tell the truth, and when parents concoct their pretty explanations are they doing it for themselves or the children? And who, she wonders, will silence the sobs and wipe the tears when alone in a foreign country their child learns the truth?

She watches Alice walk away from her along the endless platform. Her daughter, her only child, old and young in equal proportions, now being severed from everything and everyone she has ever known. And at last Renate acknowledges the grotesque truth: she and Martin are sending away their daughter to save her life. It is an utterly preposterous proposition. She wonders – no, more visceral than that, she fears she will never see her daughter again, and is horrified at the thought. It can't be forever, she won't believe it is possible. It is one thing to hate Jews as Hitler clearly does, and quite a different matter to seize each and every one of them and kill them. Barbarians in ancient times might kill a whole race, but surely not Germans in 1939. Of course she'll see her daughter again. Of course she will.

Willi and Alice, still holding on to each other, turn around for one last look. He so determinedly solemn appears suddenly very young, while Alice is old with concentration as if she is seeking to brand this picture of her parents on memory. Later she will say she began mourning her parents when she stepped onto the platform, leaving them behind the barrier.

Renate holds tight to Martin. The last they see is Alice being separated from Willi and put in a carriage with girls, while Willi is ushered into a different carriage for boys. So much for Willi will look after you, so much for any promise made with certainty.

Part II

HAUNTINGS

The *Kindertransport*

Fifty-five years later, Alice Carter, née Lewin, stood at the entrance of Drayton House in Bloomsbury, London. Upstairs, in the Central British Fund archives, was the record of her arrival in this country, the record she had travelled from America to see, the record she already knew. Hers was a history without question mark. Mother died 1943, Auschwitz; father survived Westerbork then died 1945, Bergen-Belsen; his brother, Fritz, disappeared 1938, presumed dead; aunt and uncle, Dora and Erich Friedman, slave labour in Poland then death at Chelmno; their son, Willi, Israeli citizen, married to a sabra, father of three, grandfather of seven, killed in a boating accident last year. And Hannah and Jonathon Moser, to whom Alice owed her life, died comfortably in old age, Napa Valley, California.

Nothing to discover, but here all the same and, as she pressed the elevator button, too late to turn back. With the creak and clang of a machine much the same vintage as the rest of the building, Alice opted for the stairs. She had not expected the archive to be housed in quite such a place as this. It had an institutional feel, the grey-green walls and no-colour lino suggesting a hostel or community centre from the 1960s. In America, such buildings had either slipped into slums or been renovated to within an inch of their original lives. And while there was a leap into the present at the top of the stairs with the security system, it was no more sophisticated than the number pad on her building back home in San Francisco. The whole place with its decay and its barely perceptible nod to modernity struck her as very English. She had expected a more streamlined structure, she now realised, something more along the lines of a miniature Fort Knox.

Exactly on the hour Alice pressed the buzzer. She explained her business and was admitted, only to be informed by the receptionist that the archivist had been detained. Just a fifteen-minute delay, the woman said in strongly accented English, perhaps Mrs Carter would like some coffee while she waited?

Alice declined as the English coffee did not appeal, and besides, would only send her to the bathroom again. She sat where directed, on a small chair dwarfed by the high receptionist counter, and wrapped herself up tight. After a minute of self-conscious staring at the plastic veneer of the counter, she told the receptionist she would prefer to wait in the hall. With a 'Suit yourself' barely audible above the noise of an ageing printer, Alice returned to the hall and the vinyl chair she had noticed there.

She sat stiff-backed in the dingy space. To her left was the door to reception, to her right the office containing the archive. Grimy windows, low-wattage lighting and marbled walls would have made reading impossible if she were not already too jittery to read. She rummaged in her bag for her compact, checked her make-up which did not require checking, patted her hair which was lying neatly in its waves, smoothed her suit which was perfectly smooth, and finding she was her usual tidy self, capitulated to a fretful waiting. Only for her son would she be putting herself through this, only for her son.

Raphe had always hungered for more history than was ever available. Tell me about my grandparents, he would ask as a young child. Tell me about Germany. Tell me about the war. Tell me how you and Uncle Willi escaped. At first she had been reluctant to respond. She had tried so hard to shut the lid on the past and was terrified of stirring up the old losses. At the same time she had never wanted to deprive Raphe of anything, this son who from his earliest years had borne an uncanny resemblance to her father. In Raphe it seemed her carefully packaged life was to be ripped apart.

Raphe had persisted with his questions, and eventually – he would have been eleven or twelve at the time – Alice had relented. She told him about Krefeld and the escape to Berlin, about the *Kindertransport* and arriving in England, and of course about her parents, although her memories of them were already muted. She had tried to concentrate the fading visions, would actually construct pictures in her mind, building them up bit by bit. But she knew they were not her memories, more a collage of other people's pictures and stories. For the sad fact of it was the years prior to *Kristallnacht* had been lost. Until she started talking with her son, the most vivid picture she retained of her mother was of her hunched in a chair at the window of their Krefeld flat, thin and bedraggled and grieving for her own dead mother, and the main image of her father was the knot of shivering bones that had returned from Sachsenhausen. As for the two of them together, she could still see them standing behind the barriers at Anhalter Station in the middle of a freezing night, their poor faces tight and white as they sent their only child into an unknown future.

Talking with her son brought alive other visions, other memories, and soon she experienced an unexpected pleasure in revisiting the past. She would tell Raphe stories passed on to her by others, Willi in particular, who, being so much older, remembered her parents well. Indeed, if not for Willi her storehouse of family memories would be distressingly bare. Although Raphe, with an imagination which shunned all limits, showed himself adept at improvisation. If my grandparents had survived, he would say, I'm sure they would have come to America. And they would have lived with us and taught me German. And my grandfather would have become the most famous silk maker in the country, and my grandmother the most famous silk designer. The boy crafted story after story to the delight of both mother and son.

But as he grew, Raphe wanted more history than even imagination and borrowed memories could supply, so when he was old enough he flew to Israel to talk with Willi himself. Yet still he was not satisfied, for when he returned home and to college he swapped from law to literature and ultimately the newly formed Holocaust studies, and nothing his parents said would dissuade him.

'Give him time,' Alice said to her husband, 'I'm sure he'll tire of it.'

Raphe didn't, still he wanted more history than anyone could supply.

'How much more do you want?' Alice had asked. 'Isn't the Holocaust enough?' But all-American boy she had raised, Raphe wanted his own personal narrative. And if that were not enough, he also wanted to 'make connections'.

'All I hear is death and more death,' he said. 'Let's see who's alive. Maybe a next-door neighbour, maybe the local butcher –'

'I'd have no idea of his name.'

'Then the funny man in Düsseldorf, the restaurateur Katz. Let's put a spark among all this dead history.'

Her son, now thirty-six years old, was an academic in Holocaust studies, with a passion for volcanoes.

'My history,' Alice said, 'is hardly Mt Etna.'

And yet here she was at the archives searching for history. Raphe had wanted to accompany her, and while she still rarely refused him anything, she had refused him this; not knowing what she might find and unable to predict how she might react, she didn't want her son watching. So they had parted not far from the British Museum, Raphe to wander the Charing Cross Road bookshops and Alice to head north through Bloomsbury to the archives.

At another time she would have enjoyed the walk through literary London, but today she was anxious, as had been the case ever since sending her letter of enquiry to the *Kindertransport* archives. Indeed, she had been so bound up in her anxiety as to be quite shocked at the simplicity of the procedure. After her initial contact she had forwarded birth certificate and proof of identity as requested, and they would have sent a copy of her file without further ado if she had wanted. She had told them to hold the mail, believing it preferable to be present in case there were any revelations. Better too, she thought, to be away from home for any surprises, without friends or family as witnesses, at a time known by her in advance. And even while she was making the arrangements to fly to London, she acknowledged the irony in what she was doing: that while there was no changing nor controlling any of the information in her file, she would do everything possible to take charge of the manner of revelation – rather like a drowning man who spends his last minutes deciding whether to die with his eyes open or closed.

While it might seem absurd to travel several thousand miles to see some papers that could easily have been sent, Alice had good reason. Several times during her adult years and absolutely without warning, images and events from the past had blasted in on her with the force of a cyclone. Shocking events, fearfully shocking, indeed any less shocking and she might have lived with them as she had so many of the horrors. Yet when you realise you have forgotten something so significant as your grandmother dying before your eyes, you are terrified at what else you might have blocked out. And the questions this raises about the type of person you are. For how could Alice have forgotten her grandmother climbing onto the table while the SS bashed her father to a pulp? Her grandmother standing with her arms raised high, large and stately and as motionless as a statue, then falling to the ground and the blistering crash as she hit the floor.

Forgotten, all forgotten for years, until one day when she and Phil, together with Raphe who was only a toddler at the time, had crossed the bridge into Sausalito for a picnic. After the meal, Phil and Raphe had fallen asleep and Alice had wandered off into the parklands. She was thinking how Sausalito was a nice place to visit but not a place to live when her attention was caught by an old, heavy-featured woman walking along the path, pushing a shopping cart heaped with junk. As Alice drew closer she saw the woman was more worn than old, closer still and she heard the woman's muttering, was unnerved by the utterly closed-in focus of that incomprehensible speech. Suddenly the woman let go of her cart and mounted a pile of boulders to the side of the path, stood a moment at the summit, her arms raised to the sky, then leapt or fell to the ground. A fraction of a second, then she was on her feet again, moving down the path with her trolley and her muttering. But in that moment with the woman poised high on the rocks, Alice was filled with a fear so intemperate, so uninhabitable, that it left her crouched on the grass and gasping. Recognising a lightning strike from the past, she knew she should get up and resume her life before the event materialised and left her forever changed. Yet she did not – or could not. And there it was, returned after three decades, her grandmother in an act of courage that took her last breath, and her father a pile of bloodied, wrecked flesh on the floor.

There had been many instances over the years when Alice had learned that one forgets what is unbearable to live with. So if there were a possibility at the archive of being confronted with information so dreadful she had banished it from memory, she did not want witnesses, and certainly not her son.

While Raphe was the main reason she was here, he was not the only one. It was the passage of time – two years ago she had turned sixty – which enabled her to take the risk this visit ignited. It is one thing to say your parents and friends and most of your family were killed in the war, and quite another to believe it. Unequivocally believe it. Death leaves no room for hope. But as long as you don't test the facts, it is possible, just possible you might be wrong.

And what abundant dreams have been inspired by that tiny nugget of doubt. So many joyful meetings to contrive and ever-after happinesses to imagine. Take for example, an exhibition of Chagall in New York, and you're there not to work, just as a regular visitor with a couple of hours to spare. Through the rooms you stroll, bathing in the lightness of being that is Chagall's unique touch, lingering in front of the two paintings you have worked on, savouring the pleasure which comes from knowing a painting down to its brush strokes and flares of colour. Then someone stops next to you, standing far too close and seemingly more interested in you than the painting. Finally you turn (in your dreams you always prolong this moment) and see a woman taller than you, and not unlike the women in Modigliani's later work, a woman you recognise from memory. And –

It's your mother! Can you believe it? Your mother, she's alive and in New York City, and she's not changed at all! You look again, she recognises you, her long-lost daughter for whom she has never stopped searching, has never given up hope she would find. Such a joyful reunion. You thought she was dead. She feared you were lost. And now the two of you together. Who would believe it!

So many variations of the dream. Change the paintings, change the gallery, change the city. Locate the meeting in a restaurant, a bus, a department store. Sometimes it's her mother, other times her father, on occasions Erich and Dora – so many deaths make for rich and varied dreaming. But if Alice were to possess unequivocal proof of these deaths, late twentieth-century cool reliable proof, the dreams with all their pleasures would have to be discarded.

Then she turned sixty and the situation changed. With all her dream characters now dead of natural causes should they have by some miracle survived the unnatural ones, Alice decided she could take the risk. So when her son begged her yet again to investigate the archive, she listened in a way she had not in previous years. But still, she would not have acted if not for Phil, her husband, now dead like the rest of them. With Phil gone, there was a huge gaping hole that no amount of dreaming could fill, and an unexpected slackening in her American ties.

Alice was fifteen years old when Jonathon Moser was offered a chair in British history at an American university. He and Hannah together with Alice packed up their lives and moved from Oxford to California. Alice had finished high school in America, she had attended college in America and she had married an American. It was not surprising then that throughout her adult life Alice had always felt more American than English, and more English than German. So much so that when one of Raphe's friends in grade school had commented on her accent, not an English accent but 'something foreign', Alice had been quite annoyed. But when another child made the same observation, Alice had hired an elocutionist to shape her speech into pure west coast American. She wanted no German. And no, she could not explain it, except there was a sense that if you kill off the language of the past, you also kill the past.

At high school she had read Oscar Wilde's *The Ballad of Reading Gaol*, had enjoyed it, although no more than many other narrative poems she had read at the time. But as she walked the half dozen blocks to her voice coach each week, a line from the poem marked her progress: '… each man kills the thing he loves'. And no matter how much she would vary her pace, no matter how hard she would try to pour other words into her brain, 'each man kills the thing he loves' refused to be silenced. Her parents had been German, they spoke to her in German, they loved her in German; she wondered whether killing off the language was to condemn her mother and father to a second death. And while she knew the notion was ridiculous, such thoughts, or rather moral conflicts, were not uncommon when practically every aspect of one's childhood had been uncommon. Nonetheless she persisted with her elocutionist until the deed was done, a heavyweight tolerance for guilt providing the necessary stamina to continue. Although at night in her sleep her guilt was appeased in German-language dreams – not frequently, but often enough to remind her who she once had been.

'I am not German,' she would insist to herself or anyone who might raise the issue. Yet the effort it took to deny her Germanness also kept it at the forefront of consciousness. In short, she was plagued by it. She lived much more easily with her Jewishness, despite having married a non-Jew, and despite having lost family, country and childhood because of it. She had lost so much she ought to hate it, but to hate her Jewishness was as absurd as hating her blood or bones.

It had been Phil who had quelled her factions. Phil, being so typically American, took it for granted that America was the centre of the world, history was American history and the future was an American future. The only relevant aspect of Alice's being a German Jew was that, indirectly at least, it had brought her to America. When you want no memory, America is the place to be.

But America without Phil was quite another matter; it was treading thin ice just waiting for it to crack, and nothing to protect her, not even a son, and neither would it be fair to ask. With Phil gone, America was on shaky foundations and suddenly everything was up for grabs. Which helped explain why she was here in this English building waiting for the archivist to hand over information which would either allow her memories to rest and her dreams to die, or create an almighty ruckus which at her time of life she could do without.

At sixty-two, Alice Carter was a small, trim woman, hair still brown with a smudge of grey at the temples. She dressed in a neat, ageless style with an irreverent wink at fashion's self-importance. Today was typical: black suit with a jacket nipped in at the waist, silver brooch which resembled a Miro squiggle, the skin of her neck bare and smooth, her hair cropped ('waif-like' her hairdresser called it, which struck this well-heeled sixty year old as rather quaint), dark stockings, black shoes and a fake ocelot bag.

She worked as a conservator of paintings, specialising in the modern period. Like the mother she had hardly known, Alice, too, had wanted to be a painter, but as talented as she was, could identify those who were more so. She was aware even as a twenty year old that every art form can accommodate only one or two virtuosos at any particular time, and just like Renate a quarter of a century earlier, acknowledged that being a good amateur or mid-range professional would not suit her.

It was a hard decision, but her disappointment was fortunately short-lived. From the very beginning of her career as a conservator, she had delighted in her work. She loved the detail and the focus on perfection, and the irony, how she loved the irony. Many modern masterpieces were fast deteriorating having been made with materials and techniques far less durable than those used by the old masters. Given that one of the more crucial qualities for a masterpiece was longevity, a use-by date for a multimillion-dollar work of art was more than a passing problem. Like most of her American colleagues, Alice believed the twentieth century to be the American century in art as in most things. How apt, she had often thought, that the throwaway society, the convenience society, the nation which had created Hollywood in order to reinvent history as something shorter and more entertaining than it actually was, also invented the short-term masterpiece. Although it was not without its benefits; she'd always had plenty of work and there was no sign of it letting up.

If only she were poring over a painting now, she was thinking, as she rearranged herself on the tatty vinyl chair in the tatty vinyl hall, indeed, was anywhere but here. If not for Raphe expecting a blow-by-blow account of the visit, she would slip out quietly, down the stairs, out into the anonymity of the Bloomsbury streets and gardens, stroll about at her leisure, then down to the National Portrait Gallery for an hour with the moderns, and finally meet her son as planned on the steps of St Martin in the Fields for an early evening of Mozart.

She shuffled on her chair, swallowed, and then again, as if that would remove the anxiety, and checked her watch. Only ten minutes had passed. She'd give the archivist another ten and then, Raphe notwithstanding, she would leave.

• • •

While her temperament was like her mother's, physically Alice resembled her father. She was small like Martin, with a serious, intense face, and no matter how long she lived outside Europe, she would always look European. When Jonathon and Hannah Moser had first set eyes on her in that huge dingy hall at Liverpool Station, a six-year-old girl who had travelled alone from Germany to England, Jonathon had remarked how foreign she looked, particularly when compared with Willi, a gangly adolescent who could have come from anywhere. Alice spoke no English, just stood close to her cousin, clutching her knapsack and her legends of Greece and Rome while Willi answered questions about their trip. She did not want to be there, but with the strangeness all about them and the impossible English words, she could no longer pretend.

While she had been on the train she had played a private game that as long as they were on the move she would be all right. She would travel across Europe to Asia, travel all the way around the world until eventually the train returned to Germany, Hitler would be gone and she would be reunited with her parents never again to be separated. The game made her feel less alone, less scared. She stretched it across the kilometres, through the darkness, over the landscape she mostly could not see but would not recognise anyway.

She had started the game even while she sat on the stationary train at Anhalter Station in Berlin. She knew it was a matter of survival that she and Willi were being sent away. What she did not know and could not ask was whose lives were being threatened: hers and Willi's, or their parents'? Willi would know, but he was in a different carriage; in fact, for all she knew, he might not even be on the same train. And even if he were, there were no guarantees he wouldn't be put off somewhere, leaving her to arrive in England alone. She shuffled in her seat, straightened the identity card around her neck, a standard size and far too big, checked the pouch inside her coat containing her entry certificate into Britain, and stared through the grubby windowpane. The train was still stationary and yet there were no children left to board, just guards patrolling the platform, and beyond the barriers and out of sight, her parents. She was so hot despite the freezing night with her four layers of underwear and two jumpers, and if not for her father she would have had two skirts and two coats as well. But what else could they do, her mother said, when the suitcase permitted by the authorities was so small?

The suitcase was now tucked away on the rack over her head. Alice kept glancing up to make sure it was still there. It contained the rest of her clothes, a slender wad of photographs, including one of her parents on their wedding day, and an assortment of embroidered handkerchiefs her grandmother had collected as she travelled the world playing the piano. The handkerchiefs were all Alice owned of her grandmother's and, against all manner of persuasion, she had insisted they be packed. She had also insisted on her legends of Greece and Rome, and when there was no room either in the suitcase or knapsack, had decided to carry it. The book now lay in her lap.

She could smell the food her mother had packed for the journey. She wasn't hungry, couldn't imagine ever being hungry again, had already decided that if England were really awful she would simply stop eating until she shrivelled up and disappeared. She reached into the knapsack and shoved the food beneath her scarf and cardigan; she didn't want anyone else to smell it.

She was the youngest in the carriage by several years. Some of the other girls were talking quietly, but most sat in silence looking as sad and lonely as she felt. One of the escorts, a Quaker called Fraülein Rosa, was travelling in their carriage, and because Alice was the youngest had taken the seat next to her. This was the last thing Alice wanted. Her parents had told her the Quakers were working hard to save Jewish children, so she knew they were good people, but she also knew she was less likely to cry if she didn't have to talk. Now as the train grumbled and jerked into motion and a number of the girls began to sniff, Fraülein Rosa reached across and took her hand. Alice looked up at her, 'I'm not going to cry,' she said, and pulled her hand free.

And neither she did. Not when the carriage was in darkness and hurtling through a greater darkness, not when she was desperate to go to the toilet but didn't know where it was or trust herself to ask, not when the train stopped to pick up more children and Alice in her crowded carriage worried they would toss some of the Berlin children off, toss Willi off to make room for the new arrivals. Nor did she cry when in the early morning the train stopped again, this time just before the Dutch border, and German officers boarded. She'd seen her father's face smashed in, she told herself, when the officers smashed a girl's violin looking for hidden jewels. She'd seen her family's house torn apart, she told herself, when, having discovered money in the food parcel of one of the children, the officers scattered the rest of her possessions through-out the carriage. She'd seen her grandmother fall dead to the floor, she told herself, when one of the officers searched a girl for gold and then dropped her head-first to the floor. She'd seen her father and uncle return half-starved from concentration camps, she told herself, when they took a knapsack full of food and tossed it from the train. Oh yes, she'd seen far worse, she told herself, when they ripped the cover off her book expecting to find money or jewels. And when one of the guards clenched her in his hands and shook so hard her head hurt, and would not listen when she said she had no valuables apart from the five Reichsmark they had already taken, she told herself that as bad as the fear was, she had known worse.

At last the officers were called off the train. The carriage was littered with personal belongings and distressed children. While Fraülein Rosa attended to the girls, placating, soothing, assuring everyone the worst was over, Alice searched the floor for the pieces of her book. She thought she found most of them, wrapped them safely in her scarf and placed them deep in her knapsack. The remainder of the book she kept with her, stroking it in the same way her mother would stroke her sore brow whenever she had a headache.

On the Dutch side of the border things were very different. The first people to board the train were not officials but smiling women with warm drinks and baskets of sandwiches and chocolate. And such a fuss made of Alice, she being so young, that now she was fighting to hold back the tears. She kept telling herself she would manage, must manage, although how much easier if Willi were with her. And again the terrible thought that she might never find him, that she'd arrive in England alone and be forced to struggle on by herself, a prospect so awful she pushed it aside, pretending instead she was a grown-up without a fear in the world.

The journey from the Dutch–German border to the Hook of Holland was mostly a blank, although she remembered the delight of windmills and Dutch flags instead of swastikas, and the flat wintry fields through which the train trundled as it made its way to the coast. And waiting, so much waiting that by the time they reached their destination night had again fallen. Then at last finding Willi, and he so pleased he didn't care what the other boys thought as he lifted her high in the air and whirled her round and hugged her so tight she felt all squashed like a cushion. Then followed more food and more waiting and more kindly Dutch folk, and Alice wanting to discard the food she'd brought from Germany but not daring to in case it was the wrong thing to do. And refusing to let go of Willi even for a second, until they were shepherded onto the boat and forced apart again, Willi with the boys and Alice with the girls.

And now she remembers every detail. It is night and they are on the water, a sea of water and much rougher than the river at home. She is lying on a bench rocking in the blackness, sick with leaving, sick with separation, sick with loneliness. The cabin is shrinking and Alice unable to breathe. She's scared she'll suffocate if she doesn't find air, swings her legs to the floor, can't find her balance, holds on to a pole, feels her way along the wall, loses the doorway. Think, she tells herself, think. And knowing a blind person would manage, she shuts her eyes and pretends she's blind. Stumbling, groping and slithering with the ship's swing she finds the door and lets herself out into a dimly lit passage. She sees stairs at one end, climbs them like a ladder, short legs, short arms and far too many layers of clothing, and finally to the deck and fresh air, but small relief because she's left all her belongings below and what will happen if she can't find her way back? She grabs the icy rail, her fingers stick. She pulls her cuffs over her hands, grasps the rail again and doesn't let go.

She is appalled at the vastness of the ocean, the endless dark with knives of brightness, and an incessant slush slush slush that seems to grow louder and louder. She tightens her grip and rocks with the boat, rises with its rise, sinks with its fall. She could die out here and nobody but Willi would know, and she'd never see her parents again, just an endless black nothingness like the dreadful black sea in front of her. She's terrified, but has to manage. So don't look, she tells herself, and seals her eyelids tight.

It seems like forever before she opens her eyes again. Her head is tilted back, and above her is a veritable fairyland unlike anything she's ever seen either in Krefeld or Düsseldorf or even in Berlin where, according to her mother, absolutely everything happens.

Clouds of stars like fairy dust scatter the dome. She finds red Mars and brilliant Venus, and high in the sky a golden sliver of moon. And Alice wishes herself up there, just like in the storybook pictures, to sit on the golden arc with her feet dangling, a smile on her face, and safe. She unpeels her hands from the freezing rail and steps back from the boat's edge into a protected corner of the deck. The last thing she remembers before falling asleep under a length of canvas is putting her parents up among the stars well away from danger.

When she awakens the lights of England are a foggy blur on the horizon. Alice leaves the deck and goes below. The escorts are already rousing the children. Lamps have been lit and Alice slips quietly into place. She feels as if she's been on an adventure, like Jason and the Argonauts or Diana out hunting, and has returned alone but stronger. She's not dead like her grandmother and she hasn't been bashed like her father and soon she'll be seven which is a lot bigger than six and her parents will come and everything will be all right. She recites it like a mantra: *my parents will come and everything will be all right / my parents will come and everything will be all right*. She collects her blanket, her tattered book, her knapsack and suitcase and waits with the other girls while the boat docks at Harwich.

It is still dark when they disembark, but Alice doesn't care. She pushes out of line and goes in search of Willi. So many children and she can't find him anywhere. In the end she resorts to Fraülein Rosa who promises she'll be united with Willi once they arrive in London. Shortly afterwards they are herded onto another train, an English train this time with English posters high on the carriage walls. It is still dark, but as they travel down to London the sun rises. Alice tucks her legs beneath her, better to see this new country. It could be Mars, it could be Hades, it is certainly not home. She inserts a barrier in her brain; on one side is Krefeld, Düsseldorf, Berlin, the Friedmans, Mutti and Vati, and on the other this alien land called England.

Liverpool Station is feverish with people and noise. There are trolleys piled high with luggage and fresh farm produce, and everywhere ghastly animal carcasses and shrieking birds in cages. Alice tries not to look, has eyes only for Willi, but he is nowhere to be seen. Fraülein Rosa holds her firmly by the hand and now Alice is grateful to have her close. Through the noise and the crowds, through the bewildering bustle of a world so much bigger than a soon-to-be seven girl, they arrive at a huge cavernous room. And suddenly Willi is beside her. Alice's relief is so great, the tears won't hold back any longer.

She's still clinging to Willi when, a few minutes later, Fraülein Rosa taps her on the shoulder to say goodbye. Alice gives her a long, warm hug, then watches her leave with the other escorts, all of whom will return to Germany and another transport.

Holding tightly to each other, she and Willi join the other *Kinder* in one area of the vast hall. In another area are the English people: the sponsors, relatives and strangers who have volunteered to look after the German children. In front, seated at a table, are the English officials, none in uniform, with their pens and piles of paper and booming English voices. The children are quiet, so too the guardians. Alice looks at them, trying to guess which of these strangers might be Hannah and Jonathon Moser. She makes sure her identification card is clearly visible so the Mosers can find her, then changes her mind just in case they don't like the look of her and slip away before her name is called. She holds on to Willi with both hands now: if the Mosers take him then they'll have to take her as well. He, too, is searching the crowd of English people; he, too, has covered his identification card.

'I wouldn't want that family in the corner,' he whispers to her.

Alice looks across the room. The man is dressed like a storm-trooper; the woman also wears a uniform, and the boy is dressed in the brown shorts and shirt of the Hitler Youth. And while later they will identify these people as members of the scouting movement, for now they are afraid the Nazis are here too, and England no safer for Jews than Germany.

The officials start calling the children in alphabetical order. The names toll so slowly and Alice passes the time perusing the English people and choosing those she would like to be Hannah and Jonathon Moser. By the time Willi Friedman is called, all of Alice's choices have been snapped up. Willi stands, he has to prise his fingers from hers, and an old couple with absolutely no chance of ever making Alice's preferential list come forward. Both of them look so peculiar, the man with a huge unkempt beard, dressed in a jacket which resembles a rug, and the woman with a bizarre grass-green beret Alice's mother wouldn't be seen dead in. These can't be the ones, Alice is saying to herself, surely these aren't the ones. She hears an official ask: 'Professor and Mrs Moser?' Then sees him check the papers, utter a few more words before handing Willi over.

They look better, younger, when they smile, Alice decides, but still a far cry from what she would have chosen. She watches them withdraw to the other side of the room, Mrs Moser with her arm linked through Willi's, and the Professor carrying Willi's knapsack and suitcase, watches as they keep walking – towards the exit, she suddenly realises, and is on her feet. They're going to leave without her! She's about to shout and run after them when they stop and turn and say something to Willi who points her out. Now they are smiling and waving; Mrs Moser in her green beret actually blows her a kiss. Alice sinks back in her chair and swallows her tears.

In the time before her name is called she concentrates on composing herself, not just for the next few minutes but for all the time she has to stay in England. She puts her mother's voice inside her head, her mother saying that soon she and Vati will come for her and take her back to Germany, her mother's voice telling her to be good and grown-up. When at last she is called she is quite calm. She weaves her way through the chairs to the front and walks the long strip across no-man's-land to the table.

The worst was over, Alice told herself during that long, lonely walk. But she was wrong. Six years later she was still waiting for her parents to turn up at the door, then waiting for any news of them, and finally waiting for them not to be dead. That was the worst of times, and she'd only been a child. But she managed. Then last year when her husband died and she was again alone in the world, still she managed. Compared to what she had already experienced, being here at these London archives, with her orphaned status about to be verified fifty years after the fact, should be easy.

She checks her watch and at the same time a woman appears. It is the archivist. She introduces herself and apologises for being late, then guides Alice towards the office on the opposite side of the hall.

The archivist is a short, attractive woman aged anywhere between fifty and seventy. She is also very English with a nice collection of cut-glass vowels which issue from a perfectly symmetrical

English mouth. Her hair is reddish and cropped, and her manner that of those no-nonsense English women with whom one could easily fall in love if one were so inclined, which Alice is not.

The archives area is small, cluttered and colourless. One wall is lined with squat grey filing cabinets, another is covered with shelves from floor to ceiling. All horizontal surfaces – shelves, tables, tops of the filing cabinets – are stacked with books and paper.

'A little more colour in here and it'd be just like home,' Alice says.

The archivist doesn't laugh, doesn't even smile, but neither is her face impassive; in fact, it is quite clear she is trying to fathom whether Alice is one of those rare Americans with an appreciation for irony. Alice smiles to allay any confusion and the archivist follows suit. Then it is down to business. The archivist clears the end of one of the tables and opens a file.

'The fundamentals are as you outlined them in your letter,' she begins. 'Your father escaped into Holland in 1941, and was trying to get your mother out of Germany when he ended up in Westerbork. He was transported from Westerbork to Bergen-Belsen mid-1944, included at the last minute to make up the numbers. He contracted typhus April 1945, and died in or near Belsen around the time the British entered the camp on the fifteenth of the month.' She pauses for the information to settle, then continues in her blunt, pragmatic way. 'Your mother was one of a large group of Jews, mostly factory workers actually, who were rounded up in Berlin and deported on the twenty-seventh of February 1943. She died in Auschwitz, early November 1943.' The archivist pauses again, but this time is watching Alice closely. 'As you see, nothing to add to the fundamentals. But,' another short pause, 'we do have additional details about your mother's death. New information which emerged when the archive was put on microfiche. Because of the additional cross-referencing,' she explains.

The archivist sits back, she has said what needed to be said and now waits for Alice's response. More information about her mother's death, and Alice tries to read the woman's face for clues. Surely if her mother died a hero, there'd be a smile, and if not a smile, a softening of expression. Or if there were further horrors to be revealed, the face would show a glimmer of concern. But there is nothing. Alice weighs it up. If there are horrors, they could be no worse than those she already knows, and if there are heroic acts, she wants to hear them.

She nods to the archivist, 'Please,' she says. 'Go ahead.'

The archivist lays out two sheets of paper on the table and starts to talk. She keeps her gaze on Alice, making no reference to the pages in front of her.

'The additional information came to light only recently from a woman who was in the camp with your mother.' Then, anticipating a possible query, adds, 'Some survivors have kept silent for so long, it's only when they recognise their time is running out they finally decide to speak. Of course, some take their knowledge to the grave.' She shrugs that very particular Jewish shrug with the outspread hands, palms upwards, head cocked to the side, the quizzical eyebrows.

Information from a woman who was at Auschwitz with her mother and survived, and Alice knows with absolute certainty that what she is about to hear will show that if not for some quiver of fate her mother would have survived too. She already knows that with slightly altered circumstances her father might have lived. A different barracks, another workbench, a little less typhus or simply a little more luck and both her parents might have survived. Sitting here in this archive with the information about to spill, Alice is not sure she wants to know how close she came to not losing both mother and father.

It would still be possible to wind up this meeting, return to the hotel and tell Raphe there was nothing more to learn, still possible not to know how close she came to a normal childhood. And yet she stays in her seat in this grey room recalling stories of the strong, lively woman who was her mother, a woman who would never shy away from the truth, a woman of principles, according to Willi. He often told of the time when Renate first heard about Jews being forced to their hands and knees to clean public monuments with their mouths.

'I'd refuse,' Renate had said.

'For your life you would lick,' Dora had replied.

But Renate was adamant she wouldn't.

In the end, according to the information in the archivist's file, Renate Lewin had died by her principles. Long after she had given up saying things couldn't get worse, long after she had dispensed with hope as the right arm of humiliation, Renate's strength and determination had killed her. Marching off to work one day she fell out of line. A guard about half her age slammed his baton into her, causing her to stumble. She regained her balance and rejoined the line, but only briefly before she swerved again – not through physical weakness, according to the woman who was witness, but deliberate non-compliance. Again the guard beat her, but this time Renate held her ground. When she straightened up she placed herself firmly in his path.

The archivist now paused, leaning in closer and shaking her head. 'I don't think we'll ever understand why – or when or how – some people reach their limit,' she said. 'I don't even think we can ever know for sure what that limit actually is. It might be tolerance, or fear, or courage, or simply that too much of what one values is being destroyed. I really don't know.'

She shrugged and sat back in her chair. For a while neither said a word, then the archivist glanced down at her notes and continued. Evidently Renate had remained standing in front of the guard, staring into his face and goading him to hit her. 'Hit me while I'm watching you,' were her actual words. Her face was all hollows, she was little more than a sack of bones, yet suddenly in a single slick movement she lunged for the baton. The guard yanked his arm back; plastering his face was an icy smile. Renate apparently was unfazed. Still holding his gaze, she asked whether he believed in God. The German nodded in spite of himself.

It was Renate's turn to smile. 'He's got your number,' she said.

Again she lunged, and this time – perhaps it was the mention of God – the guard was taken by surprise. The bar was in her hand, she was quick, had to be quick, and swung a calculated arc into his kidneys. It was a bull's-eye hit and it brought the German to his knees. Other guards came running. Apparently the bullets hit her just a fraction of a second after the baton slammed into the man's head.

This was how Renate Lewin died, spared the knowledge that her act of defiance ended the lives of eighteen other Jewish women.

'Your mother could not have guessed,' the archivist now says, watching Alice closely. Then more firmly, 'Your mother was not to know.'

Alice is stumbling in her own mind. Everyone knew what brutes these Nazis were, her mother must have known there would be terrible consequences. And yet if she had known, surely she would she have acted differently. Surely she would have complied and thereby prevented those eighteen women from being killed. And surely she would have continued to comply and so lived out the war. Surely. Surely. Surely. Alice has heard so many stories that expose these impossible dilemmas, but nothing she knows will show her what to do.

'Admire her,' the archivist says. 'Admire your mother. Hers was an act of extraordinary courage.'

'And the woman who told you?'

'She knew all too well that you had to be strong to survive the camps. Your mother's courage helped her. It made her stronger.'

Alice fights a sense of righteousness, a sense she would have behaved differently in the same circumstances. But would her different behaviour have been better? And who is fit to judge in these matters anyway? Such questions are the stuff of Talmudic exegesis, but this is the real thing, and besides, the Talmud has never been an option for her. She shakes off the questions, best to keep it personal, she decides. So does this new information cause her to feel differently about her mother? And she finds herself smiling, for the truth of the matter is it does.

The archivist responds to the smile. 'And I haven't told you the good news yet.'

The smile quickly disintegrates. There's more? Please God, let there be no more.

'Nothing distressing,' the archivist quickly reassures. 'Just a possible connection. In Melbourne, Australia. There's a Henry Lewin living there, a German Jew like your parents. He arrived in 1951 with his wife and young son. A daughter, Laura, was born later. We learned about him through one of the *Kinder* who's a second cousin of his wife. It's just possible he might be a distant relative, it's also possible he knew your father. He's originally from Berlin, but like your father he ended up in Westerbork and later was transferred to Belsen.' She pushes back her chair. 'It's up to you to decide whether to contact him.'

With that she hands Alice a copy of her file, including the contact details of Henry Lewin in Melbourne, Australia. She leads her to the stairs, shakes her hand and wishes her a pleasant stay in London.

The day had darkened when Alice found herself in the street again. It was tempting to read something symbolic in this given she'd only been upstairs for forty minutes, but more likely, she told herself, to be nothing other than a typical London day in October. And took comfort in so Phil-like a response, particularly with her nerves so gnarled and thin.

There was still an hour to fill before she was due to meet Raphe, an hour to digest the information and determine what to do. She had expected nothing new from her visit to the archive, this being her customary way of facing life ever since the end of the war when her parents had failed to appear. In a single afternoon all those years ago, the impossible chasm between hope and expectation had been cruelly exposed, and she was determined never again to confuse the two. But as she headed south through the Bloomsbury streets, she realised that for the first time in years she had lapsed and allowed herself far too much in the way of hope.

Her parents were gone, long gone, and she had always known it, yet the loss was as fresh as if the deaths had only just occurred. A great gaping channel had opened within her and she didn't know what to do.

Her mind was all wind and wasteland; automatically she negotiated the lumpy pavements, automatically she avoided other pedestrians. She noticed nothing. Several minutes must have passed before she was aware of a voice, quiet at first and indistinct, emerging from the blustering in her head. Go home, it said. Then louder and more insistent: Go to all your homes. And once established it would not retreat, a huge, bristling imperative to reconstruct the past: to go back to Germany and put the pieces together, properly this time, then to Oxford and lastly to America. Relive and remake her whole life without any lurking hopes.

It was a flash of brilliant illumination, clear and so evidently right. Then a moment later it was gone and Alice no longer knew why she wanted to revisit her past. No longer knew anything at all. She stepped back from the footpath and leaned against a wrought-iron railing out of the way of other pedestrians. She reminded herself of the facts: she was in London, she was on her way to meet her son, and her parents were dead as they had always been. Cold, hard facts, no illuminations, just a harsh empty landscape with the unknown figure of Henry Lewin in Melbourne, Australia, lurking in the distance. She shook him off, looked about her, could find no familiar landmarks, latched on to a street name, consulted her map, couldn't make sense of it. In the end she entered a small park and sat on a bench in a sheltered alcove. There she found herself longing for her husband – not her parents, her long-dead parents, but Phil, alive again and helping her decide what to do, Phil helping her as he had always done.

When Phil Carter first made his feelings known all those years ago in his peculiarly American invitation to 'go steady', Alice's inclination had been to resist. You don't know me, she had said, and you don't know people like me. He had met every one of her arguments with precise and practical counter-arguments entirely in keeping with the engineer he was. But it was his coup d'état – 'I make a career out of supporting buildings,' he said, 'so supporting you should be easy' – which had decided her. It was only after they were married that she realised how ridiculous his statement was, the type of support she required being of a vastly different kind to struts and concrete. Yet in his own stolid way he had stood by his word, certainly the support he gave her was no less reliable than that he cemented to buildings in trembling San Francisco. Now as she lingered in a Bloomsbury park she thought that if Phil were here he'd know what to do. Although, and more to the point, if Phil were still alive she would never have visited the archive in the first place.

'It's the past,' he would have said. 'And it's over.'

It was Hannah Moser who had introduced Alice to Phil. The Mosers had known Phil's parents for years, almost since their arrival in San Francisco. It was an acquaintance difficult to explain as the two couples had little in common. The Carters were people bereft of imagination, the wife as much as the husband: he owned a company which manufactured spare parts for vacuum cleaners and she did the books. They were reliable, predictable people who were confident of themselves and their values. Any crisis which required even a modicum of creative action would have sorely tested them, but in stable, affluent America they were ideally adapted to their environment. And their son was cut from the same cloth. One day Hannah invited the Carters for afternoon tea, and although Alice had made a prior arrangement to go to the movies, Hannah wanted her to meet Phil and insisted she change her plans.

Phil was exactly what Alice needed, so much so that Alice was forced to revise certain long-held opinions of her guardians, convinced as she was that they had engineered the match. Hannah and Jonathon had always seemed in a parallel universe when it came to parenting. Some parents are gauche, others are inept, but the Mosers simply did not acknowledge children as *children* – or so it had seemed to Alice.

This had been the case from the very beginning. Hannah would arrive home with clothes for Alice much in keeping with the grass-green beret style she favoured for herself. Alice suggested they go shopping together, but unfortunately it was not Hannah's way. She would leave the house to buy food for the family and come home with a rainbow-coloured skirt and blouse for Alice. Alice with her German accent and German ways already stood out, how much worse in the clothes Hannah chose for her. She knew she had to appear grateful, but she also knew she couldn't go to school looking as if she'd escaped from a circus. She learned from a classmate about the English system of hand-me-downs; all that was required was an older sister who was not too rough on clothes. Alice found an ideal substitute in a girl who lived down the street with no younger sister and a mother with good taste.

That fixed the clothes problem. But the Mosers did not understand about food either. Even with rationing their idea of a special tea was crumpets with sardines, so there was never any question of inviting a girlfriend home for tea. They always gave Alice exactly what they ate, even down to a glass of sherry before meals – a habit, incidentally, she still maintained. Then there was conversation: nothing was filtered or modified in deference to her age, and from 1941 when Jonathon was one of many dons recruited for the war effort, Alice knew as much – more – about the war than most adults. But the area of greatest difficulty was affection. It was not that the Mosers didn't feel it, they were unsure how to show it. In the end they settled on the same expression for Alice as they used for their adored cat, Jeoffry. They would pat her and stroke her and chuck her under the chin, and without any warning would sweep her off her feet and swing her high in the air while singing silly tamperings of well-known songs like 'Alice Alice give me your answer do, I'm half crazy all for the love of you'. It seemed to work for them and for the cat too, only Alice experienced any trouble. She remembered all too vividly how she would hug and kiss her own parents and clamber on their knees, but she couldn't do this with the Mosers, not simply because they weren't the hugging, kissing, clambering type, but because to give to them what she had given to her parents would have meant a serious act of betrayal.

Throughout the long war years Alice was careful to remain absolutely true to her mother and father. They were still in Germany and the danger worse than ever. And while in her dreams she might travel back to Germany and spirit her parents to safety on a daily basis, in reality she was helpless – except to be the best-behaved little girl in all of England in order to earn the safe arrival of her parents in Oxford.

To say she lived a childhood would be to deny its essence. She stage-managed childhood, and far from easy when first she arrived, given everything was so strange. The Mosers lived in a house not a flat. There were several heaters but they were rarely lit and the fire in the living room seemed to be perpetually in the dying embers phase. Hannah and Jonathon – they insisted being called by their first names – wore coats and gloves inside the house; for bed, they would remove their day clothes then pile more on. It was not as if they were poor, rather they approached the cold differently from Germans. It was January when Alice and Willi arrived and Alice was cold all the time, but particularly in bed. The Mosers had no quilts, just heavy rough blankets which never seemed to warm up. Like Hannah and Jonathon, soon Alice too was wearing a jumper over her nightgown, and normal socks beneath her bedsocks. But still she was cold. She hated making a fuss, kept telling herself that soon winter would be over and then she'd warm up. But that first winter in England was interminable and in the end she told Hannah how very cold she was. Later that same day Hannah produced a hot-water bottle with a knitted cover in faded purple. Off-centre and in brilliant green had been stitched 'AL' in a hand more accustomed to wielding a pen than a needle.

Gradually Alice learned how to manage; even when Willi

enlisted in the British army and moved away she managed. She made friends and she copied them. And learning the language helped. In time she felt she had an English childhood off pat while remaining loyal to her German childhood – for how else to guarantee the safety of her parents? By the time she learned there were no guarantees and never had been, she was confined by her own standards of perfection and it was too late to change.

She was thirteen at the end of the war. Hannah and Jonathon had looked after her well, and even though Willi had been away most of the time, he had written to her often and when he visited always made sure to spend most of his time with her. Yet it felt as if she had lived those war years in some pretend place, cut off from her real life. With the end of the war, her normal life, so long put on hold, would begin again.

Willi was again in Oxford and all of England was celebrating, even those like the Kerrs next door who, from Alice's point of view, had little cause for celebration given their younger son had lost a leg and their older son his life. Everyone was saying life would return to normal but how could it for Alice, a German-Jewish girl still living in England without her mother and father?

On the day Hannah and Jonathon took the train to London, leaving Willi to look after her, Alice knew this was no routine trip. She did not ask why they were going to London, had learned long ago that good news would be good whenever it happened, but even the possibility of bad news – the worst news, the news you have dreaded for six years – cannot be encouraged in any way. She tried hard not to be anxious. But there were the letters and they refused to be ignored. Or rather the silences. Her mother's letters had stopped more than a year before her father's, and the last letter from her father had arrived ten months ago. Alice knew her mother had been taken to Auschwitz, and while people had survived there, Alice was quite aware they were very few compared with the millions who had died. But when you're desperate it's easy to convince yourself that those you love will be spared. So she continued to be good, to do nothing wrong, standing calmly on the Oxford train station waving goodbye to the Mosers, so frantic with fear and worry she did not trust herself to speak.

Hannah and Jonathon returned from London the following afternoon. They entered the house looking more ragged than usual. There were brief greetings before Jonathon took Willi into one room and Hannah took Alice into another.

Hannah came straight to the point. Auschwitz, she said, had few survivors and Alice's mother was not among them. As for her father, he too was dead, although had nearly survived. Alice wanted to ask: what does 'nearly survived' mean, when anything less than 'survived' – nearly, almost, not quite – means dead? But kept quiet, and trampled her tears instead. Her father, according to Hannah, had died just before the end of the war, probably of typhus. 'Probably?' Now Alice couldn't stop herself, only to be told, *definitely* dead and *probably* of typhus. How can they be so sure? How can *you* be so sure? But said nothing: even to argue against the information was to give it more credence than she had courage for.

A half-hour later she and Willi, Hannah and Jonathon were together again in the living room. Words were hard to find. Jonathon poured glasses of sherry, Hannah turned on the wireless, the cat played with his toy teddy bear, both Willi and Alice were pale and tight. Eventually Willi spoke: he would be leaving for Palestine as soon as possible as there was nothing to hold him in England. But there is, there is, Alice wanted to protest, there's me. But trebly orphaned now, she kept her griefs to herself.

In that single miserable afternoon Alice became the person people leave. There must be something terribly wrong with her, she decided, so best to hide her flaws, hide who she really was if she was ever to have a chance at life. Although at that moment, with her parents not coming back and Willi about to leave, there was nothing she could see to recommend life. Indeed if not for the Mosers who had been so good to her, she would have taken her rotten life and tossed it to the winds. Instead, she learned how to play-act an acceptable Alice. Pretend you're someone else, the drama teacher at school used to say, and would praise Alice for her ability. Now Alice applied her talents to her everyday life. It was unbearable to think of herself without her mother and father, an orphan just like the children in storybooks, so she didn't. It was unbearable to think of being without Willi, so she didn't. It was impossible to fill the gaps left by those she loved, so she didn't. It was far easier, she discovered, to change herself.

She played the role of good student at school, and the role of good ward at home. She played the role of good English child when they were in England and good American girl once they moved to California. She played the role of good friend so well she found herself to be very popular. But in her dreams the roles fell away and she would cry for the parents who year by year were fading, and cry for a loneliness she felt she ought not feel, and dream German-language dreams of her American life. And in the morning she would wake with the shadow of her past hovering sad and unreachable in front of her.

Unlike her dreams, her public performances served her well. When a month after their first meeting Phil Carter told her he loved her, she realised she had added another role to her repertoire. Not that this had been deliberate, for she liked Phil, most of all she liked the fact that Phil was so different from her. Solid, predictable, so sure of himself, he was a man who liked people and was likeable himself. He had a bit of humour, a bit of seriousness, he played a good but not exceptional game of racquetball, a good but not exceptional game of baseball. He was practical like his parents, considerate too, but not particularly sensitive. He had no feeling for art and music, but neither, Alice had noticed, did most husbands. His passion, apart from her, was for vintage cars – Oldsmobiles, a good solid American car, according to Phil, for whom American was always best.

Phil was a man who liked what he already had, so Alice knew he would never stray and certainly would never leave her. He was a reliable man: apart from the occasional beer, he didn't drink and he never gambled. And he'd be a good provider. Following graduation he had been snapped up by one of the foremost construction companies in the Bay Area and, by the time he proposed, had been promoted twice. Phil Carter, with no connection to the Holocaust and not even Jewish, was bedrock.

Her choice of husband had served her well. Not for her the depressions and illnesses of other Holocaust survivors. Whenever her spirits started to flag, Phil would remind her of everything that was good in her life – her consolations, he used to call them.

Such a different matter with her son. While Phil had separated her from the past, Raphe seemed to reforge the connection. Running through her son was the blood of her dead parents, and emerging from his face, the face of her father. In Raphe, her past, present and future seemed to coalesce. In him more than anyone else her past had come alive.

'Tell me about my grandfather,' he would say over and over again.

And she would recall her father, the gentle man whom everyone had liked. And as she talked, Martin would re-emerge, a small, neat figure in the flat at Krefeld, drinking his coffee, reading to his daughter, playing games with her, talking with her. And she would look at her young son, 'You're so like him, Raphe. So like him.'

Phil worried about both of them. 'This dwelling on the past is not doing the boy any good,' he would say to Alice. And more gently, 'Raphe can't replace your losses.'

Alice knew this, but she knew equally that Phil had missed the point. This boy, her only flesh and blood, was doubly precious because of all she had lost. And because of the resemblance to Martin, he was also a living link with her father.

But not the only link, she was now thinking. For there was this stranger, this Henry Lewin in Melbourne, Australia. Here, possibly, was a real and tangible connection to her father. She didn't know what to do. Raphe of course would want to contact the man immediately. But there was so much more at stake, her carefully constructed life for a start. She decided it would be best to keep Henry Lewin to herself until she had thought the matter through.

It was dark and chilly in the park. Alice checked her watch, time to set off for St Martin in the Fields. With the skill and determination of an expert she directed her thoughts away from the archive, away from Phil, away from her dead parents, away from the past, and most assiduously away from the unknown Henry Lewin in Melbourne, Australia. But as she made her way down to Trafalgar Square to meet her son, Henry Lewin kept creeping in. This man who might have known her father at the very end, who might have had conversations with him, who might have heard him speak of his wife and young daughter, who might know if her father had suffered, who might reveal how very nearly her father could have survived. This unknown man kept intruding and would not go away.

A Meeting in the Woods,
Northern Germany, April 1945

The end of the war is fast approaching and the entire country is on the move. After the best six years of his life, Heinrik Heck now finds himself back on the losing side. It's a miserable situation to be in, particularly when he thought his luck had changed for good. Although given his record, he now realises, he should have known he'd chanced on nothing more than a lucky detour. But what a detour! He started as a nobody and six years later he's running the officers' mess at the Belsen camp. Not a bad war when you come to think about it: steady employment, plenty of food and a full set of dentures to boot.

'What can you do for Germany?' he was asked when he first enlisted, and always quick on his feet, said he could cook. And a good choice it was. Cooks were more essential to the war effort than almost anyone else and, as it happened, less likely to be killed. But now with peace marching through the countryside, a peace that would bring no joy to Germany, Heini guesses that a German cook from the gutter will be no use to anyone. In fact, he can see himself heading straight back to a slum room in the Scheunen-viertel and doing it tough. Which is why he's getting out of Belsen, leaving this very day. The enemy won't want him except to punish him and the Germans will simply shove him back to where he came from.

He's not the only one to predict a dim future; there's a flood of Germans leaving the camp and doing little to disguise it. The war made them all Germans no matter what their background, but Heini knows that defeat is an efficient sorter of men. Yet when he told one of the other cooks what he was planning, the fellow accused him of being a deserter. Deserting what? Heini asked. The army, the other fellow replied, a soldier to the end. But the army is disappearing as we speak, Heini wanted to say. And while you're sitting here waiting for orders from absent officers, the enemy's already within smelling distance.

It surprises him the number of men who refuse to see the obvious. After all, it doesn't require too many brains to realise that if the victorious armies do the right thing they'll reserve their best for the Jews, or at least what Jews are left, then they'll look to the people Germany conquered. As for the Germans themselves, ordinary Germans not the bosses, they'll not warrant a moment's consideration.

The Jews first, now that's a laugh. Packed in like worms one day and doing it worse than anyone, then suddenly the Americans arrive, or the British or the bloody Russians, and it's bratwurst for breakfast. Although Heini would have to admit the Jews were forced to pay up big for their luck. Not that he's ever been fool enough to believe fairness prevailed for anyone in this life, which is why he's getting out of here.

He knows he ought to try and find Agathe, but he doesn't really want to. He's got no guarantees for her, nor the kid either, and besides, it's clear they've learned to do without him. Nearly two years since he last saw Agathe, and while her letters came thick and fast at first, soon it was a scribbled note every few weeks and not even worth the postage. Then nothing for months. Yet fool that he was he kept writing and hoping, and when finally she decides to respond, he finds he's all out of patience. Now with more than a year since either made the effort, best to leave well alone. Although it's a shame about the kid. Such a pretty little thing, and old enough by now to know who her father is, though goodness knows how many fathers have been presented to her since she last saw the real one.

Agathe always knew how to charm a man, certainly she was in no doubt how to charm Heini. There they were in Berlin back in 1938, she working in a factory and a big wheel in the BDM, and he new to the army and learning how to cook. A month later she tells him she's pregnant and they're married a short time afterwards in Leipzig. Another year and this time they meet in Dresden where she's staying with a girlfriend and he sees his daughter for the first time. The baby reminds him of his sister and he says he wants to call her Hilde. That was nearly six years ago and he's only seen his wife and child a handful of times since, mostly in Leipzig where his in-laws live, and better Agathe and the kid are still there than in Dresden from what he's heard. He'd have liked to see his daughter again, no doubt about it. But Agathe would have made other plans, so best he do the same.

He makes his way back to the barracks. They're deserted, in fact, he could turn into a raving lunatic like some of the prisoners here and no one would notice. He lays out his belongings on the bunk, civilian clothes separate from the army issue. After nearly six years of war, the civilian pile is nothing more than a pair of trousers and two shirts; even his coat with the lambswool collar has gone. He adds his army underwear to the civilian pile, then takes his army coat, tears off the insignia and adds it to the pile too. These are the clothes he'll be taking, the rest he shoves in a locker. Next he turns his attention to his pack of photographs and letters. No letters, he decides, and only one photograph. Eventually he comes down to a choice between a picture of his sister and brother, and one of his daughter. He holds the photos one in each hand, looks at them for a long time, then tears both into tiny pieces. A fresh start, he tells himself, although it makes him feel a bit sad. He packs a few cooking implements – two knives, a wooden spoon and a whisk, everything else is too cumbersome – and the gear he'll need for camping out, puts everything in his pack and hides it under his bunk until later.

He doesn't know where he's headed, although it'll be out of Germany if he's got any sense. He remembers how pleased he was when he learned how to read and write. Better, he is now thinking, if he'd taught himself another language. He won't be heading back to Berlin, that's for sure, and he won't be heading back to thieving either, no matter where he stops. He's a cook now. Heinrik Heck: cook. And the rest he'll leave to chance.

Although one thing's for certain, he'll not be sorry to leave this place. He's seen more corpses than an undertaker, more starvation than would line the gutters of the Scheunenviertel, and more disease than any hospital. He's seen eyes so empty he might as well be looking into coloured glass, he's seen people on their feet yet more dead than alive, he's seen women dying and men dying and worst of all children dying and has learned for his own safety not to be moved. Although once he couldn't stop himself. A girl, twelve or thirteen years old, impossible to judge when they're starving, and he's coming from the kitchen with a full stomach and food in his pocket for later, and he sees her crouched beneath the ramp of one of the huts scavenging for scraps. He knows, as must she, there's nothing to be found there. He reaches into his pocket, has to be careful, grabs the food, kneels down to tie his bootlace, and with his greatcoat providing cover tosses the food at her. She takes it, her face without expression, and hides it in her rags. A few days later she's waiting in the same place and they do a repeat performance. And several times after that.

The girl's been missing this past month. Either she has enough to eat or the typhus has got her, and although it's unlikely, he hopes it's the former. It occurs to him he cares more for this unknown Jew girl than his own daughter. Places like this can really screw you up.

It is only midday; he plans to wait until dusk before making his move. The stench in the camp is so strong it has soaked through his clothes and into his skin. Despite the cool weather he'd do anything for a swim. He lies back on his bunk and lets his mind wander back to the days in Berlin when he would float in the river for hours on end, washing away the grime of his old, putrid life.

The Germans have left and the British are coming – or perhaps the Americans or French, no one is certain and Martin Lewin is not waiting to find out. His head is raging and there's iced lead in his bones, but he is alive. Martin has held out, twelve months in Belsen and before that Westerbork. He has kept alive minute by minute, hour by hour, but is fast approaching the point where succumbing is cruelly seductive.

Martin has stayed alive by stoking his memories of Renate, but now without something more substantial he feels his life sliding away. He needs to see his wife, needs to be with her. And Alice, too, but his daughter is safe in England, his daughter is most assuredly alive. But Renate? Please God let her be alive, for there'd be little point to his own survival if she were not. How he longs for the soft touch of her, the smell of her, how he longs to feel the weight of her in his arms, such pathetic sticks they've become but still with strength enough for his wife. He is forty years old and has survived nearly two years in labour camps, too absurd to leave this earth after just half a life, and the last part too rotten even for swill.

He tells himself it's only typhus, only typhus and he'll see it through, only typhus that doesn't necessarily kill, only typhus that most often does. He shrugs off the shadow of death as he drags himself away from the camp. The only death he allows into consciousness is useful death, the sort of death to take advantage of.

He has stripped dead people of their rags and torn the material into broad ribbons and patches to use on his own miserable body, the effort more costly with each passing hour as fatigue and malaise undermine. By the time his swaddling is complete, his arms and shoulders and his pathetic back have barely a tear left in them. But the job is good, and beneath his striped pyjamas he is a mummy. For while the thaw has come and the sun is finding its heat, Martin's bones are bleached and bare, and his skin has deserted him.

He has scavenged food from those for whom a heel of bread has come too late, will force himself to eat though his poor guts are closing. He has suffered worse, he tells himself, but in truth, beyond a certain point the immediate worse is the worst worse of all. The pain lopes through his head and lodges in his temples and every now and then a lurching in his throat. He knows he must eat for the journey to Berlin, just two hundred kilometres and how long can it take? But whether five days or ten there's no doubt he'll become sicker. Belsen has taught him what to expect. Belsen is rife with fever and rash and a head pain so piercing that even your teeth hurt. And the grating in your ears, the cough hacking your joints, the groaning muscles. And worst of all the malaise, he's seen more of it than food this past year, men lying on their backs muttering a stream of nonsense while waiting to die.

He instructs his legs to walk a little further. Soon he'll be out of sight of the camp, away from typhus and on the road, back to Berlin, back to Renate, and after that home to Krefeld to gather up what once belonged to them. Then they'll travel to England to collect Alice, before moving to one of those countries that didn't want an unemployed Jewish silk merchant before the war but after all that's happened might consider one now. So many uncertainties, among which there's only one rock-solid fact: that as surely as water relieves thirst, when Martin is with Renate once more, survival will cease to be an all-consuming issue.

He cannot believe in her death, cannot even entertain the possibility. He knows she was included in a large contingent of Berlin Jews transported to the east on the twenty-seventh of February 1943. He knows the exact date, not simply because it was her birthday, but because on that day all his efforts to get her out of Germany had finally come to fruition. If the Germans had delayed their Berlin action just twenty-four hours, Martin is positive he would have saved his wife. Just one more day was all he needed. He now knows that no matter how careful and extensive the planning, or how numerous the bribes, in the end it is chance more than anything else which determines your fate. No one ever avoided a concentration camp because they deserved to.

As he lugs himself across the broken ground, sick and debilitated but lucky to be alive, it strikes him that even if he had managed to get her out of Germany, it wouldn't have been much of a saving. A couple of months later Renate would have found herself like him in Westerbork, and nine months after that in Belsen. But they would have been together, and it is extraordinary what a difference that can make.

For most of the past two years Martin had the company of his friend Friedrich. They were each other's luck. But with Friedrich now gone, Martin is alone except for the typhus and such company he can do without. He feels like he's walking against a system of pulleys. Inside his skull the pain is kneading his brains, and the light is so sharp he might be staring into the sun. He tells himself Renate is just a few days away, sometimes he thinks he can actually hear her. Having survived the stinking rot of Belsen, he is convinced the fresh air away from the camp will revive him, and hobbles a little further, perhaps even a little more quickly. It would make no sense if he were to die now. Across all Germany, across all Europe he has no idea how many people have died, but if Belsen is any guide, the number is too great for the mind to hold. Although not my wife, he says to himself. Not my wife.

His boots, or rather Friedrich's boots, weigh a tonne. Friedrich who would be with him now if he had not died two days ago. Friedrich with whom Martin has survived and dreamed ever since the early days in Westerbork. Friedrich who has done almost as much as the memories of Renate to keep Martin alive. And now Friedrich is dead, but surely Martin is able to manage on his own until he reaches Berlin. He walks a little further, he's heading for the trees. His boots drag him back and briefly he is tempted to discard them. But everyone knows that a man without boots is going nowhere.

As the camp recedes, the fresh air hooks into his throat and hacks into his chest. He stops a moment to find an easier breath. He looks scarcely human, like a spindly insect with broken limbs staggering on the open ground, knows this from having lived with others who look scarcely human. Knows, too, that only a blind man would have compassion enough to help him.

A few more steps, a few more minutes and he reaches the trees, marvels at the clusters of new leaves sprouting in the branches. How tenacious are these plants which manage to thrive despite the death in the air. And he makes himself breathe more deeply. Inside his mummy case his body is burning, yet the chill is just a few minutes or an hour away and he does not dare tamper with the swaddling. Instead he leans down, collects some leaves still damp from last night's dew and holds them to his face. It would be cooler if he went deeper into the woods but he's afraid of losing his way. The road he is following leads directly to the main route to Berlin. He clings to the edge of the woods for protection, but never loses sight of the road.

He holds Friedrich in mind, Friedrich who gave him life and boots, and now incumbent on Martin to stay alive for both of them. Friedrich had a wife and three children, and as soon as Martin has found Renate he will search for them and give them the pen and photograph Friedrich entrusted to him. There was a diary as well – the journalist in Friedrich had stayed alive even when all else was dying – but there's only so much a man weak from typhus and starvation can carry. Martin labelled the diary and hid it among some books in the hospital where he is sure it will eventually be found. He feels he has let Friedrich down, so little bequeathed by the dying man yet already too much, but comforts himself with the knowledge that in a similar position Friedrich would have done the same. He feels beneath his jacket for the pouch he fashioned from some of the rags. Here he has hidden Friedrich's possessions with his own, so little left but more valuable than gold.

Martin continues onward, pushing one sullen step after another. He has no idea how much ground he has covered but by the time the sun is overhead he has to stop. He moves deeper into the woods, settles against a log in a sheltered grove and forces himself to eat some bread. His brain feels as if it wants to push through his skull. The pain is worse today than yesterday, and will be worse tomorrow.

Night is falling when Martin awakes. He is coughing, his whole guts threatening to erupt. He cannot believe he has wasted so much time. Hours ago when he needed this hard useless cough to wake him it was silent, now it refuses to allow him to get to his feet. He is aware of a change in the light, suddenly it is brighter, perhaps he has made a mistake, perhaps it is still only early afternoon, hard to hold on to his thoughts as he peers through the trees. The sky is flickering, the sky is mauve, although just a moment ago surely he saw the sun, and so thirsty, impossible to know anything with such a thirst, reaches for his bottle, can't find it, perhaps it's been stolen, glances towards a movement in the bushes, the thief hiding or just a shimmying of leaves, and doesn't know now what he is doing here, doesn't know anything any more.

Heini Heck watches the sick man groping for his water bottle. He recognises the familiar mix of starvation, a body in collapse and typhus. It's a Jew, and probably dying, and Heini knows he should help, but little point endangering himself when the situation is likely to be hopeless. For the umpteenth time since being stationed at Belsen, Heini thinks about the Jew pastry-cook, how when he was at his lowest the old Jew helped him, how because of him he decided to become a cook, how because of him he's probably alive today. And quickly pushes the thoughts away – no time for softness now. Instead he finds himself wondering whether as head cook in the officers' mess at Belsen Concentration Camp he's had the best life can offer. And is forced to concede he might well have. In fact, with prospects such as his, Heini is not much better off than the poor mug with the typhus lying on the ground hacking up his lungs.

Heini steps a little closer. In the wavery light he sees the grey pits where the man's cheeks used to be and a few wisps of hair poking beneath a bandage wrapped around his head. He sees how skeletal are the hands scrabbling for the water bottle, and he hears the mad raving. Heini can't stand the sound of it and turns sharply away. He covers a couple of hundred metres before he stops, stops for a long time, then makes a reluctant treading back to the man. He wants to be away from here. But for what? he wonders. For what?

Back at the man's side, he helps him take a drink. The man has some mouldy bread, Heini offers instead some sweet pastries, fine crescent-shaped biscuits that melt in the mouth. The man feels better after eating. He can't sit up without help, but says he'll be stronger tomorrow. Not much chance of that, thinks Heini, but says nothing.

The man says he's Martin Lewin, from Krefeld near Düsseldorf, heading towards Berlin in search of his wife. He pulls a photograph from a pouch. The woman is all right if you like them scrawny and dark which Heini doesn't, but he makes the right noises and the man seems satisfied. Such a small amount of talking and the man is exhausted. Heini helps him take a piss, then wraps his own coat around the pathetic body. The man falls asleep immediately and soon is muttering like a drunk.

During the night Heini goes through the man's pouch. Apart from the photograph of the wife, there's a nice pen probably worth a bit, and two more photographs. The first is of the wife with a child and a man Heini guesses is Martin, although from the picture would not have known. The second photograph shows an entirely different woman, large and blonde and much more to Heini's taste, standing with a different man and three small children. The photographs are wrapped in a small piece of material as slippery as water.

Heini tips the pouch inside out, but there's nothing else. This Martin Lewin from Krefeld could be Jesus Christ of Nazareth for all the identity he carries, and if not for the Jewish prick could pass as German. Even the way he talks: nothing like the old pastry-cook, more like rich Berliners from Charlottenburg.

The man stirs, coughs a bit then returns to his muttering. Heini wipes the sweat from his face. People do survive typhus, people do survive years of deprivation, particularly with a little food and care. Perhaps Martin Lewin from Krefeld will live. And if he lives, perhaps he'll help Heini like the old pastry-cook did so long ago. And just as quickly Heini realises how stupid he's being. The Germans have been doing away with Jews ever since Hitler came to power. This Jew, any Jew, will look at Heini and see a German – not a good German nor a bad German, just a German, in much the same way Germans didn't single out good Jews or bad Jews, just went ahead and laid into the lot of them.

Heini settles himself down and falls asleep but not for long. He is awakened by the Jew's raving, and in the jumble a veritable atlas of places: Amsterdam, Berlin, America, Canada, Shanghai, and the Danes, he keeps calling out to the Danes. And names: Renate, Alice, Friedrich, lots of Friedrich. On and on he raves. A fever of words, sometimes perfectly clear, and at other times such a slurring of memories that even if you'd been there you wouldn't recognise them. At one stage he seems to think he's in Holland talking to a woman called Gertrude about visas, then a whole scramble about 'going under', and suddenly his eyelids spring open and he is wide awake.

As Heini helps him to some water, he asks about this 'going under'. The man is quite lucid now. He explains he went into hiding in Amsterdam, not with Dutch people, they were too busy looking after their own Jews, but with a Danish family.

'Good people,' he says. 'Such good people.'

Heini has never had much time for talking, but suddenly he finds himself asking questions, lots of questions to reveal how a Jew could survive so long. And it is not as if he knows what he is going to do, but something is growing in his mind. He questions Martin about Amsterdam, and about the camp at Westerbork; and because a Jew's experience of Belsen would be very different from his own, he asks about Belsen too. He is about to start on the wife and child when Martin's eyelids begin to droop, and before long he has slipped back into his raving.

Heini leaves him to garble on while he goes for a piss. The sky is clear of clouds with a good solid chunk of moon and more stars than ever were visible in Berlin. He wanders just a few metres away, finds a low branch that's as smooth as a chair and swings himself up. Through the silence he can still hear Martin's raving, but low and steady now like the distant growl of an aeroplane. He forgets about his bladder and sinks into his thoughts. He has nothing to look forward to, even this Jew with typhus has a better future. The lowest of the low when the Germans were on a roll, what poor pickings would be left to him now Germany is on her knees? He'd do better, he realises, being a Jew.

The next day dawns bright and clear, an early summer's day. Heini offers to remove Martin's swaddling, and will wrap him up again later when it is cooler. They set off; but with Heini doing most of the walking for both of them, they don't get very far, certainly not to the main road to Berlin. At lunchtime, Heini feeds Martin from his own store, lets him sleep an hour, then they continue until nightfall. The Jew is small, and reduced as he is to his bones he's not much heavier than a child, but still Heini has had enough for one day. As for Martin, he is exhausted but different from the previous night, more alert, and now convinced he will survive.

'I don't know who you are and I don't know why you've helped me, but if there's any justice in this world you'll be rewarded.'

He tells Heini about his wife, also about his daughter safe in England, and he's talking now not raving. Heini encourages him. He learns that the wife, Renate, ended up at Auschwitz – you can kiss her goodbye, Heini is thinking – and the brother and sister-in-law were also sent to the east and were unlikely ever to be seen again.

Heini asks Martin about his papers and is told they disappeared long ago. And because Martin is so different from the pastry-cook, he asks what sort of Jew he is. He learns there was no way of telling with some German Jews that they were in fact Jewish. They didn't wear Jewish clothes nor eat Jewish food nor practise any of the customs. 'What about Yiddish?' Heini asks, thinking again of the pastry-cook, and Martin explains that German Jews like him would never speak Yiddish. He even asks about the Jewish prick, and learns that some Jews, those who were more German than Jewish, would have had a normal one, just like Heini's own. And he asks about the name, Lewin. Is it a common Jewish name? And is told, common enough. In a single hour Heini learns the sort of background a Jew from Germany might have and how such a person might have survived.

Towards the end of the conversation it emerges the men have the same birth date, although Martin is five years older. 'My special twin,' he says.

Not long afterwards, Martin falls asleep. The coughing begins around midnight and continues for a couple of hours, but between spasms he says he knows he'll live. Finally the noise stops, and wrapped in Heini's coat Martin falls deeply asleep. Heini watches. The breathing, so shallow and rapid a short time ago, quietens to such an extent that Heini bends his head to Martin's chest and listens. He wipes the sweat from Martin's face and adjusts the coat, then he settles himself down for the night.

Around dawn, Heini rises from his forest bed where he has not been sleeping and stands looking down at Martin. The Jew might survive and he might not, but whether he lives or dies he will be very sick for several days. Heini has his own future to consider. Such slow progress they will make and his food store already depleted, and the countryside filling with Americans and Russians, French and British, all of them bristling with victory. There's his own future to consider, he tells himself as he squats down and lays his hands one each side of Martin's head. He twists. It is over in a moment. He unravels his coat from the dead man and rolls him gently into a grassy hollow. Heini then gathers his belongings and turns away from Berlin, heading instead towards the displaced persons' camps in the south.

A Meeting in Melbourne

Alice Carter arrived in Melbourne in the summer
of 1995, her file from the *Kindertransport* archive
tucked into her hand luggage. She had boarded the plane not in
San Francisco but Toronto where she'd been attending a series of
meetings for conservators. She now regretted what had seemed to
be an efficient plan for a woman short of time. For the flight to
Australia had been interminable, the hours distended by dull films
and duller food, and through it all a continual debate between her
desire to meet Henry Lewin and her determination to let old
losses lie. By the time she stepped into the Melbourne morning
she had decided at least a dozen times she would see him and a
dozen more times she wouldn't. She was stale, exhausted, desperate
for a shower, and resolved to wait as long as possible before she
again travelled by air for more than a couple of hours.

Raphe had offered to accompany her but, having still not told
him about Henry Lewin, Alice persuaded him to change his mind.
As it happened, when the time came to leave, Raphe preferred to
stay home. He had met a woman he was already describing as the
love of his life. This was the one, he told Alice, the one he planned
to marry, the one who would bear his children. It was not his
failure at relationships that had kept him unmarried for so long, he

said, rather he'd been waiting for perfection. Perfection's name was Juno, and while Alice thought she was a rather loud, contrived young woman, Raphe was happy, and that was all that mattered.

So here she was in Melbourne alone. She had arranged to stay in a serviced apartment three or four miles from Henry Lewin's home and a short walk from the city's Botanic Gardens. She had rather fancied walking through tropical greenery while she decided whether or not to see Henry Lewin. She had considered contacting him from America, had toiled for weeks over a letter, but the words simply wouldn't come. And while she knew her approach was risky when dealing with a man in his eighties, in the end she decided to keep her options open. She had, however, arranged to meet with a couple of colleagues in case she needed some diversions.

A serious case of jetlag meant it was a few days before she was ready to talk to anyone. Without warning she would find herself falling asleep or rather falling out of consciousness, a mental vacancy while her coffee went cold, or the news programme she'd been watching finished, or the shopping strip she'd been strolling along became a stretch of apartment buildings. At two o'clock in the morning she would find herself wide awake, too wired to read, too wired for middle-of-the-night television, would wait out the wakefulness with a bared-teeth irritation, finally falling into a swampy blackness around six. She took long solitary walks in the Botanic Gardens, down into damp fern gullies and over wide lawns, past huge old eucalypts and beneath a multitude of fruitbats hanging from the trees like flags of sun-dried leather. A fabulous variety of flora and fauna, but not much in the way of tropical species. Indeed, when she first arrived in Melbourne, nothing about the place was tropical. It was summer, but she needed a jacket in those first days, and while soon there would be a blast of heat straight from the equator, she had not yet learned about Melbourne's jittery weather.

She woke, she slept, she wandered the Botanic Gardens and she thought about Henry Lewin. Such a jangle of thoughts, wonderful far-flung possibilities of how this man had known her father, vying with the old losses and a wad of new disappointments. To see him or not? The decision seemed beyond her. Then on the fourth evening and without knowing why, she returned to the apartment, lifted the phone and dialled Henry Lewin's number.

The call was answered by a youngish sounding woman. When Alice asked to speak to Mr Henry Lewin, the woman introduced herself as Laura Lewin, his daughter. She said her father was out taking a walk but would be home shortly. Would Alice like to leave a message? Alice explained she was a visitor to Melbourne, that it was possible Henry and her family had known each other before the war and –

The daughter's excitement burst down the phone. How she hoped there was a connection. Her father had emerged from the war with no one left, not a single relative. How exciting if after all this time … Yes, yes, she'd get her father to ring as soon as he came in. And then after a brief pause she invited Alice to join the family for a barbecue on Sunday.

Henry Lewin called back within thirty minutes. In stark contrast with the daughter, he could hardly have been less interested. He said at the outset he was sure there was no connection, but nonetheless, and with his daughter's urgings quite audible in the background, he reiterated the invitation to Sunday lunch. Alice accepted, more for the daughter than herself, and spent the rest of the evening trying to escape her disappointment. In the end she took herself off to a local cinema where she sat through two hours of a hefty Czech film which was in its finishing throes before she realised she hadn't even bothered to put on her glasses. And through the elegant drear on the screen the same old questions: When would she stop adding to old losses? When would she stop picking at old scars? And why couldn't she be satisfied with the infinite possibilities of dreams?

The next day was Saturday. Alice kept herself busy with one of her old colleagues, a gallery director, whom she soon realised was flirting with her. When Malcolm McKellar suggested lunch the following day she was sorely tempted, not only because she was enjoying his company, but she found herself increasingly reluctant to meet Henry Lewin, whose own reluctance, she decided, was all the evidence she needed to show he had nothing to reveal. But there was no getting out of it. She decided to put an appearance at the Lewin barbecue, leave as quickly as possible, and yes, she said to Malcolm, she'd be happy to meet him later in the day.

Sunday was a scorcher. Alice chose her lightest sundress, left the apartment with a jacket over her arm, then thought better of it and threw it back inside. Sitting in the taxi she composed herself into her 'I'll do the right thing then get out of there as soon as possible' mode – an adult version of the perfect child model.

And she would have succeeded if not for the daughter. If only Raphe could meet her, his girlfriend problems would be over forever. Laura Lewin was lively, attractive, a good talker and highly entertaining. Henry, in contrast, was silent, gruff and unforthcoming. Every time Laura tried to direct the conversation to the past – and it was she alone who was interested in Alice's past, she alone who was interested in making connections – Henry wrenched it back to the present. It seemed to Alice that Henry Lewin preferred to talk about anything – fishing in San Francisco Bay, the exact composition of acrylic paint, the quality of Californian oranges – anything other than the past.

The son, Daniel, wasn't much better. He wore a yarmulke, and to Alice's secular eyes seemed very religious. A friendly enough man, but reserved, and by his own admission much more interested in the future of Judaism than the past. His son, Henry Lewin's grandson, a boy in his late teens, seemed to share his father's convictions, while the granddaughter, a slender, sulky adolescent, stayed close to the mother, whose good looks and forty-something elegance she would one day inherit.

But it was Laura Lewin who charmed. She was a lawyer working in human rights and social justice – Raphe would like that – and much the same age as Raphe. There was a marriage long in the past, but no children and no desire for children – Raphe would like that too. Laura was ideal. So much so that Alice was scheming how to separate Raphe from his new love and transport him out here to meet Laura Lewin, when Nell Bartholomew arrived, similarly attractive, similarly lively, and introduced as Laura's partner.

'And what sort of business do the two of you have?' Alice heard herself asking.

But Nell, it turned out, was Laura's partner in life. Laura Lewin, perfect for Raphe in every respect, was not in the matter of sexual preference.

Soon afterwards, Alice made her goodbyes with no intention of ever seeing the family again. She stifled her disappointment, she stifled all thought as she hurried through the heat to meet

Malcolm McKellar. He was waiting for her as arranged in the café at the Botanic Gardens. She deflected his enquiries about her lunch and threw herself into art and gossip. It wasn't long before she felt herself relax. Indeed, she and Malcolm had so much in common and talked so easily that when afternoon tea drifted into dinner, she found herself thinking the trip to Melbourne had not been entirely wasted.

Perhaps it was the wine with dinner or simply that she was enjoying herself, but when Malcolm again asked about her day, she told him of her meeting with the Lewins. And soon she was talking about the parents she hardly remembered and the past she had deliberately buried, revealing far more than she ever intended. Not that it seemed to worry Malcolm. He listened closely, sympathetic-ally, occasionally asking a question, but mainly just letting her talk. She spoke about growing older, how the dreams which had sustained her for so many years were not as effective these days. She admitted how disappointed she was about Henry Lewin.

'It's hard to accept there's nothing left to discover. Or –' and a long pause as a new thought occurred to her, 'perhaps everything to discover, but no way he's going to cooperate.' The words came slowly, her voice very quiet.

Malcolm leaned forward and took her hand. 'Even if Henry Lewin does have something to divulge he might not want to in front of his family. You know better than I that some of these survivors are burdened with experiences they'd prefer to keep to themselves.'

Alice so hoped he was right. For having finally summoned the courage to look back, she didn't want the trail of her past to be rubbed out with a gruff old survivor in Melbourne, Australia. And Malcolm's point was apposite: it was possible, even likely, that Henry Lewin had plenty to reveal, just not in front of the children.

Alice was calm the following morning when she telephoned Henry Lewin and arranged to see him alone later in the day. But by the time she stepped out of the taxi and entered his front garden she was shot through with jitters. She stood on his verandah for a few seconds, pulling the air into her lungs and plastering herself with a sturdy composure, and then she rang the bell.

From the moment he opened the door, this was a very different man. He was softer, more solicitous, and while still looking much younger than his eighty-five years, his face appeared tired and his large frame was sagging. As he prepared coffee and sliced some plum cake, she saw how the muscles of his arms and legs were draped in swathes of loosened skin. There was something inexplicably pathetic about this.

Neither of them talked much as they drank their coffee and ate the cake. It seemed to Alice he was waiting for her to begin. Finally she plunged in.

'I know you knew my father.' Her voice was calm. 'So, why don't you tell me about it?'

There was a long silence during which he sat motionless, hunched forward with his elbows on his knees and his hands clasping his head. His eyes appeared to be shut. A minute passed, maybe more, and just as Alice was about to rephrase the question he began to talk, still avoiding her gaze, still turned in upon himself.

Later she would tell Raphe she thought Henry must have wanted to confess, for once he began to speak there was no stopping him. His words poured out. Yes, he said, he had known her father, had known him at the end. He told her how sick Martin had been, how he had dragged himself out of Belsen. He spoke of her father's strength, how he had been determined to find his wife and then travel to England for his daughter. He talked about her father's last days and she let him talk, she let the new information sink in. And when he started to speak about his own early life, still she listened, nothing must stop the flow of information. Here was a German who became Jewish, a German with a childhood more impoverished than anything she had ever known, a German who had fought as a German in the war, a German with no prospects as the war was ending. He told two stories: Martin Lewin's last days and Henry Lewin's life. And as he talked she struggled to bring the two of them together. On the one hand her father, and on the other, this man who shared her father's history and his name. She skirted so many possibilities, although nothing, nothing would have steered her to the truth.

'Some things will always defy the imagination,' she would say to Raphe later.

Although she had no need for guessing. Henry Lewin told her

the truth. Henry Lewin told her exactly how her father died. It was like being inside a lead-lined capsule. All that existed was this German-sounding voice intoning unbelievable, unbearable acts; the rest was blackness. Ten minutes was all it took to reveal the final moments of her father's life, and then Alice was running from the house, catching a cab back to the apartment and sitting for hours, stunned, numb, her whole body shut down. But as the night wore on, the shock began to loosen and the horror blustered in: her father killed by a low-life German, mercilessly killed as if his life were nothing more than a purse full of change. Her father murdered by a common thief, murdered by Henry Lewin. Henry Lewin now eighty-five, with his grown-up family and comfortable home in comfortable Australia. Henry Lewin with a daughter of his own with whom he could talk and laugh and shower with fatherly love. Henry Lewin who had deprived her, Alice Carter, of all his own daughter had enjoyed. How Alice wanted to make this man suffer.

She returned to his house the next day exhausted and raging and out of control. He was expecting her, this man who had murdered her father, and sat in silence while she slammed into him. All her losses coalesced in him. She attacked, she accused, she condemned, and he did not flinch.

'He knew he deserved it,' she told Raphe later.

She returned day after day. She branded him with his sins, she picked him to pieces, she made him relive every minute, every second of what he had done to her father. And she forced him to do it over and over again. Once in her rage she tripped on a rug and he reached out to save her. She felt his hand on her skin, just a moment when both felt the burn of the past, then quickly she pulled away. And on she went, a tireless machine grinding away, day after day, week after week. And through it all Henry answered her questions and bent to her will, an old man growing older as she offloaded her losses.

Finally, and not long before Henry's own death, she asked the question which had dangled like a hangman's noose throughout the long interrogation.

'Was it worth it?' she asked him, quite calm now. And said again, each word a tidy stab, '*Was it worth it?*'

He hesitated, his reluctance was painfully clear. Finally he spoke: He'd had a good life. Yes, it was worth it.

'But my father, why did he have to die? After all, it was a story you needed, not papers, not even a specific identity, just an authentic story, a credible tale. Why did my father have to die?'

Now Henry did not hesitate. 'Because he knew the truth about me, and because he would have slowed me down.' Then after a pause, 'There were two of us. But given my prospects and the state of your father's health, only one future.'

That a man should have died for such paltry reasons. Alice couldn't get away fast enough. She was out of the house and in the street, had no idea of where she was going, but could not vouch for her actions if she stayed with him a moment longer.

Only one future. Only one future. And her thoughts tripped and slithered and plunged into the darkness of a little girl being sent away from her parents. A six year old sent alone into the world to a foreign country to live with foreign people. Only one future. Such dreadful words cutting the memories. Only one future. Such happenings, such decisions have no relation to this life.

She was out of breath when she stopped at a small intersection in an undulating suburb of pretty homes and gardens. There was a light breeze playing and birds twittering, and on the verandahs of the homes were children's bikes and kennels for happy dogs. The lawns were neat, the cars were new. And it was not as if the events from the past could not be understood, they could, in all their terrible horror, they could: Henry Lewin killed her sick father in order to ensure a future for himself; Renate and Martin Lewin put their six-year-old child on a train and sent her to England to ensure her future while they lost their own. So many people and so few futures, and a pragmatism of quite a different quality than late twentieth-century pragmatism. This trading in futures, this trading in life stocks, this worth of a life.

She began walking again. She walked and walked. Sometimes there were people about, sometimes not. Sometimes she was aware of her thoughts, sometimes not. Sometimes she understood Henry Lewin's motives, sometimes not. She walked until the early evening; then, exhausted and emptied of emotion, she hailed a cab. As soon as she was seated she felt her feet burst with pain. She removed her shoes. Both feet were blotched with blisters, both were raw and bloodied. She had not known.

A half-hour later she was back in the apartment, her mangled feet soaking in the bathtub, a stiff drink in her hand. She knew she would never see Henry Lewin again, couldn't trust herself around him. And while she would never forgive him, not that he had asked, she was nonetheless aware of a strange satisfaction. At last she had the truth. No more losses were possible now. As she sat on the edge of the bath sipping her drink she was struck by a sense of finality, and a feeling of lightness as if a loaded lorry had surged out of her.

Several days later Henry Lewin, too, was dead. Alice went to the funeral to make absolutely sure, and for a moment, right there at his funeral, was tempted to tell the truth to Laura – not Henry's son, probably because he seemed so protected by his religion – but the loving daughter, so nicely vulnerable, so sharply exposed. In the end Alice decided to spare her in a way her father had not spared Martin Lewin.

There was, she decided, a point when it should stop. And as the taxi carried her away from the cemetery, she realised she was no longer angry. Now it was her turn for a better future. That night at dinner with Malcolm McKellar she arranged to meet him in San Francisco in a couple of months time, and the next day she was on her way home, leaving Laura Lewin to grieve for the father she had never really known.

Language and Silence

When the American woman turned up out of the blue several weeks before her father's death, Laura had been thrilled, not simply for her father whose severance from the past had been so total, but also for herself. At last, she thought, some facts about his early life. But her excitement was to be short-lived: Henry denied any connection with the woman, categorically denied it. So when the American lingered on in Melbourne, Laura assumed she had joined the bridge-playing, meal-providing widows who had flocked around her father in the years since her mother's death. But the American didn't play cards, and if she cooked it was not for Henry Lewin. She came to talk, and with the exception of that first lunch when she seemed so keen to meet the family, she kept her talk for Henry alone. This was, if Laura had stopped to think, sufficient to distinguish her from the customary widows who knew their prospects were enhanced if Henry's joys became their own. They would admire his coin collection and his enduring reputation as a pastry-chef, and lavish interest in his family – Laura, her brother Daniel, his wife Melissa, their two children, and if they were really keen, Nell too – poring over photographs and scrapbooks with exquisite patience. But not the American, or at least not after her initial flash of friendliness. There were no photos when she came to visit, nor admiring laughter, the topics were of her choosing and they concerned Henry alone.

For hours they would talk, the American and Laura's normally taciturn father, the answering machine switched on, bridge meetings missed, a medical appointment once forgotten. A couple of times Laura was through the back door and into the kitchen before hearing their voices, her father's heavily-accented speech low and earnest in contrast with the American's sharp, peremptory tones. She would catch a glimpse of them from the doorway, the two of them sitting on opposite sides of the living room, her father stiff and defensive, the American leaning forward poised like a bullet, a mere fraction of a second when Laura would see her blond, bearish father almost pretty in contrast to this small, sharp woman. Then they would notice her, and the American would collect her things and, with a nod to Laura and a 'See you tomorrow, Mr Lewin', would be gone, leaving in her wake a smell of unanswered questions, Henry's perspiration and a vaguely familiar perfume.

The woman was from the past, her father had finally admitted. Not a relative, he stressed, but the daughter of a man he had once known.

Laura's excitement returned. It didn't matter her father had lied, finally she had an opening. 'Someone from Berlin?' she asked. 'Someone from before the war?'

'*During* the war,' he said, before turning away and effectively closing the conversation.

Laura watched her father walk down the hallway to his office, enter the room and close the door. And even though her excitement was pushing her to follow, she knew there was no point. She was well acquainted with his attitude to the past and for most of her life had complied with it – against her better judgment, it must be said. Persecution, torture, murder, genocide all have a long and noxious half-life, yet her father seemed to think that if he didn't dwell, if he didn't talk, the horrors would go away. And who was Laura to tell him he was wrong?

If only her father had been more like her mother. Etti Lewin had believed it was important to speak. 'You can't keep the poisons inside,' she used to say. 'It's unhealthy.' An Olympian talker until her premature death at sixty-two, Etti was a poor advertisement for her beliefs. Laura had heard about her mother's family in Lodz, along with a string of neighbours, shopkeepers, peddlers, teachers, Laura had heard about them all in such detail she would recognise them immediately should there ever be an afterlife. So many words, so many stories, Etti Lewin had talked so long and so often about her past it was more real than Laura's own. But all the talking had not saved her. Eighteen years younger than Henry, she had died of cancer five years ago, reciting her well-thumbed life to the end, while Henry, who had bottled up his memories, letting them steep undisturbed in their poisons, was eighty-five when he died.

Laura, while reluctant to press her father, had never given up hope he would eventually speak. And so he had, not to the family who had loved him, but an unknown American woman who had appeared out of nowhere. Once when he was with the woman, Laura had heard her father slip into German. Immediately the American had cut him off, saying she would tolerate no German. Her voice was raised, her tone ice hard, clearly there was to be no discussion on this issue. Then the jerk and silence of her poor father trying to shape his old unspoken memories in a language alien to his early life and still too unsteady after forty years to do the job properly. How Laura had wanted to intervene, but Henry had made it clear the American was no one's business but his own.

Laura knew she could have eavesdropped, just slipped in the back door and stood silently in the kitchen listening to what Henry had always denied his family. Yet even with the curiosity pummelling the very heart of her, she couldn't do it. Throughout her life her father had sealed his past from the family behind a wall of proprietorial authority. To have listened as he talked with the American would have been a trespass comparable to reading a private diary.

And then it was too late. Henry died soon after the American's appearance, his entrenched embargo on the past broken only with a stranger.

And there was no diary.

'Although if there had been, I'd have had no compunction about reading it,' Laura said to Nell one Saturday as they were eating breakfast on their back deck. 'People who write diaries and don't burn them expect a posthumous audience.'

The two women were enjoying a leisurely morning together, the first since Henry's death. It was May, but a cushiony heat still lingered, scored by a rustling of autumn leaves in the streets and lanes.

'And where there's a diary there's the possibility of a film,' Nell said with a smile. After several years devoted to cinema studies, Nell was considering a return to filmmaking. 'I bet his story would make a terrific movie.'

A terrific movie perhaps, but a terrible betrayal of her father's wishes. And although Laura knew Nell was probably joking, could not bring herself to play along. From her earliest years Laura had bent over backwards to comply with her parents' desires, after everything they had suffered it was the least they deserved. And in the case of her father there had been no confidences, no diary, and no matter what Nell thought, there would be no film.

Which would come as no surprise to Nell, for she and Laura disagreed on most things. Indeed for six years they had regularly disagreed, yet were devoted to each other. They were a textbook example of the compatibility of opposites. Background, temperament, likes and dislikes, all different. Even here in their own slender garden their different tastes were manifest: roses, a camellia, a gardenia and a daphne in one small garden bed for Laura, grevillea, kangaroo paw and bottlebrush in the other for Nell.

Their tastes did, however, coalesce in their home. They lived in a modern townhouse, with the deep blue and terracotta colourings of the southern Mediterranean. There were swathes of honeyed timber floors, and an indoor rock pool called a Zen fountain, which Laura hoped provided tranquillity by osmosis as they blustered past in the course of their busy lives. The house was built on two levels, with ample space for two tall women with towering personalities and Wystan, a blue Burmese cat with attitude. So great was their attachment to both house and cat, they would joke that if either was foolish enough to break what they assumed was a life-long partnership, then the guilty party would lose custody of both. An easy, casual joke because neither believed for a moment it would happen.

Laura sat back in her chair sipping her coffee and breathing in the sanctuary that was this place and this partner. If she could just prolong the moment for a few days in order to regenerate – like her peace rose recovering from black spot, she found herself thinking – she would re-enter life with all her old energy and eagerness. She and Nell had been out here only an hour and already she was feeling better, aware that a lightness had displaced the grind and crush of the past couple of months since her father's death.

She had never thought grief could be so raucous. She had lurched this way and that, seeing the lawyer, the accountant, the bank manager, redirecting her father's mail, forgetting to cancel the newspaper, discovering by virtue of its smell a bin of rubbish rotting in the laundry; in short, dealing with all those aspects of a life that go on irrespective of death. And through it all going to work each day and dealing with those problems too. Day after day with so much to do and all the while wanting to stop, wanting to turn the ruckus off, wanting time just to reflect.

Her father had been old, Laura knew that, but he had been healthy and his death had come as a shock. As for his absence, she felt it like a faulty car alarm, blessedly silent for the moment but sure to return. Having to sort through her parents' house had merely exacerbated the difficulties, for it was filled not only with her father's possessions but also her mother's.

Her parents had bought the house in 1970, the same year Laura had started high school. With so much life associated with the place and over such a long period of time, the many visits Laura had made since her father's death should have been like little pilgrimages. Instead she had been aware of a stiffness, even a foreignness with both her father and mother now gone, as if she were walking through a simulacrum of the place: everything where it belonged, everything familiar, but none of it real.

The rooms were emptying and soon the house would be sold. As she sorted through her parents' possessions, Laura was reminded again and again that while her mother had no secrets, her father had behaved as if his life began at thirty-five. It had always been reasonable to assume, then, that the earlier period had simply been well hidden. But drawer by drawer, cupboard by cupboard, room by room Laura discovered nothing more than the little she already knew. She was beginning to think she had been wrong about her father, that he had no secrets, had never had any secrets, that he had kept silent all these years because he had nothing to say.

Nell would have none of it. 'Of course he had secrets, what else brought the American woman halfway across the globe to see him?' She bent her fine sculptured face to one side, and ran an index finger a thoughtful track from her chin down the long, slender neck to the notch in her clavicle. 'My theory,' she said slowly, 'is the American was a long-lost love child –'

'The woman was well into her sixties, Nell. My father would have still been in short pants when he'd gone to bed with her mother.'

'It happens, darling,' Nell said with an emphatic raising of the eyebrows, and popped a strip of roasted red capsicum in her mouth. 'All right, so she wasn't his love child, but perhaps her mother had some sort of an affair with Henry later, after he'd shed his knickerbockers for something more mature.'

Laura was laughing. 'You've been watching too many bad American movies. Not all intrigues have to be sexual –'

'But they are the most interesting.'

'Not in pre-war Germany,' Laura said as she uncurled from her chair, gathered her robe about her and walked to the edge of the garden. There she stood gazing out over their small patch, breathing in the fresh morning air.

There was a richness about Laura Lewin, a lovely feminine succulence, with her smooth full curves, the mass of blonde curls, the almost white strands framing the face, and the unnerving swimming-pool blue eyes. All of her so blonde, not a faint and watery Dickens blonde, but the tall, full-bodied 1950s version. As she stood at the edge of the garden, wrapped in her crimson robe and stretching her arms up high, she was a compelling figure.

She twisted around. 'Whatever my father was hiding, if he was hiding anything, he took great pains to keep it hidden. Maybe,' she shrugged, 'maybe it's best we don't know.'

She knelt down and started to pick at some weeds. Wystan roused himself from the warm grass, sauntered over to investigate and applied himself to dispersing the pile. Several minutes passed before Laura sat back on her haunches, a clump of violet seedlings in her hand. She dumped the violets on the pile of weeds – Nell despaired of her ever learning the difference – and with the garden desperately in need of further attention, returned to her chair.

The two women sitting together in the autumn sun comprised a yin and yang of womanhood: blonde, full-bodied Laura, and tall, angular Nell – like Audrey Hepburn, Etti had said when they were first introduced. Nell was outgoing and self-assured, Laura was far more reserved; Nell was flamboyant in everything from clothes to conversation, Laura was highly competent but preferred a set of instructions; Nell's humour tended towards the smutty, Laura's was typically wry and self-deprecating. And while both were now thinking about Henry Lewin, Laura's mind was on betrayal and loss, while Nell's was hooked into sex and affairs.

'We know your father was very poor in Germany,' Nell said. 'Perhaps he picked up some gardening work with a rich German family, or was a general roustabout on an estate, and perhaps he had an affair with the lady of the house –'

'Very DH Lawrence.'

'– and perhaps the husband started to suspect, so Henry had to be sent away and he wandered for months, which was when his teeth started to rot, until at last he was taken in by a woman who turns out to be the American's mother, and they have an affair, the result of which is the American woman's much younger sister.'

Nell sat back looking very pleased with herself and Laura knew that with very little encouragement she would fill in the gaps to the story and happily throw in a sequel and they'd be sitting here in their bed clothes at midday. Nell really had missed her calling. She was an academic in cinema studies, her published speciality the avant-garde (with such a low tolerance for boredom, she said she needed a field whose very essence was change); her passions, however, were Hollywood schlock and airport novels. Now Laura leaned over and placed a kiss on her neck.

'You could make a fortune moonlighting as the Virginia Andrews of the silver screen.'

Several hours later, with Nell at a departmental barbecue, Laura sat on the couch with Wystan curled in her lap and a pile of work beside her. She glanced at the files and decided they could wait. For she was aware of an unmistakable grievance: at the end of his life, her father had finally opened up, but to a stranger and not his own daughter. And while clearly the stranger had certain claims on the information, surely Laura who had loved her father unreservedly had different, stronger claims. She wondered if Henry might have spoken to Daniel, and then quickly dismissed the thought. Perhaps a few years ago, before Daniel became religious; but since Daniel had pledged allegiance to what Etti used to call the *meshuggeneh frummers* – fundamentalist conservatives and of quite a different breed from ordinary orthodox Jews – there had been no significant exchange between father and son. Her father had chosen to leave his own son and daughter in the dark throughout his life, and it seemed he had remained consistent to the end.

If only there had been more words from her father and fewer from her mother, Laura was thinking, or through some sleight of hand it had been possible to slice off some of Etti's and give them to Henry. For there was no doubting Etti had plenty to spare and never any sign she would run dry. Etti had talked ad infinitum about her family and friends in Lodz, all lost. She'd talked of the years in the ghetto, the drag of hunger, the threat of illness and the cruelty of rumour. And after the ghetto, the hiding, the starvation, the cold, the humiliation, and always the huge gnarled fist of fear. Etti, with an eye pressed to memory's microscope, spared her children no details. Then when the war was over, meeting Henry at Landsberg DP camp, their years in Belgium and how they nearly went to Canada but ended up in Australia because of Etti's second cousin. And how they'd been warned about the Australian heat, but within minutes of arriving at Port Melbourne were chilled to the bone. The full gambit of family life in the Lewin household had been riven through with the Holocaust, and presiding over it was not Henry and Etti together, but Etti alone, Laura's fat, hugely loving mother whose very soul had been irreparably fractured and forced to wear splints forever.

'No one listened then,' Etti would say, 'and no one listened when it was over. And people they still don't want to listen. But if you talk long enough, soon they have to hear. And if people like your father won't speak, then others have to do it for him. Me, you, even this Steven Spielberg.'

Laura had wondered whether forgiveness played a role in all her mother's talking, but Etti was scathing about forgiveness. 'Forgiveness is just an easy way of making normal,' she used to say. 'Not my life but the ones who did the wrong. Who forgives?' she continued. 'The victim forgives. Always the victim. This person who has suffered so much and lost so much and now she has to say "I forgive you" as well. Why should I bend myself over to make bad people feel better?'

With so much to say and so few reliable answers, Etti's speech was littered with rhetorical questions. Her motivation for talking, however, was much more simple. 'You talk to make people believe,' she said. 'You talk to make people understand. And you talk,' and here she would look down at her ample body, 'because the truth you cannot hold it inside.'

Laura would listen while her mother talked, and long sharp nails of tension would jam into her, and when she was alone she would find herself cut with a revenge so powerful she actually felt sick. Laura used to imagine her mother's words as pellets of revenge, although at whom they were directed remained a mystery. The Germans weren't hurting, the Poles weren't hurting, the Ukrainians weren't hurting, the Latvians weren't hurting, none of Hitler's willing helpers were hurting. And besides, neither Etti nor Henry ever spoke of revenge, which was, in Laura's opinion, as extraordinary as a condemned prisoner never talking escape.

Laura, on the other hand, had spent hours and hours pondering revenge. She would imagine German people driven from their homes and banished from their country. German people made to work as slaves for no other reason than being German. German people stripped of their dignity and herded naked to their death. German people forced to hide in holes like her mother, or put in concentration camps like her father. And instead of feeling better, she found herself feeling sorry for the poor suffering Germans of her imagination. Revenge, she decided as she wiped her mind of the false images, would simply turn the perpetrators into victims.

So she steered her thoughts towards justice, but justice was on its knees after the most cursory of considerations. Justice was, after all, what happened at Nuremberg, and while that might have eased the world's conscience, it did nothing for the loss and gruelling memories of those who survived. Certainly it did nothing for her mother and father. Justice, Laura decided, was simply too polite for genocide. So presentable in its staid abstractions, so authoritative in its ordered processes, justice fell well short when it came to dealing with the torture and killing of millions.

Laura was older, a law student at university, when she realised that in the same way language had failed to come to grips with justice, so too the official language of the Holocaust. Etti's words were heartbeats, but the public language of the Holocaust, in fact of all the horrors which pockmarked humanity, was diluted and disinfected in abstraction. Genocide. Persecution. Incarceration. Where were the perpetrators in all these words? Where the victims? Laura was studying law, she knew what to ask. But the law was silent. Only the words of her mother and other persecuted people seemed to be blooded with truth. Laura learned from them that it's only when you tell the incomparable individuality of horror, each dreadful act recited one at a time, hundreds of horrors each with its own description, each with its own location, each with its own victims, that you break genocide into its austere, blood-curdling bits. And then, only then can the sober, indecent, heart-stabbing meanings emerge.

Not that she had ever regretted pursuing law as a career, particularly when it had brought her parents so much joy. Neither of them had advanced beyond primary school yet both their children were university educated. And when Laura decided to specialise in human rights issues, they were thrilled. Later when she was appointed to the new Human Rights and Social Justice Commission they could not have been more proud than if she'd won the Nobel Peace Prize. The law fell short, but if her own work were any guide, it was not entirely useless.

Laura had prepared for her career at the family dinner table. Etti was an appalling cook and the food easy to neglect while the family sat around the table arguing the issues of the day. Etti, broad-faced and buxom, would sit at one end of the table, her pudgy hands with the dimples at the base of the fingers striking the emphasis as she talked across the congealing food. At the other end of the table Henry, straight and strong and, if the truth be known, the sort of face and figure to delight an Aryan, sparred with his wife, sometimes agreeing sometimes not. And in between, Laura and Daniel, one each side of the table, Daniel an inexplicable conservative in the Lewin household and Laura spokesperson for the oppressed and dispossessed from the time she was three years old and defending a disabled child at her kindergarten. Night after night Daniel and Laura, Henry and Etti would mix politics, economics, business, welfare and international relations with the awful food, their conversation only easing off with dessert, one of Henry's creations brought home from the shop because Etti believed 'better we eat than we waste'.

Over the years Etti had grown fat on her beliefs. Every day in the shop, with so much sugar and cream, was it any wonder, she would say, she was so fat? Henry, same shop, same sugar, same cream, same daily temptations, was built like a fortress. Even into his eighties he remained a tallish man with a strong, muscled body more suited to labour than fancy cakes. As it happened he was good at both: a legend in the kitchen and a master up a ladder. He used to joke he would live out his days with a whisk in one hand and a wrench in the other.

Whatever he did, it wouldn't have mattered to Etti. She thought the world of him, as he did of her. Even in the heat of an argument he would rise from the table to sit near her, stroking the huge pillows of her arms while she talked. 'I'm so fat,' she would say. And Henry would turn to Laura and Daniel, 'I'd love her however she was.'

And so he did, through the hard early years and the easier ones that followed, through the happy times as well as her depressions, and finally through Etti's slow dying. He held her in his arms as the cancer shrank her, his love flourishing as she became smaller and smaller. Finally it was as if she had slipped inside a sack of skin. 'All those diets,' she would say lifting a length of loose skin. 'Lucky I failed. Who would want to look like this?' But as far as Henry was concerned, Grace Kelly and Sophia Loren had nothing on his wife.

There was a toughness about Henry, but with Etti he was pure tenderness. So much love after more than forty years of marriage, of working together in the shop, of sharing a whole life together: entertainment, friends, leisure, the lot. Their friends were drawn mainly from the Polish-Jewish community and had been from the beginning. When they had arrived in Australia in 1951, Jewish Welfare had provided them with a list of local Jewish contacts both German and Polish to reflect their different backgrounds. And while Etti would have been happy to follow up some of the German ones, Henry was adamant: the Polish Jews, he said, would be quite sufficient.

He had been shedding all things German ever since the end of the war so Etti was not surprised. And besides, Melbourne's Polish Jews – the Polish contingent as Laura later dubbed them – seemed to suit him. He would sit quietly amid the swirl of Yiddish and Polish, content just to listen. It was not just a lack of proficiency with the language which kept him quiet, rather it was in his nature to keep to the edges of any group. Often on a Sunday when the Polish contingent met, Henry would leave the others to their chatting and spend time alone in the kitchen baking.

'Such a husband she has,' their friends would say of Etti. 'He spends his time in the kitchen while she shmoozes.'

When Etti died back in 1990, Henry continued with the Polish contingent much as he had always done. And all of them, together with their children and grandchildren, were there at his own funeral. It was a good turn-up: many friends, but also suppliers, other pastry-chefs, even long-time customers for whom a visit to Lewins had been a Saturday ritual. He was a good man, they said, and a great pastry-cook.

'A true artist,' one customer said at the funeral. 'Every cake a masterpiece, and the sacher torte his Mona Lisa.'

It was in 1958, the year Laura was born, that Henry and Etti had started the business. From the beginning Etti was chief assistant, bookkeeper and delivery hand while the artistry of the business rested with Henry. Theirs was a small shop in a busy shopping strip, the kitchen behind, the toilet out the back, the dwelling on top. A typical Victorian terrace which the Lewins rented from an Australian with a sweet tooth and a large circle of friends. A small alcove at the rear of the kitchen was set up for Laura and there she would play while her parents worked and Daniel, ten years older, was at school.

As a child, Laura would watch her father as he prepared his famous sacher tortes, the butter and sugar in the Hobart mixer, Hilde Hobart he called it, his thick hands on the great metal mixing bowl testing aeration and temperature, cupping the bowl with the same sensitivity as a mother supports her baby's head, knowing the slap slap slap of a mixture too wet, the white whoosh of a mixture perfectly aerated. He would lift Laura up on a stool for a better view when the chocolate was added. Listen, he would say, it sounds like mud pools with its plop and splat, plop and splat. And later when everything was prepared, her father would mix with his big bare hand in the huge bowl and her mother would add the various ingredients a little at a time: the chocolate mixture, the egg whites and now some fine almond meal, and her father's left hand on the rim of the bowl gently tipping and rolling while the right hand twisted in a deft blending of the mixture. 'Like this,' he would say, and show his hand with the chocolatey fingers slightly apart. 'You don't want to crush it,' he would always add as he scooped the mixture from the sides in a graceful arc. He had a mathematician's precision for a yield. 'There'll be nine cakes in this batch,' he would say, and with the mixture aerated to perfection there would be exactly nine tins filled. Laura would watch as he scooped from the edge and dropped the batter in the tins, dollop by dollop, with a little twist, a little squeeze. And the smell of the kitchen, the smell of baking, the smell of her parents, the smell of love. Laura would watch her father for hours on end, the stiff silent man who was all texture, all poetry when at work.

In the weeks following her father's death, Laura kept seeing Henry's hands cupped around the huge beaten copper bowl, her favourite of his implements. She would remember the faraway look in his eyes and how she used to wonder what was hidden behind that clouded gaze. Baking, Laura decided long ago, took her father back to his past. So it was significant that when the American woman turned up he was baking again, a frenzy of baking, baking up memories or baking to forget.

'What's on your mind?' she asked him one Sunday morning when she found him kneading pastry for at least half a dozen *Pflaumenküchen*. He kept up the rolling, shook his head and gave no words. She tried again: 'What's on your mind?' and again there was no answer, just a glancing up from his work and looking very old.

She was unlikely ever to find out now, she thought, as she pushed the cat aside and drew the pile of work towards her. She opened the top file and began to read but a few minutes later, with her mind still on her father, she gave up. In some peculiar way, Henry's silences during his lifetime were exaggerating his absence now. These past weeks, as she had sorted and packed at her parents' house, she had been aware of a very particular type of absence, bulky and uneasy like when you're left alone in a doctor's surgery, or those chilled moments before an examination begins and the paper is turned face down on the desk. It was an absence tinged with fear.

Nell had offered to help but, despite all they shared, Henry and Etti's house, their past, the old memories now wrenched from their moorings, and the ever-present questions about Henry were lodged in a part of Laura that not even Nell had reached. The only person who might have understood was more cruelly absent than either Etti or Henry.

Daniel's descent into religious observance had been incomplete at the time of Etti's death. He had mourned his mother according to religious guidelines although not absolutely according to the book. Henry's death provided him with the opportunity he had missed. Daniel's mourning was total, he wore it like a shroud and it blocked out his sister. He prayed at the synagogue three times every day. He loved his mourning, he seemed to love it more than he had ever loved his parents. And while daily he would share his grief with a bunch of men at the synagogue who had never met Henry, he would not with his own sister. Daniel had left the family a long time ago, but Laura had never missed him as much as she did now.

She was left to dwell on her father alone – not just the man she knew and loved, but the man he had withheld as well. She searched and searched her parents' house for evidence from his early years. She slid her fingers along the edges of ill-fitting drawers, she rummaged in his pockets and poked in the toes of shoes, she opened every container, she checked every envelope, she read the labels on his clothes. She sifted through the life her father had left and found nothing from the time before, except for the threepence, the centrepiece of his coin collection, but she had always known about that.

Her mother, even after the years of hiding during the war, had salvaged a photograph of her family now worn to a shadow, a tiny embroidered purse which had belonged to her mother, and enough memories to fill a warehouse. But Henry had nothing. 'I prefer to travel light,' he would joke. And even though no one ever laughed, it was a joke repeated down the years. Whenever a bag had to be packed, even for a day trip to the country, Henry would say he preferred to travel light.

And that was how he had quit this world. Sturdy of body despite his age, and empty of hand, and no surprises in the things he had left behind. Indeed, the only surprise at the end was the American at the funeral.

Laura had been happy to respect her father's stowing of the past while he was alive, but once he was gone she recognised a burgeoning desire to fill up his silences, which for too long had been her own. A few weeks after his death, she had telephoned her father's friends, but no one knew anything about the small American woman at Henry's funeral, few had even noticed her. Laura's curiosity tightened and a sadness too. Her father's life had been passed in two distinct channels, and when finally someone had turned up to connect the two, no one seemed to have benefited, least of all Henry himself.

Laura had been close to her father, closer than was possible with her mother. In his own quiet way he had been more of a hands-on dad than the many seemingly easier fathers of her friends. Indeed, there was little Laura had to forgive Henry in life. Despite the baggage of a survivor's life, he had supplied her with a happy childhood, leaving Etti to take care of the shadows.

Henry's preference had always been for the family. With other people, even friends of thirty years standing, he always seemed to be treading on foreign ground. So strong was his preference for family life, Laura was convinced his own early life had been idyllic. When she was a child it was invariably Henry who planned surprises and outings. In winter there'd be picnics in the Dandenongs, and on summery Sundays the family would go to St Kilda beach where Henry, Laura and Daniel would swim for hours and play endless games of cricket on the sand. Henry was a rare occurrence, an athletic Jew. 'Would warrant a whole chapter to himself,' Etti joked, referring to that slim bestseller, *The Jewish Companion to Sport*.

And there were his odd endearing rituals, like the ritual of the orange which Laura assumed had been transposed from his own childhood. Oranges, Henry used to say, were family food, already divided into those tidy segments so no one would miss out. He would peel with such care with his large gruff hands, the trick, he said, to remove the bitter pith without breaking the delicate film. And then the dividing: one for you, one for you, one for you, and one for me. And everyone ends up with three or four pieces according to Henry's nimble fingers and, if necessary, a sleight of hand.

'What happens if there are lots of children,' Laura once asked.

An orange was family food, her father said, there had to be a piece for all.

'Did you learn about oranges from your father?' Laura continued. When Henry ignored the question, she asked again, louder this time. But before he could answer, Etti stepped in as she so often did, 'Don't bother your father,' she said.

When people you love have suffered greatly, you don't want to add to their sorrows. Even as a young child Laura did what she was told and tried to avoid trouble. She trussed her days with caution, subjecting all her actions and utterances to close scrutiny before releasing them into the world; she tried, in short, to be a good and undemanding child.

Guilt, gratitude and grief, the three Gs of children of survivors – and love of course, but compared with the three Gs, the love was easy. Laura tiptoed through her childhood, not wanting to compound her parents' suffering – Etti's more than Henry's, for in the hierarchy of suffering her mother was on top. 'We were cheap children,' Etti used to say. 'We managed without food, we wore rags and were grateful, our shelter was a hole in the ground, our schooling was basic: you passed if you were alive at the end of the year.' This she would say to the daughter who once foolishly said she would die if she didn't have her own stereo, and the son who at eighteen accused his parents of a *shtetl* mentality when they told him he didn't need his own car. Unlike Daniel who had always resented his Holocaust heritage and refused to accommodate for it, Laura made a deliberate decision to keep her needs and desires private if there was any possibility of their upsetting her parents.

Which was why she married Alan Schwarz despite having been aware of her preference for girls practically since kindergarten. To present her parents with a female partner would have been beyond the pale. Not that she had used Alan: neither of them was particularly good marriage material, she had her lesbian tendencies and he had his drugs. And they had truly loved each other in their grossly imperfect ways, understood each other too, coming as they did from similar backgrounds. Then there were his looks: Alan had the face of an angel; on appearance alone butter wouldn't melt in his mouth, but as Laura would soon discover, anything with a kick in it would. Alan loved her and he loved drugs, and with parents so indulgent of their only child, he had plenty of money for the top quality stuff even while still a student.

By the time he and Laura started dating he had finished university and was working in his father's bias-binding business, with neither commitment nor reliability it should be said. As for drugs, they were a central feature of his life, although Laura thought he confined himself to grass and an occasional trip with the safer hallucinogens. And while there were plenty of warning signs even in those early days, so intent was she on keeping her parents happy, she failed to notice.

On one of their early dates Alan took her to a party. She remembered entering a basement flat (later she would wonder where on earth it could have been, given that basement flats were not common in Melbourne), a dark place with an odour of dope and sweat and people who had not moved for a long time. Ashtrays were overflowing and burgundy-coloured candles were burning, and she remembered dirty hands with black-rimmed nails and assumed that the dirty hands resulted from playing with the dark candle wax. Everyone was slow and vague and laughed a lot, and even though she felt out of place, she decided it was her fault for not being cool enough. Lou Reed waiting for the man played interminably, but so naïve was she in those early days, she had no idea why he was waiting. She smoked a little dope and thought that was all Alan did too, although when he disappeared into the bathroom with another guy she did wonder what they were doing in there together.

She and Alan were married before she recognised his heroin look: the pallid, clammy skin, the eyes that looked straight through her, his manner so disengaged. Heroin provided a shortcut to his soul, rendering her own determined attempts pathetic in comparison.

He died from a particularly pure batch at a time when he was supposed to be clean. He had left the house to do the shopping and two hours later he was dead. Laura still loved him – she was always loyal in love – and he had loved her too, although not as much as he loved heroin. Living with Alan had been shot through with problems, not the least being Laura's determination to conceal the truth from her parents. However, when Alan died, it turned out they already knew, but loving her as they did and believing she was ignorant of his problem, had chosen to speak privately with him while assuming a protective silence with their own daughter.

Love, protection, silence, it's a dangerous brew, yet Laura was never in any doubt her parents loved her, and never did she waver in her love for them. And if at times it became a little murky, that was simply a side-effect of so much love. Over the years she had watched with amusement as many of her friends had gone into therapy, each of them spending thousands of dollars trying to understand why they hated their mother or resented their father or felt betrayed by both. They would complain about not being loved enough, or being loved too much but the wrong sort of love – like the wrong sort of cholesterol, Laura once joked to Nell – and as damaging as if they had experienced no love at all. Her friends would compete for the prize of unhappiest childhood. Each would toss their childhood into the circle, then rummage through the pile, prodding, pushing, running the quality through their fingers, and in the end would retrieve their own damaged rag: it was best for being the worst. These were women and men in their twenties and thirties and forties who, with tears running down their face, would describe how at the age of four or five or eight or ten, this brother or that sister was given the book, the bedroom, the beach holiday, the bike they had coveted; or the best clothes, the front seat in the car, the mother's attention, the father's approval. 'How can you still be upset about such things?' Laura would ask. 'None of it matters any more.' But it did, it did. They were as fiercely possessive of their miserable childhoods as a miser of his bank account.

Then there were the friends who were children of survivors, all in their own way lugging around their parents' horrors whether these had been revealed or not. Laura would not condemn as she watched them negotiate a crooked path into the future, often with a great gaping chasm behind. Certainly she had never condemned Alan, although she wished he had chosen a different way. And she tried not to condemn her brother with his religion, even though

Daniel's opiate was just as effective in separating him from her as Alan's had been.

How different it was for Nell who, with her gratifyingly ordinary background, could not have predicted what trouble she had brought herself in choosing a Jew.

'So the Holocaust is sacred Jewish ground?' she had remarked in the early days of their relationship.

Just a handful of words but a mighty insult, not only to Laura but to survivors like her parents. It was indecent what her parents had paid for their survival and no one had the right to trespass. Her relationship with Alan had been far from perfect, but clearly, she realised, a non-Jewish partner was out of the question.

It was their very first holiday together and sparking with the usual excitement and fragility common to all new relationships. She and Nell had driven for hours from Melbourne to the high country of Victoria, had booked into a motel at Omeo and were taking a stroll through the main street of the historic town. It was late in the day, and although there were people about, there was that sense of space and emptiness so typical of country towns in Australia, and an odd spongy silence against which voices, birdsong, even the grating of an old ute sounded newly polished. They were passing by a stately old bank building when Nell spoke.

'So the Holocaust is sacred Jewish ground? Complete with an electric fence around it for all eternity?'

Laura stopped, a partly exposed landmine could not have produced a sharper response, and grabbed Nell's arm tight enough to hurt. And there in front of the red-brick bank, the sky blooding with the closing day and an icy chill oozing down, she took Nell on, not shouting but talking with venomous intensity. Two tall women in a country town, one startlingly fair with a mass of long blonde curls and the other equally tall, but angular and boyish with closely cropped dark hair, women who would have occasioned notice in a bustling city mall, but in this location were as obvious as performers on a brightly lit stage.

Laura, a fine arguer at the best of times, gained eloquence under pressure. It was as if a sluice gate were opened and a stream of sparklingly fluent, finely honed arguments released. With cutthroat logic and perfect delivery she ranged from trespass and betrayal, to appropriation and moral boundaries, on to ancient scapegoats and Christians with blood on their hands.

'You Jews don't do forgiveness, do you?' Nell said when Laura finally was silent.

Laura was incredulous: Nell had clearly understood nothing. And would never understand. She stomped back to the motel, leaving Nell standing in the main street of Omeo. There she collected the car, *her* car fortunately, and stormed off. She drove for hours, drove herself through the dark country, out of her rage and into the impossibility of this new relationship, only two months old after all and the two of them knowing so little of each other: Nell from her Anglo-Saxon Protestant background and Laura a Jew right down to her linen cupboard.

'Such precision,' Nell had said through her laughter when first she saw the linen cupboard. 'It deserves nothing less than posterity,' and had returned the next day with a video camera.

Laura, too, had laughed, but not any more. As she negotiated the narrow, nervy curves of this unknown region, she cursed her heritage. Other people needed to concern themselves only with a small coterie of family and friends, but Laura, *Australian* Laura, found herself defending and arguing on behalf of all those millions of European Jews who had been silenced, all of them strangers but nonetheless included in her soul's address book. It was not a role she wanted, but she seemed to have no choice. She and the six million were affronted by Nell's comments, and even though she knew Nell intended no malice, she had no right to speak in a way that on someone else's lips would be nothing less than murderous.

Hours later, having driven through ski resorts preparing for the season, down steep mountainous byways, along roads flanked by a sticky darkness, around the curves of the Tambo and the startling flash of water when her headlights found the river, she sped along the low, twisting road, could not go fast enough for the boiling inside, until in the glare of her headlights she saw a mound of dead wombat. And at last she slowed down.

Once before when driving through the country at night, she had hit a big brown male, the poor thing catapulted to the side of the road but still alive, and Laura crying and quivering and hardly able to stand but knowing she had to finish the job she had so carelessly begun. She had taken the crowbar from the car's toolkit and beaten the poor animal's head until she was sure he was dead. Would never forget the crippling horror of it all, the awful resistance of bone, the blood catching the warm fur, the legs jerking with each strike. Still shaking and crying and sickened with herself, she had dragged the animal away from the road to bury him. Her fingers proved useless against the hard dry earth, even the crowbar failed to make an impact. She pulled the poor creature a little further into the bush, rolled him into a shallow gully and covered him with twigs and leaves, and did not travel alone in the country for more than two years.

Now she kept her speed low, slipped a cassette of Bach's cello suites into the tape deck and made her way down to the coast. It was ten o'clock when she drove into Bairnesdale and the streets were quiet. From a public telephone she rang the motel at Omeo and asked for a message to be delivered to Nell's room. Then she drove back, arriving after midnight.

Wrapped in the sort of calm that feeds off tidy decisions, she informed Nell they would be leaving in the morning. But Nell would have none of it. Laura might be a neurotic Jew, she said, but she was actually quite taken by her.

They were to spend the rest of that long night talking – in later years they would call it their Isabel Archer night – and by the morning had decided to stay together. It was Henry James as psychotherapist and the only therapy Laura would ever countenance for herself.

'You're scared what you might discover,' Nell had said.

But Nell was wrong; Laura's memories of childhood were acute. Rather she was afraid what therapy might do with those memories, and she wanted to keep loving her parents. She knew about their flaws, she knew about her own flaws and she knew about the flaws in their mutual love. There was pathology aplenty in her background, enough for a lifetime of therapy, but she had made a decision long ago to live her life rather than suffer it. Being a victim, as popular as it was among many of her generation, had never held any appeal for her. Her situation was simple: there were elements in her past she could not change – the Holocaust and the cost of her parents' survival for a start – and a closer perusal would only pollute the relationships she now enjoyed.

She used to joke that her attitude must be genetic, for neither of her parents would ever contemplate therapy, although for very different reasons from Laura. Neither believed in seeking help from a stranger.

'Only yourself can you rely on,' her mother used to say. 'And your family too – although even they can die.'

Despite her family's emotional self-sufficiency, privately Laura had thought her mother might actually benefit from a little professional help. Depressions, sleeplessness, a gastrointestinal tract which helped keep the medical profession afloat, and a story of personal loss and torment too great for a multitude of people seemed sufficient to justify the services of a specialist. But Etti was of the opinion that you don't wash your dirty linen in public – or Etti's version: better the dirty clothes they stay at home – and besides, what sort of world would it be if every time you have a little problem you run off to the doctor?

Over and over she would insist: you can do anything you set your mind to if it's a matter of survival. Even when her cancer was diagnosed Etti was quite matter-of-fact: she'd survived worse.

Etti was just seventeen years old at the end of the war and entirely alone. Both parents had perished, together with her two sisters and brother, her aunts and uncles, most of her cousins, and her two grandmothers who would have died happier if, like their spouses, they had died before Hitler had marched into Poland. All alone at seventeen, minimal formal education yet a doctorate in survival. Human beings can live in a hole if that's their only option, she used to say, and feed on paper if nothing else is available. You can train your body to shut down, not to feel hungry, not to feel the squeezing of your bowels, not to smell your own filth. You can train your eyes not to see, your poor heart to go numb, your brain to go quiet.

Throughout her life she continued to believe that a person can do anything if there's a chance of survival. Although it clearly didn't work with her cancer, as the once-buxom woman with the smooth rounded face faded, too busy fighting the disease to have time for depression, too busy fighting the disease to realise she had lost this one. And still telling her past.

'I remember everything,' she said.

Etti remembered in Polish, Yiddish and English. Three languages to try and puncture the silence. Three languages better to tell the world. Three times the ammunition with which to fight evil.

With each new revisionist she despaired. 'No one else has to prove their own suffering. No one but the Jews.'

As a child, Laura used to shut herself in her wardrobe because her mother had spent half a year in a space the size of a cupboard. She would push the shoes to one side and crouch in the dark and remain absolutely still, scarcely breathing according to her mother's account.

'My feet they were always going to sleep,' Etti had said. 'My fingers I thought they would break from the cold.'

Laura's feet did go to sleep, but Melbourne was never cold enough for her fingers to freeze.

'And to know you are still alive, you have to keep thinking.'

So Laura would think: I am thinking so I must still be alive. And rolling word sequences silently over and over: days of the week, months of the year, forwards then backwards. I am still alive, she would think as she crouched in the wardrobe, counting by twos, and when she was older by threes, and older still, by sevens and nines. I am still alive, she would think as the darkness droned on.

There were times when she fell asleep in the wardrobe and knew if this were for real she might have died.

'Never a proper sleep,' Etti said. 'Always on the alert.'

And decades later, right up to the time of her death, Etti still slept poised for flight. Even the sleeping pills worked only for a couple of hours. Sleeping, Etti believed, was a state of mind which her own mind could not afford.

Laura, too, was not a good sleeper, although like so many aspects of her life, better since she'd been with Nell. In the early days of their relationship Nell would wake in the middle of the night to find Laura on the couch hitched to her walkman and the all-night broadcast from the BBC World Service. Nell would take Laura back to bed and stroke her while she concentrated on falling asleep.

'Stop concentrating,' Nell would say. 'And forget cupboards, forget darkness. Think colour, glorious colour. Think Jackson

Pollock in gorgeous rivulets. Feel it slither down your spine.' And would stroke her gently to sleep.

Everyone said it wouldn't last, Nell and Laura were simply too different.

'Why on earth would you want a partner a carbon copy of yourself?' Nell said.

Over the years Laura had come to the same opinion as friend after friend introduced their latest love, a version of themselves right down to their mother problems, or, in a recent case of two adopted women getting together, their absent mother problems.

Their differences were mostly useful and often entertaining, although Laura's lack of interest in cultural theory ('Postmodernism, poststructuralism. When does post become passé?') created tensions when it came to entertaining Nell's friends. And Nell, much to Laura's exasperation, would never learn how to stack the food in the pantry, or file the towels and sheets in the linen press. But these irritations aside, Laura liked finding what she lacked in a lover.

Coming from the the sort of background that could look after itself, Nell had always pursued a range of more creative futures. As soon as she had finished school she swapped Nell for Gaia and headed north to a commune on the central coast. But after three of the worst asthma attacks she had ever experienced, she was forced to concede that collective living close to nature fortified by love, meditation and organically grown dope was poison to sensitive lungs. Nell headed home and to university, an arts course of the English–history variety, pleasant enough but providing no future whatsoever. In her third year she enrolled in a film unit and enjoyed it sufficiently to stay for an honours year, completing a thesis on cartoons and social subversion.

Around this time she began collecting old movie posters. Her earliest acquisitions included *Some Like It Hot, South Pacific* and *Rear Window,* and over the years she had maintained the high standard. These days her poster collection was considered one of the finest in the country. Currently it was filed in fireproof trays in her study, but one day, she said, she would purchase some space and have her collection on permanent display. Nell was full of such plans.

On leaving university she bought herself some smart clothes and for a short time worked as producer–fundraiser for a number of worthy film projects. She soon discovered that hustling was not her forté, so discarded the suits for black on black and the more artistic side of filmmaking. After two years of too much wine, too much teamwork and abject poverty she did as many had before her and opted for the halls of academe.

In choice of career, it seemed Nell's blatantly ordinary past had eventually triumphed, but not so when it came to lovers. Here, too, her experience could not have been more different from Laura's. The boyfriends who had passed through Nell's adolescent heart were a motley assortment, and while none of them was out-and-out bad, she could claim more than a sprinkling of no-hopers. They prepared her well for Husband Number 1, a mistake by anyone's reckoning, although a charming mistake by Nell's. When he absconded with their joint savings and her electrical appliances, Nell said it was worth it: the savings were meagre, the appliances replaceable and she'd had a great deal of fun.

Husband Number 2 was her PhD supervisor. They started sleeping together in the same week Nell began the final draft of her doctoral thesis. The end was in sight, she said as she pulled Edouardo to the floor. The last draft was accompanied by abundant sex of the quick, illicit kind, much of it occurring on university property and in university time. The thesis was finished well before the sex wore out, and by the time Nell was appointed to her first teaching job at another of the city's universities, she and Edouardo were married.

Cinema studies is not a large field. When two of the local luminaries share the same bed even if not the same university, it can become very crowded at home. Nell rose quickly through the ranks. Those who wished her harm, and within the sleazy underworld of university departments they numbered quite a few, passed prim remarks about pretty beginners with shallow charms needing neither brains nor books to facilitate their advancement. And while it was true Nell had slept with exactly the right person at the right time, and equally true she was very attractive, she was no intellectual slouch. Within six months of completing her doctorate she had converted her thesis and had it accepted by a mainstream publisher; another two years saw her celebrating the release of her second book.

Meanwhile Edouardo had slowed down. No one it seemed was interested in his latest manuscript described by Edouardo as groundbreaking, but considered inaccessible by the rejecting publishers. Edouardo believed it was too much to expect that the backwater which was Australian publishing would recognise a work of genius so he decided to go offshore. While waiting for offers to arrive in the mail, he lounged around the house expecting Nell to show her gratitude for his seminal role in her success. Nell was happy to ladle out gratitude for Edouardo's carpentry skills, his home-distilled vodka, his nasi goreng; indeed, she was grateful to him for a multitude of things, but not her publications. Even as her supervisor his input had been minimal: he had refused to read her thesis until it was finished. As for her books, his first and only scholarly comments were reserved for what he called the 'commodified vulgarity' of the covers.

As home and hearth grew increasingly chill, Nell discovered in herself a poor tolerance for other people's envy; nonetheless, she continued to love Edouardo and to share his belief in his intellectual might. In fact, if there had been any less love or any less belief, or if she had simply listened to the warnings from practically all her friends, she would not have proposed that she and Edouardo write a joint book. By the third of the planned twelve chapters, Edouardo's envy had all but evaporated, but his attitude of un-questioned authority was, quite literally, making her sick. One evening, on the way to the Moroccan Soup Bar to meet her husband for dinner, Nell stepped off the tram and vomited. If she were vomiting at Chapter 3, she feared terminal illness by Chapter 12. Clearly something needed to be done.

Nell used to say that Edouardo's envy coated the marriage like plaque, and was just as hard to remove. If he'd been a physi-cist or an historian, even an accountant, the marriage would have survived. 'Such a stylish man,' she would say. 'And of course very clever.'

But Laura would have none of it. 'The luxury of sentiment is the luxury of she who has moved on. You left Ted –' Edouardo from Melbourne's outer north-east was definitely Ted, 'you left him because you were bored, he was driving you mad, he was old enough for prostate problems, and –' a triumphant pause, 'you seduced me.'

Laura was supposed to have been Nell's trip on the wild side, a one-night stand or a long weekend at most. But somehow the long weekend stretched into a week, then months and finally years.

'Do you think I'm a lesbian?' Nell asked Laura on their second anniversary.

Laura had laughed, 'Either a lesbian or taking a very long detour.'

For Laura, and irrespective of Alan, there had never been any doubt. From the time of her first proper kiss she knew she was in trouble. It had happened at one of the last drive-in theatres in Melbourne to survive the property boom, with Laura easing into a yawn just as the boy bent to kiss her. Suddenly his tongue was writhing around in her mouth like a motorised sponge. He loved it and wondered why she had never kissed like that before. Laura thought it served her right for not having covered her mouth when she yawned.

Then there was Stephen, the son of two very silent sur- vivors. Stephen, burdened by much blame and self-hatred, had a penchant for punishment – giving it, although in hindsight Laura suspected he gave only to receive. Whatever his rationale, she could tolerate big, bloody bruises for only so long. And there was the problem of his five o'clock shadow even before lunch. With skin as fine and fair as hers, being with Stephen meant perpetual beard-rash.

Things hardly improved with penetration, although given it required so little attention, at least her mind was free to wander. But after a well-known stud from Melbourne's Polish-Jewish community failed to get an erection with her, Laura decided she had collected enough heterosexual experience and capitulated to her interest in girls.

This was better, much better, although because of her parents it made her feel guilty. Unbearably guilty. So after an all-too-brief respite, she returned to boys, or rather she turned to Alan Schwarz, her future husband. She liked him, he was fun, the sex was tolerable, she could think of worse compromises, and it made her parents so happy.

There are pivotal events of childhood, events which crystalise complex and immutable situations. Laura could be so sure of her parents' reaction to a lesbian daughter, or rather her mother's reaction, because of an incident when she was just fourteen which would forever remind her that Etti had pride of place in the suffering stakes. No pain, and certainly not the pain of staying with Alan, would ever equal what her mother had been through; and no pain would ever justify adding to her mother's woes.

It became one of the most embarrassing moments of her childhood. A group of students at her school had been picking on her, the usual sort of school bullying but nasty as bullying always is. After several months of terror and no longer wanting to go to school, Laura decided to tell her mother. A few sentences into her tale she realised her mistake, a few sentences more and Etti had seized the narrative. When *she* was fourteen, she said, people were so mean to her they tried to kill her. Laura swallowed her words. What had induced her to speak? And over such a paltry matter? She listened in silence to her mother's familiar story and hoped it would end there. But Etti, who knew suffering better than anyone, also knew love. The next day she stormed into the principal's office and subjected him to a tirade about the suffering of her daughter at the hands of students who were behaving like Nazis. That this could happen in Melbourne, Australia, in 1972, she said, was beyond the pale, and unless the principal punished the students responsible Etti would go to the police. The principal's office was in screaming distance of three portable classrooms. By morning recess everyone knew what Laura's mother had done. By morning recess Laura wanted to change schools.

'For my children I would do anything,' Etti said at dinner that evening. And to Laura, 'No need for thanks, darling.'

Laura did not risk speaking again. Not then, nor several years later when she turned away from temptation and married Alan. She watched his drug habit grow, she dedicated herself to protecting her parents from the truth, and three years later she buried him. And only at the end did she discover her parents had known all along. But a heroin-addicted son-in-law still seemed more acceptable than a lesbian daughter, so she maintained her silence. However, a couple of years after Alan's death, when wildly in love with big, butch, out and proud Colleen, it was difficult to hide the fact she was living with a woman in a one-bedroom flat located in the next street to her parents. The time had come for Laura to say something.

On the very evening she decided to raise the topic, or rather not *the* topic but perhaps a more general discussion about the alternatives to marriage, it was her brother, not her, who found himself the focus of the family's attention. Ten years older than Laura, well married to Melissa, father to Nick and Sophie, multimedia mogul in downtown Melbourne, Daniel had developed an interest in Judaism, or, to be more accurate, was galloping towards the Yeshiva.

In a secular Jewish family like the Lewins this was tantamount to conversion. You were Jewish, no need for advertising, no need to flaunt. So when Daniel turned up for dinner wearing a yarmulke, Laura knew to postpone her coming-out speech.

Neither Etti nor Henry could look at their son much less ask him to explain himself. Instead, after a whispered exchange with Henry, Etti took Melissa into the kitchen and demanded to know what Daniel was doing. Melissa, it seemed, was as unimpressed with her husband's slide into orthodoxy as were his parents. He was unstoppable, she said. It had been a mere six months since the rabbis had first arrived on their doorstep.

'Just doing a routine door-knock,' Melissa said. 'Like the Jehovah's Witnesses, and expecting the usual curt dismissal. But fortune was shining,' she raised one impeccably plucked eyebrow, 'Daniel opened the door and they hit the jackpot. Now we receive weekly visits from bearded, hatted, black-suited men, ostensibly enquiring after our welfare but really keeping an eye on us.'

Apparently Daniel had wanted Melissa to keep kosher. When she refused, he became a vegetarian. 'And now he wants the children to go to Jewish schools,' she said. 'Not just any Jewish schools, but *meshuggeneh frum* ones.'

'And the hat?' Etti said. 'What's with the hat?'

At first he wore it only at home and a baseball cap outside. For work he went bare-headed. But a baseball cap on a pudgy man in his thirties piqued even Daniel's sense of the aesthetic. 'The yarmulke is now a fixture,' Melissa said.

'Even when he goes out he wears it?'

Melissa nodded.

'And to the office he wears it?'

Another nod.

'And the children? Doesn't he care what his children think of their father?'

'They're treating it like another of his fads,' Melissa said. 'Like jogging and learning the trumpet.'

Etti called Henry to the kitchen, filled him in and told him he had to do something. Henry, always happy to leave discipline to his wife when the children were growing up, felt very differently now. He took Daniel aside and told him he was providing a poor example for his children.

'My own son reminds me of those *Östjuden* who lived in Berlin before the war.'

'And you remind me of those *Yekkes* you've always despised,' Daniel replied. 'But when you're scratched –' and he touched his yarmulke, 'scratched very lightly, you're no different from any other German Jew.'

Laura stood back and observed the proceedings. She'd been brittle with nervousness all week over her decision to come out to her parents, and here they were inconsolable about their son being too Jewish. She interpreted their response as yet another residual Holocaust fear; after all, the Jews who copped it first and worst under the Nazis were the visible, observant ones. Daniel's thoughts must have been on the same trail, for he was now spelling out the obvious: that Melbourne, Australia, circa 1983, while not free of anti-Semitism was nothing like Berlin of the thirties. It was important, he said, that Jews made their presence felt. 'We must appear strong to the outside world.'

'What's with this outside world?' Etti's voice was booming, her face all red and glossy. 'Only *meshuggeners* who live in ghettos would do this inside–outside stupidness. Normal Jews live in the world of their host country –'

'Don't give me this bullshit about host country.' In the process of exploding, Daniel resembled his mother to an uncanny degree. 'They're lucky to have us. Look at America, it'd be nothing without its influx of European Jews. Australia too.'

He was in the process of reciting a list of familiar names from business, the professions, politics and the arts when Laura stepped in and set about smoothing the waters. Daniel's religious choices were not hurting anyone, she said.

'But they are,' Etti was close to tears. 'My son is exposing his children to ridicule. His business will suffer. How will he provide?' Her moon face had crumpled. 'What would have happened if your father and I had dressed ourselves in yarmulkes and wigs? Do you think people would have bought our cakes then?'

The conversation went on for hours. Melissa said very little, Henry seemed to be in a state of shock, Etti attacked, Laura appeased and Daniel remained firm.

Over the next few months there were many similar conversations, all to no avail. Daniel became more religious, the children transferred to Jewish schools, Melissa led an increasingly separate life from her husband, Etti and Henry fretted, and Laura lived with Colleen in the one-bedroom flat and lied through her teeth.

Twelve months later, after she and Colleen had parted, Laura delivered her coming-out speech to her parents.

They were sad — 'Such a beautiful girl,' Etti said. 'You could get any boy.' — but not all that surprised. 'Didn't I say, Henry? Didn't I say after Alan? What sort of boy now for our Laura? Didn't I say?' And because there had been Alan, they hoped the situation would change.

It didn't. After Colleen came Barbara, then Rebecca, then Tanya and finally Nell. Laura introduced Nell to Etti not long before her mother died. 'A nice girl,' Etti remarked. 'A little more hair, a little make-up, a nice dress and she'd look just like Audrey Hepburn, although she doesn't speak so nice,' this last a reference to Nell's broad Australian accent. 'But the job is good.' Etti and Henry, like so many European Jews, regarded an academic position as the pinnacle of achievement.

Her parents would have loved a professor in the family, Laura was now thinking as she sat on the couch with the cat fast asleep in her lap. They would have been so proud. For just a few weeks after Henry's death, Nell had been promoted to associate professor. How Laura missed sharing these joys with her parents. How she missed them, period.

She checked her watch. Nell would be home from her barbecue soon. Laura moved the cat to one side and flipped through a couple of the files; it really was too late to start on them now. She should spend an hour at her parents' house, there was still so much to do. Etti had been such a hoarder and Laura couldn't bear to throw anything out. Just yesterday she had brought home a tablemat made of shells, a chipped mother-of-pearl butter knife, butterfly clips to tame Etti's frizz, her mother's 'at home' shoes – comfortable scuffs that were in tatters – and her peg bag made from the material of an old floral dress.

When Etti died Henry had wanted everything to remain the way she had left it. Not that he was being morbid, he said. Rather he was a man of habit and he'd always liked the way Etti did things. In fact, he liked everything about her. Which was how it had always been from his very first sight of her, a scrawny young girl all alone at the DP camp at Landsberg.

'From the beginning,' he would say, 'Etti was the one for me.'

Daniel and Laura used to joke about their father being a cradle-snatcher, but Etti would always spring to his defence. She believed Henry had saved her life.

Laura made herself a cup of coffee and went outside. There was a honeyeater fluttering in the grevillea, she watched it as she sipped her drink. Etti had accepted everything about Henry, including his silence on the past.

'Your father has his reasons,' she would say.

Henry was beyond criticism as far as Etti was concerned.

'If not for your father,' she repeated down the years, 'who knows what might have happened to me.'

Rough Wisdom

Etti believed that Henry had saved her – not from
death but an endless, accusing emptiness. She had
survived the years of persecution but at an indecent price, for at
war's end she had no one. She would say it over and over,
incredulous: I'm the only one left. If not for Henry, she said, her
future would be fit only for the scrap heap.

It was in 1945, at the American displaced persons' camp at
Landsberg that Henry first met her. By this time Etti had so
immured herself against further loss and horror she existed in her
own separate space. She refused to see, she refused to hear, she
shunned other people. She walked with her head down, her gaze
drawn to some middle distance in the dust. She sat alone, she ate
alone. She was shrivelled into herself, all bone and crevices.
Everything about her said: stay away from me.

Life was astonishingly cruel – or God or the Germans, it didn't
really matter, for this survival she'd suffered so strenuously wasn't
worth a kopek. There was no one left and life at all costs simply
wasn't worth it.

It had been a long trek from Lodz to Landsberg. While she had
been moving there had been a sense of hope, of striving towards
something: one of her sisters, her brother, an aunt, an uncle,

a cousin, it mattered less who it was just as long as there was someone. Onwards she went, travelling from one transit camp to the next, on trains and trucks and wagons. And walking, so much walking through that spring and summer of 1945, along with a sweeping convoy of human remains from the east. She had no idea with whom she was walking, no idea whose body jerked against hers on the trains; the whole continent was moving, mostly westwards like her, but not always. She would look closely at those going in the opposite direction, desperate to find a familiar face. And at the slightest recognition she might have turned around and accompanied the person home to Lodz. But would not go back alone. Not now. Not again.

Months earlier, before the thaw, when the Russians were filling the countryside and the Germans were retreating, Etti had left her hiding place in the barn and made her way back to Lodz. It was only forty kilometres, but the weather was hard and old dangers still threatened. When would it stop? she asked herself as she trudged along. When would there be shelter and warmth and food and family? When would life be more than a fiercely guarded memory? As for the bluntest question of all – how much longer could she bear up against the dangers and deprivations? – it was never asked, for the rough wisdom of her survival was stark and simple: you keep going until you die.

Back in Lodz she went straight to the area where her family had lived before they'd been forced into the ghetto. There were people in the streets – women with parcels, a mother carrying a baby, boys chasing each other; so much was familiar yet everything had changed. Or perhaps only Etti had changed, impossible to know for sure, yet she found herself choking on the injustice of these Poles going about their normal business when her own life had been wrecked. She couldn't get away fast enough. She ran and ran, towards the ghetto she ran, the ghetto she'd been forced to, enter years ago and later risked her life to leave, the ghetto which she now realised would probably yield the best information. Under different circumstances she might enjoy the absurdity of a voluntary return. But for now she just ran.

Several minutes later and out of breath, she entered the ghetto through a set of the double wood and wire gates. How much lower were the gates now and how benign without the guards, yet she still didn't feel free and she certainly didn't feel safe. But she had to know if anyone was left, so forced herself in a stealthy movement through the dismal streets.

The ghetto appeared as if shut down. The buildings were shrouded and splintering, and so many empty rooms, the furniture fed to the stove aeons ago and now just a scattering of rags and tatters across the gravelly floors. Don't look, she told herself, don't look at the remnants, having learned during the long years of loss that the things inadvertently left behind can be so cruelly voluble. Yet at the same time she cast an expert gaze across the floor, having also learned that survival can depend on other people's dross. She missed nothing, not inside nor outside in the slush and mud. She saw the sagging wooden buildings blotched like starving skin where the shutters had been removed long ago for firewood; and still posted on some of the walls, weather-stained notices with orders and decrees in German, Polish and Yiddish. Caught in the muck and wreckage were a doll's head, a scrap of shoe, a pretty button; and among the rubbish clogging the drains a length of blanket caked with filth but still holding together. And standing idle in the streets were the carts drawn not by animals during the long years of the ghetto but harnessed to men.

Everywhere was dirt, decay and detritus. And hardly any people. Although in a sad reflection, it didn't matter much whether there were people or not, for like Jewish Lodz itself, Etti, too, was shut down. She had a single mission: to find someone who had survived, just one other member of her family would suffice, beyond which nothing else mattered.

After so many solitary months, her ability to communicate had stiffened and it took all her efforts to collect the words required for the simple questions which might lead to her family. Otherwise she kept to herself, and continued to do so even when there were more people about. She had no tolerance for others with their competing pain, no strength against those offering kindness, and most of all, no armoury left to protect her from the Poles.

At the end of her life Etti would still be trying to make sense of it. The Poles had lost millions of their own: husbands, fathers, sons, and more women and children than could ever be explained. They had watched as their homes and farms, their cities and towns were destroyed; only the Jews had lost more. You'd think, she would say, the Poles and the Jews would be united in their loss. Instead, the Poles clung to their Jew-hatred more steadfastly than almost anything else. Indeed, there were Poles who having suffered horrendously at the hands of the Germans nonetheless believed the Germans had been right in wanting to rid the world of Jews. This Etti heard with her own ears.

How different was their attitude to Jewish possessions. A quick rub and a cleansing prayer, what Etti would later call 'Polish kosher', and it seemed any Jewish taint could be eliminated from bowls, cutlery, a nice picture frame, carpets, cooking pots, a pretty bracelet.

'We were as poor as you,' Etti said, when at last she mustered the courage to approach the Poles in her family's old flat. 'We had to work as hard as you.' But such appeals were useless. She explained she wanted very little of what her family had been forced to leave behind, just a few items of sentimental value. Yet even as she spoke she saw how much had been left, how much, in fact, was rightfully hers.

With space in the ghetto so limited – two rooms between eight people when the family first moved in, and later only the one room – they had taken only the essentials. They had managed to sell a few items in the panic of those last days, but the remainder of their possessions had stayed in the flat: plates, cooking utensils, bed linen, furniture, lamps, a whole range of household goods which Etti now tried to reassure the Polish family she did not want. All she was after, she said again, were a few items of sentimental value, worthless to anyone else.

She said 'worthless', but the Poles heard gold. 'What would my family be doing with gold?' Etti said. 'If they had possessed gold, would they have lived here? If they had possessed gold, wouldn't they have used it to leave Poland?' But either the Poles did not listen or would not believe.

Etti stood in the room where she had grown up. She saw her father's chair, she saw the table where her mother had prepared their meals, she saw the two embroidered mats made by her grandmother, the picture her sister Chana had painted as a child; she saw Lena's shawl on a stranger's back and Shimon's shears in a stranger's hands; she saw this family happy together like her family had once been. To lose everything is painful enough, but to have your losses so brazenly flaunted pushes you to breaking point.

They told her to leave, but she was about to go anyway. They said the flat was theirs and everything in it. They threatened to call the authorities should she ever return. She would never return.

If Etti were not crazed with loss and loneliness she might have given up at that point, but still hiding, still under threat, still looking over her shoulder, she continued what had become a dogged habit of survival. And she kept up her search for anyone, family or friend, to give her a future by supplying something of the past. Later she would say it was like living inside a barbed-wire costume. You see everything, and everything causes pain. And you feel so exposed that despite having suffered darkness enough for a lifetime, you find yourself preferring the shade of night.

Etti remained in Lodz until the middle of May, but none of her family returned. She decided there was no point in waiting any longer, particularly given the fate of most of the Lodz Jews. She left messages with the relief groups operating in the area, did a deal with a Russian which earned her a pair of strong boots, and joined the westward flow. Sometimes she moved in a small group, sometimes a larger one, and no one asked any questions. For like everyone else, she knew that among the masses of Poles and Ukrainians and people from the Baltic states fleeing the Russians were many who had been complicit in the wartime atrocities. Everyone knew, although no one said. These traitors headed west towards Germany and Austria and the DP camps that had been hastily established there, trampling down the dirt of their involvement as they walked, so that in a staggeringly short time they were able to present a pristine and convincing past to the authorities.

And Etti moves with the flow, feeling the swarm of humans around her. She tries not to think, just pushes herself onwards. As she walks through the warming air her greenish pale skin catches the sun and turns it rough and red. She feels the tight burning, but cannot find the energy to do anything about it. A woman about the same age as her own dead mother hands her some cloth; she wraps it round her face, leaving only her eyes free. With her slitted eyes and the cloth over her face she could be anyone. All those months in the hole beneath the barn have shrunk her young woman's body into a rickety child's, her small breasts are shrivelled, her limbs tightened to bony sticks, and the months in Lodz have done little to restore her. No one would know her now. She tears off the cloth: to be seen and not recognised is a prospect too awful. The next day she replaces it, not because of her blistering cheeks, but the endless hoping and the endless searching mean endless disappointments.

Her bones ache when she sits, even more when she lies down, and with the trains so slow she prefers to walk. And the noise of the walkers far preferable to the slow punishment of the train's clickety-clack: *you're on your own/ no one left/ you're on your own/ no one left.* And how effective the scraping of ill-shod feet to drown out individual complaints, individual losses, individual fears. For she wants no tales of woe, already has quite enough of her own. The background crunch and scrape is comforting, like walking through rushing wind or a busy street − except for the foul coal and slime smell of human dejection which refuses to let her forget even for a moment where she is.

Now and then a kindly stranger will approach, and when Etti makes no response, the person tries to touch. Can't abide the touch. No one must come close, no one is allowed to set up home in her heart. She wraps herself in herself and keeps moving. There is nothing more temporary than moving over strange ground, and nothing more permanent than the awful keening of a love searching for absent targets. Etti is only seventeen, survival's most brutal strategies are tucked beneath her skin; her poor heart is punch-drunk from its incessant throttling. She'll allow no one to add to her wreckage.

It does not occur to her to walk into the surrounding woods where she might lie down and die. When you have spent every day of the past several years struggling to survive, you have acquired the habit. You breathe, you eat, you walk, you survive. None of these things is questioned. But she does miss her cow.

The hole she lived in for six months was much the same size as a ghetto corpse wagon. Enclosed by a trapdoor in the floor of a barn, it had been used to store hay. For six long months this had been her sanctuary. Across the yard in the house were Paul and his wife, together with their five children. Only Paul knew of her existence and for the safety of his family it would remain that way. As he put it: If they don't know about you then they have no reason to lie.

It was September 1944 when Etti arrived at Paul's farm. She had been surviving in the countryside since early July when she had escaped from the ghetto. At that time the ghetto was continuing to function with nearly seventy thousand Jews still alive and working, although Etti's family was not among them. Her father was dead, and two weeks before she escaped, her two sisters and brother had boarded a train that was supposed to take them to a work camp in Germany; five days later her mother had died from a brain fever. With nothing more to lose and no one left in the ghetto who mattered, the dangers of escaping were stripped of threat.

And then there was her work. Rumkowski, the leader of the elders in the ghetto, had said that work would save the Lodz Jews and her own father had agreed. But without her sisters beside her, and unable to explain exactly why, her work with the old clothes somehow became entangled with her family's safety.

About a year before she escaped the ghetto, Etti, together with her two sisters and mother, had been transferred to one of the old-clothes workshops. At around the same time, her father and brother were removed from the shoemaking workshop where they'd been since the family entered the ghetto in 1940, and assigned to the mountains of shoes in the old-shoe workshop.

The source of the old clothes and shoes was a mystery, and although there were rumours, so terrible were they, people preferred the mystery. There were clothes of men, women, children and babies. Some clothes were patched and ragged, others were practically new. There were clothes of poor people and others of such exquisite quality that Etti touched with awe. Such a variety of clothes that if you could match them with their owners you might have all of Warsaw or Krakow, even Lodz itself. There was a peculiar chill to know so much about unknown and absent people: who had painful bunions yet had to work the fields, who by their white cuffs never did any work at all; which men had wives to take care of them and which women had husbands who appreciated them. You could learn so much from piles of old clothes but the last thing you wanted to know was the truth.

When the rumours began to circulate that these were the clothes of dead Jews, no one wanted to believe such a thing, no one could believe, just kept on working – for their lives, so Rumkowski said. Huge containers of clothes brought to the ghetto, enough to keep countless people working, the ghetto Jews sorted, they repaired, they were ordered not to waste a single scrap of these clothes, and neither they did. For their lives.

It was the shoes that killed Etti's father, or more specifically a single shoe. Etti was twelve when they first entered the ghetto and growing fast, particularly in the early months when there was more food available. Later, when there was no food and with the rest of her body shrinking, her hands and feet kept on growing, her skull too. Seems that bone can grow on air.

For small children in the ghetto there were scraps of cloth and leather that could be fashioned into shoes. Adults could replace their shoes from the stock that became available when people died, and there were the ghetto's wooden clogs. But for those in between like Etti, when her shoes wore out, replacements were hard to find. Her father patched as best he could, reinforcing with upholstery hessian and his father's *tefillin*, preserved to the old man's blessed memory but now turned to more urgent use. But the winter of 1943 was harsh, and despite her careful walking through the ghetto's unpaved streets, Etti's shoes broke about her feet. Her father now working in the old-shoe workshop succeeded in stealing a left boot, perfect when stuffed with paper. But two days later when he was caught with a right boot hidden in his jacket, he was shot.

Murdered for a shoe. These Germans, so scrupulous, so efficient when it came to preserving old shoes and clothes, dispensed so easily with human life. As Etti stood at the long table sorting old clothes, her left foot in a good boot and the other wrapped in rags, it was as if she and the rest of her family, indeed everyone in the ghetto were being made to work like starving people in a kitchen: up to their elbows in what they most needed but would lose their lives if ever they were to take.

Her father was dead, and before him his mother, and within a month of his death, his mother-in-law. That left Etti, her two sisters, her brother, her mother and a welter of rumours. Many years later Etti would tell her own children that a rumour reveals something which should not have happened but is in fact true. As a girl in the ghetto, though, rather than truths, Etti was aware only of fantastic and improbable stories and tried not to dwell. So when early in the summer of 1944 notices announced that several thousand people from the ghetto were to be resettled at work camps in Germany, despite the thicket of rumours, many people, Etti's family among them, jumped at the opportunity, believing that anything would be better than the crowded, disease-riddled ghetto with its starving, demoralised inhabitants.

Such promises these Germans made, of work, of food, of shelter, but all were euphemisms for death. Their ingenuity was breathtaking. They would work you to death. Starve you. Freeze you. Deceive you. Shoot you. Bash you. Hang you. Torture you. Infect you. Gas you. Her two sisters and her brother were taken just a few kilometres to Chelmno where they were crowded into special vans. In the three hundred metres it took for the vans to roll to the mouth of the crematorium, Chana, Lena and Shimon were killed. It was like the clothes, it was like the shoes, everything must be saved except the Jews. And when she heard the truth about her sisters and brother, she knew the truth of the clothes, the clothes she had touched with her own hands, clothes that in her memory felt like human skin.

Etti did not plan her escape from the ghetto, rather a never-before-seen opportunity arose and she seized it. It was dusk, before the searchlights were lit, and two guards more interested in a jar of vodka than watching the gates. She saw, she did not think, she ran.

For the next two months she scuttled through the countryside surviving as best she could. She was lucky it was summer, and fortunate, too, she was blonde. But without the right papers and always on the run, survival exacted a shocking toll.

When she arrived at Paul's farm she was broken, starving and exhausted. Whatever Paul wanted in payment he could have, she said, just as long as she could rest for a few days. With that she started at the rags of her jacket, her bony hands picking at the fastenings. A father and good Catholic with a daughter much the same age as Etti, Paul watched horrified as this child offered her scrap of a body. What was God doing that men could be such monsters and children forced into such depravity? Paul told her to fix her clothes, that he wanted nothing from her; he spoke gently so as not to embarrass, then took her to his barn. It wasn't much, he said as he lifted the trapdoor and showed her the storage hole, but neither could he risk having her in the house.

He fixed a handle to the inside of the trapdoor so Etti could open it from below – but only at night, Paul said, was she to venture out – and loosened one of the boards so she could slip it sideways to let in some light during the day. He brought clothes to replace her rags, and newspapers to fold between the layers of her clothing. He provided hessian and straw for lining the hole, and the pièce de résistance, a quilt which looked almost new. He was far from being a rich man, he said, but as God had brought Etti to him, it was his duty to take care of her. Nearly every day he left food for her in a tin to protect it from vermin, and after nightfall she would emerge from her hole. She would make a nest with the hay and the quilt, curl into her thin warmth and eat.

At first the cows were uneasy, such lumbering shadowy beasts with their frosted breath and flicking tails, but soon they adjusted. In time it was as if her world blended with theirs: same home, same cycles of fitful sleep, same caked-on filth, same smell. How shamed her mother would have been, Etti thought as she tried to remove some of the dirt. And before the thought grew, she would shut it down, because totting up the losses made survival that much harder.

You live in your head when the obstacles of living in the world become too great. All the time Etti was in the barn, the cold hacked into her like an ice cutter. She would gather the good thoughts and separate them into stories, each story set in America where it was always light and warm with plenty of food and her family together again. The seam between waking and sleeping blurred while she lived in one or other of her storylands for whole days at a time.

She went to the toilet as seldom and neatly as possible, firstly in the barn, her smells mixing with those of the cows, but as she trained to hold her bowels, sometimes for more than a week, she would, under cover of night, venture out of the barn beneath a tent made of the quilt and find a place among the trees. As she shrugged off the hiss and spit of night noises, she was struck by how much she had changed: once so scared of creatures, now it was only people who frightened.

She made friends with the cows, one in particular, a smooth caramel beast whose stall was closest to her trapdoor. The cow would watch as Etti climbed out of her hole, the glassy brown eyes glinting as they caught the light. It was the cow who made the first move, a gentle nudge in the back as Etti sat eating at the edge of her hole. The cow must be hungry, Etti decided. She had put aside a small piece of meat to eat in a day or two, closer to when she would next have to move her bowels – she'd learned which foods settled and which ones made a fuss – and now after a brief hesitation she retrieved it; after all, this was the cow's home and she the trespasser. But the cow showed no interest in the meat, just moved closer to Etti and nuzzled into her side.

Decades later, Etti would say she owed her life to a good Polish farmer and a lonely cow. After that initial contact, Etti would eat her food, turn fresh hay in the stall and stretch out along the cow's flank, and there she would sleep for two maybe three hours, sucking in the warm alive smell of her cow, properly sleep, rather than the fitful time-filling she did during the day.

Months later, when the Russians came into the countryside and Paul deemed it safe for Etti to emerge, it turned out he had hidden a whole family as well as her. Here was a man so good that Etti's poor wracked brain could not quite assimilate it. The cow, however, was easy to understand. Etti wrenched herself from that cow as her family had been wrenched from her. And never again would she eat meat. It's not beef, she would say to Laura and Daniel, it's a cow. It's not a chop, she would say, it's a lamb. Chicken, in contrast, presented her with no such problems. No chicken, she told her children, ever saved a girl's life.

—

'Just take a look at all this,' Laura said to Nell.

It was four months after Henry's death. Etti and Henry's home was up for sale and all the contents had been dispersed, with a good proportion ending up at Laura and Nell's place. Laura was standing at the kitchen bench. Set out in front of her were a bit of blanket, a dozen old letters from Paul the Polish farmer and some more recent ones from one of his daughters. There were nine plastic cows each individually wrapped in tissue paper, a flap of old shoe, a pair of tattered mittens, the faded photo of Etti's family in Lodz, a purse, a scrap of shawl, two stones, a copy of the tape Etti had made for the Holocaust Museum and a transcript of the tape.

Nell and Laura took them in.

'They're remarkably volatile,' Nell said at last.

Laura did not answer, could not answer, just wanted the things out of sight. She bundled them up and returned them to their box, wondering when it would all stop. Her mother had been dead five, nearly six years, and still her horrors kept coming. In all Etti's telling of her past, she had never paraded this collection, or rather not as a *collection*. Laura had seen a couple of single items, but the cows, the stones, the scraps of clothes were new to her. And while she knew about the tape, she had never wanted to listen to it when her mother was alive, and after Etti died, was terrified of what new horrors it might contain.

She closed the box and moved it to the end of the bench, then a minute or two later picked it up and took it into her study. To deal with later, she told herself. Of course Daniel would need to know about these things, although she doubted he would be interested. He'd had so little involvement with the clearing of the house, had left it to his wife to lend a hand; neither had he wanted much in the way of Henry and Etti's possessions.

So much for the sentimental Jew, thought Laura, again experiencing a longing for the brother she once had. As for Etti's box of memories, even before he became religious Daniel had been critical of what he termed 'Holocaust fixations'. He believed that dwelling on a single tragic moment in Jewish history to the exclusion of millennia of Jewish learning and discovery was a greater threat to the future of Judaism than the Holocaust itself. The Holocaust, he said, had taken over Judaism. And even when Laura and Melissa insisted that sorting through Henry and Etti's possessions was about his parents not the Holocaust, he still refused to be involved.

As it happened, it had been a comfort doing the job with Melissa. Revealing considerably more foresight than her husband, Melissa had selected a number of Etti's things to keep for the children and quite a few items for herself. She had not been particularly close to Henry, she used to joke that with her

Australian background she was the wrong sort of Jew for him, but she and Etti had enjoyed a special connection.

'There's a safety zone between a woman and her daughter-in-law,' Melissa said one day when she and Laura were working together at the house. 'The relationship begins somewhere beyond that often very fraught space which is the sole domain of your own children.' She paused a moment to wrap one of Etti's pieces of fake Venetian glass. 'Your mother had nothing to lose with me. I was never dangerous ground for her so she could let herself go. And for me it was all pleasure: no guilt, no resentment, no debts.'

Melissa had wanted some of Etti's crockery, also a selection of her *tchutchkas*, that vast collection of ornaments and objects which reflected Etti's sense of the aesthetic but no one else's. Laura was amazed: Melissa and style were welded together.

'I know your mother had appalling taste,' Melissa said. 'But without her appalling taste she wouldn't have been Etti.'

Melissa had selected a coral-coloured fake Venetian glass ser-viette holder – 'I'll use it for envelopes' – a set of fruit knives with mother-of-pearl handles housed within a huge mother-of-pearl shell – 'It's a conversation piece' – a mother-of-pearl butter knife – 'Etti could have gone into the mother-of-pearl business' – and a trio of amber-coloured glass pigeons grazing on amber-coloured glass grass which doubled as a hall lamp.

As for the rest, Laura's reluctance to get rid of anything which had been important to her mother had left her with several cartons of kitchen goods she and Nell did not need, her mother's jewel-lery – most of it clunk and paste – and the remainder of Etti's *tchutchkas*.

'We'll have to move house to accommodate your mother's hoarding,' Nell said when Laura brought everything home.

It was easier with Henry's things, there being so few. And the personal items, even the everyday ones like his watch and cuff-links somehow less attached to the person he was. His baking implements, however, were in quite a different category and Laura had wanted to keep these, not that she ever baked but they had revealed a side to her father that rarely surfaced in the rest of his life.

'Here are my words,' he used to say, indicating his cakes. 'Here are my words.'

'Don't you find it odd,' Nell now said as she cleared a shelf for Henry's baking implements, 'that your father should so assiduously remove every element of his Germanness?'

Laura shook her head. It was obvious to her that extreme circumstances demanded extreme responses. But with Etti's cache of Holocaust horrors so fresh, she would prefer a change of topic, so decided not to elaborate.

'To jettison an entire language,' Nell persisted. And then a moment later: 'I wonder what language he dreamed in.'

Laura felt herself bristle: she didn't want to talk about this. And besides, Nell's comment showed that even after all these years there were things she would never understand.

'So teach me,' Nell said, responding to the exasperation on Laura's face. 'I want to understand.'

Laura sighed. All she wanted was a few hours in the sunny present. And besides, there was nothing more to say; Nell already knew about Henry's escape into Holland, his incarceration at Westerbork, the move to Belsen in 1944 where only pure luck had saved him from typhus. Peace, she found herself thinking, just give me a few hours peace. But Nell was waiting.

'I can't answer for his dreams,' Laura said at last. 'As for the rest, you know all there is to know about him.'

'And a wife?' Nell said. 'What about another wife? He was so much older than your mother. Was he married before? Were there any children?'

Nell, following her own interests in true Nell fashion, seemed totally oblivious to Laura's mood. And now it was too late. A wife? Another family? How painfully incriminating were the questions Laura never thought to ask. Her father had never suggested another family, so the possibility had never occurred to her. He had been twenty-nine when war broke out, old enough to be married and certainly old enough for children. But how completely can one block out the past, even a person as thorough as her father? Surely not to the extent of another family?

There was a chorus in her brain pleading against a first family and in its wake an echoing doubt. With her guilt gathering strength, she assured Nell there had been neither wife nor children, not simply because the habit of protecting her parents was so deeply ingrained, but because it seemed such a mark of failure that this most basic of considerations had never figured in her own map of Henry. What else, Laura wondered, had she not asked him? And had he been aware of her omissions? Had he been hurt by them?

'Are you sure?' Nell said. 'No wife? No children? Nothing stashed away behind that strong silent facade.'

Laura laughed although she really wanted to stifle. 'I'm sure there was plenty, but not another a family.'

Nell finished stacking the baking implements. 'The last of their brilliant career,' she said. And, Laura hoped, the last of Nell's curiosity.

But it was not to be. Everything was packed away and a free afternoon stretched before them when Nell brought Etti's special cache of memories back into the kitchen. Laura waved them away.

'You can't just ignore them,' Nell said. And when Laura failed to make a move, Nell took out the items and again displayed them on the bench.

Laura stood back and watched. 'Mother's memories,' she said at last, 'and now my pellets of uranium.'

She forced herself to survey the things. Precious enough to keep close, yet profoundly uncomfortable, they posed a danger to the smooth conduct of her life. She wanted to preserve them, no question of that, but she didn't want to be stumbling over them all the time. She recalled a cardboard gift box someone had given her, printed in a riot of flowers and sparkle which Etti would have loved. It would be perfect. She rummaged around until she found it, tossed aside the old bills it contained, packed up all Etti's bits of a saved life, searched for some tape, sealed the box and put it at the back of the cupboard under the stairs to glow like uranium, with a half-life that given the modern memory was not long enough. The whole exercise took less than ten minutes. She felt much more her old self when she returned to the kitchen.

She walked over to the windows and looked out. 'How about a stroll along Merri Creek while the weather's still fine.'

Then she saw the transcript in Nell's hand.

'What are you doing with that?'

'I took it out of the box.'

Laura could not believe it. She had herself paused a moment over both the tape and transcript, but the possibility her mother had held something back from the family, perhaps the worst atrocity of all, had settled the issue, and she had quickly added both to the box. Then Nell had taken the transcript out. Laura simply couldn't believe it.

Nell was now at her side, an arm around her shoulders. Laura tried to shake her off. But Nell was firm. 'By all means store the tape,' she said. 'You'll know when it's time to hear your mother's voice again. But the transcript is different. All these years since your mother's death, and how many times have you said that silence never suited her? So here's a fresh crop of her words, and nicely cushioned by print.'

Fresh or not, these were not the words Laura was wanting from her mother. She was furious with Nell. She had no right.

Nell insisted she was only thinking of Laura. 'You can't just pretend it doesn't exist,' she said.

She made a pot of coffee, talking gently and persuasively all the while. And continued to talk while they drank it.

'If you're unable to read it,' she said at last, 'let me.' She leafed through the pages. 'There's quite a lot here about your father. Perhaps there's something about the American woman.'

Laura didn't know what to do. Such fear of what might happen, how sentences lead to corners, and around every corner unexpected dangers. Or, it suddenly occurred to her, perhaps unexpected surprises, not-unpleasant surprises. Perhaps even the knowledge there was in fact nothing to fear.

'All right then,' she said at last. 'And yes, you read it to me.'

They settled themselves into armchairs, one either side of the room. Laura curled her legs beneath her, and at the first words she closed her eyes. Nell read through the late afternoon. There were intermittent storms of a hard pelting rain followed by an almost blinding sun, and in that brief brightness steam would swirl off the wooden deck. And the clouds would roll in again and more rain. As Nell continued, Laura felt herself pulled back through the years to the desolation of postwar Europe, to hordes of bedraggled people hauling themselves over rough terrain, and among them her mother, no bigger than a child and pathetically alone.

June 1945 and a burning sun and Etti is still walking. After Paul's farm, after the hideous return to Lodz, after the first of the assembly points, Etti is moving westwards. As absurd as it may seem, Germany is safer than Poland for a Jew.

She knows yet cannot believe that everyone she loves is dead. It makes no sense that she, an ordinary girl after all, would be the only one spared. Although that sentiment sparks of God and she's jettisoned him; cows are more reliable, more useful too.

As she walks through the dusty heat and insect haze, she is entirely alone. In the mornings the sun blazes hot against her back, in the afternoons it glares whitely in her eyes. Her feet burn no matter what the time of day. Members of the *Bricha*, the Jewish underground, are hard at work gathering up Jews and escorting them to safety. Or if she's to believe the rumours, the *Bricha*, comprised of hardline Zionists, will only pretend to guide you to one of the DP camps and spirit you to Palestine instead. Etti, so vague about what she wants, knows she does not want Palestine. It is, as far as she is concerned, just another Jewish ghetto despite its orchards and olive groves. She doesn't want the *Bricha's* help, she doesn't want anyone to tell her where to go or what to do, so she makes up an American relative, an aunt in New York, and if the *Bricha*, or anyone else for that matter, questions her destination, she will say she is heading towards the Americans in Germany and from there she hopes to join her aunt in America.

Etti wouldn't know where to find America on a map.

Death is everywhere, death has been a constant ever since she and her family moved into the ghetto. At first there was a stream of deaths, then with the disease and starvation and the decay of too many people in far too small a space, a torrent. And a distinctive smell, a putrid, throat-stopping, sweet-and-sour smell. And now on the move at the end of the war the death smell is everywhere, a stinking rot that clings like a damp blanket. Her own skin becomes death-wrapped; where she goes, goes death.

Etti gathers the shell of herself and for the next month, on foot, by lorry, by train, she crosses Poland down into Czechoslovakia and on to Germany. Advice is thick in the air, facts are thin on the ground. Some say go here, others say go there, and Etti decides she'll go wherever people dispense soup and care and ask no questions. As she approaches the German border she hears that

Germany has been occupied not just by the Americans and British but by the Russians and French as well. Each country has set up its own camps. To choose between the four is like being presented with four different types of potato.

As it happens there is no choice. She and her group are shepherded off a train not far from Munich and taken to a nearby camp. It is July and hot and Etti and her fellow travellers hesitant with heat and exhaustion. The camp is large without trees or grass and rimmed with barbed wire – just like the concentration camps, someone says, but as far as Etti is concerned it's just another blatantly temporary place for people who are prey to the temporary. The camp is run by Americans, and a proud lot they are. They won the war and they want gratitude. Their memories are not so much short as poorly sourced, for they seem not to know what the Jews have suffered.

In this camp Jews are not only outnumbered ten to one, they are the dregs. The Americans far prefer the Poles and Balts, so much neater, cleaner and tidier than the Jews, and more obliging and courteous as well. But even more desirable and certainly more helpful are the Germans. Etti is horrified. Germans have been given positions of responsibility in this camp. So despite all that's happened, Germans are still ordering Jews around. The Americans don't seem to understand. One day a crust of bread separates you from death, one day herded into showers and killed, one day hounded by Germans and Poles and Ukrainians, and the next day the war is over, there's food for all, the showers don't kill and you're expected to live among your murderers. Etti is not surprised to find Jews pushing themselves forward for food, or reluctant to enter the showers, or failing to obey orders given by their recent persecutors. Even with her limited education and guardedly shut off from the world, Etti has no trouble understanding the situation. But not so her keepers.

Old enemies are everywhere. In Etti's barracks there are four Jews and the rest are Poles. These Americans group DPs according to nationality not persecution. The hatred is so thick you couldn't cut it with a sharp knife. Etti hates the Poles even more than she hates the Germans – because of the betrayal, because a long time ago before living memory she had Polish friends, because they so strenuously denied her when her need for them surpassed the threat of death. A cupboard, a corner, the dark beneath a bed, she would have crouched anywhere if it were offered. But until she met the farmer it was not. 'You want to kill us?' her former friends would say. 'You want our blood on your hands?'

And what of the blood on Polish hands? she wonders. What of that invisible stain?

There's no leaving this camp and no place to hide. Etti passes the mornings wandering the perimeter of the area, avoiding the faces of her enemies. In the early afternoon when most of the people are elsewhere, she returns to her space in the long Nissen hut, wraps herself in a blanket like she did with the quilt in Paul's barn and transports herself into her imaginings. One day she observes a Jewish woman stealing food from the possessions of one of the Poles. Etti deliberately makes a sound. The woman whips around but when she sees it is Etti visibly relaxes. 'If they had stolen only food from me,' she says, 'I wouldn't be stealing from them now.'

Etti hears the situation is no better in the British camps. Why can't people understand what they've been through? But far from understanding, these Americans actually want gratitude. For what? Why should any seventeen year old be grateful to be alive? Seventeen year olds expect to be alive. And where's the gratitude in having survived everyone and everything you've ever held dear only to find yourself still at the bottom of the pile? Easy for the Poles and Balts and Germans to be grateful, they've chosen their displacement, but no one wants the Jews, not even when there are so few left. Although one of the Americans, his hands roving through Etti's blonde hair and over the soft skin of her neck, tells her she'll have no trouble. 'You don't look Jewish,' he says.

Then all of a sudden conditions change, and all because of Earl G Harrison, one of the few heroes to emerge from Etti's war. President Truman himself sent Mr Harrison to investigate conditions in the DP camps in Germany and Austria, and as a result of his report, special camps were quickly established for Jews. In early Autumn Etti arrived at the Jewish camp at Landsberg.

'And here my Cinderella story begins,' Etti would say. 'Here comes my prince.'

'Not that she made it so easy,' Henry would add at this point in the story. 'She was hardly in this world when I met her.'

In the first weeks after Etti arrived at Landsberg she kept to herself. She shared a cubicle with three other girls, all of whom like Etti preferred silence to airing their memories. She was eating well, had a period for the second time in her life, checked the lists for names she might recognise, put out searches of her own, built a small garden, started to learn English, acquainted herself with the operations of the black market, and kept her mind pinned firmly to the present. Not that she had any alternative, none of the Jewish DPs were going anywhere fast. She couldn't help but wonder if the situation were any different in the non-Jewish camps, whether large numbers of Poles and Lithuanians and Germans and Ukrainians were at this very moment on their way to America or Britain or Canada. She still had no preference as to where she wanted to emigrate, but was now thinking Palestine might well be the best option. For if there was one thing she was learning, it was that no one but Jews would welcome other Jews.

Although even among Jews, she discovered, there were some more welcome than others. German and Austrian Jews placed themselves at the top of the hierarchy, followed by the Hungarians, then the French and so on down to the Polish Jews at the very bottom. There was a hierarchy of suffering too, in which people who had not been incarcerated in a concentration camp were assumed to have faired well in the suffering stakes. Best not to talk, she decided, best not to attempt any explanation. So when Henry, still Heinrich then, first called out to her – clear what he said despite his garbled Yiddish – she made no sign of having heard, just continued on her way.

Henry was not so easily deterred. Next he called out in borrowed Polish, still no response. Finally he put speech aside, hurried past her, turned and stood in her path.

'You,' he said in his Germanised Yiddish. 'You want some cake?'

Etti stopped because she had no choice, saw the cake in his palm and deciphered his speech. She could not raise her gaze to his face and neither did she want to. She just stood there waiting for him to step aside. Then she felt his hand on her arm, felt him open her fist, felt the cake in her palm, and knew that if it were anything other than food she would have pulled away. But it was food, and food demanded a response. She closed her fingers over the cake, stepped off the path and retreated to an area at the outer rim of the huts. The cake was delicious.

'And I was still learning then,' Henry would always say.

Despite his usual reticence about the past, Henry liked to tell how as a young man in Berlin he had been apprenticed to a Jewish pastry-cook, how he had learned enough about kosher cooking to bluff his way into a job in the Landsberg kitchens. And a good thing it was too, for Etti said she married him primarily because he knew how to cook. But in truth she married him because she had no one else. No one emerged from the searches she put out through the DP network, and Henry, who was older and stronger, had no one either.

'So you weren't in love when you married?' Laura had once asked her mother.

Etti was scornful. 'This "in love" you think is so special, it happens only in the pictures. Cary Grant and Hedy Lamar, did you ever see them in a DP camp? And with eyes you can see your father is no Cary Grant, not even Clark Gable, despite the teeth. And back in those days the teeth they weren't so good. But I respected him and he could cook, and he was kind and good. This was what I was wanting: kindness and goodness. And when there was time, the love would come.'

And so it did. Etti and Henry's marriage had been full of love.

Laura sat quiet and pensive savouring her mother's story, in particular the happy ending. The drill of peak-hour traffic on the flyover filled the air, and the rattle of a distant train. Outside the sun was low. The rain had eased to the east, the air was fresh and crisp. Her mother's words lingered comfortably. She was grateful to Nell for forcing the issue.

'It's a hell of a story,' Nell said, flipping through the transcript. 'And what a film it would make.'

Laura smiled but remained silent. She wanted to stay with her mother's words a while longer. There had been nothing more to learn, she kept saying to herself. Nothing more to learn.

'A perfect human interest story with a happy ending,' Nell continued. 'Set against an important historical context. *Etti's Story*. I can see it in lights. International funding: European, Australian, and if we could find a positive role for an American, some American dollars as well.'

And still just a smile from Laura. Etti had no secrets while she was alive and of course would not have left behind a cache to explode after her death. Laura should never have doubted her.

She gazed outside, how different was the situation with her father. And as a cool breeze blew in through the open door, she was reminded of those evenings when she would pop in to see him after work and find him at his marble bench, the radio switched to the news station, and Henry murmuring to himself, invariably in German.

'The deep waters they are running still,' Etti used to say about her husband.

With no children of her own, Laura had only the one family. With her parents' death and her brother's disappearance behind his beard and hat, her family was gone. In the failing light she looked across to Nell. This woman would never replace family, but when it came to love and support, she gave in abundance. 'Enough love to be a Jew,' Nell had once joked. Laura now stretched out her arm and laid her fingers to the side of Nell's neck, drew her close and kissed her. Then, with glasses of wine, the two of them went outside to the deck.

Rainbow lorikeets flew overhead in flashes of noisy brilliance. Under the darkening sky the two women sat with their thoughts, sipping their drinks.

It was Nell who broke the silence.

'Your father was not an easy man to know.'

Laura had been thinking much the same thing – a little resentfully it must be said. And now feeling guilty, as if Nell had read her mind.

'Survivors like my mother made a life out of their memories,' she said, determined to make amends. 'While others, my father among them, could only live if they deliberately forgot.'

Although she wished it had been otherwise, for his choices had been her losses. 'When he shut down his language,' she now added, 'he also shut down his past.'

'But to such an extent?'

Laura unpinned her heavy mass of curls, let the hair fall briefly over her shoulders, then twisted it back into a tighter knot. She knew what Nell was implying. So much evidence in recent years of how only the strong survived, and how survival always came at a cost. She took Nell's hand and held it a moment before replying.

'If he wanted to keep his secrets, then so be it. There's nothing I wouldn't forgive him.'

But even as she spoke, Laura knew she was lying. It was true, there was nothing she would not forgive him, but now he was gone there was nothing she did not want to know. She thought of the American, that hard little woman, and felt again the temptation to discover who she was. This woman had known Henry, and no matter what she might have said, it was clear now to Laura that her visit halfway across the world was specifically to see him. This woman had lost both parents in the Holocaust. Henry had admitted to knowing her father. There were people alive in the world who had more information about Laura's own father than Laura did herself. She was prepared for the worst, although if asked could not have said what that might be, but suddenly she needed to know what in Henry's past was so explosive that half a life had to be shut down.

Part III

THE NEW CENTURY

Hooked on the Holocaust

Early in the new millennium Alice Carter's son, Raphe, is standing at the lip of a volcano on an island off New Zealand, gazing into a blast of billowing ash and steam. You need to choose carefully whom you take to a volcano, he thinks, as he watches a long-established husband and wife team who began their quarrel back on the mainland, continued it throughout the ninety-minute boat journey, suspended it briefly when they first stepped on the island and again a short time later when forced to don gas masks. Now against the hiss and rush of the volcano they are shouting at each other and shoving too, and Raphe wishing they would take their blustering to a safer part of the island.

He turns ever so slightly to remove the couple from view. He mustn't let them spoil this visit, this highly symbolic visit, he reminds himself, to mark the new century. He redirects his attention to the fizzing crater, trying to forge the physical connection he always feels when in the presence of a volcano. All around him is ash and cracks and plumes of steam, and the hiss and bubble of boiling water. Against such devastation he has a sense of being so small, neat too, in his jeans and cropped jacket, his thick dark hair slicked back from his face, and his red sweater so bright against the deep grey of the island. He turns further from the feuding couple and deeper into the boiling landscape, and at last he feels himself settle.

Raphe Carter loves volcanoes. Their power, the detonated shock of them, their utterly inescapable lethal beauty promote in contrast an exquisite peace. It was precisely because of this he had wanted to mark the new century with a new volcano, set the right tone from the beginning. For only with the whole of the earth's innards heaving and raw do his abbreviated family history and sorry absence of relatives, even his unremitting failure at relationships become irrelevant. Only here is the truth about his grandfather, Martin Lewin, drowned out by a larger noise. Of course he loves volcanoes, with their reliable respite from a life stretched on the rack.

He glances again at the couple. So intent are they on their hatred they seem unaware of how close to the edge they are. A little shove from him, a little nudge from her and only one of them will be walking back to the boat. Raphe pictures it now all so clearly, but instead of the warring couple, it is he and Laura Lewin who visit a volcano and only one of them returns. And in a flash his sense of peace explodes.

A couple of years earlier, following the second of her heart attacks and not long before her death, his mother had revealed how his grandfather had died.

Her exact words were: 'When I went to Australia, I met the man who killed my father.'

Alice had paused, just the briefest of moments, but long enough for the words to strike. Raphe's grandfather, his alter ego, the one member of her family she had bequeathed to him, his own guardian angel. And when she told the story it was not as if his grandfather were being killed all over again, it was as if he were being killed for the very first time.

She related the events of Martin Lewin's death as calmly as if she were describing a visit to an art gallery. She told the tale so vividly Raphe might have been in that German wood himself, along with his grandfather and the man who should have been Martin's saviour but was not. The story was long in the telling and Alice extremely weak. Sometimes her voice dropped to a whisper but she never faltered. Only when she was finished did she succumb to exhaustion, sinking into her cushions, her eyes firmly shut.

Some time passed before she spoke again. 'Now Henry Lewin's dead too.'

Although not before he'd led a full and active life, Raphe was thinking, eighty-five years of a full and active life. He clenched on his hostility, and asked whether this Henry Lewin had shown any repentance. His mother had shrugged as if to say: What would be the point? How could a man repent an action that had provided him with his own life?

Raphe was outraged. 'So in similar circumstances he might do the same again?'

Again his mother shrugged. 'I don't know. I think he was sorry for what he'd done.'

'And what about the son and daughter? Any contrition there?'

His mother doubted they even knew the truth. 'He seemed too close to the daughter, Laura, to want to upset her, and too distant from the religious son to bother.'

Passions are buxom, rambunctious things which rarely play second fiddle to reason. His beloved grandfather, the best part of himself: Raphe's rage sparked and boiled and burst through his skin and clung to him like ash from a volcano. And revenge, how he longed for revenge, he, who would have preferred a more admirable response but simply couldn't find it in himself. Certain wrongs would always be wrongs, murder in the past was no less murder now, and most crucial of all, no one had paid for his grandfather's death and someone damn well ought to.

'Jehovah is a kind and benevolent judge compared with you,' Alice used to say when as a boy Raphe would pass judgment on another child, or a relative, or the man who ran the drugstore; in fact, anyone who acted contrary to Raphe's definition of right. While still in elementary school Raphe had decided to study law when he grew up, and that had remained the plan until he went to college and suddenly opted for English and history. His father was unhappy about the decision, he saw no future in it, but his mother was clearly pleased. She'd often talked about her own father's love of books, and here was her son following in his footsteps.

He told his parents he had lost interest in the law, but in truth, post-Vietnam, post-Watergate, and with crowds jostling for air on death row, the law had failed to live up to his expectations. Words, he decided, were more powerful; words, as history had so persuasively demonstrated, could drive people to commit unpardonable atrocities; and words, Raphe concluded after immersing himself in literature and the grand historians, could also bring about a better world. He loved words, he loved everything about them. Above all, he loved their independence and durability – both vital attractions for a young man with aspirations.

Raphe still carried in his wallet his reading list of 1978, the books which convinced him to toss in the law and become a scholar. They included Canetti's *Auto da Fe*, Sontag's *Against Interpretation*, Arendt's *Eichmann in Jerusalem*, Goethe's *Faust*, and Kafka's *The Trial*. He had read and reread these luminaries, memorising the passages which spoke most urgently to him, and with their words filling his mind, he was convinced he had not simply found his mission but also possessed the ability. Twenty years on he still believed words could change the world, although not his words, not an academic in Holocaust studies with a side in volcanoes. And while a glance at last year's reading list might suggest he had only himself to blame, he knew he was not alone in believing, or wanting to believe, that an appreciation of great works would translate into an ability to produce the same himself. But he was disappointed: one always wants to achieve the best and he knew he had fallen well short of that. Although in the bright hours of his dreaming he still saw himself walking among those same luminaries he had long admired.

If he had fallen short of his dreams, he believed it was not entirely his fault. His had been a fraught life, one which for the first dozen years had been shot through with silence; even at forty-two he still suffered the deprivations of his early years. Juno, his live-in partner and personal critic, accused him of using his childhood to excuse all his adult failings. 'And how bad was it really?' she said. 'You received ample love, plenty of food, a fine education. You had a roof over your head, a substantial one from what I've gathered. In fact, you never wanted for anything much at all.'

Juno was head of black studies in his own department and well-versed in deprivation and suffering. But in this instance she was wrong. For the fact was, the first half of his childhood had been plugged with secrets, like living in a space lined with locked doors. He'd had to fight hard for his history, and he'd put up the biggest fight for his grandfather.

'It's not fair to tell me how much I resemble my grandfather and just leave it at that,' Raphe had complained from his earliest years.

'You have to understand, your mother has a lot to forget,' his father would say.

Alice's forgetting clearly suited Phil, but it did not suit Raphe. In fact as Raphe grew, little about his parents' life suited him. It seemed so dreary. With the exception of a trip to Canada, Phil had never travelled outside the United States, and although Alice's work took her to Europe, she never stayed longer than a few days. They followed American sport, they saw only American movies, they drove American cars, they talked American politics. Plenty of his friends had been to Europe, plenty could speak more than one language, and when Raphe visited their homes he would eat food that would never find favour in the Carter home.

'We have to look after your mother,' his father was quick to say whenever Raphe suggested they try something different. And Raphe would look at his mother, that strong, self-possessed woman who refused him nothing except an escape from ordinariness, and think she needed very little looking after.

'He's so like my father,' she'd say when she observed Raphe buried in a book. 'He's so like my father,' she said when he got his first pair of glasses. 'He's so like my father,' when she saw how popular he was with his friends. But when Raphe pushed for further information, he was always disappointed.

'Your mother wants to protect you,' his father said.

But from what? Raphe would wonder. From what?

At last he found an opening: his first year of high school and a project which required each student to write their family history. It was the major social studies assignment for the year, and no matter what his parents' preferences, it had to be done.

'You wouldn't want me to fail,' Raphe said.

His father was unstoppable. Born and bred in California as were his parents and their parents before them, he produced a gaggle of clerks and shopkeepers and small business people going back more than a century.

This was not the history Raphe wanted. 'How about a cowboy?' he said. 'Surely after all that time in the wild west, there's a cowboy. Or maybe an outlaw. Or a sheriff. What about a sheriff?' But the best Phil could produce was the sheriff's bootseller or dry goods supplier.

Raphe turned to his mother. 'It's your turn,' he said. 'Tell me about your family.' And when she remained silent, 'All right then, just tell me about my grandfather. Why am I so like him?'

If it had been left up to her, Raphe suspected she might have spoken. But Phil was adamant: 'Don't bother your mother.'

For a twelve-year-old imagination, silence is a rich canvas. Raphe knew his mother had been born in Germany, that she'd left in a hurry before the war, and that none of her family had survived. He also knew there was a Jewish connection because of the Mosers and his uncle Willi, but attempts to learn anything more had been firmly stymied.

In his own short life the only information Raphe had stifled quite as strenuously as his parents had stifled Alice's past concerned actions he was ashamed of. Like the time he had told on a boy for cheating, or when he had stolen some candy from the drugstore. People hide bad things. Raphe turned to his empty project book and with a mind swirling with Jews, Germany, killings, aggressive silence, and a rich diet of westerns and comics, he started to write.

A month later his parents were summoned to the school and shown the project. They were advised in the strongest terms to seek help for the boy. That night both parents sat him down and attacked him, there was no better word to describe it. How could he have made up such lies? And after all his mother had suffered. He'd dishonoured her family and he'd reserved the worst for his grandfather. A man who never hurt anyone had been portrayed as a spy and child deserter, all for the sake of a school project.

'We protected you,' his father shouted, 'and this is how you thank us.'

Raphe was bewildered. Why were they attacking him? He'd done nothing wrong, he'd merely tried to work out his mother's history.

'You know nothing,' his father kept shouting.

'And whose fault is that?' Raphe yelled back.

Phil was all fury. His scalp shone red and glistening through his thin hair, his hands were clasped into fists. 'You should have done your project on my family,' he said. 'You should be proud of your long American heritage.'

How could Raphe say it wasn't enough? How could he admit he wanted something different? How could he own up to a curiosity that simply would not lie down? His mother's story dangled just out of reach, rather like a brand-new, state-of-the-art television locked away in an attic.

Throughout the drama Alice had remained tight and quiet. Now she whispered something to Phil, then turned to Raphe and told him to go to his room. He sat on the floor squeezed in the narrow channel between his bed and the wall listening to his parents argue in a way he'd never heard before. And when he couldn't bear to listen any longer he turned on his transistor, stuck the earpiece in one ear, a ball of bubblegum in the other, and turned the volume up high.

It was late when his mother entered the room. His legs were cramped and his stomach rumbling. She helped him from the floor and hugged him long and hard. But it was only when she admitted she and his father had been wrong and she was so sorry, that he returned her hug.

The next day he began to learn about his mother's background, and how he preferred it to his father's, who could not help where he had come from but neither could he expect his son to feel the same pride. With his mother's story he had something special, a mark of distinction, but most of all he had a hero. Martin Lewin managed to fill the spaces in Raphe's humdrum life.

Raphe would imagine long talks with his grandfather about all manner of thing: friends, teachers, books, baseball, worries, decisions, hopes, dreams. Nothing was out of bounds. Unlike his friends, Martin was always available, and Raphe was never made to feel a fool. Even when he grew into manhood it was invariably Martin he turned to in times of trouble. It was as if his grandfather lived inside him, protector, conscience, guardian angel. In fact, until his mother's revelation about Henry Lewin, Raphe had never really experienced his grandfather as being dead.

His grandfather had infiltrated every aspect of his life, even his fascination for volcanoes owed something to him. Raphe had never wanted the same passions as everyone else, just like he'd never wanted the same family history. Juno said the differences he was wanting were all very safe. But where, he wanted to know, was the safety in volcanoes? Where in the Holocaust? Where in being Jewish? She was a tough judge, his beloved.

The Jewish connection at first had little impact, but once he entered college and fancied himself as an intellectual, he made more of it. He found himself gravitating towards Jewish students, exchanging Holocaust stories, reaching for certain books, being involved in Jewish-related discussions. He stepped further and further into a milieu spiked with Jewishness, so by the time the new discipline of Holocaust studies was established, Raphe slipped into it as if he had been waiting for it to happen. And such a fit it was. Finally he could delve deep and long into areas relevant to his life and history and make a career of it.

There was so much excitement in those early days as an academic, a flood of ground-breaking research, and his own con-tributions making quite an impact. And discussions like he'd never had before or since as he and his colleagues quarried the new area. Such heady days they were.

The reality today was far more mundane: too many classes, too many lackadaisical students, too many meetings, too many hostile colleagues, and too little time for research. Although it was research he had first turned to after his mother's terrible revelations. He was enraged over what had happened: a piece of German scum had stolen his grandfather's life. Suddenly there was a voice in his head demanding revenge, trying to goad him into action and accusing him of cowardice when he tried to silence it. Raphe knew it was the voice of his grandfather appealing for justice, but he didn't know how to respond. He immersed himself in his research, he read, he made notes, but the rage beat a hot storm through him and he found he couldn't concentrate. Even Juno, who had never failed him in the time they had been together, was unable to restore him. In fact, nothing was the same after his mother's revelation.

As to the extent of its effect, Raphe was to discover this a few weeks later. He was standing at the Bart waiting for a train when he heard Australian voices along the platform. Two men, young, gay by the look of them and minding their own business, and Raphe suddenly wanting to march up to them and shove them on the rails for no other reason than they came from the same country that had harboured his grandfather's murderer. And when the three of them entered the same carriage, the rage was so overpowering it threatened to strangle – either him or them, two young Australians who probably knew nothing about the war or Jews. At the next station Raphe moved to another carriage because he did not trust himself, and besides, he could not breathe.

Juno believed his rage was part of the whole survivor package and not specific to the wrong done to his grandfather.

'You simply can't leave the Holocaust alone,' she said.

She was quick to remind how she would have got nowhere if she had chosen to immerse herself in the rage of generations of black women. There are victims and victims, she went on, and Raphe was turning himself into a dangerous one. He might also have added he was turning himself into a person he did not like, but he didn't want to fuel her arguments.

Although without the Holocaust he would be nobody. As it was he was a second-rate academic at a second-rate college forced to spend far too much time vying for promotion with younger and hungrier colleagues. In fact, if there were a grand master handing out grades for life, despite all his hopes, Raphe knew he would be awarded a B. Better, he thought, to have failed properly, at least that would have been a definitive statement. Instead, he was condemned always to be a smudge behind the best.

He was employed at his second-rate university as deputy head of the Culture and Identity Studies Centre – Victim Studies by any other name. The centre had replaced the Holocaust studies department of a few years earlier, despite his vocal opposition. Clearly a B grade at argument too. With each passing year he was forced to watch his own specialty become ever more diluted as it was lumped in with Armenian massacres, the Irish troubles, KKK lynchings, South African apartheid, Palestinian exile, Rwandan genocide, Kurdish oppression, Yugoslavia's entrenched hatreds. So many new atrocities, and as soon as each was tidied up in the field there was another new unit to offer the students, or in the words of the university administrators, a new product for enhanced market penetration.

With bloodshed and brutality on every continent of the world, the Culture and Identity Studies Centre was bursting its seams. But worse than the huge classes, even worse than collegiate competition for top victim status, was the loss of integrity which had given rise to departments like his in the first place. When a new professorial position to be occupied by Raphe was approved earlier in the year, it was endowed by an armaments company. Raphe was being paid in profits from nuclear weapons!

No doubt about it, definitely a B for work. And a B for love, too, although he desperately hoped this had changed with Juno. But before he met her, serial partners, none of them lasting longer than five years, and among them not one Jewish girlfriend.

'You wouldn't want any competition for your Holocaust,' Juno said.

A B in all aspects of life, although after learning about Henry Lewin he was heading towards an A in violence. He, Raphe Carter, who not so long ago had been a man whose violent impulses extended no further than squashing a mosquito, a man who felt protected by the benign presence of his beloved grandfather, now understood how men could hurl their children at walls, bash their wives senseless, and kick their animals to death, how the anger could build until you had no option but to let it out. Raphe could understand this and it terrified him. And it was getting worse; his imagination without the restraints of reality was making freedom of movement a dangerous privilege – witness the event with the Australians on the train.

And then his mother died, far too young like most members of his family, and no one to blame this time. He was already filled with anger over Henry Lewin and now with grief as well. Juno did her best, but in the end she ran out of patience. Six months after his mother's death, Juno suggested they take a break.

'You need to temper all this emotion,' she said. 'Or rather, you need to temper the rage. I can cope with the grief.'

Juno, Juno, Juno. He couldn't bear to think of life without her. He pushed Henry Lewin out of his thoughts, he tried to silence his grandfather's demands, and he turned all his attention to Juno. They went to concerts and the theatre, they had a weekend away at the beach, they made love more often and with much the same vigour as they used to. And when a bequest arrived at the college specifically tagged for Holocaust teaching, even work started to look better.

One evening at the end of a particularly enjoyable dinner,

Raphe poured a sauterne and the two of them sat at the table surrounded by maps, planning their first trip to Europe together. Germany was on the proposed itinerary.

'And you'll show me Krefeld,' Juno said. 'It'll be different, less disturbing, seeing it with me.'

Raphe, wrapped in the mellowness of the evening, answered without thinking: he'd never visited Krefeld before, he said, nor Düsseldorf for that matter. He'd always imagined his grandparents in Berlin – he had visited there twice – and in various concentration camps – Auschwitz, Sachsenhausen and Buchenwald had each received a visit.

Juno was appalled. 'It's as if you've let the Nazi years erase all the life which came before.' She found it macabre that the regime which had killed his grandparents was now being given exclusive licence to define them. 'Perhaps you Jews ought to excavate a little deeper.' Her whole pose was a mix of bewilderment and derision. 'Where do you think African-Americans would be if we'd looked no further than slavery?'

All mellowness was gone as Raphe tried to explain his position, how despite his efforts the Holocaust seemed to stand like an impenetrable barrier between him and his grandparents' early life. How with only a handful of objects from that life remaining, the public knowledge – history – had an uninterrupted opportunity to dominate.

Then there was the not inconsiderable matter of interest, although he would never admit this to Juno. But the fact of the matter was he was much more interested in his grandparents' wartime experiences than their unremarkable earlier life. Their lives as he knew them were braced with history; it lent them a solidity, an authority he welcomed.

Over the next hour he tried to justify his omissions, tried to justify what he didn't fully understand himself, but Juno remained unconvinced.

'So many sick fixations,' she said. 'And I thought you'd moved on.'

Despite his best resolve, Raphe's attention started to slip again, and within a day or two of their argument his grandfather's voice had returned stronger than ever, his demands for action infused with a new urgency. This battle was endless; Juno didn't understand, could never understand. And Raphe had only dwelled on half the story. There was his grandmother, Renate, also murdered, and in evil's own front parlour. Raphe justified his focus with the Auschwitz aura. Auschwitz was millions, Auschwitz was horror on the grandest scale. Auschwitz was synonymous with mass atrocity, mass murder, mass barbarity. He could leave Auschwitz to humanity. But not the single, one-to-one confrontation which made up the last hours of his grandfather's life.

Which brought him to justice. If justice had been done, Raphe would not now be wearing the tragedy like a lead-lined vest. But justice wasn't done, either for the whole Nazi era or specifically for his grandfather. So here he is, a different country, a different hemisphere, on the precipice of a hissing volcano and as fixated as ever on his grandfather and the circumstances of his death. Somebody should pay. Nothing less would let his grandfather rest in peace, nothing less would loosen the grip of Raphe's own inherited responsibilities. There is Henry Lewin's son, Daniel, but according to his mother's account it is Laura who was close to her father, so in Raphe's imaginings it is Laura who should pay. But how? Raphe is no Nazi and it is not the 1940s any more. How should the daughter pay?

Raphe stares into the crater of the volcano. With so much activity, the sides are falling away. If he were to return in a year or so the crater would be unrecognisable. If only life moved in the same way. Raphe brushes the fine velvety ash off his jacket. The movement makes him think of his grandfather too weak at the end even for this small action. Laura Lewin should suffer her father's wrongs, Raphe is just not clear how.

In contrast, what is perfectly clear is his failure to live with history. Here he is, a generation removed, and shuffling through his days lugging a great load of hatred and resentment because no one has paid for what happened to his grandfather and all the other millions. Or at least none of the guilty have paid. Plenty of Jewish survivors have paid, he's seen that first-hand, and their children have paid, and now their grandchildren are paying too. When it will all stop? he wonders as the volcano roars about him. What will make it stop? Not forget, must never forget, but stop the sufferings from being handed further down the line. Even he bears the scars, a man in his forties, not unattractive nor unintelligent, but the longest relationship he's ever had is with a dog who left him after seven years for a more congenial home a couple of blocks away. There are leavers and leftovers and Raphe sees himself as one of the latter – although not any more, he pleads silently, not after five years and Juno still putting up with him.

It used to be that given all his girlfriends left him sooner or later, he was very careful how attached he became in the first place. Juno had identified this quality early in their relationship. She accused him of living, and loving too, with his gaze pointed in the wrong direction. She said he reminded her of those drivers who spent their time looking in the rear-vision mirror rather than through the front windscreen.

'They wouldn't see disaster coming in sequins and tiara,' she said to him. 'And neither would you.'

'Someone has to watch over the past,' he said in his own defence.

Although since learning the truth of his grandfather's death, Raphe has done considerably more than watch. It's as if he and his grandfather are connected by a tight leash and Raphe not quite sure who is leading whom. With his gandfather no longer the benign protective presence of his younger years, Raphe has wondered what would happen if he were able to untie the old man and let him go. Would Martin run off, dragging Raphe behind? Or released from his bonds, would the Raphe who remained blossom and flourish? There are times when the force of his grandfather is so intense that all Raphe wants is to step out of the old man's skin into his own reduced but contemporary life. And is ashamed at the thought.

For whatever resentment Raphe feels, none of it belongs with his innocent grandfather. It is all too clear where the blame lies. Martin Lewin's life was so brief, cut short by Henry Lewin. Raphe's own mother was orphaned by Henry Lewin, and Raphe was deprived of the grandfather he always wanted. So much loss and all because of Henry Lewin. It doesn't matter the man is now dead; the wrong he committed still requires restitution, and it is now up to his descendants to pick up the tab.

As the volcano hisses and steams in front of him, Raphe imagines two people at the edge of a fuming crater. And then only one. Laura Lewin and Raphe Carter go to a volcano and only Raphe returns. Ashes to ashes, dust to dust, and no evidence to condemn. He is unnerved by his thoughts, but feels no shame.

Over and over he has envisioned it, and again now as the warring couple continue to throttle each other at the edge of the volcano. When the man raises his arm, Raphe finds himself dashing forward to save the wife. But the man's arm comes to rest across his wife's shoulders, then he is kissing her and the two of them, all quiet and loving, start back to the boat together. An hour of yelling and screaming in front of one of the natural wonders of the world and now it's all peace and harmony.

Raphe follows at a distance. His anger has subsided too; he's beginning to understand what must be done. He moves across the ashen landscape, treading carefully around the steaming cracks. The air quivers, the gases lighten, he breathes more deeply. He has a week before he has to return to work. Juno won't miss him if he stays away a few days longer. In fact, she's all spark and wire at the moment, firing off at him at the slightest provocation. And while she's quick to blame him and his fixations, a book which is dragging its feet as is hers at the moment, does nothing for the mood.

He stops near a craggy slope encrusted with sulphur deposits and picks up a bright lemony lump dusted in a layer of dove-grey ash. He wraps it carefully in a tissue and puts it in the pocket of his jacket. It's toxic and he registers an odd sort of comfort. As he walks onwards to the rickety jetty, the crushing responsibility he feels for his grandfather becomes more and more manageable.

On the way back to the mainland he keeps to himself, sitting at the back of the boat where he can watch the volcano shrinking on the horizon. He feels calm, he feels inspired, he feels his grandfather's plaint as a clear and gentle urging, like the press of a lover's hand between his shoulders. As the volcano grows smaller and smaller, Raphe vows to make amends.

As soon as he arrives back at the hotel, he telephones Juno to let her know he will be staying away an extra week. Then he calls Qantas and arranges a return flight to Melbourne. At last he is ready to meet Laura Lewin.

A Seinfeld Lookalike
with a Side in Volcanoes

At the Human Rights and Social Justice Commission no one entered the building without a serious encounter with security. But Raphe Carter did. He skirted around the posse of neo-Nazis protesting outside, slipped into the building, sweet-talked the man on the information desk, took the lift to the inner sanctum of offices, and within two minutes of entering the building was standing in the open doorway of Laura Lewin's office.

It was just after nine. Laura had been at the office since seven trying to finish a report before the day began in earnest. She was in that glazed space of prolonged gazing at her computer when she glanced up and saw a strange man standing in her doorway. He was smiling and uttering her name. She stared at him as if through clouds, then a fraction of a second later her years of training kicked in and she hit the emergency switch.

In the time it took for security to respond, the man with dazzling American fluency explained his business with her. He was in Melbourne for only four days, he said, and needed to speak with a Jew. He had seen her name mentioned in the newspaper that morning, so she seemed an obvious place to start.

'What about the telephone directory, under Jewish,' she said.

He was reading the newspaper not the telephone directory, he said. And besides, not any Jew would do. He needed a Jew with clout.

'A synagogue then. And an authoritative rabbi,' Laura said, intrigued in spite of herself.

The man shook his head, he wanted results not religion, and would have continued but for the arrival of two security officers. The male officer frisked him, while the female officer checked his passport and other documents. Then each grabbed an arm and were about to escort him from the room and the building when Laura asked them to wait. Not that she needed any more work, but she admired *chutzpah*, something Raphe Carter from San Francisco, California, had in abundance. And she was curious to know what a well-dressed, thirty-something maybe forty, sweet-looking, sweet-talking man wanted from her – or not specifically her, but a 'Jew with clout'.

The security officers consulted each other then nodded to Laura to go ahead. They positioned themselves against the wall, one either side of the door, and waited.

Raphe Carter was a man who needed no encouragement, his words slipped out like silk. He told Laura he was an academic, mentioned a couple of book titles she'd never heard of, then without a trace of a smile said, 'The Holocaust is my gig. And I do a side in volcanoes.'

Laura caught the expression on the female officer's face, an unambiguous are-you-sure-you-don't-want-me-to-get-rid-of-this-geek grimace. But Laura didn't, or at least not yet. Raphe Carter from San Francisco, California, was providing an entertaining break in what had been a horror week. Here was a man who could have walked off the set of an American sitcom, not simply the lines so earnestly delivered, but the compact body, the clothes worn with ease, the make-up smooth skin, the dark, almost pretty face.

'I'm Jewish,' he said.

Seinfeld, Laura was thinking, Raphe Carter could be Seinfeld's brother. As for Jewish, everyone on *Seinfeld* is Jewish.

'Well actually part-Jewish,' he said.

'Nothing special about that around here,' she said. '*Our* gig is minorities.'

Although no one within these ideologically pure walls would put it quite like that. The Human Rights and Social Justice Commission had been established in the 1980s to deal with a range of ethnicity-based human rights issues. Throughout the nineties its brief had grown to meet an ever-expanding repertoire of bigotry and intolerance. Now in the new century the extent of the commission's purview was reflected in its scrupulously nondiscriminatory board of commissioners. There was one of everything: one Greek, one Italian, one Vietnamese, one Chinese, one indigenous Australian, one Malaysian Muslim, one Jew, one Lebanese Christian and, at the present time, two vacancies and a stampede of lobbying in high places.

Not that any of this concerned Raphe because his business had nothing to do with the commission. His mother's family was Jewish, he explained, but had been severed from their roots in the move from Europe. He gave a you-know-what-I-mean shrug to encompass the entire Holocaust and its devastations. 'My immediate family's gone now. So as I was out this way I thought I might try Australia.' Then, to ensure Laura had not missed his point, 'To see if anyone's left.'

With the American woman of a few years ago and her own investigations since, this was not a point Laura could easily miss. Although for what he was wanting she couldn't help. 'Wrong sort of Jew,' she said. 'Wrong sort of clout.'

Again he mentioned she was the only identifiable Jew in the morning paper, again he mentioned he was short of time. Laura consulted her watch, so was she. 'Some traces take years and you've got –?'

'Four days.'

The sweet-faced renegade from *Seinfeld* had fast become a nuisance. As Laura rummaged in her desk for the phone number of the Jewish Historical Society, she wondered what sins she had committed this past week for her Friday morning to be saddled with such a schmuck. At the same time she realised how much she must need a break that she gave him the benefit of the doubt in the first place. She found the number and wrote it down, then couldn't resist, 'For a four-day search,' she said with an exquisite lack of facial expression, 'you'd have done better to arrive earlier in the week.'

Raphe Carter looked confused.

'Friday,' Laura explained. 'It's Shabbat. The Jewish organisations all close early and tomorrow they're shut.'

She watched as the frown was replaced by an utterly symmetrical smile.

He was, he said, a seasoned researcher. 'If there's anything to discover, I'll know by the end of the day.'

She too smiled, very dry and very wry, as if that might highlight the irony he clearly was missing. 'Maybe so, but a week would have clinched it.'

She watched as he slipped the information into his wallet, a satisfied expression on his face, and knew he was in for a rude awakening. The searches took years, even a lifetime, particularly if the searcher chose to interpret every failed attempt as a flaw in the search rather than there being nothing to discover. Laura had observed this among a number of her friends, on and on they went, lurching between eager anticipation and dazed disappointment as they hunted down their lost past. And just when they thought they'd exhausted all possible leads, along came the Internet with website after website bristling with promise, and conveniently linked to on-line loss and grief counselling when hopes took a whipping.

In the period following her father's death when she'd been desperate to uncover the truth about him, Laura had been caught in the on-line search maze. Almost every night while Nell slept, she would cruise the survivor sites, perusing names, dallying in chat rooms, following leads, searching always searching. While she was at the computer, while she was scanning lists, while she was searching for her father's lost past, the immediate reality of Henry's death with all its accompanying pain was somehow pushed aside. On and on she would go, often ending up at sites with only the faintest connection with the known facts about Henry. But it didn't matter. She had hope and it pulled her onwards, away from her mourning, away from the gaping hole of the present, towards the answers her father had so strenuously concealed.

It was some months before she realised how very seductive hope can be and how great its stamina to withstand disappointment. So much time wasted: for she discovered nothing. In the end she forced herself to give up her on-line excursions, to turn away from the alluring echo of her father's silence. But it was hard, very hard, both the knowing and the not knowing, the searching and the not searching. And here was this cocky American bitzer wanting to uncover his European roots in Australia this weekend. He was, Laura decided, either very naïve, very arrogant, or very crazy.

And fortunately he was leaving. He thanked her and shook her hand. But at the door, dwarfed by the two burly officers, he twisted around, 'I know what you're thinking, but it won't be as difficult as you think. Lewin, for example, your name. My mother was born a Lewin. I could start with you.'

And with that he was gone.

Months later, after her own life had collapsed, Laura would recall those words: *I could start with you*, and wonder whether that was exactly what he had done. He was neither so arrogant nor so naïve that his Jew-with-clout-in-the-newspaper story should be believed. Although on the day of their first meeting it was not that she believed him, she simply did not have time to doubt.

It was in the heat of yet another multiculturalism backlash, spearheaded this time not by ratbags from the far right but the country's own elected political leaders. Every month saw another boatload of desperate asylum seekers risking their lives to travel to Australia because their lives were under far greater threat in their own countries. And instead of welcoming these people, instead of recognising the shocking brutality they'd suffered under some of the most repressive regimes on earth, many of the nation's leaders were accusing them of queue-jumping and turning them away. But what queue was this when the oppressors in their own countries had no queues? What astonishing twists of reason had supposedly humane citizens talking of queues when people were being maimed and slaughtered at random?

Laura was witnessing slurs and slogans which could have graced the pages of *Der Stürmer*, and violence too, this spilling onto any Australian who looked and sounded different from those of a white European background. 'Australia for Australians' was the catch-cry. But what sort of Australia was this? And how limited the definition of Australian. Some of the flag-wavers were extremists such as the neo-Nazis outside the commission at the time of Raphe Carter's visit, but most were just ordinary citizens who had been doing it tough.

People had been quietly seething throughout the nineties as their jobs disappeared and social services were cut. They stood by powerless as their local hospital was shut down, together with kindergartens, schools and neighbourhood banks. As their standard of living plummeted, it was with bitterness they heard how the nation had never been so prosperous, that the budget was in surplus for the first time in years, and a financial institution far away in the United States had rewarded Australia with a triple A credit rating. Immigration levels and multiculturalism were easy targets in such a climate and, with an election in the offing, were being used as political cards by the nation's leaders. 'Australians will decide who lives in Australia,' the prime minister had said recently as yet another boat of desperate people was turned away from Australian shores. And riding the waves of his thinly disguised racism, a level of violence to keep plenty of people locked in their homes.

Raphe Carter was quickly forgotten as Laura dealt with the latest attacks. The Jewish targets had been fewer than the Asian and Muslim ones, but sufficient to place her usual work on hold. Anti-Semitic obscenities had been daubed on the walls of the Yeshiva as well as on a number of houses in the main Jewish area of the city. One of these was occupied by a terrified Indian family from Fiji who had not expected to experience in Australia the same racial hatred which had forced them from their own country. Mid-morning Laura met with her colleagues and together they devised a plan to meet the most pressing of the current problems. The rest of the day Laura spent lobbying parliamentarians and bureaucrats for a special one-off grant to pay for increased security. With the impending election and many politicians not wanting to be strongly identified with either side of the refugee issue, it was a day spent talking in euphemisms. But home-grown violence on the front pages was not conducive to a conservative government running for re-election on a platform of security and stability, so by the end of the day Laura had the funds she needed.

It was after seven when she rang home to say she was running late. The answering machine was on and Nell clearly running later. With Nell not at home pouring the drinks and preparing the dinner, Laura decided to walk herself out of the hectic day into a calmer evening. Her brain was a tangle of hot acid circuits and she fairly bolted out of the building into the Friday-night bustle. The traffic was heavy, the air cluttered, and the footpaths thick with impatient shoppers and weary workers. With a graceful swerving to avoid other pedestrians, Laura swept past shops and bars and cafés with bright lights and blaring music, heading towards the park. From there it was just a short tram ride home.

Laura Lewin had changed little in the five years since her father's death. With her tall elegance, the full proportioned body, the black tailored suit setting off the pale hair and pale skin, she was still a woman not easily overlooked. She, on the other hand, took an increasingly pragmatic approach to her appearance, a no-frills person except for the hair which she categorised as a non optional extra.

It was this blonde Polish fuzz, as light and wild as one of Turner's skies, that had saved her mother in the war. 'You and me,' Etti would say to Laura, 'we look like Poles not Jews.'

That life could depend on the colour and texture of hair was an obscenity, Laura had said.

'I can tell you worse obscenities but you wouldn't want to hear.' And then without any encouragement Etti would go ahead and relate the obscenities in all their gory details.

It was now more than ten years since her mother's death, but Etti's voice was as clear as it had always been, the familiar utterances framing old memories and keeping them vivid. How different it was with her father, more recently dead, but fading, less as a result of his own reticence during life than the shadows which had crept over him since his death.

How Laura wished she had left well alone after the Internet fiasco, but she simply could not stop herself when she heard about a group seeking restitution for those forced into slave labour for German firms during the war. Another possibility, she thought, another chance for the truth. She contacted the group, she waited for news, and when the news came through she castigated herself yet again for not leaving the past in peace. For the fact of the matter was her father had not been at Westerbork despite what he had said, nor at Belsen. There was no record of him among the survivors of either place.

It had been a madness after that. Laura returned to her searches with the force of a runaway train, and with about as much thought. Camp after camp, list after list, documents, books, survivor groups, she plunged ahead, looking for something, anything, and would have continued if not for an incident involving some friends of her parents, a couple who had been part of the Polish contingent. Both of them had been survivors of Auschwitz. They had made a good life in Australia, had raised two children, one a lawyer, the other an architect, and were settling into a healthy and active old age when they were dragged back to Poland by their children, back to where they had lost everything, back to Auschwitz, back to deliberately buried memories, all because their adult children had wanted 'to connect with their roots', had wanted first-hand experience of 'their tragic history', which is to say their parents' tragic experience, and insisted their parents act as guides. The mother, always prone to depression, did not recover from her children's pilgrimage and was now in a nursing home; the father, poor man, could not re-forget the same unimaginable horrors twice, and his children wouldn't forgive him for what they had learned he needed to do to survive.

Suddenly Laura was shredding notes and erasing computer files, destroying all the leads and dead ends she had collected in the years since her father's death. Suddenly it was all very clear: only something truly awful, truly shameful would have necessitated Henry's lies. She had loved her father, and in order to keep loving him she carefully corralled her thinking about him. As for the Seinfeld lookalike who had appeared in her office that morning, she would have done him a favour if she'd shared some of her hard-won lessons. Even presumptuous Americans did not deserve the disappointments she had suffered.

A blast of wind blew her hair across her face as she left the main city precinct. She twisted her hair into a rope and tucked it down the collar of her jacket. Once in the park she slackened her pace, and at last she felt the tangle of an impossible week start to loosen. Night had now fallen, but with a clear sky and a near-complete moon, not darkly, and Laura was not at all nervous. She knew this park, the well-lit paths littered with the first autumn leaves, the open spaces, the shadowy alcoves, recognised the old-fashioned drunks who lingered here, as opposed to the jittery young junkies in the other park a block away. The most dangerous creatures were the feuding possums. So a sense of unease which seemed to grow as the noise of the day subsided struck her as odd. It did not concern her parents, nor politicians who would do anything to stay in power; it was the American, Raphe Carter. *I could start with you*, he had said. And in the cool of the evening, as she walked beneath the yellowing canopy of elms, her skin sparked and prickled as if someone had scratched her.

'He sounds like your standard quick-fix American,' Nell said as she topped up their drinks. 'I should know, the university's full of them.'

Nell launched into the latest idiocy of her head of department, Don from Oregon, whose memory had rotted after years of dedicated dope smoking. But Laura interrupted.

'There was something else about this Raphe Carter. He was so sure of himself and so sure of his right to be in my office. He seemed to know exactly what he was doing.'

Nell brought the drinks over and sat next to her on the couch. 'It's got nothing to do with the Seinfeld lookalike,' she said putting her arm around Laura. 'It's these bloody politicians, not a humane heartbeat between them. They're threatening everything you've ever worked for.'

This was exactly what Laura wanted to hear. As a source for her current unease, the known danger of reactionary politicians was far preferable to the unknown Raphe Carter. And yet those last words of his with their whiff of threat, *I could start with you*, would not go away. With her anxiety again on the rise, Laura decided to do a search on Raphe Carter, easy enough to discover if he really was who he said he was, and was already on her feet when she stopped. It had been a shocker of a week, dinner was in the oven, and as a cause for doing anything, anxiety was rarely productive.

She returned to the couch, nudged Wystan aside and stretched herself out. 'Play me something soppy and romantic,' she said.

Nell settled at the piano and played some Schubert, then a little Schumann and finally Chopin, playing with the same vigour as she did everything else. Laura lay back on the couch, content just to watch. Even after all these years, more than a decade now, just the presence of this woman could mollify her. She watched and listened and floated on waves of Chopin, found herself thinking that Raphe Carter had the same physical appeal as Nell, the same smooth, androgynous features. Disaster with the face of an angel. Can you see it coming? And wondered at this voice, these strange words.

She turned on her side, away from the piano, away from her lover, and forced herself to shift back to the last American. Such an effort it took, as if her mind were an ageing gearbox. Back she went, back to the woman who had turned up not long before her father died, the woman who had laced up Henry and held him captive, the woman whose name had until this minute not connected. The woman who was Alice Carter.

A moment later Laura was on her feet and ringing her brother. Alice Carter and now Raphe Carter, surely too much of a co-incidence. Daniel met the American woman, Daniel would surely remember if she had a son. She dialled a wrong number, then dialled again. The phone rang and rang, eventually an answering machine. Of course, Friday night, Shabbat, and Daniel as likely to answer the telephone as convert to Christianity. Laura blurted out a confused account of the meeting with Raphe Carter and was cut off mid-tale. She rang again, an engaged signal while the answering machine reset. Then she remembered Nell had met the American woman. But Nell couldn't recall whether she had a son. Laura pleaded with her to try and remember.

'I expect you'll never hear from this Raphe Carter again,' Nell said in an attempt to calm her.

Laura shook her off. She returned to the phone and left a short and what she hoped was a coherent message on Daniel's machine. Then she excused herself and went for a walk. She moved briskly through the dark streets, pacing off her anxiety, and felt considerably better when she returned. She poured herself a fresh glass of wine and tried to settle into the evening. But half an hour later she knew it was hopeless. She pleaded a headache, swallowed some painkillers and went to bed. When next she awoke it was 1.50 a.m. and Nell was fast asleep beside her. Laura lay in the dark for almost an hour, eyes wide open to the blackness. Finally she lifted herself from the bed, wrapped a rug around her and went to the couch. There she worried about the two Carters until dawn.

It was nearly a week before Laura spoke to Daniel as he was away on business, a difficult week made even more so with Nell curiously absent even when she was present. Nell assured her there was nothing to worry about, rather she was flat out at work and simply didn't have time or energy for what she termed the 'Carter fantasy'.

As it happened, the whole Carter issue fizzled. When finally

Laura did speak to her brother, he remembered the woman but little else, and certainly not whether she had a son.

'Leave it alone, Laura,' he said in a voice uncharacteristically gentle. 'Leave the past alone.' And after a pause, 'There are other ways of filling up silences.'

Raphe was full of the past when he returned home to San Francisco, and charged with a new energy. He'd faced his worst enemy and found her not the least bit terrifying. And it helped to have a real and tangible target for his sometimes out-of-control imaginings. But with a clamour of modern-day problems awaiting him, he had absolutely no time to dwell on the past. He spent his first week back in student selection, interviewing a stream of eighteen year olds with brains like music videos. Juno said he had only himself to blame, given he was the instigator of the selection process. He disagreed: there was nothing wrong with his system, it was the applicants who were at fault.

The system involved a short interview for all prospective students of Holocaust studies. Raphe had designed it a couple of years earlier to weed out the lazy sentimentalists who had been signing up for his courses expecting a Hollywood guide to atrocity. And while it demanded a lot of time initially, it paid off in much more rewarding classes throughout the year.

'You're crazy,' Juno said. 'What teacher in their right mind would lose a week, lose even a day of valuable research time if they didn't have to?'

But he wanted only committed students, young people who were struggling to understand the long shadow of the Holocaust, people who would approach the material with the sensitivity and respect it deserved. A few years earlier one of his students had written Holocaust blasphemy for her final assignment, an odious short story about a modern-day trip to Auschwitz-Birkenau, during which a couple had sex in the wooded area alongside crematoria four and five. A couple having sex on the very spot where Jewish women and children had waited their turn at death. It was outrageous, and Raphe wanted no more students like this, thus the mandatory interview. But the new system was powerless against the crop which greeted him on his return from Australia. Only a handful made the grade, yet if he didn't meet his quota, his budget would be cut.

'Forget your principles, Raphe, just take the lot of them,' Juno said. 'They're students, for God's sake, and you're treating them like little scholars. Deal with them as quickly and with as little effort as possible, and get down to the real business of your own research.'

Juno's argument was less than judicious given that research was not a happy topic in their household at present. Or rather Raphe's research. Juno was well satisfied. Through arcane and devious methods known only to academics, the money donated for Holocaust studies which Raphe had hoped would buy him out of teaching while he wrote his next book had miraculously appeared in the black studies' budget. And Juno, his own beloved, was using it to write her next book. His money, her book.

He had tried to be fair, he had tried to be understanding, but it was clear that yet again the importance and specificity of the Holocaust was being eroded. Juno not surprisingly disagreed. She was very sorry about his grant, but if he were to miss out, then better she benefit than some of their colleagues.

She was, however, less understanding on the larger issue.

'We can all learn from each other. Putting the Holocaust, or rather your Holocaust, the Jewish Holocaust, in a class of its own, is dangerous. For a start it has you siding with those who suggest that homosexuals and gypsies were lesser victims.'

In fact he did have some opinions about this but it was not the time to admit to them. He watched Juno as she tried to persuade him out of his misery, watched rather than listened, and what he saw was a movie stretching into the not-too-distant future. Juno, whom he had believed to be the love of his life, would soon, he feared, be the most recent in a long line of failed relationships.

What sort of man reaches forty without at least one child and one marriage? What sort of man has a track record with women that is at best hideously untidy and at worst grounds for long-term therapy? Yet it should have worked with Juno. She was beautiful, she was intelligent and they'd managed well together for five years. But as he focused more closely on what she was saying he realised there was little hope. She was lambasting him about 'his' Holocaust, how without it he would lose his primary reason for living, and referring to his 'damned grandfather' who, according to her, wouldn't thank his grandson for his obsessive attention.

'Just leave him in peace,' she said. 'And the Australian girl too. She's done nothing wrong.'

It was ludicrous to have ever thought Juno would understand. Juno, the love of his life. Juno, exotic right down to her name.

'What sort of name is that?' he had asked when she first took over black studies at the centre.

'The sort of name you'd choose if you had scholarly aspirations and your parents had saddled you with Jill,' she had replied.

Raphe had fallen in love with her before the week was out. She was so vibrant, she seemed to spill her very own edges. 'You're so *big*,' he would tell her later. Everything she said was fascinating and new, everything about her was so passionate.

Five years, five good years, but with her now pocketing his research money and slandering the Holocaust as some sort of personal pathology, it was easy to regret the merging of his private life with his professional. He had arrived home from Australia full of Laura Lewin and the wonderful life she had gained courtesy of the murder of his grandfather. And while he may have presumed a little too much on Juno's interest, he was nonetheless shocked when out of the blue she said she refused to countenance his madness any longer. She went on to accuse him of some sort of bizarre appropriation of the Holocaust.

'You'd be as slight as air without it,' she said.

He went berserk. But whatever he could dish up she could always dish up better. In the end he decided she would certainly achieve higher billing than him in the madness stakes. 'I've had your Holocaust,' she said as she cut his Armani shirt into neat hexagonal patches. 'I've absolutely had your Holocaust,' she said when she tried to cut him into neat hexagonal patches. She said she'd prefer to tear him into slender strips, but given he was nothing more than a huge lump of gristle, she was not about to waste her energy.

Juno had a wonderful turn of phrase even when angry. Particularly when angry.

The Armani shirt, as it happened, was just the beginning. They made up, but a few days later it was on again.

'At times you act as if you are your dead grandfather,' she said. 'The rest of the time you're perfectly happy just to play God.'

Attack after attack, but it took the destruction of his Mies van der Rohe chair to break him. They were having another argument, she was attacking the memory of his grandfather and Raphe was attacking her in return, and suddenly she was spreading the contents of the pantry over his Mies van der Rohe chair. The chair was so new that before the onslaught it still smelled of the store. As he attempted to remove jelly and horseradish, peanut butter and a trattoria's worth of virgin olive oil, he told her he wanted her out by morning.

Always a step ahead of him, she left the same night. The door shut behind her and immediately he regretted it. She was the love of his life. They had their differences, but they were not irreconcilable. And given she was a black American and he the son of a German-born Holocaust survivor, they had done remarkably well.

He did not go to work the next day, instead he spent it in front of the computer writing her a mammoth email. He sent it off during the afternoon. The following morning, a Saturday, when there was still no reply, he sent it again, together with a long but eloquent footnote: he loved her and would always love her being the general gist. Two more chapter-length emails were sent off before he learned from a colleague she had moved in with the professor of German.

Juno always knew where to stick in the knife.

Suddenly Raphe was awash with reality. Five years with a two-timing, anti-Semitic black woman who had been on his back from day one. 'There's no malice in it,' he used to say to his friends when she was so critical of him. But that's where he was wrong, there was malice and plenty of it, and long before she massacred his chair and shacked up with a Kraut.

He should have been warned. From the beginning she had wanted him to be a different Raphe Carter. She had insisted on a new wardrobe, a shorter hairstyle, a change of cologne. Even before she moved in she had rearranged his kitchen cupboards and his bedroom drawers. And while both of them were aficionados of junk food, her McDonald's always won over his Burger King, similarly her KFC over his Taco Bell. 'You wouldn't have the problem if you were a vegetarian,' one of Raphe's vegetarian friends said, but with his world already upside down Raphe wasn't about to help it along. She had killed his collection of bonsai, they were unnatural she said, and she had tried to kill his volcano love, comparing it with a ten year old's fascination with fire crackers.

'Come with me and see for yourself,' Raphe said.

So she came, and he should have called the relationship off there and then. You have to be careful whom you take to a volcano and with Juno he was not careful enough. He had chosen his favourite, Kilauea in Hawaii, but he might as well have shown her a barbecue for all her response.

'You're so fucking attached to your own fucking narrative,' she said when he complained.

'No other life interests you,' she said as she attacked his Mies van der Rohe chair.

And then she was gone, but not before accusing him one last time of living with his head turned in the wrong direction. And possibly she was right, but someone had to watch over the past, and at least the past, unlike Juno and all the women who preceded her, hung around for the long haul.

Juno moved out and the semester dragged on. Raphe wasted hours and energy trying to avoid her at work, his students were the worst ever, his nights were long and solitary, and his dreams were haunted, not only by Juno, but by Laura Lewin whom he really blamed for Juno's departure. It no longer helped that he had met her, nothing seemed to help any more. Every night the same turmoil, the two women shouting at him and making demands, and his ever-present grandfather, once his guardian angel, the most demanding of all.

One night on his third trip to the toilet in as many hours Raphe stood in front of the mirror and saw what was happening to him. He had lost several pounds, which he could ill afford, and deep creases had formed down both cheeks. He hadn't had a decent shave in weeks because his razor needed replacing and he couldn't be bothered going to the store. He couldn't even be bothered masturbating. He was turning into a lovesick eunuch whose deepest relationships were with ghosts.

Enough, he told himself, he had to move on. He had his hair cut and bought some new clothes, he put in a proposal for a new course and made notes for a new journal article. Then Juno's

German professor accepted a position in Brussels, and without language or job prospects Juno announced she was going with him. It all happened so quickly: one week Raphe was avoiding her in the corridors, the next she was gone.

The semester rolled on. A couple of students started to show promise, his new course looked as if it would be accredited, his article was shaping up nicely, he was going out regularly with friends, he'd even had a couple of dates. Life was looking up. But no matter how hard he tried he could not silence the voice of his grandfather, could not placate those old demands for justice. In the end Raphe decided that unless he was prepared to live like his mother, forever turned away from the wrongs, he needed to settle his dues.

With the semester's end in sight he started to make plans. He arranged some study leave, closed up his apartment, and almost three months to the day, Raphe Carter found himself again flying across the Pacific to Australia to meet Laura Lewin.

Feuds and Fallout

It had been the warmest winter in living memory and a great disappointment to Laura who preferred Melbourne's winters to be wracked with winds off the Antarctic. Afterwards she would say the peculiarly warm weather was an omen, for those three months were shot through with disappointments, and of them all, the weather was the least malignant.

Raphe Carter was quickly forgotten as bigotry continued its ride through the backblocks of the nation. Laura's workload reached mammoth proportions. Passions were high, demonstrations flared, righteous supporters clashed with righteous objectors. The everyone-has-a-right-to-an-opinion-in-a-democracy justification for inaction was uttered with prim authority by the prime minister, who had seen the polls and wasn't about to alienate further all those voters who under his administration had lost so many of their community services. Every time he appeared on the evening news Laura would rail against him. In the past there had been political leaders she had not liked, but the present prime minister, a remarkably unprepossessing man who did not know how he would act on an issue until he had seen the polls, revealed an ethical emptiness that was truly frightening.

'He couldn't possibly believe this "everyone has a right to an opinion" crap,' Laura said to Nell during a walk along the Merri Creek trail on a rare evening both were home early. She paused a moment to watch a pair of red-rump parrots, but not even her favourite bird could calm her. 'This man is pure politician. Blood, bone, muscle and gore. He'd do anything to stay in power.'

Apart from a handful of courageous community leaders and a few liberal voices in the now almost universally conservative press, racism was being given a dream run.

'Why can't people see what's happening?' Laura continued as she and Nell turned around and headed for home. 'We're turning into a nation of inhumane, jingoistic, selfish, mindless cretins, while desperate people die a short boat ride from our shores and our prime minister fashions himself to appeal to the lowest common denominator. What needs to happen before this man will act?'

Laura had been asking similar questions of colleagues, friends, shopkeepers, even strangers on the tram. She could talk about little else. It was incredible to her that anyone, even reactionary leaders like the present PM, would allow the current situation much less promote it, 'And in the name of bloody democracy too.'

She continued her diatribe back home while she prepared dinner. 'There's a case for political assassination, although you wouldn't want to risk making a martyr of the man.' She went on to suggest a chronic but not life-threatening disease instead. 'One of those bowel conditions which cause uncontrollable wind would do quite nicely.'

Laura was standing at the stove with a knife in one hand and a leek in the other, her indignation turned up to extreme. Hers was a passion sparking with incredulity, the sort which renders the speaker, if not blind, then largely insensitive to anything else, so the outburst which followed took her by surprise. Only later, as she travelled through the last months of her relationship with Nell, would Laura find several subtle signs.

'Can't you talk about anything else?' Each of Nell's words was a bullet. 'I'm fed up with the refugee situation, I'm fed up with the bloody prime minister. And,' this said more slowly, 'I'm fed up with your raging.'

Her voice was low and threatening and hardly recognisable as Nell's. Laura was immediately silenced. She turned from her cooking and for an embarrassingly brief moment their eyes met.

'I'm going for a walk,' Nell continued. And as Laura went to speak, 'No, don't offer to join me. I suggest you stay here and think of some new topics of conversation.'

Before she left, however, there were a few other issues she wanted to get off her chest, and through them all her voice remained quiet and controlled and frighteningly fluent; clearly her sights had been loaded and on target for quite some time. As for Laura's sights, they'd been directed elsewhere and not monitoring her own behaviour as one who experienced personal criticism as a catastrophe always should.

She had no desire to defend herself, not with the fear rising faster than the PM's approval rating. She'd hurt Nell, that much was clear, annoyed her too, and was prepared to accept the blame. In fact, she would agree to anything as long as Nell stopped attacking her. She interrupted Nell's tirade: she was sorry, terribly sorry, she said.

But Nell didn't want her apologies. 'Apologies roll so easily off your tongue, Laura. You'd apologise for murder and mayhem if you thought it'd stop someone yelling at you.'

Nell opened the door, then paused for a parting shot. 'No one's as affronted as you are over this refugee business, Laura. And do you know why? It's the whole Jewish thing. But as bad as he is, the prime minister is not Hitler, and today's Australia is not thirties Germany, and the sooner you get that into your bloody child-of-survivors head the better.' And the knock-out blow just before the door slammed: 'If you're not careful, Laura Lewin, you'll end up raging alone.'

Laura stood at the stove stunned. The threat of those last words. She couldn't move, she couldn't step back into a life which had turned so hostile. Minutes passed before the crackle and smoke of burning oil broke through. And then came the tears: over Nell and her attack, over the gutless prime minister, over the fact that no one had learned a bloody thing during the past brutal century. But most of all she cried over Nell. She cried as she finished slicing the leeks, she cried as she wiped the mushrooms, she cried as she cooked the linguini. By the time she was adding black olives and salted capers and tossing the lot in a pasta dish she and Nell had bought in Florence, her tears were finished and a decision made.

For a month or so things settled. Laura monitored her outbursts and kept her criticisms of the prime minister away from home. Not that Nell was often there. The old days of a leisurely drink together after work, sitting on the deck with the lorikeets squawking overhead, were a distant memory. So, too, the pleasurable evenings which used to follow, with Laura whipping up a meal from the jangle of food in the fridge and cupboards, the two of them lingering over dinner to talk, and then to the couch together and a spot of TV.

Laura would do anything to have that life back again.

'If I didn't know you better,' Laura said one Friday evening as they were driving to her brother and sister-in-law's for Shabbat dinner, 'I might suspect you were having an affair.'

They both laughed, but there was no hilarity, and Nell drifted off almost immediately into her own thoughts.

Was an affair so improbable? Laura wondered, then quickly brushed the thought aside. While there was little certainty in this life, Laura was sure about Nell. And while neither was so naïve to think they wouldn't have their ups and downs, the relationship was rock-solid. And rock-solid meant no affairs.

'I'm so bored.' Nell's voice burst out loud and accusing. 'I'm so bloody bored.'

It was a bull's-eye hit. Laura slammed on the brakes in the middle of impatient end-of-week traffic and brought the car to a standstill – a brief breathless moment sidelined from the rest of her life, before she regained her senses, shuffled behind the wheel as if that would dislodge the knife, and moved back into the traffic. Immediately she riffled her mind for possible explanations, had to understand, had to stop the panic. And of all the possibilities, she decided the most likely culprit was work.

Nell had made several comments recently about how she wished she had never left film production, that if she hadn't she would now be one of the foremost filmmakers in the country. And while this had been a regular lament in the past, with the cutbacks at universities it had gained momentum in recent times. She had started picking at some old unfinished scripts, had actually spent a couple of days revising one of them, but while she always had good ideas and good twists on ideas, follow-through had never been Nell's strong point. The whole filmmaking issue always tended towards a slow frustrating collapse and, as far as Laura was aware, it was proceeding no differently this time.

Perhaps work was not the problem, perhaps given they were

on their way to Melissa and Daniel's place, Daniel's new pro-
hibition against non-Jews was to blame.

'I don't have non-Jews in my house,' he had said recently. 'And
I'm no longer prepared to make an exception of Nell.' He held
nothing against her personally, he said, in fact he had always liked
her, but it was inappropriate for her to enter his home.

'*Our* home,' Melissa had corrected. And proceeded to remind
him of all the changes she had made because of his Judaism, which
was not, she stressed, her Judaism. 'In my home I'll have the friends
and family I want. I'll have llamas if it suits me.'

Melissa had reported the conversation to Nell and Laura earlier
in the week, and Nell had been furious. Daniel could stuff his
religion up his kosher arse for all she cared, she wouldn't want to
enter his home now even if he were to beg. '*My* home,' Melissa
reminded her, and added that as far as she was concerned, her
increasingly absentee husband had no rights in this matter. The three
women had ended up laughing together over women power,
chicken soup performance-enhancers and potential uprisings in the
mikvah, and this had been the flavour of the two or three comments
Nell had made to Laura since. So perhaps Daniel's appalling attitude
was no more likely to explain her outburst than her dissatisfaction
with work. Laura wracked her brains for a few moments longer,
then decided to forgo the guesswork. As loathe as she was to have
this conversation, she realised she had no choice.

'What do you mean "you're bored"?'

'I don't know how to be any clearer,' Nell said, making no
attempt to disguise her irritation. 'I'm bored, Laura, I am, quite
simply, bored. Look at our life, look at our friends. Every day, every
week, every bloody year, the same people, the same places, the same
conversations.' Nell spoke with a fluency which suggested her
thoughts had benefited from considerable rehearsal. 'I look at us and
rather than the lively, cutting-edge, we're-going-to-change-the-
world sort of people we always planned to be, or rather I planned to
be, I see two women slouching towards middle age, drab and dismal
and dragging their best years behind them.'

Clearly she and Nell had very different perspectives, indeed Nell
would be hard-pressed to find any support for her view. As for the
whole middle-age caper, Laura had made a conscious decision
before she turned forty to jettison middle age forever. Middle age

was a figure in a sensible skirt with twinset and pearls, a figure which had passed away along with earlier generations, a figure which had nothing in common with Laura.

'Speak for yourself,' she now said. And as she turned into her brother's street, 'Can we postpone this talk until after dinner?'

'Of course,' Nell replied. 'Who am I to upset the Jewish family?'

If the feeling in the car had been bad, worse was lodged within the timber and glass interior of Daniel and Melissa's home. The atmosphere was crisp and careful, with Daniel and Melissa skirting round each other like athletes before a race. Their twenty-three-year-old son Nicholas was the immediate source of tension. During his schooldays Nick, like his father before him, had been drawn to a greater observance of Judaism – although more of a hobby than his father's energetic calling. But in the past few years the hobby had become an all-embracing commitment. Not only had Nick overtaken his father, he had decided to study for the rabbinate; worse still, he'd chosen a college in America. Daniel was elated, but Melissa together with Sophie, a cool, slender twenty year old studying at the Film and Television School, were not impressed.

'Daniel's defection was one thing, and took some adjusting,' Melissa said to Laura and Nell as she prepared the dinner. 'But it's far worse when it happens to your son. God knows we have little in common now, but when he's finished with this rabbinical nonsense we'll have nothing. And he'll find himself one of those wives with a wig and the clothes sense of a nun, who'll have baby after baby and she and I will have as much to talk about as I now have with Daniel's *meshuggeneh* pals.' Melissa took a hefty swig of non-kosher vodka and tonic. 'My son tells me nothing. Nothing. If I ask, he says there's no point talking to me because either I won't understand or I'll ridicule. And when I mention I've stayed with his father all these years and have provided a home in which both of them have lived as observant Jews, he looks at me as if he despises me.'

She was sobbing now and, when the tears would not stop, excused herself. A few minutes later she returned to the kitchen red-nosed and dry-eyed, refreshed her drink and applied herself to some California rolls and some bite-sized fishy things – 'For we girls,' she said indicating the platter. 'To have with drinks. *Our* drinks. My husband and son won't go near this stuff.' She added a clump of chives, a couple of curls of lemon peel, a small dollop of something dippable and stood back to appraise. The platter was, as with all Melissa's platters, a work of art. She slid it along the bench, then pulled a couple of bowls from a cupboard, slammed them on the bench, filled one with olives, including two olives which had fallen to the floor – 'A dollop of non-kosher botulism would be good for them' – and the other with sliced dill cucumbers reeking of garlic. If the expression on her face could have translated to action, she would have spat in each bowl.

Melissa was clearly out of patience.

'You know Daniel's planning an extended trip to Israel?'

Laura did know because Melissa had mentioned it several times.

'And now that Nick's going to America, Daniel will probably spend some time there too. I may as well not have a husband.' She looked from Laura to Nell. 'I envy you, I really do.'

As she finished arranging the hors d'oeuvres she talked about what it was like to have a husband who put so many things ahead of her, who would prefer to spend his leisure with a crop of men smelling of chicken fat, men who not only didn't know her but wouldn't want to know her.

'Daniel and I used to have so much fun. Films, picnics, jazz concerts. We used to mesh so well together, but now –' Suddenly she stopped, her gaze directed to the door. Daniel had entered the kitchen.

'And we could have a life together again,' he said. 'Even better than before.'

He spoke softly, but each word was clear and resonant, eerily so. And then he turned away. He left the kitchen, he left the house and walked down the path to a sheltered alcove at the end of the garden. To be alone, to collect himself, to try and find his balance in a life which was crumbling. It had come to this, he was thinking, the wife who had once been his saviour was now ridiculing him and demeaning his choices, and making no attempt whatsoever to bridge the gap between them.

'Share this with me,' he had begged when he first became interested in Judaism. 'Come to *shule*. Join one of the women's study groups.'

But she had never been interested, not then nor now. She knew she was Jewish, she said, she didn't need to eat it and wear it, and she certainly didn't need to make a lifetime's study of it.

He brushed some leaves off a garden bench and sat in the shadows watching the house. In the early years he had persisted, hoping she would change her mind. And then one day it dawned on him he liked having his religion to himself. Indeed, if she were to change her mind now, and the arrival of the Messiah was far more likely, Daniel would be at pains to talk her out of it. His religion was his only comfort and she would spoil it for him, not through deliberate malice, he had never believed she wished him harm, but through a certain shallowness. It was an awful observation to make about your own wife, but there was no avoiding it: Melissa seemed without passions, without longings, or at least none he could discern. As for his own yearnings, as obvious as a face without a nose, she had always been blind to them.

His parents hadn't noticed them either. Yet from his earliest years he had been aware of an emptiness cutting deep within him, an abrasive hollow which filled so much space and yet demanded itself to be filled. He remembered as a young boy drawing a picture of his family: mother, father and himself – Laura was yet to be born; the parental figures had bodies shaped and clothed, but his own torso was an empty circle.

It was how he had always been, a person with a hollowness hard within him, and spawning a yearning so amorphous yet so voracious, and little notion how to satisfy it. Yearning not wanting. Wanting knows its target, yearning is far less specific – although he had known since boyhood that lining his emptiness was the Holocaust. It was a reluctant knowing and one he preferred to avoid, yet he was convinced if he could somehow fill the gaping hole inside him he would submerge, quieten, his Holocaust heritage. He saw an analogy with the Eildon Weir, a vast man-made catchment not far from Melbourne which had drowned out an unwanted landscape. What worked so well in geography and metaphor he hoped would work for him.

But despite his efforts it didn't. While still a boy he tried friends, but they were so unpredictable that sometimes the yearning cut even deeper. And Etti's terrified opposition notwithstanding, he had tried horseback riding, but soon he learned it was the idea which appealed, the freedom of bare-backed speeding over a deserted beach, not the uncomfortable reality of falls and aching muscles and a face full of flies. He tried sex when he was older, but this was before the sexual revolution reached Melbourne, and the abandon which might have made sex a useful solution was strangled in guilt and elastic girdles. He had tried dope too, so much dope that the five-year period before he met Melissa was a soggy blur.

Finally he tried Melissa, and at last he seemed to settle. She was Jewish but without a Holocaust background, a good-looking woman who wore her Jewishness as elegantly as her silk shirts and Georg Jensen jewellery. She was fun, she was spirited, and she threw herself into sex with an abandon of the highest order. She blanketed the emptiness and he thought he was cured. But then they married, and Nick and Sophie arrived, and there was money to be made, and with Melissa always so involved with the children the yearning started to gnaw again.

He drowned his pains in work. He had been drawn to computer technology for much the same reason he would later be drawn to religion: it seemed such a private and benign source of succour. By the time Nick and Sophie were at school, his company was a major computer payroll supplier and he was already exploiting the possibilities of the new digitalisation. At the age of forty he was a millionaire several times over. But despite his successes he was still restless, his chest still gaped achingly, and he was lonely too. Not surprisingly, when the rabbis turned up at his door he welcomed them in.

And so he came to Judaism, not the Judaism of his parents, a watery, secular, ham-in-the-fridge, Holocaust-defined Judaism, but a Judaism which meant something, and now meant everything to him. It replenished him, it gave him hope and meaning, and it gave him comfort. And he was no longer lonely. He could talk at length with the other men at the synagogue about any subject, including the Holocaust. This was the Judaism Melissa disparaged.

His parents' Holocaust had been so painfully personal, you couldn't question or discuss it; in fact, the only permissible role in the face of such suffering was to listen. Or at least with his mother. It was worse with his father whose silence, suggesting as it did experiences too dreadful for words, made the whole business even more untouchable. But at the *shule* he met survivors and children

237

of survivors, many of whom, like him, had come to orthodoxy as adults. Daniel talked and prayed with the men at the synagogue and the hollow deep within him started to fill.

Only Jews care about Jews, he now believed, and the strength of Jews lay in their acting together and speaking in one voice no matter where in the world they lived. He could go to New York, or Rome or London or Belgrade and find Jews just like him, all with the same values, the same beliefs, the same vision. He truly believed that the greatest threat to the future of Judaism was not anti-Semitism, but liberal and secular Jews like his wife.

Twenty-five years together, half a lifetime, and so little in common, not even the children. Sophie, so like her mother, rarely said a word to him, and Nick, so much his father's son, hardly acknowledged his mother's existence. They lived like two couples under the same roof: Melissa and Sophie, Nick and himself. Even their past, his and Melissa's, was no longer shared. An event of ten or fifteen years ago might be mentioned and Daniel would find himself recalling a vastly different situation and for entirely different reasons than Melissa. In short, what once was important to him about their life together was not to her. As to what she valued, much of the time his memory simply failed him.

He had asked himself whether he still loved her, and was too afraid to answer. There were times when she showed him a kindness, or would look at him with warmth, and his heart would leap and he would want to take her in his arms. But suspecting that old habits were stronger than new resentments, he kept his hands to himself. He wondered whether he had ever loved her, whether he had ever loved anyone properly. Certainly not his parents. He had respected them and admired them, but also resented them in equal measure. And with your children it is so difficult to know whether you have loved them properly, loved them in the best possible way. As for Laura, ten years is a huge gap between a brother and sister and love didn't really come into it.

But he did love God. And he did love his Judaism. And he loved those Jews who greeted him at morning and evening prayers as if he really mattered. He felt at home in their little synagogue in a way he did not in his own home or his parents' home before that. And he loved the certainty of his faith, and all the arguments, the ideas, the conundrums which filled the books of learning.

The people of the book were his people and he loved being part of it.

He looked towards the house. The lights were on, there were shadows behind the blinds, a normal family home except the husband and father was loitering outside in the dark. He should go inside, part of him really wanted to, but so many things had been said, so many angry, cruel words, the most recent just two nights ago, a violent slanging match over Israel, and he and Melissa had hardly spoken since. It had been largely his fault, he had been blunt, far too blunt about his plans to spend some time in Israel before – and he could recall his exact words – 'Those idiot Labour supporters hand over the whole country to the Arabs.'

He wished he had shown more restraint, after all, he would make his trip no matter what she thought, but sometimes his frustration burst out, surprising him more than anyone else. He was hardly aware these days of how much he bottled inside. So he exploded and she was shouting at him that Labour was the best hope for Israel, in fact, the only hope. And if only *meshuggeners* like him – 'My own husband,' she said in a voice oozing venom – stayed out of it, peace was a real possibility.

The argument had continued for hours. At one stage she said the best solution to the conflict was to take the *meshuggeneh* Arabs and the *meshuggeneh* Jews, stick them all in a compound, arm the lot of them, lock the gates and let them kill each other; then the moderates on both sides could get on with the negotiations. He could hardly believe what he was hearing, and from his own wife too. He yelled at her, she yelled back. He yanked her arm, she kicked his shin. She threw his Shabbat goblet across the room and dented it, he threw her Lalique sculpture to the floor and shattered it. They shouted cruel and horrible words to each other and neither made any attempt to retract.

Soon the Middle East conflict was left far behind and he was attacking her secularism and accusing her of shallowness, and she was attacking his orthodoxy and blaming his Holocaust background for it.

'I'm a Jew,' he had shouted at her. 'Not just someone once removed from genocide.'

And when she shouted back she was as much a Jew as he was, he plunged in the knife.

'Show me,' he said. 'Just show me what sort of Jew you are.'

But she couldn't, for she had nothing whatsoever to show for her Jewishness. As for the Jewish sensibility she waved at him, it was laughable.

'A little bit of guilt, a little bit of neurosis, a fondness for disinfectant and a belief in the restorative powers of chicken soup? That makes you a cliché, Melissa, it doesn't make you Jewish.'

She accused him of Holocaust superiority: 'All you descendants of survivors think you're so much more authentic than the rest of us.'

It showed how little she knew: he had chosen religious observance not the Holocaust to inscribe his Jewish identity. Melissa knew nothing about his choices, like she had known nothing of the yearnings which had precipitated them. She was wrong in everything she had said the other night, had been wrong about everything she had said for years. His bags were half packed, he already had one foot outside the door, and he knew that driving him away was not that he and Melissa shared so little but that she disparaged what he valued most.

He looked up as the back door clicked open. Silhouetted against the light were his wife and his sister. He guessed they would either call out to him from where they stood, or Melissa would send Laura to find him. He watched as they exchanged a few words, then Laura turned and went inside. His wife lingered a moment on the doorstep and then she advanced slowly down the path. She would know exactly where to find him. He knew he should meet her halfway, but he couldn't. He watched her draw closer, he could hear her shoes on the gravel, he thought he could smell her perfume. He sucked in hard, sucked in his life and sadness, and tasted memory. He sighed, deep to his heart he sighed, and at the last moment stepped out of the alcove to meet her. Without a word the two of them walked back to the house together.

From the kitchen Laura watched them come up the path. There was something deeply moving about the scene. She turned to Nell, 'Melissa will never leave him,' she said quietly.

Nell assumed her irritated expression. 'You're such a romantic, Laura. It doesn't take a genius to work out that Melissa stays with Daniel because she gets something out of it. Quite a lot actually, particularly for a strong-minded woman like her. She leads a life entirely separate from her husband. She could go out all day and half the night while he's at his prayers and never have to account for herself. She has all the trappings of marriage and, as long as she's discreet, none of the constraints.' Then still totally oblivious to Laura's mood, her face softened into a grin. 'There's a lot to recommend it.'

Was Nell tiring of their relationship? Laura found herself wondering, and quickly brushed the thought aside: of course they were all right, just going through a rocky patch.

Later when they were all congregated around the Shabbat table with Nick leading the service, Laura looked at Melissa and Daniel. There was every reason for them to separate, but whenever that had seemed a real possibility, something always prevailed. Perhaps Nell was right, perhaps it was pragmatism not love, but alternatively there were the mysterious ties of long-term couples. Whatever the reason, the two of them would draw back from the precipice, at least for a short time.

And so it happened that evening. Melissa decided to ignore her son's desertion, while Nick himself confined his conversation to secular topics. Sophie shed her anger at her brother sufficiently to allow a dark and sprightly humour to surface. Even Daniel was more his old self; he complimented his wife on the meal, and passed a few jokes with Nell. There was only one fragile moment when Sophie raised the topic of the asylum seekers. 'You must have your work cut out for you at the moment,' she said to Laura, who simply nodded and went to change the topic.

Daniel, however, was too quick. 'This sort of racism is why Jews have to start behaving like Jews,' he said. 'Be seen as Jews, make an impression as Jews, present a strong united front as Jews.'

Laura was tempted to say that black coats and shaggy beards and umpteen children and out-moded dietary laws and time switches on Shabbat and living in modern *shtetls* and burying your head in the Talmud would do little to stop any sort of violence and bigotry, but could anticipate her brother's retort: Jews who don't deserve to be called Jews have no right to an opinion on Jewish issues. And besides, for the sake of her relationship with Nell she'd made a private pact to leave her politics at work.

It was little more than a thumb print on the mood of the evening and soon the jollity returned. Daniel even did a shortened *bentshing* after the meal because they wanted to continue an hilarious discussion about the film each of them would make if they had Steven Spielberg's money and connections. By the time they said goodnight even Nell was her old self, and when in the car Laura picked up the dangling threads of their earlier conversation – Nell's boredom, her obvious discontent – Nell brushed them aside. 'It's probably hormonal,' she said.

Whatever it was, it refused to go away. The next day, after an awkward breakfast together, Laura attempted to talk about the tensions between them. But Nell refused, accusing Laura of nagging.

'You're making trouble where there is none,' she said. 'Just leave it alone.'

Laura might have persisted, out of fear more than desire, but at that moment the doorbell rang.

Standing in the doorway was the part-time tutor from Nell's department, a woman young enough to be called Cyndee. Nell was suddenly her old charming self. How nice it is, Laura was thinking as she watched the two of them, that Nell has a young friend in the department. And how fortunate, given that Nell has alienated quite a few of her other colleagues. Nell invited the girl in, made the introductions, and as the three of them chatted together, Laura felt the recent tensions fall away. This was better, she was thinking, much better; perhaps all they needed were some new friends. But soon the conversation turned to departmental matters, which was, as far as Laura was concerned, the fast track to boredom. Several times a week for several years now she had heard about this or that idiot in the department, or this or that incompetent, or this or that sleaze. In fact, if Nell were bored with their friends, perhaps she should take note that many of their friends were, like Nell, academics, and wanting, like Nell, to talk university issues ad infinitum. It was like a mutual dabbing at weeping sores and Laura not up to it today, so when Cyndee suggested they continue their talking on a walk, Laura made an excuse and let them go alone.

A few minutes later Laura, too, prepared to leave the house. She had a huge amount of work to do, but she needed to unwind. She was about to shut the door and head off to Dight Falls, the rapids in the centre of Melbourne and a place always conducive to thought, when she heard the phone ring. She hesitated a moment, then re-entered the house and bounded up the stairs to interrupt the message mid-flow.

It was the American, Raphe Carter. Laura had not heard from him since that day several months ago when he turned up at her office.

'Four days not enough to unearth the family history?' she now said.

He was laughing. Not nearly enough, and besides, it left no time to see anything of the city. So he was back in town, and with no special plans.

Laura found herself agreeing to meet him for coffee; not simply the dull moan of the recent tensions with Nell, but something about the American, his newness, his humour and ease, suddenly seemed exactly what she needed.

But first she had to know about Alice Carter. 'She's an American like you,' she said. 'Also from San Francisco. She knew my father.'

His response was quick and uncomplicated. He'd never heard of an Alice Carter, and then added that Carter was not an uncommon name in his part of the world.

Laura was more relieved than surprised. When there had been no word from Raphe after their first meeting, she decided he had no sinister motives, that he was probably nothing more than an American accustomed to easy solutions and immediate gratification. In fact, she'd hardly given him a thought these past three months. Now, however, she found herself looking forward to seeing him again. She directed him to her regular café, changed her clothes, and set off immediately to meet him.

Intimate Betrayals

He liked her, he liked her very much, and would prefer not to. He liked her humour, her ideas and her politics. He liked her tall womanly figure, her mass of blonde curls and her fine pale skin. As they sat opposite each other drinking their double espressos, the ideologically suspect Australian 'long black', Raphe reached across and touched her hair. 'Something caught in your curls,' he said, surprised at how wiry it felt.

He liked her so much it would be easy to forget why he was here. He had to keep reminding himself that certain wrongs would always be wrong, that murder in the past was no less murder now, that no one had paid for his grandfather's death and someone damn well ought to. But while his thoughts were set firm, the rest of him was wavering. It was far easier, he decided, to be an effective hater in the confines of your own mind. For in the presence of the very real Laura Lewin, reason had deserted him. What on earth had made him return to Australia? What on earth did he think he could achieve?

He wanted to go home and return to the drawing board. At the same time he wanted to stay right where he was, drinking coffee with Laura Lewin who was so different from the Laura Lewin of his imaginings. Calm down, he told himself. No one is forcing you to do anything, no one even knows the real purpose of this trip, and managed to settle himself sufficiently to ask about her work, a topic designed to keep her talking while he regained his composure.

As soon as she began to talk, so he began to feel better, although not in the way he had hoped. His anxiety and conflicts disappeared because Laura Lewin occupied his entire attention. Such an expressive speaker, he couldn't take his eyes off her; the tiniest movement of her face, the lift of an eyebrow, the flicker of a grimace, emphasised and elaborated her words. She was equipped with that special skill of exposing brutality and injustice through reference to individual stories. She guided him through some terrible narratives, sparing him nothing but at the same time ready to lend a hand should he falter. He saw the dust and disease of refugee camps, he felt the stink and cramp of rotting trawlers, he knew the loss of whole families, whole villages, he saw death and mutilation in all their cruel diversity. As she told the stories it was as if the victims themselves were speaking and his own urgency fell away.

Hearing about her work at the commission, Raphe couldn't help but wonder if he had judged the law too quickly all those years ago, for Laura, it seemed, managed to operate within a framework of justice.

'Although it takes regular beatings,' she said. 'Revenge – a form of rough justice by any other name – is so much easier than justice, and certainly less encumbered by rules and regulations.'

Rough justice. And suddenly Raphe found his feet. Rough justice, and Laura Lewin's attractions fell away. Rough justice, and Raphe knew exactly what he was doing here.

So many times had he imagined those last dreadful moments in a wooded area not far from Belsen, two men, opposites in every respect, one his grandfather, sick, but perhaps not dying, and the other Laura's father, strong and healthy – and still strong and healthy in his eighties according to Raphe's mother. A crime had been committed yet no one had paid. The courts had failed, and with the increasing passage of time, soon they would stop bothering. Which left only rough justice.

As Laura chatted on about her work, he wanted to grab her by the arms tight enough to hurt, grab and shake and squeeze her to the bone. He wanted to tell her the truth, make her listen, make her understand who her father really was. Now that would be a form of rough justice.

More than sixty years ago and another era, two men in a wood, one on the side of the barbarians and the other among the persecuted, and, despite his mother's account, Raphe still tormented by the possibilities. Was his grandfather forced to lie in his weakness as Laura's father came towards him? Might there have been a stick, or a gun, or perhaps a knife? Or did the brute rely only on his bare beefy fists. Did Martin Lewin in a sweat of fear and helplessness watch his own death drawing closer? Did he with his last breath beg to be spared?

Raphe had spent a good many nights lying in his own sweat gnawing at the unfairness of it all. As he lectured his students, or worked at his keyboard, even on occasions when he was with a woman, he was aware of the weight of his grandfather's suffering, a leaden cladding as snug and heavy as custom-made armour. He felt the torment so intensely, he couldn't help but wonder if there was something specific to him, some nugget of madness or idiocy that had him choking the present in the long reach of the past. Even his mother had handled the knowledge better. What you can't change, she used to say, you have to accommodate. You have to move on. And while Raphe had tried, his grandfather refused to be left behind.

All so different from Laura Lewin. No extra identities had attached to her, no suits of ancestral demands were weighing her down. And again he was struck by the unfairness of it all. He felt wronged, personally wronged, like when he was a boy and someone stole his new football, or later at college when a fellow student pinched his ideas and received a higher grade. But this was no football or college essay, this was a life. His grandfather had been wronged; his mother deprived of her parents had been wronged; and he, Raphe, the only one now remaining, had been wronged. Someone ought to pay.

Yet as he sat in the small café across from Laura Lewin, the woman he had charged as responsible, the woman who was talking about work he found admirable, sat with her here rather than viewing her in the glare of his private and unrestrained imaginings, he found it impossible to make his sense of wrong coalesce in her.

For years he had lived with an imagined woman, a prototype Laura Lewin already guilty by virtue of who she was. In his mind she had existed only as the daughter of Henry Lewin, and his only interest in her had been as the grandson of Martin Lewin. But now the flesh-and-blood version was invigorating quite a different set of interests. She was so vibrant, so funny, so engaged, and her work had a real effect in the world. She was the sort of wide-screen, irresistible woman who had always appealed to him. And young in a way that he, almost exactly the same age, was not.

As she talked, it was as if she wrapped him in her voice. He was surprised to see the café had filled, including a pair of squealing children at the very next table. He wondered how it was possible to experience a description of work as an act of intimacy, particularly when uttered by someone he wanted to find abhorrent. It was not that the words she used were so unusual, rather she selected them with special care, like a painter choosing colours. Earlier she had described her friend Nell as 'the wellspring' of her life, and the religious brother as 'a performer in his own tragedy'. Now she was talking about travel, how much she enjoyed it. 'Boredom,' she said, 'is the most barren of soils. And complacency,' she paused a moment, 'complacency is like a top of the range coffin.'

She asked him about some of the volcanoes he'd seen. As she listened she was smiling at him across the table, which felt more like a smiling *into* him.

'With your love of volcanoes,' she said at last, 'I expect you wouldn't do a good complacency.'

And while he managed to smile back, more for her turn of phrase than anything else, he wished he could be as certain as she.

He had let his coffee go cold and Laura went to order some more. As she waited at the counter to place their order, she was thinking how less sure of himself he was than the man who had appeared in her office all those months ago, less brash too. And unlike that other time, far more interested in her, or at least making a good pretence of it. Not that she cared: any interest, even feigned, was welcome these days. Nell was working flat out on a grant proposal and hardly ever home, and when they did spend time together, she was so critical of Laura and the life they shared, there was scant pleasure in it. In fact, the scene in the car last night had been typical of recent times. Laura would screen topics for discussion and rehearse her opinions beforehand; she'd cut interesting snippets from the paper and make a note of gossip, but none of her attempts improved the situation. She would scour the entertainment guides for activities to appeal to Nell: a new multimedia exhibition, moonlight cinema, fish and chips down on the wharf, a series of avant-garde short films. But few were taken up, and those that were often provided a new source of criticism rather than the pleasure for which they were intended.

So this time with Raphe was a welcome respite. She ordered their coffee and on returning to the table asked about his background. She listened as he talked of his mother's experience as part of the *Kindertransport*. He spoke so movingly about the little girl sent away by the parents she was never to see again, the hurt and loss of the child, and the hopes which had helped make the loss bearable. He seemed to feel so much of what his mother had suffered it did not surprise Laura he'd not had children of his own. And through it all she was aware of an intense empathy with him. He had loved his mother deeply although not always easily.

'Sometimes I was too much the centre of her world,' he said. And laughed, 'Of course I would have forgiven her anything.'

Laura could have used exactly the same words in relation to Etti.

She encouraged Raphe to talk about his mother, such a different experience from her own and yet somehow illuminating it. And when he digressed to speak about his grandfather, a man with whom he clearly felt a strong bond, Laura was quick to steer him back.

They talked until the sky darkened and the owners of the café were stacking tables around them, a strange, fervid time, during which both were driven to greater confession by that hothouse intimacy which often happens when strangers meet. They were in this together, this life, these mothers, these sunderings, or so it seemed to Laura, who felt a closeness to Raphe she did not feel with many of her old friends. And, she realised, a fresh closeness with her mother as well.

Raphe had not treated his mother with the same kid gloves Laura had used with Etti. He'd never seen the necessity for it, he said. 'After all my mother had suffered, I was sure she'd be able to manage anything I might dish up.'

And of course he was right. But it had never before appeared to Laura to be that simple.

When they finally left the café, Laura insisted on driving him to his hotel, a way of thanking him for a special afternoon. They walked in step to her car, close but not touching. He must feel it too, she was thinking. This connection, he must feel it too.

The house was quiet and still when Laura arrived home. There was a note from Nell on the bench: with the grant proposal due to be submitted soon, she and Cyndee had decided to have a work dinner. Laura was quite pleased, she needed some time alone. She gathered up Wystan and stood at the glass, stroking the cat and staring through her reflection to the darkness beyond. A long time passed before she put the sleeping animal on the couch and went to the filing cabinet for her mother's transcript. Raphe's account of his own mother had aroused a longing for hers. The transcript and – it was hardly a decision after all this time – the tape as well. She was ready to listen to it, ready to hear her mother's voice. Even if she were never to see Raphe again, she'd be grateful to him for guiding her to this moment.

But it's not there. The transcript's not there. She knows the exact file. The file's empty. The transcript's not there. She checks either side of the file, it's not there. She checks every file in the drawer, it's not there. Then every drawer and back again to the first one where it should be, where it has been ever since that afternoon years ago when Nell read it aloud to her. It's not anywhere.

She searches the cabinet a second time and a third, then the drawers of her desk and after that her bookcases. She excavates her mother's box of treasures from beneath the stairs: everything in its place but no transcript. She slips the audio cassette in her pocket and returns to the filing cabinet for yet another fruitless search.

So many times of clawing the same ground before conceding that no matter how closely she looks, the transcript is simply not there and disbelief won't make it suddenly appear. She starts on the rest of the house – the linen cupboard with its neat stacks of towels and sheets, then the broom cupboard and after that the liquor cabinet, then the kitchen cupboards and drawers. It's like losing her mother all over again. She searches behind chairs and couches, among the sheet music on top of the piano, through the rest of the bookcases. It's the only transcript. Daniel didn't want a copy, Daniel didn't even want to read it. One copy in all the world, although, and she pats her pocket, the tape still exists, she forgot in her panic the original exists, so she could transcribe it herself. But it's not the same. She wants her mother's transcription, the one her mother read and approved. She searches the bathroom, the laundry, she searches handbags and suitcases, she even looks under the living-room rug.

She's faint with desperation when finally she finds it, in Nell's study of all places. Lying there on her desk. Etti's story on Nell's desk. She grabs it, clasps it to her chest, and with the relief plunging through her, she slumps to the floor. It is unbelievable that Nell would have gone to Laura's filing cabinet, riffled through until she found the transcript and then taken it without asking. What could she be thinking? Nell who has been so cool these past couple of months and so critical of Laura, what could she be thinking of?

And suddenly it occurs to her, the only possible explanation: Nell must be wanting to make amends. They've been going through such a rough patch, round and round, and when one has wanted to make peace the other has been too hurt to respond. So difficult to know how to stop the cycle. But Nell has finally done it. She's been critical about everything concerning Laura, but particularly what she sees as Laura's overreaction to the political situation, so what better way to try and understand than a return to those experiences of Etti's which helped shaped Laura in the first place? What other explanation could there be? It's Nell's way of showing she's sorry for her recent behaviour, Nell's way of reaching out to Laura in the most elemental way, Nell's way of showing she understands.

The transcript is safe and Nell as committed as ever. It's the only possible explanation. Laura wipes her eyes and clears her throat, and with the transcript tight in her hand and the tape tucked deep in her pocket goes into the lounge. She slips the cassette into the tape deck, curls up on the couch with the cat, and with the transcript in front of her, finally – again – listens to her mother's voice.

~

'Who in your family do you most resemble?' Raphe asks Laura as she drives the rugged contortions of the Great Ocean Road around the southern coast of Victoria.

A week has passed since their first coffee. In the interim they have met for drinks and dinner as well as some local sightseeing. Raphe has not met Nell, neither it seems has Laura much over the same period, but he knows who she is and her relationship with Laura. Times are tough, he said a few days ago, when good-looking women who could have any man opt for a female partner instead. Laura's response was sharp: lack of success with men did not turn women into lesbians.

Raphe decides that despite their vulnerabilities, family relationships are a safer topic. 'So who in your family do you most resemble?' he asks again.

Her answer surprises him, and she is quick to add, 'But not to such an extent the lines were blurred between my father and me. And,' she says with a smile, 'don't think for a moment my father made me a lesbian.' She goes on to explain that identification with Etti was impossible. 'My mother guarded her identity so fiercely. She could never let us forget she'd been shaped by hardship not only worse than anything my brother and I had ever experienced, but worse than we could even imagine.'

Towards her mother, Laura says, she always felt an overwhelming love mixed with an overwhelming responsibility. Although, and she keeps this to herself, so much has changed since listening to the tape, and changed so absolutely and with such positive effects that Laura cannot help but wonder how different the past few years might have been had she found the courage to listen to it earlier.

It was an alchemical experience, three hours of spellbinding intensity, with Etti speaking directly to her in a voice so much quieter and calmer than her old puff and bluster. Finally, it seemed, Etti had no need to prove anything about her past, the very fact the Holocaust Museum had commissioned the tape meant she was believed. In those three hours so many of the burdens passed to Laura while Etti was still alive were diffused. She even dared think that rather than the less than perfect daughter she had long judged herself to be, she had probably been as good a daughter as was possible to such a long-suffering mother. As to why the tape had a far more profound effect than Nell's reading of the transcript, she could not with absolute certainty say, except it was her mother's own voice in the conversation she never managed to have with her daughter.

Laura told no one about listening to the tape. It was a private experience, a revelatory experience; indeed, if moments of epiphany could stretch to several hours, it was one such moment. She replaced the transcript exactly where she found it on Nell's desk, and a couple of days later it reappeared in her filing cabinet. Now with Raphe sitting next to her in the car, she realises she would be more inclined to tell him about listening to her mother's tape than Nell. She glances across at him and smiles: he has entered her life at exactly the right time.

His own face is solemn as he meets her gaze. 'So you identified with your father then?'

She nods. 'By keeping his losses to himself, my father harnessed me to none of the same burdens as my mother.'

I bet he didn't, Raphe is thinking. He has prepared himself carefully for today. No falling for her charms, no failing in his responsibilities towards his grandfather. For it is incomprehensible that Laura, a highly intelligent woman fully aware of life's complexities, could not know the truth about her father. If Phil, Raphe's own all-American father had been a Nazi and a murderer, Raphe is sure he would know. Either Henry Lewin played his stolen identity to perfection or, far more likely, Laura was in cahoots with him and deserves to share the blame.

At the beginning of this visit Raphe had resolved to approach the topic of Henry Lewin with restraint, not wanting to arouse Laura's suspicions. But now he casts his caution aside, he simply can't wait any longer, and soon he is conducting the complete survivor's questionnaire. He asks about Henry's background, his family history and early social circumstances, his movements during the war, how he ended up in Australia, who of his family survived, what searches he did and what reparations he received.

Laura's answers are neat and sure and lacking detail; her father didn't talk about these things, she explains. And when Raphe persists, she stresses there is no more information to give.

'You're just like Nell,' Laura says, surprised and saddened by his sudden brusqueness. 'She's convinced my quiet, reserved father was neither so quiet nor reserved, just hiding something.'

'And what do you think? Was your father hiding something?'

Hiding is such a sweetly innocent word, Raphe is thinking. Two simple syllables to cover a multitude of sins. He holds his gaze hard ahead, sketching in his mind's eye a clearing, not in a German wood, but here on this jagged Australian coast, a pocket hidden from the road, with the steep cliffs rising on one side and the steep drop to the ocean on the other, and he and Laura standing together in the blustering wind. And coinciding with a heavier gust, a gentle shove, and at long last blessed justice for a crime committed more than half a century before. Not trusting himself, yet knowing that within the courageous confines of his imagination he wouldn't hesitate in that nonchalant, calamitous nudge, he keeps his gaze away from her and his hands locked painfully together.

'Was your father hiding something?' he asks again.

The road is narrow and treacherous. A metre to the left and the car will bounce down the brutal cliffs to the ocean below, a metre to the right and it will be in the path of oncoming traffic, yet Laura twists her gaze from the road and looks at him, clearly deliberating whether to speak or not. And suddenly he is afraid of what she may know and equally afraid of what she may not know. Wishes he had not asked the question, wishes his mother had not bequeathed him this terrible knowledge, wishes history had left him alone to mosey on through life without these wrestlings with revenge and justice. And now he's met Laura Lewin who makes such an unacceptable enemy, there's forgiveness to grapple with as well. Forgiveness after all these years, as if he doesn't have enough to lug through his days. I'm not my grandfather, he wants to shout. I'm not my grandfather. Yet against the hum and whoosh of the car on the curling road he feels the beat of his grandfather's blood in his veins.

It jerks him back to reality. He reminds himself this quest is not his alone, that he has no right to dwell on fear. Fear is his grandfather's province, real fear in the face of life-threatening dangers. Raphe sucks in his breath: if he won't act on behalf of his grandfather, no one else will. Yet with Laura Lewin sitting just inches away from him, no amount of logic will alter the fact that enemies should feel different from her. When it comes to the real, very much alive Laura Lewin, Raphe simply does not want to shoulder his responsibilities.

'What do you think?' he says again, trying to grasp a new determination. 'Was your father hiding something?'

Laura begins to speak, so slowly that it seems to Raphe she's deciding with each word whether to continue. She says she doesn't believe her father ever revealed the whole story – a long pause – but he resisted all her attempts to discover more. A longer pause now, and Raphe already sparring with his own demons doesn't need to put up with impatience as well. He wants to drag the words out of her. But he remains silent, he does not even look at her, just wills her to continue.

The road is very high at this point, the plunge to the ocean sharper than ever, and it occurs to Raphe that he is as much at Laura's mercy as she drives this precarious Australian coast as his grandfather was with her father in that wood outside Belsen. For a moment the possibility is terrifyingly real, then the road widens and bends briefly inland. The word 'mercy' lingers; it strikes him as peculiarly un-Jewish.

'My own investigations,' Laura says, 'small as they were, suggested there was more to be learned.' She checks the rear-vision mirror and slows the car down. 'But my father's gone now and,' there's a slight hesitation, 'I suppose I'm resolved to let him have the last word.'

She pulls in at a scenic observation point and stops the car. She's picking at a knob of loose plastic on the steering wheel. 'I loved my father,' her voice is no more than a murmur. 'I loved him enough to accept his version of his life, even though I knew –' Raphe leans forward, a small interrogative explosion escaping his lips. 'Oh yes,' she continues, 'I always knew we didn't have the whole truth. But it was, after all, his life. And who needs to know the almost unthinkable? Who can afford to remember it? I never wanted to force that on my father.'

She's lucky to have had the choice, Raphe is thinking. He swallows the bile and forces himself to listen as she tells about her so-small investigations, how there was no record of her father ever having worked in labour camps.

'And now I've stopped searching,' she says. 'Both my parents are dead, I've never had any grandparents, my brother's thrown in his lot with the *meshuggeners*, I can't afford to lose any more.'

There follows a long silence, with Laura still nagging at the knob of plastic and Raphe assaulted by questions and objections, and through it all a mess of fear, self-pity, resentfulness, envy and, as much as he would prefer otherwise, fatigue. At forty-three years of age Raphe finds himself a psychiatrist's delight, when all he wants is to do his duty by his grandfather and get on with his life.

Longing is such an effective gauge of a person's value and how Raphe has longed for his grandfather. If only, he used to think, longing were sufficient to disinter the dead. But now, high above a lethal coast, sitting with the daughter of his enemy in a car buffeted by stiff southern winds, he wishes there were someone else to take on his grandfather, just for a short time, to give Raphe a break: a trouble-shooter for the psyche, a Freud in the field.

He starts with a touch, her hand on his shoulder. Feels it through his clothes. A touch which pulls him into the present and spirals clean through him, a touch which spills onto his skin in a flood of hot prickles. A touch which, whether he likes it or not, blots out the old pains.

'Look,' she says. 'Take a look at this magnificent view.'

He gazes through the windscreen and sees where he is. Not simply a lethal coastline, nor a succession of threatening cliffs, but a brazenly beautiful stretch of clay-coloured crags and broad bleached sand. A coastline ringed with a wide collar of whitest foam, and beyond that the endless green of a wintry sea.

Her hand is still on his shoulder. He looks at her, she is not his Holocaust, she simply cannot be his Holocaust.

He makes himself smile, 'It's almost as good as Big Sur,' and notes the relief in his voice.

Laura stifles her laughter. Raphe Carter: academic, writer, volcano lover, Jew, American, and of them all the American clearly dominates. She smiles back at him, and the tensions of a moment ago are fortunately gone and in their place a ferocious hunger.

She starts the car and follows the coast a little further where the road dips to sea level. Within a few minutes she and Raphe are propped on a rug in the shelter of some low dunes just a few metres from the breaking waves. They had stopped at the Victoria Market before leaving Melbourne – food heaven, Laura had promised – but with Raphe clearly more interested in hygiene than food ('Nothing's covered in plastic,' he kept saying) she'd gone ahead with a selection to suit herself. And it's a veritable feast, she decides, as she spreads out the food.

'Not too cold?' Laura asks, and seeing he is, pulls off her scarf and gives it to him.

For the next hour or so, and despite the cold, they sit together on the wintry beach, dipping into the food, talking, laughing, arguing, and now and then retreating into their own thoughts.

At one point Raphe asks about Daniel and the religious choices he has made. Laura says she feels his loss much like an amputation, that she's aware of a shadow, an echo of how he used to be at the same time as she mourns his absence. She talks about feeling so powerless. He's the one who's deserted, she says, he's the one who's rejecting her, and she hates it, hates what he has taken from her.

She slurps a fat oyster from its shell. 'He's lucky it's not pork.'

Yet even as she speaks she realises how ridiculous she sounds. Just as Daniel's dietary laws will not make one iota of difference to his rewards from God, neither will her denial of those same laws have any effect on her brother's behaviour. It's just that she misses him so much.

'I see him passing his life in a capsule, like those bubble babies you read about. So safe and sterile, but the outside world will get him in the end.' She adds some smoked salmon and dill cucumber to a crust of rye and takes a hefty bite. She chews long and slowly. 'I've as much in common with a Jewish fundamentalist like my brother as I have with a Muslim fundamentalist, and each of them, incidentally, would have far more in common with each other than either would have with me. In fact, throw in a Christian fundamentalist, and you'd have the ultimate triumvirate, one with a nasty penchant for violence.'

Raphe's response surprises her. While he agrees with everything she says, he also believes that if she wants a brother she'll have to accept his choices, 'As he has accepted yours. I'm sure a lesbian sister was not on his agenda.'

And while it's true, Daniel has always accepted her lesbianism, it's now tainted by his lack of acceptance of the non-Jewishness of her partner. Although her brother's acceptance is not the main issue.

'Daniel's religious cohorts wouldn't accept me,' she says.

'But that's no reason to sink to their level.'

And the two of them burst out laughing. Something quite humorous about secular Jewish Laura being morally superior to the extreme orthodox.

And yet it isn't humorous, nothing about her brother's religious choices is humorous. 'His choices are downright dangerous, and not just for him but for all Jews,' Laura says. 'Observance has never saved anyone, it just makes you more obvious. More vulnerable too. All that communication exclusively with your own kind and the group never takes a critical view of itself, never tries to understand itself in relation to anyone else.' She slurps down another oyster. 'My brother and his mates are making it impossible for diverse people to live together.'

Raphe is quick to respond. 'But these sort of orthodox don't want to live with people who are different from themselves. They don't want diversity and pluralism. And they certainly don't want the likes of you.' He leans forward and touches the side of her face, a fleeting moment and then he is sitting back again leaving her with his touch on her cheek. 'But this doesn't alter the fact that Daniel's your brother, and if you want a brother then you'll have to make some concessions for him.'

A short time later they start for home. They have only travelled a few kilometres when Raphe indicates an uncleared area stretching inland from the road.

'I can't visit Australia and not experience the bush,' he says.

Laura pulls in at a narrow opening near a walking track and the two of them rug up and head off. She is happy for a walk, happy to slough off the familiar conflicts of her brother and enjoy the unexpected comforts of this new friend. The trees shelter them from the wind; she takes in the fresh, wet smell and the rustling of branches, the squelching of their boots and the crash of distant waves. And she takes in Raphe, his presence so strong that the side of her nearest to him is scratchy and hot. He has such a strange effect on her. There have been times during the past few days when she has felt so close to him that if someone were to prod him she would know the pressure, so close that when he has begun a sentence she could finish it. Indeed, the connection has been so pronounced that if she believed in reincarnation she would think they had met in a previous life. Then in a moment the harmony will disappear and there'll be the sharp bite of his interrogation about her father. And in another moment, the knowing empathy about her brother. So many moods, yet invariably intense. And exciting too, in a strangely charged yet strangely disturbing way, like being back in high school with a secret crush on one of the boys. She finds it all rather peculiar.

If there were something feminine about him she might better understand, but there is not. He is much the same height as she, shortish for a man, tallish for a woman, a neat, caramel-coloured man. She likes his compactness, his firmness, or at least she thinks he would feel firm, is tempted to touch and stops herself just in time. It's odd to be so aware of him physically and certainly not her usual response to a man, not her usual response to a woman come to that, and moves ever so slightly away.

Such a careful distance now between them, and is he aware of it too? Again she is reminded of high school ditherings: does he like me as much as I like him? And a flickering through her like wings she has not felt since the early days with Nell. He seems happy to walk in silence, and while he looks to be quite composed, perhaps he, too, is experiencing the same jangling as she is. She hopes so. And quickly stifles the thought, all these peculiar thoughts. Not what she wants to be thinking, a self-respecting, permanently partnered lesbian who has happily left her heterosexual days far in the past. She manoeuvres her attention to the bush, the slender, blue-grey eucalypts, the dripping ferns, the wombat hollows, but her body tugs her back to less environmentally sensitive topics. It's their conversation, she decides. They talk so closely, so intensely, and not the first time she has experienced the arousal of words. For there is something indisputably erotic bridging that careful distance between them. It was there on the beach as well; in fact, several times this past week she's been aware of it. And a pleasure in watching him, in hearing the soft nasality of his speech, even in his smell, a faintly herbal aroma.

And all because of the intensity of their talk? Who does she think she's fooling. And exactly on cue, there's a peal of laughter from a pair of kookaburras.

'Look,' Raphe says, stopping on the track. 'Look, two of them, up there on the branch and having such a good time.'

'Laughing at us, I bet,' Laura says, laughing herself.

'Oh I hope so, I do hope so,' he says.

Such a sweet man, she finds herself thinking, earnest but very sweet. And as disturbing as these feelings might be, they're far preferable to anything she has experienced with Nell these past couple of months. She is enjoying Raphe's company, not anything she can really explain, and neither, she suddenly realises, does she care. He's an unexpected gift, something in addition to the rest of her life, and very grateful she is too.

'May I hold your hand?'

She stops, so deep in her own thoughts, and wonders if she's heard correctly.

Then said again. 'May I hold your hand?'

The moment is magically prolonged. She is forty-three years old, has done a good deal more sex than she ever needed to do, and here is a grown man asking if he can hold her hand. It's like hitting the jackpot at spin the bottle, and there you are paired with the only boy in the room without pimples and adolescent whiskers. She is blushing and confused and very aware of his maleness, not as something to avoid, but as a beacon of erotic light. And a sense of intimacy far greater than if he suggested they go to bed together.

She wipes her palm against her jeans and puts her hand in his, and the two of them walk hand in hand down the track. She moves in closer, or perhaps he does, better to establish a shared rhythm. Her arm brushes against his coat, against his torso, and with it a charge as if they were suddenly naked and his skin grazing hers, that clutching in the blood, that squeezing deep inside. The initial unease quickly falls away as she becomes utterly rolled into this man whose voice, whose language, whose entire presence is pulling her closer and closer. That and the warm, slightly sticky grasp of his hand.

For ten minutes they walk, hands clasped, without speaking. She has no idea what he is thinking but hopes he feels as knotted to her as she does to him. If she could see into his face she might know, but she does not dare disturb their rhythm by even a glance. The track rises higher; every now and then they catch a glimpse of the sea. They're walking the edge of the world and Laura happy to take this moment out of time and prolong it for as long as possible, when they are suddenly brought to a halt by a fallen log.

They could clamber over and continue along the track, but nightfall is not far away. She sees him glance at his watch, he knows it is late. They sit together on the log, neither of them saying a word; her hand feels cold without his touch and she wants him to take it again. You're a grown woman, she tells herself, if you want to hold his hand go ahead and do it. But something about that request of his: may I hold your hand, makes her not presume.

They are half a body length from each other, his breathing has quickened. It occurs to her that with a cigarette and a glass of wine they might well be postcoital, and in the next moment she changes her mind. There is an energy between them, and a tugging curiosity, but it's not like lovers, not like soon-to-be lovers either. It is as if she and Raphe are diving far out in the ocean, using only the quiet hush of snorkels. Underwater and together in a world utterly beyond imagining, floating together in a closed, muted, sensual wonderland. And why this man and these sensations, she cannot explain, but for one day in an otherwise stormy month, she decides not to interfere.

It was dusk when they arrived back at the car. They were both very cold and content to sit in the warming cabin wrapped in their own thoughts. Raphe in particular, who couldn't believe he was falling for a woman whose father had been responsible for so much harm to his family, a woman for whom he had travelled half the world in order to seek retribution. But he had been desperate to touch her, had wanted to all week. Five small words: may I hold your hand, just the touch of a hand when he yearned for so much more, five small words requiring several minutes' rehearsal, and then: to hell with it. But this was not what he wanted, not what he had come to Australia for. It was not that his eye was drifting off the ball, it was more he had stumbled onto the wrong playing field. Yet he couldn't stop himself.

As they walked hand in hand through the bush, he had let his mind fly. He had imagined the weight of her breasts, the swell of her hips, the slither of skin, the stroke of her nipples down his chest. He imagined cupping her face in his hands, twisting his fingers through her hair, tasting the cool-hot damp of her mouth, entwining those long lithe legs with his. And even while he was soaking in his thoughts, he knew what a fool he was being. On the way back to the car and no longer hand in hand, he shook his mind free of her body but not free of her, and found himself wondering how she lived, the style of her house, the pictures on her walls, the books on her shelves, the colours of her furnishings, the indoor fountain she had mentioned. Even her cat, Wystan, he wanted to meet the cat and he didn't even like cats. And long before they reached the car he had seized her hand again, grabbing even a flicker of that body he had imagined so vividly.

Now as they made their way along the twisted road back to the city, Raphe held himself as far from her as possible and forced himself to see reason. He had once read that when family members were separated – siblings when young, or parents from their babies – then met up later in life, often a sexual relationship sprang up. The desire was there even though it should not be. And so too with him and Laura: a desire where it did not belong. And while it felt as good as any desire he had ever known, he had a job to do. He did not know exactly what he planned, but for the moment he needed to get away from her before he lost his way completely. So when Laura asked about his movements for the next few days, he told her he would be leaving early in the week for the Philippines to see one of his favourite volcanoes, and then would be flying home.

His leaving seemed to have no impression on her whatsoever, but not so the volcano.

'One day before I die I'd love to see one,' she said. 'I expect volcanoes remind you who you are.'

*

Laura dropped Raphe off at his city hotel and drove home through Fitzroy. At seven o'clock on a Saturday night the Brunswick Street cafés were filling fast. The footpaths were flush with strolling *flâneurs* of the twenty-first century variety, and Laura tempted to join the throng, although only fat cats and parking attendants ever found a car parking space in Brunswick Street. Besides, she wanted to be strolling with Nell.

After the odd, hot-house wonder of the day, Laura was feeling good. The time with Raphe had reminded her what was important between people, what she and Nell had neglected recently. She was eager to be home, and hoped Nell had shut the door on her grant proposals, her PhD supervisions, her strategic planning, all the work that had increasingly colonised their private life. Then together they could come back to Brunswick Street, have a cocktail in one of the bars, followed by a leisurely meal and a browse in the bookshops, then home to bed for the first sex they'd had in months – which was, she decided, not only the best way of diffusing all that erotic confusion with Raphe, but making the best sense of it as well.

A few minutes later, with her hopes reinforced with a heady anticipation, Laura arrived home. The house was in darkness and bloated with that stretched noiselessness of a place not disturbed for some time. Laura turned on lights, turned up heaters, turned on music, injected some life into the stillness. Then to the refrigerator to store the food left over from the picnic. The refrigerator was empty save for a few old jars of pickles, some mayonnaise and a bottle of undrinkable wine given to them by a stingy acquaintance. It was the sort of refrigerator that reeked of single person and no cooking, and just as eloquent as the supermarket basket with cans of cat food, packet soups, prepared freezer meals, and toffees to chew while watching TV alone. Bloody Nell, what was she thinking? Jobs come and go, grant applications and graduate students too, but their partnership was forever.

And suddenly, and leaving her so giddy she had to sit down, she knew something was terribly wrong, knew it with absolute clarity. Perhaps it had required this special day with someone else to open her eyes, but something was wrong, and not a manageable I'm-busy-at-work wrong, but a fundamental wrong, and had been for a long time.

Over the past couple of months Laura had made regular enquiries about the progress of Nell's grant application, about the dynamics at work, about the new tutor. But only now did she realise she had kept her questions, her intellect too, on a short rein, because there were some things she never wanted to name, never wanted to canvas. This was how it had been between her and her father, and now she suspected she was loving Nell in the same way, a deep love, even all-consuming, but skirting the edges as if she were afraid of confronting the truth. Laura, it seemed, was an expert in loving profoundly and misguidedly.

The answering machine registered just one message, and even while the tape was rewinding Laura was hoping it was not another excuse from Nell. But of course it was. Nell said she was determined to complete her grant application and would be home only when it was finished. The message had been phoned in at 4.46 p.m., much the same time Laura was walking hand in hand in the bush with Raphe Carter. It seemed like an age ago. There was no apology from Nell, and Laura was suddenly very lonely as only one can be after a stimulating day. But worse, far worse, feeling very scared, and an old familiar fizzling in her stomach which she recognised immediately.

She grabs her coat, leaves lights, heat and music turned on, and walks up to the corner shop. She buys her first packet of cigarettes in years, is appalled to discover they're the same price as a dozen oysters. She smokes the first cigarette slowly as she walks home. It tastes like the gutter. She perseveres for a few more drags then throws it away.

Back home she perches on the front doorstep and lights another. This time memory, or perhaps old entrenched habit is a winner, and she manages to smoke most of it. Too bad love is not so durable.

Inside the house it is all chill and glare. The cigarettes have lodged in her right temple as a dull accusing ache. It was Nell who insisted she give them up, said she didn't want Marlboro Maid in her bed. And she still wouldn't. Laura shakes herself into action. She goes to the bathroom and washes her teeth, scrubs the smell from her fingers, applies scented hand cream. She sniffs at her jumper and decides to change it, chooses a hot pink polo neck Nell likes. She dabs on perfume, changes her watch for one Nell gave her and returns to the lounge. She wants Nell home, she wants to tell her how much she loves her, she wants to ask all those open-ended, risky questions she has avoided these past few months.

She turns on the TV – Saturday night and it's all sport or drivel – puts on some music but even Bach fails her, tries to do some work but her brain is itching to do something else. Reading will provide a better diversion. On the way to the bedroom for her book she walks past Nell's study and notices some posters have been left on the display board. Nell is most particular about her posters, and without giving it much thought, Laura unclips them and files them away. Then to the bedroom for her novel, an early Iris Murdoch which should see her through the next couple of hours. Her bookmark has fallen out and one of the pages is turned down. Laura reads books as if they are priceless manuscripts, never a drop of coffee or a Vegemite smear on her pages, never a dog-eared corner or cracked spine. Nell used to say that if she were to have her time over again she would like to return as Laura's collected Shakespeare: plenty of attention, plenty of admiration and first-class care. Which makes the state of Laura's book noteworthy. If Nell was reading it she would have treated it with far more deference.

A moment later Laura grabs her keys, dashes out to the car and she's on her way to the university. She knows what's wrong, she knows with heart-stopping certainty what's wrong – not the particular someone Nell is seeing, although she has her suspicions. The university is deserted. Nell always parks in the same area. But not tonight. The building where Nell works is spotted with the occasional light, but the cinema studies floor is in total darkness. Ten o'clock and Nell is not there. Back home at ten fifteen and Laura is checking the dishwasher – yes, she's positive there's an unaccounted mug in there, and surely those are sugar grains in the bottom. Neither she nor Nell takes sugar. And the shortbreads, ultra-expensive, pay-by-the-piece delicacies and only one left in the jar. Last night there were five. It's simply not possible Nell could eat four pieces in a single day. And then back to the bedroom and Laura sifting through the bits and pieces on Nell's bedside table, and only when she's inspecting the sheets and then bending down to smell them does she pull back. She sinks to the carpet, swamped not by grief nor anger, but terror, gut-strangling terror. Time passes but with no proper thoughts to measure it, might be hours or minutes. Eventually Laura goes downstairs, pours herself a large whisky, lights another of the cigarettes and does not go outside to smoke it. She turns on the TV with the mute control activated, replaces Bach with Jeff Buckley, and amid the sorrowful insistence of someone else's knowledge, waits for Nell to come home.

The Purloined Narrative

On another Saturday night twelve weeks later, Laura is at Melissa's house for an evening of food, wine and comfort. With Daniel attending a religious gathering in Sydney led by a Brooklyn rabbi considered to be the last word in Messianic predictions, it is just the two of them.

They have taken possession of the Lewin living room. Melissa, dressed in designer beige, provides elegant contrast with the charcoal leather armchair, while Laura, in close-fitting black, is draped over a startling rug whose coloured patches and squiggles recall the later Matisse. Both are in easy reach of a long, low table messy with the remnants of assorted delicacies: scraps of smoked salmon dotted with the occasional caper, the pickled onions of what were originally pickled herrings and onions, a seriously mauled selection of cheese, a roasted vegetable salad reduced to its zucchini – neither of the women like zucchini – and the slimy remains of a spinach and bocconcini salad. Little restraint in the way of eating has occurred, and with Melissa now filling glasses from a newly opened bottle of wine, not too much in the way of drink either.

'An Anglican Steven Spielberg from Australia! Spare me.' An extremely gaunt Laura reaches for the smoked salmon. 'I think I'm rediscovering my appetite. Do you mind if I finish this off?' And with a nod from Melissa, cleans the plate. 'It's difficult to know if Nell's worst crime is (a) leaving me; (b) for a girl fourteen years my junior, or (c) the fact she absconded with my mother as well.'

'Your mother's *story*,' Melissa says.

But given the circumstances Nell deserves no allowances. Nell Bartholomew, Laura's partner of twelve years had, nine weeks previously, removed herself from their relationship. This she had done with promises of a hypothetical permanent friendship to replace their very real permanent partnership.

'You're irreplaceable,' she said to Laura over and over again. 'And I'll always love you.'

She also, as it turned out, loved young Cyndee, and if that were not betrayal enough, she loved Etti Lewin's life story too. Such a good film it would make, Nell had said when first she heard it all those years ago, and had not changed her mind since. Wisely, she did not emphasise her filmmaking aspirations in the early weeks of the break-up, instead she stressed the inviolate nature of her con-nection with Laura – daily reminders as it happened, over the phone, over coffee, over meals, during walks down to the Merri Creek, and all the while she was forging a new connection with the twenty-nine-year-old Cyndee.

'It's absurd to think you can slice the friendship component from the partnership,' Melissa now says. 'Like preserving the orange peel with the old girl while eating the juicy flesh with the new.'

'I thought I was happy.' This Laura's mantra of the past three months since finding out about Cyndee.

There were three hellish weeks between Nell's confession and her packing her bags. Three insultingly short weeks for Nell to throw away twelve years of a well-rounded, multifaceted relationship. Nell left, and Laura lost her confidence, her sense of security, her mother's life story and an eighth of her body weight, this last despite Nell's concern to leave the cupboards full. 'For you, Laura,' she kept saying, indicating the full pantry, the full linen press, the shelves of crockery and cutlery. But Vegemite, pasta, tablecloths and soup plates are poor substitutes for what Laura really wanted, which was the old Nell. 'For you,' the new Nell said, indicating the full cupboards, but really for Nell, because she anticipated moving around over the next few months while she raised money for her film.

As for the topic of her film, according to Nell, Etti's story was too good to waste. When Laura objected, Nell's answer was swift: 'What were you going to do with it, Laura? You couldn't even bring yourself to read the transcript.'

Her mother's life was being used as Nell's ticket out of academe, her mother's suffering reduced to a career move.

'How can you steal my mother's memories?' she said to Nell. 'How can you steal my heritage?'

'How can you be so melodramatic?'

Nell then proceeded to argue her case by quoting Laura's own words: that the lessons from the Holocaust needed to be shared; that we have to find new ways of entering the old material. 'You've been harping on about these things for years,' Nell said. 'And even if you hadn't, your mother's story is simply begging to be filmed. It has the lot: pathos, hardship, death, sex, all capped off with a happy ending. And so many benefits in a non-Jew doing the story,' she added. 'For a start, no one can accuse me of pushing my own bandwagon.'

Laura was too upset for restraint. 'You mean you're more interested in ambition than atrocity.'

'That's so like you Laura. Give me one good reason why I, or any non-Jew for that matter, can't put her stamp on the Holocaust.' She proceeded to provide what she believed to be a water-tight justification for her film. So far, the Holocaust had stayed in the hands of the Jews, she said. Yet not only was anti-Semitism as rife as it had ever been, given the number of atrocities that had ripped through the world these past sixty years, clearly the lessons of the Holocaust hadn't been taught particularly well. 'It mightn't be such a bad idea to take the Holocaust away from the Jews. Or at least loosen their monopoly.'

Laura was too horrified to speak. Such sentiments belonged to the extremist groups she spent her days fighting, not to the woman she had loved these past dozen years. Nell, however, interpreting her silence more positively, reached across the kitchen bench and squeezed her hand,

'Don't worry, I'll do justice to your mother's story.'

Nell strips Laura's heart, she steals the family history, and with the young thing on her arm and Hollywood in her sights, she turns a firm back on the past.

'Let's drink to the film never getting off the ground,' Laura says to Melissa filling their glasses.

'And if it does, may it be a real turkey, a case of *Cleopatra* meets *Holiday in Auschwitz*,' says Melissa.

'And may the young thing wear her out – Nell's old enough to be her mother.'

'And may Nell, infamous cradle-snatcher and committed urban dweller, find herself prematurely located in a lesbian nursing home at the back of Bourke,' Melissa says.

'And may the nursing home be infested with spiders and ants,' adds Laura, who after twelve years has an intimate acquaintance with Nell's phobias.

And so they laugh their way through the last of the food and the second bottle of wine. But the laughter has to stop some time, and an hour later, with misery lurking like a cyclone off the coast of Darwin, Laura prepares to leave. And yes, she knows she's welcome to stay at Melissa's, but equally she knows she'll never adjust to an empty house unless she spends more time there.

Laura drives with the studied care of the nearly drunk, avoiding the roads she knows to be favoured by the police. She feels trebly bereft: she's lost Nell, she's lost the future they would have shared, and in some weird sense she has again lost Etti. Her life is shuffling backwards: the empty house, the memories, the longing, and before she sinks too low, she quickly slips a tape into the cassette deck, and just as quickly ejects it: the music reminds her of Nell, all the music she has in the car reminds her of Nell.

She arrives home chilled and suddenly sober. She finds an old bar radiator and huddles over it with Wystan. Distraught woman with cat, it is not a pretty study, and Laura decides to accept Melissa's offer of a bed for the night. A moment later, she changes her mind: she has to learn to manage. She keeps up what she hopes is a sane and humorous commentary to Wystan while rummaging in the cupboards for some valerian tea. Nell used to drink it on the rare occasions she couldn't sleep. Laura, a chronic nonsleeper, tried it just once before deciding that such foul stuff made insomnia a preferred choice.

She can't find the tea, hates the search, hates seeing their possessions, hates the memories attached to them. When Nell first moved out, Laura selected a mug, a glass, some cutlery and crockery from her pre-Nell period, and confined herself to an old rocker of Etti's to avoid using the lounge suite she and Nell had bought together. Their bed was full-strength arsenic. She told Nell to take it, but again, on the pretext of thinking of her, Nell said she'd leave it with Laura.

'But I don't want it,' Laura had yelled.

The house is full of memories and none are welcome. Either they are infused with the devastation of the past three months or the now-tainted pleasures of the previous twelve years. Laura longed for the day when she would stop missing her, or rather stop yearning for her. Longed for the day when she would wake up and recognise a lightness, a freedom, like the morning after a migraine, or the sloughing off of jetlag.

It was not so much that everything she did reminded her of Nell, rather she slotted Nell into all her moments. She would linger in front of a travel agent's window decked out in posters of London and feel the pleasure Nell would feel. In their first year together they spent a month in London and Nell loved it so much that Laura kept showing her more of the city, just for the joy of seeing Nell's joy. Or she would pick a book at random and start to read, and the words would inflame her longing. Or another time and another book and a rash of new insights into their life together replete with new arguments to bring Nell home. If only I knew then what I know now, Laura would think as she read and read, for Nell and to Nell, while she sat alone in the house they had once shared.

In a peculiar sort of way, Nell had a stronger presence now she was gone. Laura would sit on the couch, their couch, eat food Nell had enjoyed, watch TV programmes Nell preferred, wear clothes Nell liked. Nell was gone but was ever-present in all Laura's moments. I love you, Laura would find herself saying aloud in the shower. I love you, as she put out the rubbish. I love you, as she pulled the weeds from the garden. I love you, as she tried to work. She maintained a constant conversation with Nell. No matter where she was or who she was with, Nell was there too. Laura was holding on to her as hard as she could, hanging on to Nell who had gone.

And waiting, always waiting. For the knock at the door, for the familiar figure sitting in their favourite café, for the woman walking towards her on the Merri Creek path, or the film aficionado at the late night showing of Kubrick's *2001*. And waiting for Nell's car to appear in the street outside, with a chastened Nell in the driver's seat hoping to be seen. And daily, hourly, waiting for an email, and when the server crashed, wild with frustration, knowing, knowing it would be at that very time Nell would be trying to contact her. And in the sudden silence of cyberspace, composing email after email, queuing them up for when the system was up and running again. And when finally it was, the thumping disappointment of junk mail, work memos and trite messages from friends. And her own relay of white hot emails would be transferred to the 'never sent' category to cool down with all the others never sent.

And waiting for the phone, willing it to ring, refusing invitations so as not to miss Nell's call. And in the early mornings when Nell did most of her telephoning, watching the clock, watching the minutes drag by, carrying the phone when she went to the toilet or took a shower or watered the pot plants or picked out a tune on the piano which was already sounding hollow and unused. Waiting and waiting for that phone call, for that familiar voice, tentative now but loving, telling Laura of her change of mind. She'd made a mistake, Nell would say, and wanted to come home; she'd acted in a moment of madness, had never stopped loving Laura. And of course she wouldn't be making her film. And only then, exhausted with all her waiting, exhausted with all her yearning, only then would Laura pause to gather in her worn-out suffering and consider if she wanted Nell to return.

But an hour later, two hours later, three hours later, and it would begin all over again. In the aftermath of Nell's desertion, the very best times, indeed the only times when the knife stopped turning were when she was daydreaming her and Nell back together again. She played the daydreams from morning to night. She would wake before dawn and start one of her 'together again' narratives. She would develop it further over the breakfast she didn't want to eat, followed by more elaborations in the shower. She would talk out loud, tender conversations with her absent beloved, conversations which ignored Nell's desertion and theft and kept her place warm. Scenes and more scenes as she walked to the tramstop, and padded out further in the crowded tram. Then all day at work between meetings, waiting for phone calls, walking to the toilet, waiting at the lift, the dream would forge ahead. And back at home in the evening and nothing to interrupt her now, and if walls and cats could speak, such tales of happiness they could tell, such bleatings of woe beneath.

Laura wanted to be with her fantasies more than she wanted to be with her friends, more than she wanted to be at work, even more than she wanted to sleep. Just another fifteen minutes she would tell herself at two in the morning while in the middle of a scene where she and Nell finally make the trip to India they had long planned. Just another fifteen minutes as Laura's imaginings guide them through a landscape they would never now see.

Then one morning a couple of weeks ago and for no reason at all, it hit her: Nell wasn't going to ring begging forgiveness, Nell wasn't going to turn up with two tickets to India, it was a waste of time and money to check her email hourly, Nell wasn't going to email. Nell had neither desire nor reason to contact her. Nell had left. Nell was well and truly embarked on the next phase of her life. Nell was gone.

And the next moment: might she be wrong? Surely there was still a chance? Laura could not bear not to think about her.

But she wasn't wrong. The phone wouldn't ring, the email wouldn't arrive, there'd be no more trips together. They were non-us, they were kaput. They were not even a 'they' any more.

She had gone into Nell's study, no Nell but still her study and still full of her books and papers, for Nell needed to travel fast and light these days in order to be in pole position for the hotly contested film money. But she'd be back, and besides, she insisted, she couldn't make the film without Laura's help. This was meant as a compliment, but would have been said no matter what the subject of her film. 'You're my soul mate,' Nell had said over the phone soon after she left. 'You understand the workings of my mind.'

Nell simply could not see she'd done anything wrong. As far as she was concerned, she hadn't really dumped Laura; indeed, Laura was as important as she had always been. A beloved sister, even a twin, was how Nell referred to her. And she certainly hadn't stolen anything. Etti's story was taped, it was transcribed on paper, it was in the public realm. Anyone could have used it, and surely, she kept saying, you would prefer it was me.

As Laura opened the first drawer of Nell's poster collection, she felt a surge of hatred for this new Nell, although in the absence of drugs and mental illness, and Nell was a stranger to both, she knew this new Nell had been there all along. This woman had shared her bed – Laura grabbed the pile of posters in the top drawer and tossed them to the floor; this woman had eaten her food – she emptied the second drawer; this woman had been privy to her private joys – now the third and fourth drawers; and her private fears – now the fifth; this woman had been embraced by Laura's parents – she cleared the sixth and seventh drawers; this woman had been given more trust, more love than Laura had ever thought she was capable of; this woman – and the contents of the last two drawers crashed to the pile – this woman had left her for good.

She surveyed Nell's precious posters all in a jumble on the floor. What she wanted was to take them outside, stuff them in the old metal rubbish bin and set them alight. She wanted to see the posters burn, she wanted to see them reduced to ash, she wanted Nell to know an irreplaceable loss. This was what she wanted. But try as she might she couldn't, not Nell's precious poster collection. Love can make such a fool of you, she thought, and spent the rest of the morning putting the posters back in their drawers.

Laura swings with the memories and struggles against them. She has considered drugs, not tranquillisers but heroin, guaranteed, so she learned during her marriage to Alan all those years ago, to block any pain. Considered, but only briefly, not simply because she faints with injections and has no idea how to smoke the stuff, but because memory of Alan, long dead and forever young, would have erected an insurmountable barrier between her and the drug dealer. And so she's reduced to valerian. Finally she finds it, wonders if aged valerian is still effective, decides it must be given it smells and tastes as foul as ever, is just dropping off to sleep when she realises she has forgotten to check the answering machine. And fortunate she does because the light is flashing, just one call, but sufficient enough for hope.

The voice surprises. It's not Nell, it's Raphe Carter ringing from his home in San Francisco. He's not been entirely out of her thoughts these past three months. She's used him, quite deliberately, as a kind of retreat, a safe, welcoming place far from what she has come to regard as Nell's hell. She's indulged in a few harmless 'if only' scenarios, has even toyed with the idea of ringing him. And here he is, again at exactly the right time, with a proposal. He says he is going to Kilauea in Hawaii next month and wonders if Laura would like to join him.

'You said you wanted to see a volcano before you die. Well here's your chance.'

At the Volcano

The eleven o'clock plane from Honolulu to Hilo was cancelled, with all passengers being transferred to the next flight. Raphe paced the open-air corridor of the airport, wishing the passengers had been cancelled too. His mother used to accuse him of acting impetuously, but inviting Laura to Kilauea wasn't so much impetuous as just plain idiotic.

He had thought she wouldn't come, which was why it was so easy to make the offer. Just lift the receiver and dial her number, Saturday night Melbourne time and Laura unlikely to be home. Come volcano watching with me, he says to her answering machine. So easy, so uncomplicated, and the special touch that he was only responding to something she herself had initiated. But now she was coming it was clear he had given far too little thought to the post-answering-machine events.

She had called back almost at once, seemed so pleased to hear from him. Yes, she'd love to join him, such a wonderful idea. When? Where? What should she bring? And in that blaze of spark and excitement from the real-life Laura, he realised he had again forgotten whatever was inconvenient to remember about her. He worked to temper her enthusiasm, suggesting she should give the proposal a little more thought. After all, it was not just a beach picnic, and was about to add 'or a walk in the bush', but decided it would be wiser not to mention that queer, heated time. He turned to other objections. What about the commission? With so many people reliant on her, surely she would need to choose her absences carefully. And her personal commitments: what would Nell think about her embarking on such a dangerous excursion with a relative stranger? Which was when she told him Nell had left her, and something extraordinary like a volcano was exactly what she needed to wrench her out of her misery and point her in the direction of a new future. She proceeded to rebut all his objections and soon he was providing dates, flight information and advice on what to pack. In short, Laura Lewin was accompanying him to a volcano and the moment of reckoning he had rehearsed countless times was to have a real run.

Fantasies lose their athleticism when they are forced into the ring of the possible. Raphe had experienced this when he last met Laura, but he had conveniently forgotten it these past three months as he worked full-time on his grandfather's team. Safe at home in San Francisco, Raphe had imagined standing with Laura above a lava lake, his hand on her shoulder, a gentle push and over she goes. Or a fast-flowing lava stream and a wayward spark shoots out and she stumbles the wrong way. Or a too-firm foot on an unsteady escarpment and suddenly she disappears. Unencumbered by explanations or recriminations, accidents are so elegantly effected in fantasies, but until Laura Lewin agreed to accompany him to Kilauea, he had not realised they were designed to provide sole allegiance to his murdered grandfather. These fantasies readily removed identifying details from Laura: her face, her voice, her laughter, her *humanness*. And they eclipsed the ethics of justice and revenge, managing to right all wrongs in the absence of any conflicting considerations. But now Laura was coming to Kilauea she would actually be walking near fissures and lava tubes, she would be within arm's reach of so many different dangers she could really die several times over. What exactly was he thinking when he made his invitation? What did he want with the real, the very much alive Laura Lewin?

He checked his watch. The next flight was due in an hour. Too little time to go anywhere else and, with no other choice, he went inside. He was not tempted by the café and so wandered over to the newsstand. There was a short row of bestsellers. He picked up the latest John Grisham and began to read.

Laura had flown into Honolulu late the previous night and stayed near the airport after what had been the most enjoyable flight she had ever experienced. She'd had her own movies, plenty of leg room, and all manner of food and drink delivered to her with a courtesy and alacrity only dreamed about at the back of the plane. She was, she decided, definitely a business-class sort of girl. Sitting next to her had been a small, antisocial man with a laptop, who, after a curt nonverbal greeting, had devoted himself to a reconfiguring of America's tea-drinking habits. He drank only coffee, Laura noticed, and plenty of it while he gazed at his screen. No lover could be more attentive than this man with his computer, and no person made a more desirable travelling companion.

Twelve perfect hours. No telephone, no work emergencies, no accusingly empty house, and with a steady flow of food, drink and entertainment, no unwanted memories. Rather than going into therapy when disaster struck, a long trip taken up the front of the plane was far more effective. As Laura settled back for a snooze, she decided that even if Kilauea suddenly went dormant, the trip would have been worthwhile. Although she was looking forward to seeing Raphe, this man who seemed to turn up just when she needed him. She knew that if not for him, she might never have listened to her mother's tape (certainly she had no desire to hear it now with Nell's greedy fingers all over it), and because of him she was about to see an active volcano. She felt very much indebted to him.

She was the first to disembark when the plane touched down at Hilo. It was a moment before she found him, standing towards the back of the small crowd. He on the other hand saw her as soon as she stepped off the plane, and with that first glance the familiar clutching in his stomach he'd come to associate with her. She had shed pounds and years, and he happy simply to take her in as she walked across the tarmac. But as soon as she saw him she slung her bag over her shoulder, ran towards him and threw her arms around him. Her excitement and pleasure flowed over him in an unexpected comfort.

She pulled away long before he was ready. She wanted to see everything, and she wanted to see it now. 'I have to know I'm at Kilauea volcano and not just any lush tropical isle.'

He found himself laughing, he couldn't help himself despite his resolve. She seemed to have that effect on him, one minute he's struck dumb with fear and anticipation, and the next he's on top of the world.

'You and Kilauea will be on intimate terms before I've finished,' he said. 'And that's a promise.'

As they drove the thirty miles south from Hilo to the Volcano Village past shuttered stores, ramshackle houses and unkempt fields, he told her about the collapse of the sugar industry, how it had been disastrous for the island, with dozens of plantations a few decades back and not a single one left today. He spoke of the ruinous development, particularly on the west coast, and much more still on the drawing board. And he told her about the resurgence in Hawaiian nationalism after years of almost nonstop erosion of their culture. 'There aren't many Hawaiians left, but they sure as hell have vision and determination.'

'Clearly they're not following the victim trail.'

Her response caught him up short. That word 'victim'. Was she being critical of him? She, who had no right to criticise. And might have lost himself in his old imaginings except she pulled him back with an avalanche of questions about their itinerary on the Big Island, about the current volcanic activity, about the likelihood of a new flow starting in the next three days. And every now and then an incredulous, 'I can't believe I'm about to witness the world's most active volcano.'

As they approached Volcano Village, he thought it only polite to ask about Nell. Laura was disinclined to talk about her; however, she did tell him about the film.

'That's all the Holocaust has become for a good many people,' she said. 'A leg-up the career ladder, Hollywood entertainment, an up-for-grabs myth. March up, march up, and take your pick – which is what my former partner certainly did.' And no, she didn't want to discuss it any further; she wanted to leave Nell and her grubby deceptions behind.

Back at the bungalow he carried her bag into the bedroom. His own possessions were packed neatly on a chest.

'I'll sleep on the couch, of course,' he said, nodding in the direction of the living room.

She looked at the double bed. 'There's ample room here, and you'll be a lot more comfortable.' She smiled, 'I trust you, even asleep I trust you.'

And suddenly Martin filled his mind, Martin asleep with typhus in the woods outside Belsen, Martin with Henry who couldn't be trusted. And for the first time Raphe was sure Laura didn't know her father's crimes. Strangely, it afforded him little relief.

He waved the bed question aside, for now he'd prefer to be out of here. Volcanoes, he decided, were safer than this woman.

He had arranged for a helicopter to fly them over the area, as much for him as for her. It had been nearly two years since he was last here and the eruption had changed considerably. He didn't expect any of the pyrotechnics seen on his previous visits, and neither did he care. It was the changing eruption he had always found so seductive about Kilauea.

As he and Laura headed off in a hire car to the volcano park headquarters, he told her about the lava fountain he had seen on a previous visit, a huge jet of brilliant fire spurting a couple of hundred metres into the night sky. At its core was a blazing orange-red radiance framed by a cloud of darker, cooler fragments; like a vision from Blake, he said. He shaped its brilliant fall, he told of the flying globules of molten fire spitting onto the blackening earth and collecting in a flow down the slopes.

She listened mesmerised, as if in the presence of the volcano itself. 'The path we walk is both beautiful and dangerous,' she said finally.

Again she caught him up short. It was one or other in his sort of life: beauty or danger. In fact his entire life was rent by polar opposites: real Laura or imagined Laura, ideal fantasies or unpredictable reality, and given his grandfather had been silent since Laura's arrival, his grandfather's demands or Laura Lewin. He tried to understand as she did: beauty *and* danger, but it was an unnerving experience, like free-falling without a parachute, and he was quick to return to familiar territory.

'I'm afraid you'll see no lava fountains this trip.'

'No dangers at all?' Laura asked.

'Different dangers,' he said as he turned into the car park.

• • •

An hour later they are flying over Kilauea towards a remote area of the park where the current activity is occurring.

'Pele's been a busy girl since you were last here,' the pilot, an old acquaintance of Raphe's, says. 'New vents, new flows, new breakouts. Nothing too explosive, more her subtle, subversive side.'

Raphe tells Laura about Pele, the volcano goddess who lives beneath Kilauea. 'We'll see the exact site, her home and hearth so to speak, tomorrow at the Halemaumau crater,' he says. 'She's one tough and angry gal this one. Hasn't had a moment's rest since 1983 when the volcano started erupting.'

He has always liked the stories of Pele, the uncompromising, high-spirited woman who every now and then wakes up and bursts out of her home. Pele the volcano goddess who caused the volcanic eruptions on the ocean floor which formed the Hawaiian islands in the first place, and ever since has exacted a Faustian price. Pele gave Hawaii life, but in one of the most volatile places in the world, she can also take it away. It's a type of justice, Raphe is now thinking as he looks at the glorious panorama below. A type of justice.

The first glimpse of Kilauea is awesome. All those years ago when he first came here, he had expected a symmetrical, cone-shaped mountain with its peak neatly chiselled off, a puff of smoke at the top plus a bit of fire if he were lucky. But Kilauea is a vast volcanic landscape of multiple craters and solid black lava flows which actually form the hills and plateaus of the south-east section of the island.

'It's not human-sized,' Laura is saying. 'It makes you want to burst out of your skin.'

Raphe smiles in spite of himself. When he least expects it, and often when he least wants it, she shows herself as not so different from him.

He tells her about the lava tubes which flow like giant arteries a few metres beneath the earth, and points to a brilliant pool of liquid fire where the roof of the main tube has collapsed. Laura is transfixed, the great gaping orange pool beneath the black blisters of cold *pahoehoe* lava.

Raphe, too, is looking. 'This always reminds me of a cremator-ium,' he says.

Her response is sharp. 'Don't bring your Holocaust here.' And quieter, 'I want to see this place as it is.'

Immediately his fury rises. Who is she to be angry? Who is she to tell him what to do? For unlike her he doesn't have the luxury of choice when and where to think of the Holocaust, no choice at all since he found out about her father and his grandfather, no choice since he learned justice doesn't have a use-by date. Indeed if not for her father, the haunting of his entire life might never have occurred. And he's back in his familiar groove, even here flying over Kilauea he's counting out his wrongs. And if he were to avenge Martin Lewin's murder, avenge it in this place – 'She slipped,' he would tell the authorities. 'Didn't listen to my warnings.' – would he feel any better? Would he feel liberated? Righteous? Relieved? Would he feel he had done the right thing? As he gazes at the terrors of this landscape, he senses more strongly than ever the two people who comprise him. His Martin side might for the first time be calmed if Laura were made to pay for her father's sins, but the Raphe side would be horrified. And again the familiar resentment, again the desire to live his life without the righteous clamouring of the dead.

They are flying over the main tube towards the sea where the lava empties in a furious cloud of white steam and a scattering of rock. Raphe shakes off his thoughts. He wants today off. He's flying over his favourite volcano and he wants it simple, just for today.

'That's much bigger than when I was last here,' Raphe now says, referring to the lava bench formed where the molten lava discharges into the sea.

Although not as big as it was, according to the pilot. A month or so earlier a parcel of the cliff had broken off and disappeared into the ocean.

'I wouldn't want to be standing on that,' says Laura. And yet that's exactly what Raphe is imagining. Laura Lewin standing on the lava bench, and suddenly it breaks off and she disappears into the turbulence.

'What's wrong?' Her hand is on his arm, she's staring into his face. 'I wouldn't return to those thoughts,' she says. 'They're clearly not good for you.'

The helicopter is heading inland again towards Kupaianaha shield, the second eruption site but quiet now for many years.

'It's like huge billowing black blisters,' Laura says of the smooth bulges of cold *pahoehoe* lava in the treeless landscape. 'And a sense of devastation and creation all at the same time.'

Raphe hears the wonder in her voice. It is exactly how he feels. Life and destruction side by side, and an energy that swells and enters you like a magical, life-giving elixir. He is always seized by the marvel that is this place.

And perhaps that might explain the mood of the evening. You simply cannot gaze at a volcano and be untouched by either the volcano or your companion. Back at the bungalow, they prepare dinner together. They linger over the meal, plenty of good food and wine with old blues crackling in the background. And he doesn't know quite how it happens, but one moment they are talking together, and the next she is turning up the volume and moving to the music, her eyes closed, her head flung back. And he, too, is on his feet, and the beat is billowing through him and the heat is flushing his skin, his feet tripple like piano keys, he sways with her, he mirrors her movements, their hands are entwined, her breath hits his face, the hot flicker of touch, the two of them turning and turning and turning again on and on until the music finishes. And in the sudden silence they remain clasped together, still moving gently to the beating in their bodies and the echoing music.

She pulls away first. 'What a great partnership we make,' she says with a smile.

He quickly collects himself, returns her smile without, he hopes, revealing the embarrassment he feels, and applies himself to the cleaning up.

With the room tidy, the glasses washed and put away, it is time for bed.

'Don't be silly,' she says when he starts to move bedding into the living room. 'We're both grown-ups.'

He decides to accord her a commonsense he does not himself feel and they prepare for bed quickly. She chooses her side, which fortunately is not his side, they say goodnight before hopping into bed and the lamps are immediately extinguished. He lies as far from her as possible. She falls asleep within minutes – so much for her tales of being an insomniac – while he lies awake trying to shut his mind to the sinewy music and the slow synchrony of their dancing bodies. He tells himself to ignore her presence, doesn't want to feel her so close, stuffs his mind with diversions: a list of currently active volcanoes, a list of students in his classes last semester, a list of the students in his college graduation class. Finally, irritated beyond belief and no closer to sleep, he lets his thoughts settle, not with Laura, but with the man who brought him here, his long-dead grandfather who seems more in control of Raphe's actions than is Raphe himself.

So, Grandfather, I'm here, and the girl's with me. Death in a myriad of costumes is in easy reach. I hear the bell tolling, it's pay-up time and I don't know what to do.

And for his pains? No clear direction, just the ever-present squeezing of his guts and a voice of conscience Raphe cannot locate. It's times like this, he is thinking, that God would be useful, an authoritative voice from the dark with a prescription for action. But there's no one to help him, the quest is his alone. Who is he fighting though? And what is he defending? He seems locked into his old thoughts, his old beliefs, in a way, it suddenly occurs to him, not dissimilar to a religious fundamentalist. It is not a happy thought: Raphe Carter, fundamentalist Holocaust survivor once removed. Yet it seems inescapable. He walks the same groove over and over, and the groove becomes deeper, and the walls, the walls he creates himself, grow higher. He imagines only what he has imagined numerous times before, and his imaginings, although so clear and certain, take him nowhere. And beyond these walls of his making? It hardly bears thinking about. He's set firmly within the concrete of his mind.

If he stretches his arm across the bed, he can touch her. He is as close to Laura Lewin as was her father to his grandfather, and soundly sleeping, she is just as vulnerable. He looks at her, this woman who cut her teeth on her mother's grief, and touches her lightly. She shuffles in her sleep and he withdraws his hand. With the feel of her on his fingers, it occurs to him that far from being his enemy, she might actually be his providence. But the thought is so alien, that in the same way the immune system gathers itself against foreign microbes, so too his old thoughts against this frail new possibility.

The night hours slog on with Raphe wandering through his conflicts until he has completely lost his way. He fears he will hold on to his pain until the last drop in the glass. Again he reaches across and touches Laura on the warm sleepy skin of her shoulder, again she shuffles, but this time he does not withdraw his hand.

In the morning when he awakes, she is curled against him, her head resting on his shoulder. She is gently snoring. He rolls her out of his arms and she opens her eyes.

'You purr,' he says.

She smiles, 'That's what Nell used to say when she still loved me.' And leans across – he wishes she wouldn't – and pecks him on the cheek. 'And you,' she says, 'talk in your sleep.'

He is frantic, what on earth could he have said?

'Everyone has their secrets,' she says, smiling. 'And you're entitled to yours.'

Later in the morning they are standing at the rim of Halemaumau crater, a huge quarry-shaped pit at the top end of the caldera, with steep, sulphur-stained slopes. And everywhere are steaming fumaroles puffing their heat and energy into the air. There is a rim, like a watermark, high on the sides marking the level of the boiling lava lake which once filled the crater. Here is the heart of the vast Kilauea volcano, this is Pele's home. And this year, next year, in ten years time the lava will again ooze out of the ground and fill this vast pit.

Laura stares into the huge gaping space: it is marvellous, quite marvellous, with a wild singing energy; it makes her feel strange and wonderful. There are some people, she finds herself thinking, who derive a sense of belonging, of continuity, by reminding themselves of the familiar. They touch the gate each time they arrive home, and the doorframe, they run their fingers across a bench or over a banister, a range of actions to remind themselves that things are as they ought to be. And when they travel they return to the same places to tread familiar pavements, visit familiar shops, stay in the same hotels. As she gazes down into the vast, other-world of the Halemaumau crater, it occurs to her she used to be that sort of person. But no more. Life is fragmented, no point in denying it. Life is uncertain and that is that. And nothing, nothing is forever. The thought fills her with a quiet exuberance. She glances across at Raphe; he keeps coming back here, so he too must feel the power of this place. Yet with his furrowed brow and the gloomy set of his mouth, it is hard to know what he is experiencing.

All those months ago when they shared a picnic together on a wintry beach he had described himself as saturnine. I could teach you happiness, she had thought then, and in her gratitude for all he has done, she would still like to, although it occurs to her that happiness may not be on his agenda.

His hand is on her arm: if they are to make it across the caldera and back, he says, they had better begin. She turns to him, startles him with a hug, and the two of them set off.

A couple of hundred metres from the rim of Halemaumau crater they begin their descent into the Kilauea caldera. There is a sign: 'Thin crust – keep to trail'.

'How thin?' she asks Raphe.

He turns to her and he's not smiling. 'Best not to test it,' he says.

As it happens, the trail is nonexistent, just a way marked by stone cairns through the lava-clad landscape. The paradox strikes immediately. Cairns, which she has always associated with death, are marking a safe passage through one of the most lethal landscapes on earth. She treads carefully, the solid *pahoehoe* flow, like smooth interlocking carapaces from a distance, is far rougher, far more organic up close. Some parts are like solid black slabs of liver, others like hard ropy swirls of intestine, and all of it is curved and sensual and infused with a silvery, oily sheen. Carefully she climbs and descends the bulging ground.

The wind is furious across the caldera floor and the sun very hot. There is no shelter whatsoever. She walks this blackened cracked landscape, this volatile not-quite-comprehensible landscape, and despite being racked through with its marvels, it is Laura who is now reminded of the devastations of the Holocaust.

She looks ahead at Raphe. She is sure he, too, has made the same connection, yet finds it perplexing that with all his miserable fixations, he has arrived at so few understandings. It's like being caught in the eye of a storm with no awareness of where you are and consequently no desire for escape. How else could it be possible to dwell on the same issues for years and years and not resolve them?

He is waiting for her to catch up. He is standing at a long, smoothly sculptured fissure. 'Look,' he says as soon as she joins him. 'Look how deep it is. You can't see the bottom.'

The jagged edges of the crack run neatly and precisely parallel. She looks down. About a metre below the surface, and clinging greenly to a small barren ledge, is a fern.

Raphe sees the darkness, while she sees the fern.

It's a small miracle in the devastation of this landscape. She files it in memory, turns away and continues across the hard lava. You see what you want to see, you think what you want to think. How guarded had been her thoughts about her father, how guarded her thoughts about Nell. But even within these limits and despite having just been betrayed by the love of her life, she is happier than Raphe. She feels his undercurrent of misery even here, the earth boiling beneath his feet, a place with so much life but none of it touching him. She is sorry for him, wants to insert herself behind his eyes and show him what there is to be seen.

Later, when they are back at the bungalow Raphe is quiet and withdrawn. Laura makes several attempts at conversation, but he is shut off from her. 'Frozen' is how he would put it, and nothing he can do about it. He pours them both a glass of wine, is wondering how he will get through the evening, when she leaves the room and returns a moment later with a volume of poetry. It is a collection of the Russian poet, Anna Akhmatova.

Laura begins to read, poem after poem addressed so personally to a series of people Akhmatova had loved and most often lost, and to a country she had similarly loved but refused to give up. Poems written during a time when each day was a struggle for survival. There are moments when her voice wavers and he finds himself envying her. He knows why she is reading these poems, but it isn't so easy for him to reach for a book and through someone else's sufferings settle his own pains. He simply cannot see how to use this Russian woman's poems to still his own demons as Laura clearly has done. So he gives up trying and turns his attention to Laura instead. He listens to the melody of her voice, he studies each of her features, he studies the whole, he engraves her every movement on his mind. Laura reads Akhmatova and Raphe reads Laura.

By the time they go to bed he feels at peace. And as she lies next to him asleep, he makes himself envisage a different set of Laura imaginings than his old revenge narratives. If he would only let her, he tells himself, perhaps she could quieten his storm.

The room is lit by a near-full moon. He shifts to the edge of the bed in order to observe her better. She sleeps in a patch of light from the window, lying on her side and facing him. Her hair is knotted on top of her head, wisps curl about her face and down her neck. There's a slight sheen to her skin, her eyes flicker behind the lids. He moves closer, runs his forefinger down the fine skin on the side of her face, from her left temple down to her jaw, his fingertip on that utterly soft skin. It's a caress he hasn't dared imagine since their walk together in the Australian bush all those months ago, too much a betrayal of his grandfather.

Her eyes open, he snatches his hand away. In the faint light he sees she is smiling. A moment later he startles at the touch of her hand on his neck. The tips of her fingers stir his hair, sparks slither down his spine, and then she is guiding him towards her. It's like sinking into pillows, her lips soft yet tensed, and moving so surely and taking him with her, like dancing, he is thinking. And he gathers her up, a shudder as he feels her full loose breasts beneath her T-shirt, and is kissing that sweet wet mouth, eking out the moment, not wanting to finish. Finally she draws away, and with a sigh, burrows into his shoulder and falls back asleep.

Raphe is wide awake, he can hardly believe what has happened. But soon the satiety of a moment ago, of that utterly enveloping shut-out-the-rest-of-the-world kiss is replaced with the hungry retrospective gaze of wanting more, of not remembering exactly how it felt, of not attending to this or that – her breath, her taste, her hand as it moved, did it move? – and in his dissatisfaction over that ever-so-fleeting satisfaction, a desire which swarms through him and has him clasping her against him as she sleeps. His hand is in her hair, her body lies loosely against his, he leans into her, breathes in the smell of her and, impossible to explain these things, but suddenly his conflicts melt away and the future emerges with an amazing new narrative. She is his future, and not in the way he had previously thought: Laura Lewin is his salvation.

So many years absorbed by his grandfather, so many years stifling in the same scenes, and all he has to show for it is his own blackened self. It is as if he has been charred by his own imaginings, and no one, not one single person has benefited. But Laura offers another way. She is his salvation, and must realise it too. Her lips told him, her kiss told him. She must realise it too.

Hours later he has worked it out. Hours later he has played and replayed the life they will make together. He has never felt this alive; the old groove of his grandfather's rights and demands has been filled by this astonishing new story. Through their own lives, Laura and he will make amends for the wrongs of the past, and they'll do it together. At last he sees the purpose of his grandfather's haunting, at last he understands why his grandfather is now silent. He knows what do. It makes sense, it makes such perfect sense.

He feels both calm and excited as he lies close to Laura, turning the possibilities in his mind. And when finally he falls asleep, it is a deep and peaceful sleep. He awakes late; the sun is already quite strong and he can hear Laura rustling about in the kitchen. He quickly pulls on some clothes and soon is sitting in the kitchen ready to talk. He has barely begun when the telephone rings. It's the commission for Laura with an urgent problem only she can solve. It occupies the next four hours and, as soon as it is resolved, Laura is eager to be started. Their plan is to hike over the lava bench to the point where the molten lava enters the ocean.

Raphe tries to hold her back, he is bursting to speak. 'There's no point in leaving too early,' he says. 'You won't be able to see the lava until after dark. And there's no shade, not a place to be lingering on a warm day.'

He is so excited about his plans, *their* plans, everything else pales in comparison. And at last he can tell her what happened outside Belsen all those years ago, because it doesn't matter any more. *It doesn't matter any more*, he can hardly believe it. By being together they will atone for the past in a simultaneous apology and act of forgiveness. It makes sense to him in a way the revenge option never did. But Laura won't stay still, she wants to be started, a close-up view of flowing lava and she doesn't care if she can't see it clearly, she doesn't care if she gets sunstroke. So an hour earlier than he planned they are in the car and driving the Ring of Craters Road. As for speaking with her, he's waited so long for his peace, another few hours won't make any difference.

The Ring of Craters Road curves and winds down towards the sea through a permanent display of the recent eruptions of this mighty volcano. In many places the lava has flowed over the road and has had to be cut away, so they find themselves driving between low bulbous canyons of lava. Eventually the road disappears entirely beneath a huge flow. Now the lava clads the ground ahead of them as far as the eye can see, and in the distance their destination: a cloud of ash and steam where the current lava flow hits the sea.

They park the car and start off immediately. Raphe carries a pack containing water, a light supper, torches, a cellular phone. Laura had watched him with his preparations and wondered whether he wasn't being just a little too cautious. He assured her they would be going to some of the most dangerous land on the face of the earth. She thought it was probably hyperbole but kept her thoughts to herself. But now as they start walking over the lava bench and she sees signs everywhere warning of a multitude of hazards, and other signs strongly warning against walking over the lava bench at all, she is fast changing her mind. Raphe assures her that as long as you know what you're doing it is perfectly safe.

From the very beginning the going is rough. The ground is like a solid turbulent sea, huge swells falling to low curving swirls of rippling lava. But before long she gets herself into a pattern, a sort of nimble goat pattern despite her sturdy boots, and although very watchful, feels her feet and legs learning the lie of this terrain. Nell would never have come here, she finds herself thinking. Nell by her own reckoning was not much interested in nature. And it occurs to her that not so long ago a future without Nell was as inconceivable as this volcano. It's a satisfying thought.

She looks across at Raphe with his clouded desires and his bittersweet sadness, Raphe clinging to his losses for fear of what might happen if he were to let them go, Raphe who seems some-how hobbled to himself. If he could only forgive all the wrongs he feels have been done to him he would be a far happier man. But forgiveness, requiring as it does such an awesome muting of self, a moral victory, in fact, over one's desires and self-interests, is, she suspects, beyond Raphe's reach. Forgiveness, Laura has long thought, is really among the most unnatural of acts. Yet she has always known how to forgive, has done so many times over the years. Out of love she would have forgiven her parents anything. And perhaps it is out of love she has managed to forgive a good many of Nell's actions. But not the theft, she can't forgive the theft of her mother's story. That act, so instrumental, so self-serving, so unequivocally cruel, has cast a shade over all their years together. That act was unforgivable.

The sun is sinking, but still so hot. She removes her hat and wipes her brow, and immediately Raphe is by her side offering her the water bottle. They both sit on a huge swell of lava while she drinks, their legs occasionally touching. With him now so close, she recalls the kiss of last night, a long, close kiss, yet oddly chaste, she is now thinking, and a relief after the erotic charges of some of their past meetings. She reaches for his hand. She doesn't know why, but she has an overwhelming desire to help him. It could be she simply wants to repay her gratitude – for she is grateful, is aware at this very moment of standing at a fulcrum in her life, behind her a weary, depleted landscape and in front unknown dangers and unknown excitements. How different it is for Raphe. You have to grab your understandings wherever you can get them, but you have to desire them first.

He helps her to her feet and they are walking again. Closer and closer to where the boiling lava streams from the tube into the ocean. The fountain of steam is larger now, the crash of waves too. She forges ahead, driven by excitement and a strange sense of recognition. The warning signs are now so numerous they stand like sentries along the cliff edge. At one point where the road reappears briefly, a huge chunk of land has fallen into the sea. Raphe takes her arm and leads her back from the edge, and keeps his hand on her until the rough terrain requires them both to clamber on all fours. The sun is sinking but the wind remains hard. They stop again for water. She wishes the sun would set; at the same time she's fearful of this place in the dark. Pele is rather like the Old Testament God, she is thinking, protective to those who obey, but angry and vengeful when provoked. From the little she knows of Raphe, he seems to share some of the same qualities. Gods and humans, and both yet to understand the utter futility of revenge.

Night is falling as they approach the end of their journey. The sight is awesome. A huge fountain of shooting steam and sea spray spiked with hydrochloric acid, and beating the air a thunderous noise. And finally, her first glimpse of lava, a stream of black and orange liquid shooting into the spray. And she cannot remove her gaze for a second, stands buffered by the wind as the sky darkens and the lava spilling from the tube into the ocean becomes brighter. Raphe is alongside her and when she steps forward he pulls her back.

'You don't know the danger,' he says.

She smiles at him. 'I'm not here to be safe. If I wanted safety I'd be back in Melbourne with my job, my house and my cat.' She leads him forward to gaze into the fiery stream. And the cold ocean fizzes and steams with the molten fire from the centre of the earth.

They are standing close, he puts his arm about her shoulders. Her body is tensed, alert to the breathtaking display, but he's kept his silence long enough, he's desperate to speak to her. During the walk over the lava bench his thoughts kept returning to their future, he even tried to engage his grandfather, but his grandfather remained silent. And Raphe so pleased he did, for through the silence he heard Laura and she was saying yes, to his plans, yes, she feels as he does, yes, she will return to America with him.

She's pulling away from him, wants to go still closer. 'You can't,' he shouts over the noise. 'You can't.' Just the previous week a young couple were killed here, a storm, the night dark, the steam and lethal spray more violent than usual and they were washed off the bench. He pulls her back. 'You can't,' he says again, and she smiles at him, a smile of utter radiance. At him.

'Wouldn't it be extraordinary to stay the night here,' she says.

He tells her it is far too dangerous, and besides – at last, at last – there's something they need to talk about. And with the crash of the water against the new rock, the fizzle of fire as the molten lava hits the cold sea, and the storm inside him, he pulls her close and begins to talk right into her ear, talk beyond the tumult outside. He simply can't wait a moment longer.

He tells her he has worked it out. 'You said how much I'd helped you. We can help each other, we'll be each other's strength, our old demons will be silenced together.'

She is trying to interrupt, she is pulling away. He has to make her understand. He talks and talks like he's never talked before, he loves what he is saying. These are dreams actually happening. He talks about his grandfather, a man her own father knew, he talks with tears filling his eyes, he talks to her, *to her*, whom he now knows to be his salvation.

'I always knew there was something more. I thought it was my grandfather, I even thought it was Juno. But now I know it's you. You're the one I've been groping towards.'

She is shaking her head. No, she is saying. 'It's a moving story, and I know it's heartfelt, but it's not mine. It has nothing to do with me.'

It has, it has, she doesn't understand. 'Your father,' he says, 'I'll tell you about your father.'

She is fierce in her refusal. 'Don't you dare.'

'But it's your story,' he's pleading with her. 'It's our story. You have to listen.'

'No I don't.' And now taking his hand. 'I'm not your answer,' she says. 'I am not your answer. And —' this last said firmly, defiantly, 'I don't want to know.'

She's wrong, he knows she's wrong. He'll not give her up. He's worked it all out. She turns away. She's walking back over the lava bench. He sees the play of her torch, the flicker of her body in the jiggling light. It's too late for her to leave now. He starts after her, he's calling above the hiss of lava, the roar of the sea.

'You have to know. Your father, my grandfather, you have to know.'

She doesn't stop, she refuses to listen.

'I've worked it out,' he shouts over the boiling sea. 'I've worked it all out.'

She continues walking over the lava bench, walking away from him. He stares after her a moment longer then turns back to gaze into the shooting fire and steam. She'll come around, she has no choice. He sees it all so clearly. Their future. He is aware of a rare contentment as he stands alone on the rock, and, amid the tumult of the boiling sea, he hears a clear voice speaking to him, placating him, protecting him. The voice belongs to her.